Ford Madox Ford

FORD MADOX FORD (the name he adopted in 1919: he was originally Ford Hermann Hueffer) was born in Merton, Surrey, in 1873. His mother, Catherine, was the daughter of the Pre-Raphaelite painter Ford Madox Brown. His father, Francis Hueffer, was a German emigré, a musicologist and music critic for *The Times*. Christina and Dante Gabriel Rossetti were his aunt and uncle by marriage. Ford published his first book, a children's fairytale, when he was seventeen. He collaborated with Joseph Conrad from 1898 to 1908, and also befriended many of the best writers of his time, including Henry James, H.G. Wells, Stephen Crane, John Galsworthy and Thomas Hardy. He is best known for his novels, especially *The Fifth Queen* (a trilogy about Henry VIII; 1906–8), *The Good Soldier* (1915) and *Parade's End* (his tetralogy about the First World War). He was also an influential poet and critic, and a brilliant magazine editor. He founded the *English Review* in 1908, discovering D.H. Lawrence, Wyndham Lewis and Ezra Pound, who became another close friend. Ford served as an officer in the Welch Regiment 1915–19. After the war he moved to France. In Paris he founded the *transatlantic review*, taking on Ernest Hemingway as a sub-editor, discovering Jean Rhys and Basil Bunting, and publishing James Joyce and Gertrude Stein. In the 1920s and 1930s he moved between Paris, New York and Provence. He died in Deauville in June 1939. The author of over eighty books, Ford is a major presence in twentieth-century writing.

SARA HASLAM is a Senior Lecturer in the Department of English at the Open University. She studied at the University of Liverpool, and King's College London, and was a founder member of the Ford Madox Ford Society, of which she is currently Chair. She is author of *Fragmenting Modernism: Ford Madox Ford, the Novel and the Great War* (Manchester University Press, 2002) and *Life Writing* (Routledge, 2009, with Derek Neale), and editor of Ford's *The Good Soldier* (Wordsworth, 2010) and *England and the English* (Carcanet, 2003) as well as *Ford Madox Ford and the City*, the fourth volume of International Ford Madox Ford Studies (2005). She has published essays on the literature of the First World War, on Modernism, and on Ford, Thomas Hardy, the Brontës and Henry James.

FORD MADOX FORD

Parade's End

VOLUME III

A Man Could Stand Up –
A Novel

Edited by Sara Haslam

CARCANET

A Man Could Stand Up – was first published in Great Britain in 1926 by
Duckworth & Co.

This edition first published in Great Britain in 2011 by
Carcanet Press Limited
Alliance House
Cross Street
Manchester M2 7AQ

A CIP catalogue record for this book is available from the British Library

ISBN 978 1 84777 014 1 (*A Man Could Stand Up –*)
ISBN 978 1 84777 021 9 (*Parade's End* volumes I–IV)

The publisher acknowledges financial assistance from Arts Council England

Supported by
ARTS COUNCIL
ENGLAND

Typeset by XL Publishing Services, Tiverton

CONTENTS

ACKNOWLEDGEMENTS

My first thanks are due to my fellow editors, Max Saunders, Joseph Wiesenfarth and Paul Skinner. I have found this a hugely rewarding project, not only because of the brilliance of Ford's text, but because of the collaborative nature of the endeavour. My initial notes date from a balcony meeting at a conference in Genoa in 2007. Though I recall the sense that we were embarking on an important and necessary edition I had little idea then how fascinating the project would become – or how much collective concentration would be required. I am extremely grateful to all three friends and colleagues for making the experience such a positive one, and for the astute and detailed comments that they have made on all aspects of this text. Max Saunders assumed the vast majority of the burden of chairing electronic and face-to-face discussion, and produced much of the editorial material that we then refined together. I should like to thank him for this, and, more generally, for all the professional generosity he has extended to me since we first met.

I have been greatly assisted throughout by my mother and stepfather, Olwen Haslam and Paul Bywaters. My mother has, once again, proved to be an invaluable proofreader (much better than Ford), and many of the notes contain material she researched either alone or alongside Paul. I shall not forget the semi-complete patrol of their grandchildren marching around a kitchen in North Wales singing 'Some talk of Alexander' as a result of one reference in Ford's text. My husband Paul, as well as building a spreadsheet to help me make sense of the typescript, has provided insightful comments throughout. My thanks go to him for this, and for the weekends he spent with our children Maisie and Caspar (I missed you) so that I could work.

Ashley Chantler deserves special thanks for his editorial

advice, especially on the comparability of work across all four volumes. I am also very grateful to other friends and colleagues who helped by providing information and discussing editorial issues, including Jason Andrew, John Attridge, Pete Clasen, Tony Hume, Kate Lindsay, Bob Owens, Martin Stannard and Shaf Towheed.

I have had most direct contact with Laura Linke at the Carl A. Kroch Library, Cornell University, and I am especially grateful to her for her detailed answers to questions concerning Ford's typescript. I should also like to thank Katherine Reagan, and other staff at the Library, as well as staff at the Royal Artillery Museum and Apsley House for their assistance. Cornell University, Michael Schmidt, and the estate of Janice Biala have granted kind permission to quote from Ford's translation of Euripides and from Ford's and Biala's letters.

Our editor at Carcanet, Judith Willson, deserves special thanks for all her valuable advice. Finally, I'd like to thank Michael Schmidt, as director of Carcanet Press, for his confidence in the project; and, as Ford's executor, for contributing in this and many other ways to the general knowledge and experience of his work.

LIST OF ILLUSTRATIONS

LIST OF SHORT TITLES

A MAN
COULD
STAND UP

By
FORD MADOX
FORD
(Ford Madox Hueffer)

7/6
NET

A MAN
COULD STAND UP

FORD · MADOX · FORD

DUCKWORTH

INTRODUCTION

Ivor Gurney's poem 'War Books' imagines his fellow writers at work at Corbie Ridge, or Fauquissart, or Ypres. Yet he himself was writing after the First World War was done – 'War Books' was drafted between 1922 and 1925. By the end of this period, two volumes of Ford Madox Ford's *Parade's End* had already been published. Ford's war tetralogy was therefore one of the earliest, as well as one of the most impressive, examples of how 'men would gather sense / Somehow together', as Gurney put it in his poem.[1] Ford's four books were called by William Carlos Williams the 'English prose masterpiece of their time'.[2] *A Man Could Stand Up –*, volume III, appeared in 1926. As this Introduction is intended to show, it built on the strengths of its predecessors, and contributed to Ford's overall success in his treatment of the war, in a number of notable ways.

On 12 January 1927 *Punch* magazine carried an unsigned 'review' of *A Man Could Stand Up –*. It began as follows:

Provided you've—wisely, I count it—kept trace
Of FORD MADOX FORD on the War,
A Man Could Stand Up will fall into its place
As Tale Three in a series of four.

---

1 Gurney's poem was not published at the time. He was held in asylums throughout this period, and wrote in notebooks from which later editors then worked. P. J. Kavanagh, one of those editors, has written that the nearest thing to the version of war that Gurney experienced 'is in prose, in the opening pages of *No More Parades* [volume II of *Parade's End*], which is set in Gurney's part of the front'. See his introduction to *Ivor Gurney: Collected Poems* (Manchester: Carcanet, 2004), xxix ('War Books', 258).
2 Similar judgements have been offered by Anthony Burgess, Malcolm Bradbury and Samuel Hynes, among others. See Williams, 'Parade's End', *Sewanee Review*, 59 (Jan.–Mar. 1951), 154–61 (155); reprinted in *Selected Essays* (New York: Random House, 1951), 315–23 (316).

Two further verses point readers towards volumes I and II, in case of any difficulty as to plot or character. The review then concludes:

> But you'll find, when you've sorted each separate clue
> That the story (from DUCKWORTH) is such
> That life in the trenches is brought to your view
> With a wholly remarkable touch.

It is a humorous, positive piece, its composer appreciating the novel's individual – 'wholly remarkable' – merits as a war book, as well as its contribution to the larger fictional project of which it was a part: 'Tale Three in a series of four'. Perusal of the previous volumes (*Some Do Not* ... and *No More Parades*) is recommended. At the same time, the rightful 'place' of volume III is emphasised, one that it holds by virtue of and in relation to its companions. This is an advertisement for *A Man Could Stand Up –*, for Duckworth, and also for what would become *Parade's End*.

A Man Could Stand Up – in the Series

The focus of this Introduction will be *A Man Could Stand Up –*, but *Punch*'s notice should serve as a reminder that the novel was not intended to be seen or to stand alone. Furthermore, the magazine's reviewer was sure about the quality of volume III, as well as the number of volumes that should be read alongside it. (Although *Last Post* was not yet out, Ford described *A Man Could Stand Up* – as the 'penultimate' in the series in its dedicatory letter.)[3] Different opinions have been expressed on both counts. This is to be expected regarding reviews, of course, and the novel's critical reception forms a later section in this Introduction. Less predictable, though, were the occasional presentations of Ford's magnificent series as a trilogy instead of a tetralogy.

---

3 Isabel Paterson's column in the *New York Herald Tribune* on 21 November 1926 eagerly anticipated the fourth volume. 'All will be revealed,' she wrote, 'in two or three years'; especially the 'ultimate fate of Christopher Tietjens'.

Details can be found in the Introduction to *Last Post*; suffice it to say here that (the clue being in the title) *Last Post* is an integral part of *Parade's End*.[4] 'Tale Three', however, as *Punch* called *A Man Could Stand Up –*, was always going to be its climax. *A Man Could Stand Up –* treats the reader to at least two high points. The first comes when protagonist Christopher Tietjens, at war, has been under bombardment, narrowly escaping death. After rescuing one of his men he undergoes a transformational experience, in which the 'complete taciturnity' to which we were introduced in *Some Do Not . . .* is overthrown. (Ford made it clear there that Tietjens believed not only that you didn't 'talk' about how you felt, but it was possible you didn't think about it either, I.i.)[5] Forced by a combination of hellish circumstance and his own instinctive response into new psychological territory, Tietjens does now consider how he feels. He appraises his physical performance, realises 'for the first time' that he is grateful for his strength and capability, and thanks God resoundingly for them (II.vi). The second, related, high point of the text is the formal climax, found in the last lines of the last page, as Valentine, the woman Christopher loves, celebrates her approaching union with him. It is Armistice Day. They are not alone. Fellow soldiers who promised to 'look old Tietjens up' have kept on arriving at the door. Accordingly, though not seamlessly, the celebration expands to take account of them all. The strains of a French nursery rhyme help to conjure this specifically post-war reconstruction of a 'domaine perdu' – 'Ainsi font, font, font / Les petites marionettes / Ainsi font, font, font / Trois petits tours'.[6] There is noise and dancing, and smashing glasses, and faces swim in and

---

4 The most famous example (which draws on some of Ford's expressed views too) is Graham Greene's 1963 Bodley Head edition, which omits *Last Post*.
5 And in *No More Parades* Tietjens surmised that '[h]e would, literally, rather be dead than an open book' (I.iii). Neither Tietjens, nor those upon whom he was modelled, were alone in their 'taciturnity' of course: 'The English habit of managing difficult feelings was to suppress rather than to discuss them, as if by remaining silent the feelings would disappear', writes Juliet Nicolson in *The Great Silence 1918–1920: Living in the Shadow of the Great War* (London: John Murray, 2009), 6. Cf. Ford's description of the 'national characteristic' of repression in his book *The Spirit of the People* (1907), volume III of *England and the English*, ed. Sara Haslam (Manchester: Carcanet, 2003), 313–15. The story Ford tells here relates to the 'germ' of what is, perhaps, his most famous novel, *The Good Soldier* (1915).
6 See the footnote to the text for more on this rhyme.

out of focus before her.[7] Above all, Valentine experiences the happiness and hope of the only kind of wedding the two of them might know: there is no priest and there are no vows, and Tietjens is already married, but 'They were the centre of unending roaring circles' (III.ii), and this is a wedding in all but name. As *A Man Could Stand Up –* comes to a close Tietjens is dancing (Tietjens is *dancing!*) with Valentine. The English language alone cannot do justice to the joy, so there is French too; prose, and speech, cannot achieve it either, so there is rhyme and song; and Ford deploys ellipsis one final time, unwilling to complete the picture of the future filling Valentine's head and heart.[8]

The tripartite structure of *A Man Could Stand Up –* is carefully planned, and certainly contributes overall to the deep satisfactions the novel provides in scenes such as these. There may be no beginning, middle and end in classical style: Ford's modernist use of time-shift prevents it. There are, however, clearly developed patterns of character interaction as well as individual protagonists who progress. Parts I and III take place on Armistice Day, while the much longer middle section returns us in time and space to the Front during the war. Part I gives us Valentine in her work at the school – during which she thinks and talks about Christopher; Part II concentrates on Christopher at war – often reminded of Valentine. Part III, later on Armistice Day, brings the two of them together, realising or anticipating their congress sexually, intellectually, and emotionally. Valentine is welcomed into the soldiers' 'family', a stark contrast to the common projection in war writing of an unbridgeable divide between those who fought, and those who did not.

The sense of optimism and excitement in this novel is testament to Ford's focus on his fiction and belief in its potential, and it is true to say that none of the other three volumes achieves its heights in these respects. Close attention to his life during 1926, not to mention his devastating experience of war, mean readers

---

7 Smashing glasses was a popular pastime at Armistice Day celebrations. At the Savoy, the more adventurous members of the RAF were swinging from the chandeliers and there were nearly three thousand smashed glasses in the hotel's dustbins the following morning (Nicolson, *The Great Silence* 35).

8 Valentine could not possibly have imagined how things would go that night. *Last Post* provides the details of their 'nuit de noces' (I.vii), as well giving the longer view.

might expect a considerably more murky and complex picture; and the threat posed by Tietjens' absent wife Sylvia is still very real in volume III, as are the fear and suffering in the face of war. Overall, though, its structure and its hope can only mean that Ford is seeing some things, at least, clearly in this novel and, in the final analysis, positively too. In *Some Do Not* . . . Ford had found the perspective necessary for treating the war in fiction. This had been facilitated by the passage of time, and by his leaving England for France in 1922. (His swift interpretation of the need for such a move contributed to the fact that his novels came out earlier than many of the other 'big' war texts.)[9] The individual qualities of *A Man Could Stand Up* – represent a development of that same perspective, one which enabled him, in addition, to acknowledge and at the same time imagine moving on from the mental suffering caused by the war, itself complicating an early history of agoraphobia and neurosis. A man could stand up, in order first of all to show that he had endured and survived; and then he would look properly about him. Siegfried Sassoon, also an infantry officer in the war, believed something similar, though like Ford took several years to work it out, and say so:

I saw [Armageddon] then, as I see it now – a dreadful place, a place of horror and desolation which no imagination could have invented. Also it was a place where a man of strong spirit might know himself utterly powerless against death and destruction, and yet stand up and defy gross darkness and stupefying shell-fire, discovering in himself the invincible resistance of an animal or an insect, and an endurance which he might, in after days, forget or disbelieve.[10]

---

9 *Death of a Hero, All Quiet on the Western Front* and *Goodbye to All That* were all published in 1929, for example. In R. A. Scott-James' preface to the 1948 Penguin edition of *A Man Could Stand Up* – he writes that Ford's novels came 'too soon', perhaps, for the buying public, who were being asked to 're-live the painful years of the Great War' (Harmondsworth: Penguin, 1948), 5.

10 George Sherston [Siegfried Sassoon], *Memoirs of an Infantry Officer* (London: Faber & Faber, 1930), 216–17.

Though I will return to Ford's choice of title in more detail later on, it is this related writerly aim of being able to see the subject clearly, without fear or flinching, that is perhaps most important in the initial approach to the book. 'It is unbearable to exist', as Ford put it later, 'without some view of life as a whole.'[11] War had taken this ability away from him in a variety of terrible ways.

Biography

Ford was born in 1873. He began to publish his writing well before the century was out. At first there were fairy tales, inspired or illustrated by the painters of his grandfather's circle. He wrote poetry too, and initiated what would be a lifelong interest in recording lives and impressions when he published a biography of his grandfather, Ford Madox Brown, in 1896. He married young, and he and Elsie had two daughters. When he enlisted in July 1915, he was forty-one years old.

At his age and at that date (conscription was not introduced until the following year) he didn't need to fight, and he was not really fit enough to do so, but his decision was founded on more than one aspect of his life in those times. It is important to remember that he was still known then as Ford Madox Hueffer. His father was a German émigré, but even in the year of the sinking of the *Lusitania*, when atrocity-mongering and anti-German feeling became increasingly prominent aspects of the cultural milieu, he did not feel the need to change his name before joining up.[12] Later he himself described 'Hueffer' as both

11 Ford, *The English Novel: From the Earliest Days to the Death of Joseph Conrad* (1930) (Manchester: Carcanet, 1983), 12.
12 Circulation of those newspapers which ran most atrocity stories, and the ripest of rumours, increased steadily between 1914 and 1916. The *Daily Mail's* figures, for example, rose from 946,000 before the war to 1.4 million in June 1916. In January 1915, Ford (still Hueffer of course) was ordered to leave the county by the chief constable of West Sussex. The order was revoked a few days later, and Ford suspected that it had its roots in personal animosity because Ford had satirised the violently anti-German Edward Heron Allen in a story, 'The Scaremonger', published three months after the outbreak of war. See Max Saunders' biography of Ford: *Ford Madox Ford: A Dual Life*, 2 vols (Oxford: Oxford University Press, 1996), I 472–3. Alan Judd's biography of Ford records that he attracted 'unpleasant attention' because of his German name and ancestry, and was 'insulted in the street' (*Ford Madox Ford* [London: HarperCollins, 1991], 246–7).

'suspect and unpronounceable',[13] yet, citing 'native stubborn-ness', he did not choose to become Ford Madox Ford until after the war.[14] It would have been hard to question seriously his loyalty at this point – though, as I will suggest later, such ques-tioning would have led to an interesting discussion. After all, he enlisted, and soon afterwards he produced two volumes of propaganda when asked to by his friend, the Liberal Cabinet minister C. F. G. Masterman. One of these, *Between St. Dennis and St. George*, reported the sinking of the *Lusitania* as well as the horrific possibility that German sailors had filmed the deaths of women and children as it sank.[15] And Ford believed in the war, increasingly through its first months. When he had finished with the propaganda, that belief – widely shared, as it turned out – became more evidently nuanced and complicated. *No Enemy*, which he began writing in 1919, and then *Parade's End*, show how.[16]

There are at least three discernible stages in Ford's early response to the First World War. The first was brief. It belongs to the weeks following the declaration of war on 4 August 1914 and was characterised by a lack of understanding and acceptance of its aims, mainly contextualised by Ford's perception of himself as both a 'cosmopolitan' and a poet, a member of a supra-national 'republic of letters' dedicated above all to the cause of great liter-ature. (At this time, too, he expressed his belief that his 'own heart is certain to be mangled' whichever side won.) Ford felt he could trust nothing he read in the newspapers, and experienced only 'depression' at the bellicosity of the language employed to

13 Ford, *It Was the Nightingale* (1933) (New York: The Ecco Press, 1984), 136.
14 The reasons were more complex than that, and included the ending of a relationship and the beginning of a new one (see later in the Introduction for details). Ford's refer-ence to 'native stubbornness' came in a letter to his agent, J. B. Pinker, in June 1919; see *Letters of Ford Madox Ford*, ed. Richard M. Ludwig (Princeton, NJ: Princeton University Press, 1964), 93.
15 Ford Madox Hueffer [Ford], *Between St. Dennis and St. George: A Sketch of Three Civil-isations* (London: Hodder and Stoughton, 1915), 111. The companion volume, also published by Hodder in 1915, was *When Blood is Their Argument: An Analysis of Prussian Culture*. Since September 1914, Masterman had been co-ordinating the War Propaganda Bureau from his office at Wellington House. Adding to the discussion about names above, it must have been useful to him to have an author with a German surname producing pro-Allies propaganda.
16 *No Enemy*, which presents the war reminiscences of the fictional poet Gringoire, was not published until 1929.

describe what he still wanted to call 'the gallant enemy'.[17] At this time he found himself unable to write a poem about the war, though he tried, because of 'the hazy remoteness of the war-grounds', and because he could believe nothing of what was said about the conflict.[18] In the second stage, he wrote 'Antwerp', the war poem T. S. Eliot, among others, so much admired. The city had surrendered to the Germans in October 1914, and Ford saw with his own eyes the resulting refugees. He found that he did begin to believe some of the things he heard about the experiences of these civilians, or, at least, could not ignore them. This ushered in a third stage, which resulted in the following section from his 'Literary Portraits' series in the *Outlook*, as well as the (somewhat idiosyncratic) propaganda he would write for Wellington House:

> Three months ago [he wrote in January 1915], I remember – and it seems as if it were a dream of another age on this planet – I wrote that I wished the war could be conducted in terms of 'the gallant enemy'. Now I should thank God to know that a million Germans were killed; and my gentle companion would have thanked God, and every soul in that building would have uttered words of gratitude to that Most High, Who presumably made the Germans as well as ourselves.[19]

Despite the strength of feeling expressed here, Ford never completely lost his sense of the 'good and kindly Germans'[20] who co-existed with the spirit of Prussian militarism that he was

---

17 All these quotations are taken from his series 'Literary Portraits', published in the *Outlook*. Relevant extracts (those quoted appeared between early August and mid-September 1914) can be found in Ford, *War Prose*, ed. Max Saunders (Manchester: Carcanet, 1999), 207–9.

18 While this inability to believe in and write about the war was superseded, Ford did experience later periods of doubt, and sometimes simultaneous difficulty with words. A good example is provided by the essay 'Arms and the Mind', written in the Ypres Salient in 1916, in which he describes looking from Max Redoubt, on the Albert–Bécourt Wood road, up to Martinpuich, and over Mametz, Fricourt, Bécourt-Bécordel – all key locations in *A Man Could Stand Up –*. He thinks of the men in that territory, 'moving one against the other and impelled by an invisible moral force into a Hell of fear', and confesses that he has no explanation of why this is so. 'It is the Will of God', he concludes (*War Prose* 38).

19 *War Prose* 210.

20 *War Prose* 207.

writing against in *When Blood is Their Argument* and *Between St. Dennis and St George*. This combination would resurface in key scenes in *A Man Could Stand Up –*, when violence and fearfulness can also be matched with pity and understanding for the men in the trenches opposite. It is, in part, what his long-term partner Stella Bowen responded to in Ford after the war: 'I soon found that if he was a militarist, he was at the same time the exact opposite.'[21] Receiving his commission in the Welch Regiment, however, he felt he was, at least, ready to fight.

Ford had other motivating factors for leaving London. His relationship with Violet Hunt, the novelist and socialite with whom he had begun an affair, was deteriorating.[22] He wanted to leave her, and it was proving very difficult to do. He was also still married, to Elsie, who did not want to grant him a divorce. Emotional difficulties like these would be persistent throughout his life.[23] Perhaps you cannot create a character like Sylvia Tietjens without having experienced particular kinds of torment first. (One hopes it was never as dramatically awful in reality for Ford as Mark Tietjens imagined it was for his brother: Sylvia, according to Mark, 'was as thin as an eel, as full of vice as a mare that's a wrong un, completely disloyal'; what's more she's a 'harlot' and a 'bitch', *Last Post* I.v.)

The War

Having received his commission as a second lieutenant in the Welch Regiment (Special Reserve), Ford went first (probably) to the Chelsea Barracks, then to Wales for training: Tenby and Cardiff. He left for France on 13 July 1916. In an essay written later about the journey, its scenes are reconstructed in Pre-Raphaelite and cubist pictures (the 'clouds, shadows, pale faces,

21 Stella Bowen, *Drawn From Life* (London: Collins, 1941), 62.
22 The affair had begun by 1909, when Ford was editing the *English Review*. It caused, or helped to cement, rifts with some of the most important figures in his life: Arthur Marwood, for example, who would prove particularly significant to the history of *Parade's End*, and Joseph Conrad.
23 See Joseph Wiesenfarth, *Ford Madox Ford and the Regiment of Women: Violet Hunt, Jean Rhys, Stella Bowen, Janice Biala* (Madison, WI: University of Wisconsin Press, 2005).

spirals of violet smoke, out of which loomed the iron columns supporting the station roof' at Waterloo station; the meadows under the summer sun and the small pink clouds in France).[24] In Rouen he found time to focus on Flaubert, before being attached to the 9th Battalion and sent to the Somme. He was stationed with battalion transport near Bécourt Wood – a key location in *A Man Could Stand Up –*. From here, he provides less evidence of his responses to colour (although the landscape and its trees are detailed), but his very first letters signal a total attention to the soundscape of war that would mark his writing about it for good.[25]

It is the overwhelming experience of sound that Mary R. Habeck argues was most commented on by soldiers, particularly novices, as they arrived at the Front. 'I'm going stark, staring mad because of the guns', is how Siegfried Sassoon put it in one famous example.[26] This experience was mostly related to the shells and other forms of artillery. The noise often terrified Ford, and yet the results of his simultaneous literary alertness can be seen in the precise transcriptions of different artillery sounds – in the air, and exploding on impact – throughout his war books. In fact, Ford used his own responses to the noise to test his skills, writing to his friend Joseph Conrad in September 1916 about his experiences during a terrible storm in what he hoped was a 'constatation of some exactness' – he was under artillery bombardment too.[27] The sense of writers' exercises persisted in subsequent communications to his friend; one letter begins 'I will continue, "for yr information and necessary action, please," my notes upon sound' and proceeds to detail the noises made by different forms of artillery meeting specific landscapes.[28] Though Tietjens 'was

---

24 See the essay 'Pon... ti... pri... ith', first published in French in 1918 (*War Prose* 30–5).
25 Those to Conrad which I go on to discuss, but also to Lucy Masterman, Charles's wife, *Letters* 66–76.
26 Mary R. Habeck, 'Technology in the War', in *The Great War and the Twentieth Century*, ed. Jay Winter et al. (New Haven, CT: Yale University Press, 2006 [2000]), 104. Sassoon's poem is 'Repression of War Experience', in *Collected Poems 1908–1956* (London: Faber & Faber, 1984), 89–90; see also Ivor Gurney's 'On Somme': 'No flame we saw, the noise and the dread alone / Was battle to us', in Kavanagh (ed.), *Ivor Gurney: Collected Poems* 206. '[N]oise rushed like black angels gone mad; solid noise that swept you off your feet' in Christopher Tietjens' trench in *A Man Could Stand Up –* (II.i).
27 *Letters* 71.
28 *Letters* 73–4.

never much good at identifying artillery by the sound' (II.iv), it was evidently crucial to Ford that he did so – and who better to write about it to than Conrad, his mentor and erstwhile collaborator, who professed faith in both the 'force of a word' and the 'power of sound'.[29]

Ford's soundscape, however, was also made up of birds: the swallows and larks in particular that would punctuate so pointedly the action of *A Man Could Stand Up* – as well as numerous other accounts of this war. To Lucy Masterman he wrote of the way he was able still to hear the singing of the 'innumerable larks' through a bombardment, and of how the sky was full alike of 'sausage balloons, swallows, larks & occasional aeroplanes'. 'I have jeered against the nature-love of the English', Ford was to admit in *It Was the Nightingale*, 'but I will confess that I am never completely easy unless I have the sense of the feathered things near me.'[30] Birds bring blessings (the flight of birds means they have long served as symbols of the links between heaven and earth). The year is 'sanctified' once the nightingale's song has been heard for the first time, and Ford weaves birdsong into his understanding of the creative spirit. The 'amazing bouquet of sounds' is like 'an incredible spray of sparks from an anvil' but does not disturb his 'tranquil penmanship'.[31] In his war writing, Ford is also clear about the beauties and benefits of swallows and thrushes. The experience of walking through a field of thistles, full of swallows, makes both Gringoire (Ford's *persona* in *No Enemy*)[32] and Tietjens feel immortal, like Greek gods, as the rush of beating wings, the colour and the sensation combine in something like a 'miracle' to exalt them.[33] To Ford, however, 'larks were less inspiring' (II.vi). While some writers use them in ways

29 See Conrad's preface to *A Personal Record* (1912) – originally serialised, of course (having been requested) by Ford in his *English Review* (Dec. 1908–June 1909). Particularly effective examples, as well as variations, of Conrad's views on sound can be found in Chapter 15 of *Lord Jim: A Tale* (1900) and Part III of *Victory* (1915).

30 *Nightingale* 246. On nature, cf. his account of the English landscape, and the effects of familiarity with it, in the *Heart of the Country* (1906), volume II of *England and the English* 164–5.

31 *Nightingale* 248.

32 Paul Skinner's description in his Introduction to *No Enemy: A Tale of Reconstruction* (Manchester: Carcanet, 2002), viii.

33 *No Enemy* 25; *A Man Could Stand Up* – II.vi. In both cases the effect depends on the sense of mortality that is also made present by Ford.

one might expect, as a reminder of life beyond war (in Sebastian Faulks' novel *Birdsong* (1993), a lark 'singing in the unharmed air above him' signals the end of the war for protagonist Stephen Wraysford),[34] there is often ambivalence here. Commentary on John McCrae's poem 'Flanders Field', written at Ypres in 1915, for example, picks up on the way that the ubiquitous larks, singing 'bravely', sanction defiance; and yet some soldiers took potshots at them because of the unbearable contrast they made in their song and flight with the men's earth-bound experiences.[35] In Tietjens' mind, they also provide a symbol of the differences between him and his men. Rendered almost paranoid on more than one occasion, he feels that they are hostile towards him, that they are 'screaming imprecations and threats', and that they make a 'heartless noise' which he relates to a poem by Mathilde Blind (a poet known to Ford who scared him to death: see the relevant footnote to the text in II.vi).

Ford would return repeatedly to this aspect of the war – its sounds – which impressed him immediately. But his war moved on very fast. Either later the same day on which he wrote to Lucy Masterman about the larks, or on the following day, he was blown up by a shell. In the Introduction to *No More Parades*, volume II of *Parade's End* and the first of the series to feature the war, Joseph Wiesenfarth points out that Ford 'was on the scene of the two bloodiest actions of the Great War': the Somme and, later in 1916, Ypres. It would have been miraculous if he had escaped injury in both, though he was with battalion transport and there-fore removed from the front line (his C.O.'s decision, due to his age). His physical injuries cannot have been too serious, because he was at Ypres by 16 August, but he was suffering from shell-shock. The regular relapses he suffered, along with the damage to his memory – he forgot his name and lost completely and for good the narrative of three weeks of his life – also contributed to the

---

34 Sebastian Faulks, *Birdsong* (London: Hutchinson, 1993), 392.
35 See http://www.ppu.org.uk/learn/poetry/poetry_ww1_1.html (accessed 22 May 2009).
    This contrastive quality of the larks can be seen in other poems: Edmund Blunden's
    'Two Voices' ('as thus he broke / The death-news, bright the skylarks sang') and Isaac
    Rosenberg's 'Returning, We Hear the Larks', for example. Ford quotes in *No Enemy* a
    letter of Gaudier-Brzeska's – 'Today is magnificent, a fresh wind, clear sun, and larks
    singing cheerfully ...' – immediately before describing how he learned of his death in
    1915 (110).

fact that it took Ford Madox Ford some years to write in any prolonged way about the war.

Later war duties included training and lecturing, in France and back in England and, as he would later re-imagine in *A Man Could Stand Up –*, guarding German prisoners at Abbeville. He left the army in January 1919. Though he started off living in London once more, recovery for him meant the country and his new love, the Australian painter Stella Bowen. Red Ford, his first stop, was a 'leaky-roofed, tile-healed, rat-ridden seventeenth-century, five-shilling a week, moribund labourer's cottage'.[36] He had some writing to attempt, and though he felt very much as though he was starting again at his craft, he did write.[37] He also had some reading to do. While he had absorbed himself in fiction during what Tietjens calls the 'eternal waiting that is war' (II.ii), he now wanted to turn – in what would become an obsession with notions of perspective – to 'the events of war and of the world outside my own three inches on the map'.[38] And his lungs needed to heal. First of all, though, Ford grew vegetables, got to know locals and animals, especially pigs, and cooked simple food. Simple things, because whatever he was doing at that time he was also contending with a 'horde of minor malices and doubts' that were alive in the shadows, and 'whispering beings that jeered' behind his back through the 'dark, gleaming panes of the windows' – the main psychological legacy of his war.[39] These 'malices and doubts' were inextricably linked to his sense of his abilities as a writer and, therefore, whether or not he would be able to make a living post-war. (He and Stella were expecting a child by the beginning of 1920.) This most vivid account of them comes immediately after he has remembered an experience at the Somme when, 'during gunfire that shook the earth', he prayed that his reason might be preserved, in order that he could, later, just continue to do his job. Yes, he needed the money. But he also wanted others to know what war was like. More than that, he

---

36 *Nightingale* 23.
37 He feared his readership would have deserted him as well as his skill (*Nightingale* 17).
38 *Nightingale* 27. In *No Enemy* it is 'that eternal "waiting to report" that takes up 112/113ths of one's time during war' (33). Stephen Crane's *The Red Badge of Courage* is one book that was particularly important to Ford at war.
39 *Nightingale* 116.

would eventually be prepared to put aside his maxim that a writer's job is not to moralise and write a work with a purpose: of 'obviating all future wars'.[40]

Considering the title Ford chose for volume III of *Parade's End*, one might have expected him to begin writing it, or something similar, at the house he and Stella bought together after Red Ford. It was called Coopers Cottage and was in Bedham, Sussex, in what Bowen described as an 'extravagantly beautiful and quite inaccessible spot on a great wooded hill'.[41] It had an amazing view – locals said twelve counties, Ford would almost swear to three from one window. Even this setting, combined with such peace, was not enough to kindle the next great creative phase of his writing life. A greater remove (from the war, but also from the hard physical labour of running a smallholding) in the end proved necessary. But he had to earn a living, and there was other writing he began with: a translation of Euripides' *Alcestis*; poetry, including the prize-winning 'A House', which celebrated his life with Stella at Red Ford; some articles for the *New Statesman* (later to be re-worked into *No Enemy*); reminiscence, and some fiction too. His production rate does seem, on the face of it, to have slowed. In the period 1910–14 he published seven novels, three volumes of poetry and five other works. In the war years he published one novel – that first masterpiece, *The Good Soldier*, mostly written before the war began – one volume of poetry and four others.[42] Between 1918 and 1923 there was only one novel (*The Marsden Case*), poetry publications, including the long poem *Mister Bosphorus and the Muses*, and *Thus to Revisit: Some Reminiscences*. Though he was certainly writing, if not publishing so much, in this period, it is clear that he needed to wait until he could write properly about the war.[43] Three books came in 1924, one of them *Some Do Not . . . .*

---

40 *Nightingale* 225. See, for his expression of this maxim, the epilogue to *A Call* (1910)
   (Manchester: Carcanet, 1984), for example, or the beginning of Part III of *Joseph
   Conrad: A Personal Remembrance* (1924) (New York: The Ecco Press, 1989).
41 Bowen, *Drawn from Life* 69.
42 On the question of the date of completion of this novel see Martin Stannard's Introduction to *The Good Soldier* (London and New York: Norton, 1995).
43 His work from the time includes the uncompleted novel *True Love and a GCM*
   [General Court Martial], and the complete but unpublished *Mr Croyd*, for example,
   as well as the material that later became *No Enemy*.

Stella Bowen describes in her letters her life with Ford in ways that reveal how much he must have needed her at that time, to live, but also to work. He acknowledged that debt often, but particularly movingly in a letter he wrote to her from America in November 1926 when he was ill: 'So, as this is a quiet moment I'll seize it and say that if I've done anything during these last years and if I am anything it has been entirely due to you.'[44] Aspects of Bowen's forthright intelligence are clearly drawn on by Ford in his creation of Valentine Wannop's character, though there are other likely sources too.[45] Her care was fundamental. He did not begin his 'immense novel', however – it is intriguing to wonder if he ever would have done if they had remained in Sussex – until the poet and editor Harold Monro offered them the loan of a small villa at Cap Ferrat, near Villefranche.[46] 'I was no sooner installed on those heights from which one could throw a biscuit on to the decks of the men of war in Villefrance bay – and see the octopus and mullet swim beneath those keels ... than, at once [...] I wrote the first words.'[47] Another hill, then, with a different view, and a rediscovery of his identity as a writer, and he could begin.

Writing A Man Could Stand Up –

The detail as to Ford's composition of volumes I and II of *Parade's End* can be found in the Introductions to *Some Do Not ...* and *No More Parades*. Their appearance set the scene for his writing of *A Man Could Stand Up* – in more ways than those obvious ones of character and plot. First of all, they were very popular.[48] *Some*

---

44 *The Correspondence of Ford Madox Ford and Stella Bowen*, ed. Sondra J. Stang and Karen Cochran (Bloomington and Indianapolis: Indiana University Press, 1994), 229–30.

45 He charts his development of both Valentine and Sylvia in *Nightingale* 210–11. Bowen does not feature here, but he does mention the actress Dorothy Minto. See Saunders, *A Dual Life* II 267ff. for more on the links between people in Ford's life and the characters in the tetralogy, as well as Saunders' introduction to *Some Do Not ....* Ford points out in both *It Was the Nightingale* and *Return to Yesterday* that Christopher Tietjens was based on Arthur Marwood, who died in 1916.

46 An interesting use of 'novel' in the singular here; and in some respects, *Parade's End* is one novel.

47 *Nightingale* 193.

48 Ford hadn't experienced sustained critical success since the *England and the English* trilogy nearly twenty years previously. See my Introduction to *England* xiii–xx. The other works he was producing in the twenties, *A Mirror to France* (London: Duckworth, 1926), for example, did not do as well.

Do Not ... sold 'like hot cakes' Ford said, and was reprinted in 1924.[49] The reviews of *No More Parades* were even better, and it sold very well indeed, making Ford proper money – the Boni first edition in the United States sold 9000 copies and went through five reprints before the end of 1926 (when volume III came out). Ernest Hemingway called Ford at this point one of 'the two most generally admired novelists in America'.[50] Hemingway's description is interesting, because of the intense rivalries of their relationship perhaps, but also, when coupled with those sales figures, because of his precise use of 'America'. In the time between the publication of *Some Do Not* ... and his writing of *A Man Could Stand Up* – Ford had become a novelist who sold well, with all the attendant benefits to his confidence and self-esteem.[51] He also became a novelist who sold better in the States. His life as a writer and editor in Paris/Provence in the early twenties expanded accordingly, and – tiring and disruptive as it was – he began to travel regularly to the US. Elements of all these transformations fed into the tone and structure of *A Man Could Stand Up* –, and also allowed him, I suggest, to write this novel as fast as he did. He knew he was at the top of his game.

Ford began *A Man Could Stand Up* – in January 1926, at Toulon. He and Stella were on holiday while work was completed on their new Paris studio. They both worked as they travelled, visiting Ezra and Dorothy Pound at Rapallo as well. It was not just building work that they were leaving behind them. Ford was involved in a new affair, with the novelist Jean Rhys, and she had been staying with them. Though it is entirely possible that Rhys gave Ford some assistance with the novel in its later stages – perhaps it was she who took Ford's dictation, as I suggest in the Note on the Text – it must have been easier to write away from that particular domestic set up. By Easter, though, he and Stella were on their way home. *A Man Could Stand Up* – is not a long novel (around 70,000 words), but he may not have been quite as far on with it as he thought when he wrote to his publisher, Gerald Duckworth, on 9 March from Toulon saying 'A month's

---

49 *Nightingale* 351.
50 Saunders, *A Dual Life* II 288.
51 Unfortunately it also gave rise to a different series of problems with publishers over royalties, in particular Seltzer in the US with regard to *Some Do Not* ....

good work will finish it'.[52] It is likely that he completed a draft in mid-May. This would mean that if he had worked steadily, in his usual routine, he would have been almost halfway through when he wrote to Duckworth, a short while before returning to Paris. (The signs of possible dictation begin at roughly mid-point.) Five months later, the novel was published in the UK and the US.

Publication and Reception

In the UK *A Man Could Stand Up* – was published in the second week of October, most likely on the 8th or 9th.[53] Duckworth made sure the launch emphasised the series of which it was a part. The back of the dust-jacket ran with two reviews of each of *Some Do Not . . .* and *No More Parades* (as well as one of *The Marsden Case*), while the inside flap provided a summary of the novel:

> In this novel Mr. Ford continues the survey of his own times which began so brilliantly with "Some Do Not" and "No More Parades". The whole series constitutes the most remarkable picture of the reactions of the civilian and military populations, and, more particularly, of the sexes one to the other, in a prolonged war. "A Man Could Stand Up—" is a vivid and startlingly outspoken description of the state of men's minds during the period of growing disillusionment which ended in the Armistice.

The publisher also made sure that readers knew Ford had previously been known as 'Ford Madox Hueffer', bracketing this name both on the spine and on the inside flap after the first reference to the title and author. The design on the cover makes it one of the more interesting jackets of the series; there is a line drawing of the top half of a soldier, in profile, seeming to duck, and holding onto the edge of his tin hat (see image, p. xii).

---

52 *Letters* 168–9. See also the early footnote to the Dedicatory Letter in the text for more on Duckworth.

53 There is a limited amount of pre-publication material for these novels, as explained in the Note on this Edition. What we know about the date of the first publication of *A Man Could Stand Up* – is drawn to a significant degree from the reviews, which themselves may have been based on advance copies.

The American edition, released by Albert & Charles Boni, came out shortly afterwards, possibly only a week later. The dust-jacket of this edition carried the title front and centre, in large bold white type in a black box. A write-up of the volume, and the series, ran from the top down to the bottom, around the edges of the title box. It began, 'The Third in a series that is, to put it mildly, a breathtaking, Herculanean project …'

The first review of the novel cited by Ford's bibliographer was penned by Gerald Gould, in the *Observer* on 10 October. (Though a few more reviews have been uncovered since David Harvey published his bibliography, none of them predates this one by Gould.) It is a very favourable write-up, which calls Part II 'the best thing that Ford has ever done—and that is saying a lot'. Gould evidently did not appreciate the presentation of Tietjens' character in the previous volumes, but feels that here something has changed: 'It is as if his hero […] who in the previous volumes […] was a nightmare of almost incredible incredibility, had come to life under the urgent threat of death.' The *Times Literary Supplement* review four days later agreed: 'the second part is magnificent', with its 'wonderfully blended mosaic of incidents, speeches, reflections'. H. C. Harwood, in the *Outlook*, felt that the book was not as consistently impressive as its predecessor, but admitted that Ford's 'genius' continued to command 'an almost awed attention' nevertheless. Isabel Paterson's name has featured already, and she was one of Ford's most vocal champions in the United States. Writing in the *New York Herald Tribune* in the first American review (17 October) she takes a similar line to Duckworth on its dust-jacket. She emphasises the vast social shift that Ford had taken for his subject and had then gone on to realise in what she called an 'astonishing achievement'.

Though there is undoubted warmth in the reviews of *A Man Could Stand Up* – and some high praise ('it is about the most exciting thing to have happened to the novel since "The Way of All Flesh"' was John Crawford's response in the *New York Times*) it was not, overall, as acclaimed as *No More Parades*. If reviewers stated a preference as to its constituent parts, they found its strengths to be in Part II, at war; if they liked this section, they tended to like it greatly. Too much 'psychology', or its rendering in overly impressionist style, formed the basis of the criticism of its first and last sections, though on one occasion in terms that sound rather like success instead (Valentine's 'confusions are too faithfully reproduced', according to Harwood's *Outlook* review). *Time* magazine (10 January 1927), among others, however, appreciated greatly the effect of this very style: 'The total effect is vivid, clear and all the stronger for its slow fusing.' 'Each moment,' L.P. Hartley had said in the *Saturday Review*, 'is like a re-birth, a re-awakening to pain and perplexity.' 'We are sorry,' he continued, 'to say goodbye to Tietjens.' He didn't know yet that he didn't have to.[54]

The novel had its second printing in the US in December 1926, and it sold well there, as *No More Parades* had done (Boni gave Harvey figures indicating that the first three novels of the series all sold over 10,000 copies). In the UK the figures were lower, as one might expect, and the total, of around 1000, was a disappointment to Ford despite his success elsewhere. His autumn trip to the US to publicise the novel convinced him of his popularity, however. The audiences he pulled in at clubs and colleges were sometimes very large, and allowed him to write home to Bowen on his birthday in 1926 saying that he had been 'speaking *triumphantly*' every day that week.[55] *A Man Could Stand Up* – sold 200 copies the morning after the first weekly article he wrote as a visiting critic in the *New York Herald Tribune Books*, and 600 orders came in on 27 December.[56]

Summary of the Novel

Despite being only the third of the series, *A Man Could Stand Up* – acts climactically, and cathartically, in ways related to form as

---

54 All the reviews from which I have quoted, with the exception of *Time* magazine's, can be found in David Dow Harvey's bibliography of Ford, *Ford Madox Ford 1873–1939: A Bibliography of Works and Criticism* (Princeton, NJ: Princeton University Press, 1962), 366–70. See also Max Saunders, 'Ford Madox Ford: Further Bibliographies', *English Literature in Transition 1880–1920*, 43.2 (2000), 131–205, and Ashley Chantler's more recent supplement, accessible via the Ford Madox Ford Society website at www.open.ac.uk/Arts/fordmadoxford-society

55 Ford/Bowen 256.

56 The figures were given to Ford by Albert Boni, and he passed them on to Stella in a letter on this date (*Ford/Bowen* 276).

well as content. Most obviously, perhaps, it contrives a final scene on Armistice Night, but the conclusion is not, of course, quite as simple as that implies. Nor is the tripartite structure as neat as it might first appear. Parts I and III, which take place on Armistice Day, number three and two chapters respectively, and Part I is longer as one might expect. Part II takes the reader back in time. It is significantly longer than the other two parts put together, containing six out of eleven chapters and 164 out of 275 pages in the UK first edition. It bears the weight, then, and might be said to halt the sense of progression, retaining more of the reader's attention on its prolonged presentation of Tietjens and his men at war. How does *A Man Could Stand Up –* contribute to Antony Fowles' description of 'the decorum of the tetralogy's handling of time'?[57] There are, on the face of it, a couple of glitches in relation to the chronology of the previous volumes. Such glitches might bear witness to the difficulty of handling a series of four novels over five such years in Ford's life,[58] but more to the point is that his protagonist has been suffering from memory loss and shell-shock. In fact, time itself is seemingly both stretched and foreshortened in all kinds of ways throughout the tetralogy as a deliberate component of Ford's technique. It is worthy of particular comment in *A Man Could Stand Up –*. The action of Part I takes place during approximately twenty minutes of 'real time'. The whole six chapters of Part II occupy a real-time slot of around forty-five minutes. During Part III Armistice Day evening turns into night. Ford's creative debt to the man he had recently termed 'the Master from New England', Henry James, most particularly his interest in the detailed representation of consciousness, is starkly visible here.[59] Overall, though, its struc-

57 In his book, *Ford Madox Ford* (London, 2002), 87.
58 Ford began writing *Some Do Not . . .* in 1923; *Last Post* was published in 1928.
59 Ford knew Henry James, and had also published a book about him in 1914. His quoted description came in 'A Haughty and Proud Generation', *Yale Review*, 11 (July 1922), 703–17. The essay is reproduced in Ford, *Critical Essays*, ed. Max Saunders and Richard Stang (Manchester: Carcanet, 2002), 208–17. James' rendering of human consciousness is of evident relevance to Ford's project – and the opening sentence of volume III is an excellent place to begin to make comparisons between the writers. But despite its beginning in a London schoolroom, and concluding in a London house, *A Man Could Stand Up –* represents a dramatic extension of what Ford calls in the same essay the 'Jamesian-At-Home sphere of life' (212). The life of the mind in the face of extraordinary danger and stress is Ford's métier in *Parade's End*. Five months after the essay on James, Ford published an equally relevant one, on James Joyce's *Ulysses*.

ture is such that it realises very effectively Arthur Mizener's description of A Man Could Stand Up – as a novel in which Christopher and Valentine both 'reach the climax of long struggles' and move on, consciously, from their Edwardian selves into a new world.[60] Sylvia is notably absent throughout.

A Man Could Stand Up – opens with Valentine on the telephone, having been called away from her duties in the girls' school where she is a physical instructress. It is around 11 a.m. on Armistice Day. There is excessive noise, from the street and from the girls in the playground, though she has missed the bells, sirens and maroons signalling the eleventh hour.[61] At first unclear as to whom she is talking, it eventually transpires that Edith Ethel Duchemin (now Lady Macmaster) is informing her that Christopher Tietjens is in London once more and in need of help. It is a tortuous conversation, as well as a cunning device. Edith Ethel is malicious, and has managed to link Valentine's name compromisingly with Tietjens' in an earlier part of her conversation – with the headmistress of the school. By the end of this call, and the other conversation in Part I that completes the triangle (Valentine talks to her headmistress face to face; all three women thus talk to each other),[62] we have been reminded of significant events from Some Do Not . . . , as well as of the characters of those involved. Valentine has also reflected on her place in what is now the after-war world, and decided that if he still wants her she will attach herself, for good or ill, to Christopher, whom she loves.

Part II shifts time and place dramatically, returning us to the Front, though not immediately to a bombardment, on a morning in April 1918. Soon the noises of war begin, first of all a 'sulky' cannon; then, immediately, the larks. The conversations between men follow on – paralleling those between women in Part I – as Tietjens discusses the larks, among other things, with his sergeant and also feels, like Valentine, alienated: '[the men]

---

60 Arthur Mizener, The Saddest Story: A Biography of Ford Madox Ford (New York: Carroll and Graf, 1985), 506.
61 The Daily Mail recorded that 'bells burst forth into joyful chimes, maroons were exploded, bands paraded the streets followed by cheering crowds of soldiers and civilians' (12 November 1918). Maroons (small fireworks) are mentioned in the first pages of A Man Could Stand Up –.
62 The men may feature in their conversations, but in the first Part of A Man Could Stand Up – it is women who are running the show.

look at me as a sort of atheist', he thinks, shortly before he begins to brood on his statistical chances of surviving the imminent massive German attack (II.i). The bombardments, when they come, are perhaps less bloody and desperate than in *No More Parades*, though Tietjens does remember at one point the terrible death of O Nine Morgan. Up to and even including the final explosive scene, with one notable exception (in a flash-back to when a German soldier invades their trench and Christopher prepares to stab him),[63] his emotional and psychological responses through the several periods of shelling are subject to a greater sense of an evolving character. Ford, against the background of high tension, is carefully setting out the ways in which his subject will change. From the start of Part II the process is in train that culminates in Tietjens' own declaration as to his place in the post-war world: he will retreat from his professional and personal encumbrances in order to live with Valentine and sell antiques to make a living. Pictures from the past help him to believe in, and enact, this transformation. He recalls some of the same scenes as Valentine from their previous time together; their consciousness-raising is intertwined with similar memory and feeling, though it occurs in different times and – particularly – places.

Part III of *A Man Could Stand Up –* begins as Valentine comes to Gray's Inn in order to meet Christopher. The one remaining hurdle to their becoming lovers is presented by Mrs Wannop, Valentine's mother, and the wife of Christopher's father's oldest friend. She telephones them, in an echo of that first triangulate of telephone conversations which insinuated an adultery that had not taken place. Both Christopher and Valentine talk to Mrs Wannop, and there is a nice irony in the fact that she, in fact, eases the whole matter forward for them by inadvertently letting Christopher know that Valentine is prepared to become his lover. Valentine begins to learn about his war experiences as men from his unit arrive, honouring their promises to look him up; Tietjens, meanwhile, has confessed something of his continuing psychological and emotional terrors to Mrs Wannop on the phone. The drunken celebration and dance that ensues contains

---

63 He does not need to do so because the German is hit by artillery and collapses into the trench. Tietjens aids him immediately.

within it all the tensions of the inter-relationships between the men, as well as their combined experiences. Valentine has found herself thinking of Sylvia more than once. This is why the energy of the dance is so compelling, its level so high. They dance together, and it is as though the 'whole world round them was yelling and prancing round': a microcosm of Armistice Day, and a temporary conclusion to *Parade's End*.

Communication

The organising principles of absence and presence around which *A Man Could Stand Up* – coheres, and related issues of communication, are effectively signified by the repeated use of the telephone in the novel. The conversation between Valentine and Edith Ethel with which it opens has often attracted the attention of critics, because of the ways in which this particular technology amplifies gossip, exacerbating Valentine's fear and doubt. That scene ends with Valentine 'smashing' the telephone, and severing the connection between her and Edith Ethel's world of social climbing and hypocrisy (I.ii). Its use in Part III is as significant. When Valentine adapts Shakespeare ('It broke the word of promise to the ear, the telephone'),[64] she is still caught by her fantasy of Tietjens as the murderous Bluebeard while wrestling with her own agency in the affair. She imagines his telephone has been disconnected, so she will not be able to scream for the police through it when his 'madness caused by sex obsessions' means he tries to strangle her. She, so the fantasy goes, cannot escape. When it actually rings, proving her wrong, she is no longer in the same psychological place. Thanks to her exploration of the house and its furniture – with all they symbolise of Tietjens – she is, instead, prepared to be caught. She answers the phone, and in this mediated fashion, Ford lets us know she will

---

64 As I point out in the footnote in the text, this reference from the beginning of Part III is to Macbeth's words to Macduff in the final scene of Shakespeare's play, on discovering that Macduff had been born by what we would now call caesarean section. Macbeth answers: 'Accursèd be that tongue that tells me so, / For it hath cowed my better part of man; / And be these juggling fiends no more believed, / That palter with us in a double sense, / That keep the word of promise to our ear / And break it to our hope. I'll not fight with thee' (V.x.17–22).

sleep with Tietjens. Readers who are familiar with Ford's Edwardian novel *A Call* (1910) will make a different connection at this point as well, identifying a development between Ford's pre-war and post-war fiction. Robert Grimshaw suffers a prolonged nervous breakdown as a result of answering a telephone when in a very similar situation, though the sexes are reversed. Valentine does not care who knows she is there: 'Her voice might be recognised. Let it be recognised. She desired to be known in a compromising position! What did you do on Armistice Day!' (III.i). The fact that it is her mother on the phone does, however, test her resolve. The plot slows, as it becomes more fraught (and Ford's difficulty with writing this section of the novel is detailed in the Note on the Text), and then Christopher takes over, meaning that her resolve, whatever its status, becomes temporarily irrelevant. Instead of being with her, he will talk to her mother about her. Those most directly involved in a situation rarely discuss it with each other, Armistice Day or not.

In the Introduction to *Some Do Not ...*, Max Saunders discusses the characteristic conversation pattern between Valentine and Christopher in its hesitations and obliquenesses. Ellipsis, signifying suppression, repression, doubt, hesitation, nervousness or expectation, remains Ford's most frequent stylistic device here.[65] Valentine and Christopher are seen together even less in *A Man Could Stand Up* – than they are in that first novel and, despite the different tone overall, the telephone is also an important symbol of the indirectness of communication (between them, but not just between them) that persists into volume III. They do not talk to each other on the phone, though they pass a receiver between themselves in order to talk to Mrs Wannop about each other – and Valentine, remember, was telephoned about Tietjens by Edith Ethel in Part I. On first being reunited, they leave sentences unfinished, necessitating ellipsis of course, and almost immediately Valentine's mind is elsewhere, thinking about the telephone. When they do speak directly, as the novel comes to a close, they are saying something completely different (and more boring, less passionate) from what they had wanted to

---

65 Ford also employs this device frequently in *The Good Soldier*, which has a similar focus on repression. See note 5 above, and my Introduction to *The Good Soldier* (Ware: Wordsworth, 2010).

say, creating another level of running, unspoken dialogue. There is, therefore, a notable contrast when Tietjens begins to talk to Mrs Wannop on the telephone and discovers some fluency.[66] Each hears what the other is saying and is able to respond. It is tempting to read this as a deliberate reference to the comparative simplicity of the past world in which their relationship is rooted: his father and Mrs Wannop's husband were each other's 'oldest friend'. The fluency and self-expression do not last for long, however: the interruptions from drunk soldiers begin, and our attention is taken away from Tietjens' honest and open expression of his war experience. Its most compelling and pitiable aspect ('It's that that's desperate. I'll tell you. I'll give you an instance. I was carrying a boy [...]') is relayed in the next section, by Valentine. From then on, we are left with Valentine's overheard snippets until, in the following chapter when the subject has changed again, Tietjens himself becomes the focaliser. Now he constructs his own dual dialogue, thinking slowly yet desperately on his feet about how to continue this conversation with a mother 'pleading with infinite statesmanship for her daughter', while retaining his intention to make love to Valentine. When, finally, he hangs up, he cuts himself off from Mrs Wannop's rather desperate perception of the 'high-minded', and their particular brand of 'irregular union' (III.i). He smiles as he comes downstairs.

Communication was, of course, vitally important to Tietjens as a commander at the Front. Although there would have been scope for Ford to persist in his use of the telephone to express the difficulty of communication at war too, there are only passing references to telephone calls in Part II.[67] That difficulty of communication is still very much shown through ellipsis (though this device is deployed as regularly in Part II to show the internal

---

66 See *Joseph Conrad* 200–6, in which he details the rules they developed for rendering realistic conversation. Notably, considering what I go on to say about the scene in Ford's novel, this included the maxim that a speech must rarely actually answer that which came before.

67 There is an allusion to this capacity of the telephone to confuse things at the Front in *No More Parades*, when Cowley lets Tietjens know about 'a rumour ... round the telephone in depot ordering room' that threatens to countermand the draft (I.ii). In an essay forthcoming in the new *Edinburgh Companion to Twentieth-Century British and American War Literature* (ed. Adam Piette and Mark Rawlinson), I discuss telephones at war in more detail.

hesitations and problems Tietjens experiences as he responds to or thinks about his world and his place in it) but also in the dialect conversations, which presented copy-editors and American publishers with evident difficulty.[68] Tietjens does not ever seem to struggle to understand the cockney that Ford renders so phonetically. But it does have the effect of increasing his sense of isolation at the times when that is most apparent. A good example occurs in II.i, two pages after one of the most problematic renderings of dialect – 'was it n smashed. Hin a gully; well beind the line' – with no apostrophes.[69] Tietjens remarks at the end of this exchange with his sergeant:

> "Do you mean to say, then, that your men, Sergeant, are really damned heroes? I suppose they are!"
> He said "your men," instead of "our" or even "the" men, because he had been till the day before yesterday merely the second-in-command – and was likely to be to-morrow again merely the perfectly inactive second-in-command of what was called a rag-time collection that was astonishingly a clique and mutely combined to regard him as an outsider. (II.i)

Though he understands it, the use of dialect does help to reinforce this sense of himself as the outsider. As he is an officer, this is about his rank too, one that he is proud of but cannot inhabit for fear of its impermanence, as indicated in the quotation. However, there is something else going on here that has a more profound, though subtle, effect on the text, and on our understanding of Tietjens' character and the extent to which he is marginalised. Between the instance of dialect and the passage quoted above, the sergeant's speech over several lines is rendered in free indirect style. Tietjens' viewpoint has been temporarily invaded; taken over in fact. The novel's editors did not know what to make of this, and the confusion in their decisions as to what to do with speech marks, for example, can be seen from the relevant textual notes accompanying the chapter. Ford, however,

---

68 Its extent can be traced in the textual notes to the novel.
69 As discussed in the Note on the Text, this led the American editor to come up with 'was it not smashed', instead of the first phrase.

knew exactly what he was doing (the typescript is far less confused than any other of the textual witnesses): he was forcing home this impression of a man under siege, and bending the rules of narrative to do so.

Though the sergeant is not aware of the effect he is having on his senior officer, McKechnie is not such an innocent. He worries away at Tietjens' sense of himself and his authority ('whispering in the ear of the C.O.' says Tietjens, II.ii) in a deliberate attempt to destabilise him, thereby totalising the assault. In many cases, Tietjens manages to deflect the tensions in his relationship with this character away from direct verbal encounters into the intellectual constraints of Latin composition, but McKechnie's paranoid nervousness threatens to break out into full-blown mutinous behaviour on more than one occasion. Tietjens must develop an effective psychological trick for dealing with him, based on his anachronistic understanding of feudal order – and ability to translate it into forceful military parlance.[70] One wonders often, when reading the six chapters that make up Part II of the novel, whether any real leader of men during the war could possibly have been as beleaguered as Tietjens. And this is before discussion of his problems with his commanding officers, complicated as they are by Sylvia's notorious behaviour.[71] His alienation – from his peers, from his superiors, and sometimes from his men – is what turns his final transformation in Part II from being merely impressive into a miracle. It also makes Valentine's acceptance of him seem all the more tender, especially when it occurs (Valentine is 'amazed' that it does, and so, perhaps, are we) in the context of similarly complex communication.

---

70 The fact of feudalism being 'finished' is something that Tietjens returns to more than once in the novel.

71 Some of what he experienced was drawn from life: Ford had bad relations with at least two of his own Commanding Officers, Lieutenant-Colonels Cooke and Pope – the latter back in Yorkshire when he was posted to a training command in 1917. While Campion sends Tietjens up the line to near-certain death, however, Ford wanted frontline experience that his C.O. would not endorse because of his age.

Regeneration/rebirth

Pat Barker's celebrated series of books about the First World War
is known as the Regeneration Trilogy.[72] Long before W. H. R.
Rivers, the real-life doctor who features prominently throughout,
had anything to do with shell-shocked soldiers' minds, he had
been engaged in more practical experiments, such as the one in
1903 with his colleague Henry Head at Cambridge, in which a
cutaneous nerve in Head's forearm was severed. The ends of the
nerve were then rejoined, sewn together with fine silk sutures,
and the men commenced their task: to chart the healing process
of the separated nerve. In his later writings on this medical exper-
iment, Rivers cited his 'observations on the sensory changes
which accompany the regeneration of a divided and reunited
nerve'.[73]

The keyword in Rivers' description is 'regeneration', and it is
one that Barker exploits in all its symbolic strength in her trilogy.
(Ford worked with this idea rather earlier, as I go on to suggest.)
Biological processes serve as a foundational layer in her fictional
exploration of what war can do to a man's mind. Unlike in the
experiments of the pre-war world, however, the fractures of shell-
shock, memory loss and repression are not easily balanced by the
curative processes Rivers and others are able to bring to bear upon
them. In *A Man Could Stand Up —* there is no Rivers, nor anyone
like him. Tietjens bears his psychological wounds alone, but
knows in the end that he needs to talk about them — not to a
doctor, but to Valentine, and to her mother as well.[74] Tietjens,
though, despite suffering from nightmares and flashbacks, and

---

72 The first novel in the trilogy, *Regeneration*, was published in 1991. *The Eye in the Door*
    and *The Ghost Road* (winner of the Booker Prize) followed in 1993 and 1995 respec-
    tively. *Regeneration* has at its centre the encounter between Rivers, then an army
    psychiatrist, and Siegfried Sassoon, who became his patient at Craiglockhart Hospital
    for Officers, near Edinburgh, in 1917.
73 W. H. R. Rivers, *Instinct and the Unconscious: A Contribution to a Biological Theory of
    the Psychoneuroses* (Cambridge: Cambridge University Press, 1922), 22.
74 The evident psychological and emotional importance of the relationship between Mrs
    Wannop and Christopher in Part III of the novel renews speculation as to its precise
    nature. When she calls him 'my dear, almost son', for example, is she both unwittingly
    letting Christopher know that Valentine desires him, and also possibly revealing that
    an affair between Christopher's father and herself produced a child — Valentine — thus
    rendering his love for Valentine an incestuous one? (See Saunders' Introduction to
    Some Do Not . . . .)

physical injuries too, has been spared the worst traumas the war could inflict. War itself is also regenerative for him, and this emphasises the size and scale of the character with whom we are dealing.[75] As the key scene in Part II approaches (in which he is rescued and then in turn rescues one of his men), Tietjens works out that the real reason he hates the Germans is because they are preventing him from being with Valentine, whom he loves. As a 'Younger Son' the word 'love' has been very little in his vocabulary, along with anything else reflective, ambitious, driven or self-interested. Until now, this defining sense of himself has only been compounded by his role in the war: 'He had been a sort of eternal Second-in-Command' (II.vi). Tietjens' moment of regeneration in A Man Could Stand Up – is, therefore, as dramatic as any healing of a nerve could be. It is as though some connection is effected that has been missing in his make-up; a systemic link is forged between mind and body that allows him to inhabit himself, to feel all his extremities, and to contemplate 'standing up', which he then does, under fire, carrying the wounded Aranjuez. His relationship to the world around him is simultaneously changed, because it 'was a condemnation of a civilisation that he, Tietjens, possessed of enormous physical strength should never have needed to use it before' (II.vi). (Protected, as he was, from physical labour by his background of course.) Rather than fear any increased alienation, a reader at this point is only aware of his increased potential, immediately fulfilled when he 'felt tender, like a mother, and enormous' in charge of the boy.[76]

There is one final and important stage to be worked through before Part II ends and the reunification scene in London can begin, and this takes place around the near-death experience of Duckett. Lance-Corporal Duckett is seriously wounded (and, unlike Tietjens, quasi-comedically buried) in the bombardment during which Aranjuez is saved. Duckett has reminded Tietjens throughout the novel of Valentine. Tietjens has noticed things

---

75 It is important here to consider the Tietjens with whom we were presented in *Some Do Not . . .* and all that has been said about his politics, his class and his background since then. In many ways, Tietjens embodies a previous age and so it takes a cataclysmic force to move him forward, through time, into the new world Ford is trying to depict.

76 This scene is problematised, however, by the loss of Aranjuez's eye as Tietjens is carrying him to safety.

about him, character traits, such as the way he rubs his ankles, which have at times been expressed very affectionately. Although, first of all, the 'nice, clean, fair boy' suggests Valentine Wannop, and then assumes a position in Tietjens' mind where he '*was* Valentine Wannop', it does not take Tietjens long to understand that, in fact, this confusion of identities is 'mere subterfuge'. Duckett is the route his unconscious is taking to a longed-for post-war world, and life, that are gradually taking shape within it. (It is a world in which Tietjens will not take orders, and there will be no more feudal atmosphere.)[77] Tietjens is quietly obsessed by Valentine, he realises, and the 'rest' and 'repose' that she represents (II.iv). So what are we to make of the fact that Duckett then almost dies?

It is, in part, the mechanism by which Ford recombines Tietjens' and Valentine's separate wartime existences: the 'nice, clean, fair' soldier Captain Tietjens cares about is almost sacrificed as part of the process by which he comes to his real love object. But there is more at stake too. Tietjens, newly maternal (his men had spotted this quality in him some time previously),[78] does genuinely and independently care about Duckett, and at first we think that Duckett is most likely to be dead. He has been buried for ten minutes, and the Company Commander is revealed as dead, shot through the head, while they are still trying to dig Duckett out. Tietjens himself is not sure whether, when he does emerge, he is dead or unconscious. The ambiguity, overall, of this whole scene makes a forceful point about the fragility of life (and, in turn, about the fragility of much else that is life-giving, like his reunion with Valentine). The fact that Duckett does not die is then rendered simultaneously both more surprising and more affirmingly ordinary – it is down to the methodical and efficient

---

77 Duckett also acts catalytically in this respect, and it is crucial that he knows Groby. Immediately after they have been discussing the estate, and life there, in II.vi, Tietjens states that he 'was never going to live at Groby. No more feudal atmosphere! He was going to live […] [w]ith Valentine.' Duckett's habit of ankle rubbing has reached a 'paroxysm' just previously, as if in anticipation of Tietjens' own excitement (earlier in the novel, in I.i, Valentine too is linked with this habit when, just before she rhapsodises about the post-war condition, she notices the girls in the school playground indulging in it).

78 '[H]e mothered the lot of us as if he was a hen sitting on addled eggs', says Lieutenant Cowley to (of course) Sylvia in *No More Parades* II.ii.

attention of the 'small Cockney Tommy' called, with robust humour, Cockshott.

Finally, it is crucial to the climax of this novel that Duckett, in part representing Valentine, both undertakes and then emerges from his journey underground and into death. Marvellously alive, thanks to Cockshott's artificial respiration, he gives us leave to hope that the death Tietjens has often anticipated (it was a funeral at the end of *No More Parades*) has now been removed to a safe, and liberating, distance. At the same time, the social funeral Valentine imagined in I.iii is given new substance. She and Tietjens will be living openly together – 'reprehensible!' says Tietjens – in this strange new world as man and wife.

The regeneration scene in which Tietjens is rescued could equally well be described as a symbolic rebirth.[79] Tietjens' rescue is not dwelt on, particularly, in this way; but that of Aranjuez certainly is:

> They were low. In a wide hole. There was no reason for furious haste. Especially on your hands and knees.
>
> His hands were under the slime, and his forearms. He battled his hands down greasy cloth; under greasy cloth. Slimy, not greasy! He pushed outwards. The boy's hands and arms appeared. It was going to be easier. His face was now quite close to the boy's but it was impossible to hear what he said. Possibly he was unconscious. [...] He lifted the boy's arms over his own shoulders so that his hands might clasp themselves behind his neck. They were slimy and disagreeable. He was short in the wind. He heaved back. The boy came up a little. He was certainly fainting. He gave no assistance. The slime was filthy. (II.vi)

In the end, two others help Tietjens deliver Aranjuez, but the primitive, physical, miraculous nature of their initial struggle is one of the unforgettable scenes of the novel. Ford does not allow its momentum to be lost. It is preserved by Duckett's crossing and

---

79 W. H. R. Rivers was fascinated by the symbolism of rebirth, and took it for his focus in a lecture about the universal importance of symbols in human behavioural history in 1922. The lecture is reproduced, nearly complete, in Richard Slobodin, *W. H. R. Rivers: Pioneer Anthropologist, Psychiatrist of The Ghost Road* (Stroud: Sutton Publishing, 1997), 247–59.

re-crossing of the boundary between life and death, and sustained into Part III in which, further augmenting Tietjens' own transformation and unification with Valentine, a very particular inter-textual relationship is at work: that with Euripides' *Alcestis*. Ford translated the *Alcestis* as one of his first literary tasks after being demobbed. Its symbolic role in the pattern of his career is thus, perhaps, evident. However, the play has particular relevance in a discussion of volume III of *Parade's End*: because of its content, because of its form, and because of the way the two combined to break the rules of classical tragedy. Alcestis being brought back from the underworld helps in part to explain the hope and optimism of *A Man Could Stand Up –*.[80]

The *Alcestis* begins with a picture of a marriage, and the themes of domesticity remain important throughout. Alcestis and her husband Admetus, king of Pherae, have been married for some time, and have children, but the play opens on the day on which Alcestis must die. Emotional scenes relate her leave-taking of her children and her husband, before she is escorted to the underworld by Death. As the household mourns, Hercules passes by, on his way to perform heroic deeds. Admetus offers him hospitality despite his grief; unable to bear the shame of turning him away he lies about the causes of the household's obvious distress. Hercules, finding out the truth, is so moved by Admetus' courage and forbearance that he undertakes to vanquish Death. Bravely, he will journey into the underworld in order to release Alcestis and return her to her husband. This he does, she in disguise, and the two are reunited in great joy.

The *Alcestis*, with what one editor has called its 'fairy-tale plot and happy resolution', did not follow the usual tragic pattern.[81] The undoubted misery of its early scenes is overwritten by the comedy of Hercules' drunken revelry and later mortified rescue of the doomed wife. While this formal characteristic might be

---

80 But cf. also the reference to Eurydice 'sinking back into the shades' in *No More Parades* I.ii; and Sylvia likens Christopher to Alcestis in *No More Parades* II.ii in his care for their son, who almost died from measles.

81 Euripides, *Medea and Other Plays*, trans. John Davie, ed. Richard Rutherford (Harmondsworth: Penguin, 2003), xxiv. The play was also unusual in that it took the position of the usual 'satyr-play', which would normally have been fourth in a tetralogy of plays. The satyr-play tended to be shorter, more frivolous and boisterous than its companions (3).

said to relate to aspects of *A Man Could Stand Up* – the relationship between the texts is more well-developed than that. The
nature of life's boundary with death as Ford constructs it in his
novel is increasingly insubstantial, increasingly wonderful:
Duckett, like Alcestis, comes back from the dead. But it was the
emotion of the *Alcestis'* early scenes that most impressed Ford. As
he begins to discuss Euripides in *The March of Literature*, Ford
focuses on his 'humanity' and 'vitality', before proclaiming
Alcestis' farewell to her marriage bed his 'favourite passage of all
Greek drama'.[82] To a reader of *A Man Could Stand Up* – (as well
as then of *Last Post*), his choice is not surprising. While the play
receives at least three mentions at the end of *A Man Could Stand
Up* –, it is the bed Ford found so compelling that most occupies
Valentine's thoughts as well.

'So she kissed the bed whilst the tears fell upon it,' Ford writes
in his translation of Euripides, '[a]nd she went away; and she came
back again; and she lay down upon the bed as if she would never
leave it. Over and over again […].'[83] Valentine's own 'nuptial
couch' (III.ii) may be a humble camp bed, but there is nothing
prosaic about it. 'What an Alcestis!' she thinks, as she watches,
closely, the three officers who are sitting on it, springing up from
time to time as they do to join in the celebrations. In Euripides'
drama this piece of furniture symbolises the strongest of Alcestis'
ties to life, as well as her life-giving potential, realised in the children she conceived and bore there. The contrast with the death
she is anticipating is felt most keenly, and can be expressed most
dramatically, there. Ford borrows this contrast, updating it – it is
Tietjens who comes closer to death and who has also, thus far,
been associated with new life; it is the future that the bed symbolises here, not the past.[84] But Ford also preserves very effectively

82 Ford, *The March of Literature: From Confucius to Modern Times* (1938) (London:
    George Allen and Unwin, 1947), 117–19. In *It Was the Nightingale* he says that until
    1914 he used to read 'at least Alcestis' address to her bed once, and possibly more often,
    every year' (149); the fact that contemporary women would be unlikely to find inspi-
    ration in Alcestis' address to her bed when contemplating matrimony is one cause of
    the regret he expresses in *English Novel* (19).
83 'The Alcestis of Euripides: freely adapted for the Modern Stage', 1918–19; typescripts
    at Cornell University. Quoted with the permission of the Carl A. Kroch library,
    Cornell University, and Michael Schmidt.
84 Tietjens wants to make a living out of antiques, specifically furniture, in the post-war
    world.

the sense of desperate odds in Euripides' play, and the fundamental importance of the sexual relationship between husband
and wife.

Title

Much of the material in this Introduction could have been
related to the title that Ford chose for his novel. Its final punctuation, a dash, is less suggestive of hesitation than of a range of
potential subsequent clauses or illustrations.[85] The sexual pun has
become most obvious, perhaps, in the recent discussion of the
marriage bed – Tietjens and Sylvia have not made love in five
years. Ford's title can also be linked powerfully to ideas of regeneration. A vision of a man standing 'in a high place in France'
initiated *Parade's End*, Ford's greatest achievement as a writer
post-war. In a vivid account of the early stages of the work, Ford
realises his 'intrigue' is a resurrection of his great friend Arthur
Marwood, who had died in 1916. As he works away at the nature
of his protagonist, Ford suddenly sees Marwood in his mind's eye,
'during the period of hostilities taking in not only what was
visible but all the causes and all the motive powers of infinitely
distant places'. 'It was as if he lived again,' writes Ford, 'I had my
central character.'[86] Tietjens stands like Marwood in volume III.
    Earlier in this Introduction I talked about the importance of
Ford being able to see things clearly in and with this novel: his
own recent experience, the world around him, the past and the
imagined future. Hills are, of course, symbolic of this activity, and
had been for Ford since the very beginning of his writing career.[87]

---

85 The dash, or hyphen, does indicate a break in grammatical structure, but a sharper
   one than the dots Ford so commonly employs to indicate hesitation, doubt or suspense
   (and which feature in the title of volume I of the series, and related discussion in my
   Note on the Text).
86 *Nightingale* 222.
87 The 'Victorian great figures' of Ford's childhood (Thomas Carlyle, say, who features
   in *A Man Could Stand Up –*, or John Ruskin) were held up as standing 'on unattainable heights', overwhelming him as a youth, but Ford also wanted 'Great Writers' to
   elevate their readers, making the world a better place by providing a new point of view.
   He thought similarly about other kinds of artists too: Holbein and Dürer 'stand up like
   lighthouses out of the sea of Germanic painters'. See *Ancient Lights and Certain New
   Reflections* (London: Chapman & Hall, 1911), viii–ix; *Letters* 15 (a letter to Edward
   Garnett in 1901); *Hans Holbein the Younger* (London: Duckworth, 1905), 1. In *A Call*,

His post-war domestic locations in both Sussex and France are
relevant in this respect, and Ford also places himself conspicu-
ously at the top of a hill as he begins to construct his post-war
vision in *It Was the Nightingale*.[88] When a man is talking about
'standing up' in volume III of *Parade's End*, he is most often imagining standing up on a hill:

> The name *Bemerton* suddenly came on to his tongue. Yes,
> Bemerton, Bemerton, Bemerton was George Herbert's
> parsonage. Bemerton, outside Salisbury.... The cradle of the
> race as far as our race was worth thinking about. He imagined
> himself standing up on a little hill, a lean contemplative
> parson, looking at the land sloping down to Salisbury spire. A
> large, clumsily bound seventeenth century testament, Greek,
> beneath his elbow.... Imagine standing up on a hill! It was
> the unthinkable thing there! (II.ii)

One must stoop at war, as his sergeant soon laments (like the
figure of the soldier on Duckworth's dust-jacket). Head wounds
from snipers were frequent. Tietjens himself states later that he
can't 'apparently, get away from them' when the Company
Commander is killed. That is one reason why standing up is
'unthinkable', but it is also, at the level of imagination, about the
impossibility of a long perspective. At war, Ford felt constrained
by his necessary close attention to three particular inches on the
map – such was the 'grindstone of affairs'. Post-war, he read vora-
ciously to correct that narrowness of vision.[89] In Ford's case,
however, there is also the business of how he felt about the
Germans. If you gain enough height, after all, perhaps it is
possible (or even required) to see both sides.

In March 1926 Ford wrote to Gerald Duckworth. In this letter
he detailed his progress with *A Man Could Stand Up –*, and it has

---

Robert Grimshaw appreciates his encounter with a Greek Orthodox priest because it
enables him to 'come for a moment out of the ring, very visible and circumscribed, in
which he moved'. It gave him, 'as it were, the chance to stand upon a little hill and
look down into the misty "affair" in which he was so deeply engaged' (121). See also
the early poem 'A Great View' (1904) in *Selected Poems*, ed. Max Saunders
(Manchester: Carcanet, 1997), 21–2.

88 *Nightingale* 63.
89 *Nightingale* 27.

been quoted from already, but he also had another matter to raise with his publisher: a German translation of *No More Parades*. He's uneasy about the idea, because he fears that the novel might be interpreted as representing a political critique of 'England' during the war. He accepts it eventually, however, on the understanding that the un-named German publisher will also take *A Man Could Stand Up* – 'which is rather nasty to the said H[uns], redressing the balance'.[90] From the evidence in the novel, it is hard to know exactly what Ford means. While Tietjens feels disgusted by the prisoners he is guarding, and there is the odd reference to the 'beastly Germans' or the 'bloody imbeciles', much of the material directly treating the Germans seems to belong to that code covering the 'gallant enemy' that Ford regretted the loss of in the face of early reporting of the war and Germany. Though one reading of Ford's choice of title has to acknowledge, along with the implications of sexual expression, its connotations of manly duty (it is 'in the trenches' that Tietjens 'is a man', noted the *New Statesman*),[91] moral courage and perhaps even patriotic aggression, there is less of all this here than one might, perhaps, expect.[92] Where it does appear, as in a discussion of influenza in II.vi, or in the case of the 'fat Hun' on a hillside, it is swiftly mediated by some expression of sympathy or common humanity in the face of the trials of war. This is not an anti-German book. Ford's vision of hills in the novel anticipates peace above all, the renewed breadth of vision of all the 'kingdoms of the earth', as Gringoire puts it, that is, in its completeness, closer to the truth.[93] 'On a huge hill, / Cragged, and steep, Truth stands, and he that will / Reach her, about must, and about must go', wrote Donne in one of his satires, and there is a sense of that kind of progres-

---

90 *Letters* 168.

91 This was P. C. Kennedy on 23 October 1926.

92 Conrad's exhortation that 'a man should stand up to his bad luck, to his mistakes, to his conscience' (*The Shadow-Line* [London: Dent, 1923], 131–2) must, however, have been in Ford's mind. References to passages of the Bible occur fairly frequently in *A Man Could Stand Up* –, and on this particular point see also Ephesians 6:13–14, 'Wherefore take unto you the whole armour of God, that you may be able to withstand in the evil day, and having done all to stand. Stand therefore, having your loins girt about with truth, and having on the breastplate of righteousness'; and Revelation 6:17, 'For the great day of his wrath is come and who shall be able to stand?'

93 In the gospels, the devil takes Jesus up onto 'a high mountain' to show him 'all the kingdoms of the world' and tempts him to renounce the Lord (see, for example, Luke 4:5); *No Enemy* 35.

sion as Gringoire details his landscapes at the start of *No Enemy*, pausing to anticipate sight of his own preferred kingdoms (England and France) en route to considering his view of the Germans.[94] Those who instigated the war Gringoire feels antipathy for; those he was fighting against were different: 'But I don't think many people in the trenches actually, and except at odd moments, ever felt active hatred against the men in the opposite lines or even those who militarily directed their operations.'[95] Tietjens expresses a very similar thought, but first of all he has to find a long view of the 'whole vast territory that confronted them' (II.vi), one that brings with it, more notably, sympathy for the 'most miserable human beings that had ever existed': he means not the Tommies but the underfed Germans who are stricken by illness.

Important as it was to Ford, this is not just about political morality. He needed this view, personally and, more specifically, psychologically. In *Provence*, published in 1935, he writes about his experience of claustrophobia, associated not with London locations but with life in Sussex post-war, where the 'dreadful greennesses of the countrysides' frightened him: 'My chest will burst. I shall suffocate if I cannot get to a hard, hot stone, flat on an iron, parched hillside, looking, between olive, almond and mulberry trunks, over the Mediterranean.'[96] The necessity of hills, the way they are built into the fabric of *A Man Could Stand Up –*, takes on a different resonance in a context like this, one that is reinforced if we think again about the fear of the 'malices and doubts' in *It Was the Nightingale*. Deep in Sussex, Ford felt himself to be hemmed in by ghosts, by time present and time past, as imagined voices and images bounce back and forth in the reflective panes of the windows.[97] This is very different from the crippling fear of open spaces he experienced as a much younger

---

94 Donne, Satire 3 ('Kind pity chokes my spleen') in *The Complete English Poems*, ed. A. J. Smith (Harmondsworth: Penguin, 1980), 161–4, ll. 79–81.

95 *No Enemy* 47.

96 Ford, *Provence: From Minstrels to Machine* (1935), ed. John Coyle (Manchester: Carcanet, 2009), 289.

97 I have written elsewhere at more length about this key section in Ford's work, and its relationship to others of his texts. See, for example, *Fragmenting Modernism: Ford Madox Ford, the Novel and the Great War* (Manchester: Manchester University Press, 2002), 209–15.

man.[98] Though Olive Garnett recorded one of his more serious agoraphobic attacks as having occurred on Salisbury Plain, Ford wrote in *Return to Yesterday* of how in the 'vastnesses of London one has the impression of being infinitely alone'.[99] One effect of the trauma of war is that rather than fearing those 'vastnesses', he seeks them out. They prove curative not solely for the enforced narrowness of perspective at war, but existentially, for the stooping and fearful existence in the trenches and its legacy of terrors that crowd his mind. He found them in Provence.

Ford's ultimate achievement in the literary imagination of Christopher Tietjens, I would like to suggest in conclusion, is rooted in the fact that once Tietjens has learned how to stand up in a critically changed environment, expediting that very process of change as he does so, he alters direction again. 'A man could now stand up on a hill,' he exults, 'so he and she could surely get into some hole together!' (II.vi). Tietjens is thinking about a still place, a protected space – a foxhole, a dugout, something like that 'antiquity shop' near Bath. It may be the noise of the dance, and Valentine's thoughts of the bed, that draw *A Man Could Stand Up* – to a close, but 'he and she' go about their peace together quietly and fruitfully, ushering in the very different world that is *Last Post*.

---

98 His unpleasant and sometimes very strange treatments for this, and for other bouts of neurasthenia, are detailed in the memoir *Return to Yesterday* (1931) (Manchester: Carcanet, 1999), in the chapter 'Some Cures'. They included diets of pork and ice cream, cold baths, and being suddenly shown 'indecent photographs of a singular banality' as doctors attempted to prove that his agoraphobia and depression had a sexual origin (202–3).

99 *Return* 230.

A NOTE ON THIS EDITION
OF *PARADE'S END*

This edition takes as its copy-text the British first editions of the four novels. It is not a critical edition of the manuscripts, nor is it a variorum edition comparing the different editions exhaustively. The available manuscripts and other pre-publication materials have been studied and taken into account, and have informed any emendations, all of which are recorded in the textual notes.

The British first editions were the first publication of the complete texts for at least the first three volumes. The case of *Last Post* is more complicated, and is discussed by Paul Skinner in that volume; but in short, if the British edition was not the first published, the US edition was so close in date as to make them effectively simultaneous (especially in terms of Ford's involvement), so there is no case for not using the British text there too, whereas there are strong reasons in favour of using it for the sake of consistency (with the publisher's practices, and habits of British as opposed to American usage).

Complete manuscripts have survived for all four volumes. That for *Some Do Not ...* is an autograph, *A Man Could Stand Up* – and the other two are typescripts. All four have autograph corrections and revisions in Ford's hand, as well as deletions (which there is no reason to believe are not also authorial). The typescripts also have typed corrections and revisions. As Ford inscribed two of them to say the typing was his own, there is no reason to think these typed second thoughts were not also his. The manuscripts also all have various forms of compositor's mark-up, confirming what Ford inscribed on the last two, that the UK editions were set from them.

Our edition is primarily intended for general readers and students of Ford. Recording every minor change from manuscript

to first book edition would be of interest to only a small number
of textual scholars, who would need to consult the original manuscripts themselves. However, many of the revisions and deletions
are highly illuminating about Ford's method of composition, and
the changes of conception of the novels. While we have normally
followed his decisions in our text, we have annotated the changes
we judge to be significant (and of course such selection implies
editorial judgement) in the textual notes.

There is only a limited amount of other pre-publication material, perhaps as a result of Duckworth & Co. suffering fires in 1929
and 1950, and being bombed in 1942. There are some pages of
an episode originally intended as the ending of *Some Do Not* . . .
but later recast for *No More Parades*, and some pages omitted from
Last Post. Unlike the other volumes, *Last Post* also underwent
widespread revisions differentiating the first UK and US editions.
Corrected proofs of the first chapter only of *Some Do Not* . . . were
discovered in a batch of materials from Ford's *transatlantic review*.
An uncorrected proof copy of *A Man Could Stand Up* – has also
been studied. There are comparably patchy examples of previous
partial publication of two of the volumes. Part I of *Some Do
Not* . . . was serialised in the *transatlantic review*, of which at most
only the first four and a half chapters preceded the Duckworth
edition. More significant is the part of the first chapter of *No
More Parades* that appeared in the *Contact Collection of Contemporary Writers* in 1925, with surprising differences from the book
versions. All of this material has been studied closely, and informs
our editing of the Duckworth texts. But – not least because of its
fragmentary nature – it didn't warrant variorum treatment.

The only comparable editing of Ford's work as we have
prepared this edition has been Martin Stannard's admirable
Norton edition of *The Good Soldier*. Stannard took the interesting
decision to use the text of the British first edition, but emend the
punctuation throughout to follow that of the manuscript. He
makes a convincing case for the punctuation being an editorial
imposition, and that even if Ford tacitly assented to it (assuming
he had a choice), it alters the nature of his manuscript. A similar
argument could be made about *Parade's End* too. Ford's punctuation is certainly distinctive: much lighter than in the published
versions, and with an eccentrically variable number of suspen-

sion dots (between three and eight).[100] However, there seem to us four major reasons for retaining the Duckworth punctuation in the case of *Parade's End*:

1) The paucity of pre-publication material. The existence of an autograph manuscript for *Some Do Not* ... as opposed to typescripts for the other three raises the question of whether there might not have existed a typescript for *Some Do Not* ... or autographs for the others. Ford inscribed the typescripts of *A Man Could Stand Up* – and *Last Post* to say the typing was his own (though there is some evidence of dictation in both). The typescript of *No More Parades* has a label attached saying 'M.S. The property of / F. M. Ford'; although there is nothing that says the typing is his own, the typing errors make it unlikely that it was the work of a professional typist, and we have no reason to believe Ford didn't also type this novel. So we assume for these three volumes that the punctuation in the typescripts was his (and not imposed by another typist), and, including his autograph corrections, would represent his final thoughts before receiving the proofs. However, without full surviving corrected proofs of any volume it is impossible to be certain which of the numerous changes were or were not authorial. (Janice Biala told Arthur Mizener that 'Ford did his real revisions on the proofs – and only the publishers have those. The page proofs in Julies' [*sic*] and my possession are the English ones – no American publisher had those that I know of.'[101] However, no page proofs for any of the four novels are among her or Ford's daughter Julia Loewe's papers now at Cornell, nor does the Biala estate hold any.)

2) Ford was an older, more experienced author in 1924–8 than in 1915. Though arguably he would have known even before

100 In general Duckworth seems to have attempted to standardise Ford's punctuation in *A Man Could Stand Up* – by using three dots (with a preceding space) when they occur in mid-sentence or end an incomplete sentence; and four dots (with no preceding space) when they follow a completed sentence. However, it isn't always clear that a sentence has been completed even if it isn't grammatically incomplete. Nor is the convention always applied consistently. I have only intervened occasionally, therefore, when the grounds for doing so do seem clear. See the relevant textual notes in this respect.
101 Biala to Arthur Mizener, 29 May 1964, Carl A. Kroch Library, Cornell University; quoted with the kind permission of the estate of Janice Biala and Cornell University.

the war how his editors were likely to regularise his punctuation, and had already published with John Lane, the first publisher of *The Good Soldier*, nevertheless by 1924 he certainly knew Duckworth's house style (Duckworth had published another novel, *The Marsden Case*, the previous year). More tellingly, perhaps, Ford's cordial relations with Duckworth would surely have made it possible to voice any concern, which his correspondence does not record his having done.

3) On the evidence of the errors that remained uncorrected in the first editions, the single chapter proofs for *Some Do Not . . .*, and Ford's comments in his letters on the speed at which he had to correct proofs, he does not appear to have been very thorough in his proofreading. Janice Biala commented apropos *Parade's End*:

> Ford was the worst proof reader on earth and knew it. Most of the time, the proofs were corrected in an atmosphere of [. . .] nervous exhaustion & exaperation [sic] with the publisher who after dallying around for months, would suddenly need the corrected proofs 2 hours after their arrival at the house etc, etc, you know.[102]

At the least, he was more concerned with style than with punctuation.

4) Such questions may be revisited should further pre-publication material be discovered. In the meantime, we took the decision to retain the first edition text as our copy-text, rather than conflate manuscript and published texts, on the grounds that this was the form in which the novels went through several impressions and editions in the UK and the US during Ford's lifetime, and in which they were read by his contemporaries and (bar some minor changes) have continued to be read until now.

---

102 Biala to Arthur Mizener, 29 May 1964, Carl A. Kroch Library, Cornell University; quoted with the kind permission of the estate of Janice Biala and Cornell University.

The emendations this edition has made to the copy-text fall into two categories:

1) The majority of cases are errors that were not corrected at proof stage. With compositors' errors the manuscripts provide the authority for the emendations, sometimes also supported by previous publication where available. We have corrected any of Ford's rare spelling and punctuation errors which were replicated in the UK text (the UK and US editors didn't always spot the same errors). We have also very occasionally emended factual and historical details where we are confident that the error is not part of the texture of the fiction. All such emendations of the UK text, whether substantive or accidental, are recorded in the textual endnotes.

2) The other cases are where the manuscript and copy-text vary; where there is no self-evident error, but the editors judge the manuscript better reflects authorial intention. Such judgements are of course debatable. We have only made such emendations to the UK text when they are supported by evidence from the partial pre-publications (as in the case of expletives); or when they make better sense in context; or (in a very small number of cases) when the change between manuscript and UK loses a degree of specificity Ford elsewhere is careful to attain. Otherwise, where a manuscript reading differs from the published version, we have recorded it (if significant), but not restored it, on the grounds that Ford at least tacitly assented to the change in proof, and may indeed have made it himself – a possibility that can't be ruled out in the absence of the evidence of corrected proofs.

Our edition differs from previous ones in four main respects. First, it offers a thoroughly edited text of the series for the first time, one more reliable than any published previously. The location of one of the manuscripts, that of *No More Parades*, was unknown to Ford's bibliographer David Harvey. It was brought to the attention of Joseph Wiesenfarth (who edits it for this edition) among Hemingway's papers in the John Fitzgerald Kennedy Library (Columbia Point, Boston, Massachusetts). Its rediscovery finally made a critical edition of the entire tetralogy possible. Besides the corrections and emendations described above, the editors have made the decision to restore the expletives that are frequent in the typescript of *No More Parades*, set at the Front, but which were replaced with dashes in the UK and US book editions. While this decision may be a controversial one, we believe it is justified by the previous publication of part of *No More Parades* in Paris, in which Ford determined that the expletives should stand as accurately representing the way that soldiers talk. In *A Man Could Stand Up* – the expletives are censored with dashes in the TS, which, while it may suggest Ford's internalising of the publisher's decisions from one volume to the next, may also reflect the officers' self-censorship, so there they have been allowed to stand.[103]

Second, it presents each novel separately. They were published separately, and reprinted separately, during Ford's lifetime. The volumes had been increasingly successful. He planned an omnibus edition, and in 1930 proposed the title *Parade's End* for it (though possibly without the apostrophe).[104] But the Depression intervened and prevented this sensible strategy for consolidating his reputation. After Ford's death, and another world war, Penguin reissued the four novels as separate paperbacks.

The first omnibus edition was produced in 1950 by Knopf. This edition, based on the US first editions, has been reprinted exactly

---

103 If the decision to censor the expletives in *No More Parades* is what led Ford to use euphemistic dashes in the typescript of *A Man Could Stand Up* –, that of *Last Post* complicates the story, containing two instances of 'bloody' and two instances of 'b—y'.

104 Ford wrote to his agent: 'I do not like the title *Tietjens Saga* – because in the first place "Tietjens" is a name difficult for purchasers to pronounce and booksellers would almost inevitably persuade readers that they mean the Forsyte Sage with great damage to my sales. I recognize the value of Messrs Duckworth's publicity and see no reason why they should not get the advantage of it by using those words as a subtitle beneath another general title, which I am inclined to suggest should be *Parades End* so that Messrs Duckworth could advertise it as PARADES END [TIETJENS' SAGA]'. Ford to Eric Pinker, 17 Aug. 1930: *Letters* 197. However, the copy at Cornell is Janice Biala's transcription of Ford's original. The reply from Pinkers is signed 'Barton' (20 Aug. 1930: Cornell), who says they have spoken to Messrs Duckworth who agree with Ford's suggested title; but he quotes it back as 'Parade's End' with the apostrophe (suggesting Biala's transcription may have omitted it), then gives the subtitle as the 'Tietjen's Saga' (casting his marksmanship with the apostrophe equally in doubt). These uncertainties make it even less advisable than it would anyway have been to alter the title by which the series has been known for sixty years.

in almost all subsequent omnibus editions (by Vintage, Penguin, and Carcanet; the exception is the new Everyman edition, for which the text was reset, but again using the US edition texts). Thus the tetralogy is familiar to the majority of its readers, on both sides of the Atlantic, through texts based on the US editions. There were two exceptions in the 1960s. When Graham Greene edited the Bodley Head Ford Madox Ford in 1963, he included *Some Do Not . . .* as volume 3, and *No More Parades* and *A Man Could Stand Up* – together as volume 4, choosing to exclude *Last Post*. This text is thus not only incomplete but also varies extensively from the first editions. Some of the variants are simply errors. Others are clearly editorial attempts to clarify obscurities or to 'correct' usage, sometimes to emend corruptions in the first edition, but clearly without knowledge of the manuscript. While it is an intriguing possibility that some of the emendations may have been Greene's, they are distractions from what Ford actually wrote. Arthur Mizener edited *Parade's End* for Signet Classics in 1964, combining the first two books in one volume, and the last two in another. Both these editions used the UK texts. Thus readers outside the US have not had a text of the complete work based on the UK text for over sixty years; those in the US, for forty-five years. Our edition restores the UK text, which has significant differences in each volume, and especially in the case of *Last Post* – for which even the title differed in the US editions, acquiring a definite article. This restoration of the UK text is the third innovation here.

With the exception of paperback reissues of the Bodley Head texts by Sphere in 1969 (again excluding *Last Post*), the volumes have not been available separately since 1948. While there is no doubt Ford intended the books as a sequence (there *is* some doubt about how many volumes he projected, as noted here in the Introduction to *A Man Could Stand Up* – and discussed at more length in *Last Post*), the original UK editions appeared at intervals of more than a year. They were read separately, with many readers beginning with the later volumes. Like any writer of novel sequences, Ford was careful to ensure that each book was intelligible alone. Moreover, there are marked differences between each of the novels. Though all tell the story of the same group of characters, each focuses on a different selection of people. Sylvia

Tietjens is, for example, completely absent from *A Man Could Stand Up –*, which centres on Valentine in its London scenes. The locations and times are also different in each of the four novels. In addition, and more strikingly, the styles and techniques develop and alter from one to the other. The time-frame of *A Man Could Stand Up –* is tightly compressed, and the relationship between thought and time, as treated in *Some Do Not ...*, evolves in volume III: 'Later [Valentine] realised that that was what thought was [...] in those ten minutes you found you thought out more than in two years' (*A Man Could Stand Up –* p. 29). Returning the novels to their original separate publication enables such developments and differences to be more clearly visible.

Parade's End in its entirety is a massive work. Omnibus editions of it are too large to be able to accommodate extra material. A further advantage of separate publication is to allow room for the annotations the series now needs. This is the fourth advantage of our edition. Though *Parade's End* isn't as difficult or obscure a text as *Ulysses* or *The Waste Land*, it is dense with period references, literary allusions and military terminology unfamiliar to readers a century later. This edition is the first to annotate these difficulties.

To keep the pages of text as uncluttered as possible, we have normally restricted footnotes to information rather than interpretation, annotating obscurities that are not easily traceable in standard reference works. English words have only been glossed if they are misleadingly ambiguous, or if they cannot be found in the *Concise Oxford Dictionary*, in which case the *Oxford English Dictionary* (or occasionally Partridge's *Dictionary of Slang*) has been used. *Parade's End* is, like Ford's account of *The Good Soldier*, an 'intricate tangle of references and cross-references'.[105] We have annotated references to works by other writers, as well as relevant biographical references that are not covered in the introductions. We have also included cross-references to Ford's other works where they shed light on *Parade's End*. To avoid duplication, we have restricted cross-references to other volumes of the tetralogy to those to preceding volumes. These are given by Part-

---

105 'Dedicatory Letter to Stella Ford', *The Good Soldier* 5.

and chapter-number: i.e. 'I.iv' for Part I, chapter IV. We have, however, generally not noted the wealth of cross-references within the individual volumes.

Works cited in the footnotes are given a full citation on first appearance. Subsequent citations of often-cited works are by short titles, and a list of these is provided at the beginning of the volume. Otherwise, full details can be found in the Bibliography. A key to the conventions used in the textual endnotes appears on p. 219.

That in effect was love. It struck him as astonishing. The
word was so little in his vocabulary..... Love, ambition, the desire
for wealth. They were things he had never known of as existing -
as capable of existing within him. He had been the Younger Son,
loafing, contemptuous, capable, idly contemplating life, but ready
to take up the position of the Head of the Family if Death so arranged matters. He had been a sort of eternal Second in Command.

Now: what the Hell was he? A sort of Hamlet of the Trenches?
No, by God he was not!..... He was, now, perfectly ready for action.
Ready to command a battalion. He was presumably a lover. They did
things like commanding battalions. And worse!

He ought to write her a letter. What in the world would she
think of this gentleman who *had once* made improper proposals to her; balked;
said "So long!" or perhaps not even "So long!". And then walked off.
With never a letter! Not even a picture postcard! *Fortunzeus!* A sort of a
Hamlet all right! *Or a curse!*

Well then, he ought to write her a letter. He ought to say:
This is to tell you that I propose to live with you as soon as
                    You will
this show is over.   ~~Please therefore~~ be prepared immediately on
cessation of active hostilities to put yourself at my disposal; we
~~will inhabit a flat because I shall be presiding.~~ Please. Signed
Xtopher Tietjens Acting O./C 9th Glams. A proper military communication. She would be pleased to see that he was commanding a
battalion. Or perhaps she would not be pleased. She was a pro-
German. She loved these tiresome fellows who tore his, Tietjens',
sofa-cushions to pieces.

That was not fair. She was a Pacifist. She thought these

A NOTE ON THE TEXT OF
A MAN COULD STAND UP –

The Typescript and its Status as Pre-publication Material

The earliest extant version of *A Man Could Stand Up* – is a typescript, as is that of its predecessor in the tetralogy, *No More
Parades*.[106] Part of the Loewe Collection[107] at the time David Dow
Harvey produced his *Bibliography of Works and Criticism* of Ford
(1962), the typescript is now housed in the Division of Rare and
Manuscript Collections, Cornell University. It is complete, with
a total of 249 leaves. The two-page dedicatory letter and the title
page are additional to this total, which is written in hand on the
last leaf of the typescript.

It is very likely that the extant typescript, aside from the
sections of it that have been revised, was the first version of *A
Man Could Stand Up* –. Or, to put it another way, Ford probably
did not produce an autograph manuscript of this novel in addition to (and predating) the typed draft. Max Saunders argues in
the Note on the Text to *Some Do Not . . .* that the existence of
an autograph MS of the first volume of the series does not mean
his fellow editors should expect to find one in the pre-publication textual history of the later novels. His reasons can be usefully
repeated here. The first is Ford's complaint of writer's cramp,

---

106 *Some Do Not* ..., however, was handwritten. Like *Some Do Not* ..., the title of
volume III of *Parade's End* contains punctuation, and in what was perhaps at first a
conscious echo of the earlier book, Ford opens the typescript with *A Man Could Stand
Up*.......: a total of seven dots. In a further twist, Ford wrote in a letter to his agent
in 1926 (in self-admitted 'haste and complete exhaustion') 'The title then is: 3 A
Man Could Stand Up? Or had you some other form?' opening up at least the possibility – one can't be more definite than this because he's also addressing a question
to Bradley – that he'd considered a question mark too (*The Ford Madox Ford Reader*,
ed. Sondra J. Stang [Manchester: Carcanet, 1986], 489).

107 Julia Loewe was Ford's daughter with Stella Bowen.

which became more serious following the completion of *Some Do Not . . .* and which led Ford, as he admits in *It Was the Nightingale*, to write with a 'machine' (a typewriter) or to dictate.[108] Second, in a letter in December 1926, two months after the publication of *A Man Could Stand Up –*, Ford displayed anxiety as to the whereabouts of particular manuscript material. He asked Stella Bowen to find 'the m.s. of <u>Some Do Not</u>'; 'a great part is amongst the papers still at the Quai d'Anjou – in among the proofs of the <u>T.R.</u>' (the *transatlantic review* was the periodical Ford had been editing at the time in Paris).[109] In the same letter he says that 'The typed m.s. of <u>A M.Cd.S.U.</u> is in my escritoire – or was when I left.' His equation of the 'typed m.s.' of the later novel with the 'm.s.' of the earlier certainly suggests there was no autograph manuscript of volume III. As far as the cause of this anxiety goes, Saunders surmises (partly because of the contemporary bump in his sales figures) that Ford is concerned about each of these manuscripts 'because they are, for the moment, valuable properties; and if he wasn't considering selling them, he may have worried that someone else would try to'.[110] If Bowen's hunt is indeed to protect commodities, Ford is specific about where the value lies. Convincing as all this is, there is a further important point to be made about the typescript's status. Its initial leaf, like that of *Last Post* after it, is inscribed in Ford's hand. He writes, in ink, 'This is the typescript – my own typing – from wh. the novel was printed FMF.' Even brief examination of the TS serves to confirm that it has not been produced by a professional typist (though small sections of it may in fact have been dictated by Ford). This is not simply because of typing errors, but because of the fact that revisions, and sometimes quite detailed ones, are made in type. And a professional typist would have baulked at a machine that was working as imperfectly as that used in II.vi, when, for example, '%' has to stand in for a full stop. For these reasons I assume that this only known typescript of *A Man Could*

---

108 *Nightingale* 239. Here he says that he dislikes writing with a pen because 'writer's cramp has never left me and every word I write is accompanied by a little pain', but see also a letter to Stella Bowen in November 1926 in which he explains he is using pencil because his 'cramp is rather bad' (*Ford/Bowen* 227).

109 The letter was written on 6 December (*Ford/Bowen* 252–3).

110 See Saunders, Note on the Text to *Some Do Not . . .* lxxviii.

Stand Up – is not only the version sent to the publisher, but almost certainly for the most part the first draft.

It is, however, just possible that more than one typed version of *A Man Could Stand Up –* was produced. Two (or even, conceivably, more) different versions might have been condensed to form the sequence of 249 leaves that was used to set the proofs of the novel. In I.ii, for example, there is no typed '28' (in one of the two series of numbers on the leaves of the TS to be described in more detail below), but a page with a typed 36 is in its place. This page bears no resemblance to the later page 36, which is in the right place. Is this an insert from another version of the text? It is possible, of course, that Ford simply temporarily forgot where he was up to in the sequence, and reverted to the correct number on the next leaf. (A likely explanation, it must be said, given the lack of revision to the text at the end of the previous leaf and the start of the next.) Much later in the volume there is a different case, however, in which there are three TS leaves given the number 182 in type. One also receives a rather half-hearted 'A', but though the text is sequential overall, there is a problem with the transition from leaf to leaf as some text which is in UK is missing from the end of the first 182. Again, could one or more of these leaves have been imported from another version? Rather more dramatically, the typed sequence shifts after the typed page 163, switching to a much lower number, 145, and beginning a new sequence which is then followed, more or less, to the end of TS. Page 163 is clearly a later insert. It contains only nine lines of type, breaking off mid-line after the words 'the Germans' to produce the necessary link to the following leaf (beginning 'would strain themselves'). It also looks very different from its predecessors. The print is very clear, while earlier leaves are blurred. The next few leaves follow its lead (with the odd exception of 146), in one or two cases enjoying very sharp print indeed. Did Ford rewrite all of the first 144 pages, substituting a couple from the first version here and there, overall producing a longer first half of the text which were rejoined with the original via 163? The answer to both this question and those above might possibly be 'yes', of course, suggesting in turn an especially detailed and painstaking approach to this third volume of his series. Other explanations are more likely, however – especially

given what we know both of Ford's life at the time he was writing
the novel, and the speed at which he completed it.

The changes such as I have described above in the clarity of
the type from leaf to leaf of the typescript are due to the use of
carbon paper for the purposes of duplication.[111] As a rule with this
method, the top copy is sharp, then those produced through the
carbon paper become increasingly blurred. Ford's typescript is a
mixture of top copies and carbon copies. Some idiosyncrasies in
the number sequence, though not the most dramatic shifts, might
be explicable as a result of the various copies being separated, and
then one copy later being grafted onto another, perhaps with
additional text. We know that Ford separated out his copies. In
the same letter in which he wrote to Bradley about the title of
volume III he explains why he is sending him a nearly complete
version of *A Man Could Stand Up –*: 'when I get towards the end
of a book I always hate to have all the copies of a ms in one place
for fear of fire'. He also took the opportunity to remind him that
'[y]ou have already had duplicates of the earlier chapters – to Part
II.1'.[112] What is beyond doubt is that Ford retyped particular
leaves, or sections, as he redrafted and edited the book. Those
very leaves or sections that he subsequently rewrote might
already have been separated out, and perhaps sent to Bradley, or
elsewhere.

When Ford wrote to Harriet Monroe in November 1926, he
was in New York, on a tour to promote his work ('Ford Madox
Ford Arrives'; 'Ford Madox Ford Here for Three Lectures',
reported the press).[113] The Tietjens novels had done particularly
well in the US and Monroe, editor of Chicago's *Poetry* magazine,
was one key to that success.[114] She had written asking Ford to
come to Chicago but the letter took some time to find him. When

---

111 In *It Was the Nightingale*, Ford relates the traumatic story of a producer's request for a
    replacement copy of his first post-war work (a translation of Euripides' *Alcestis* – for
    more on which, see the Introduction here). 'For economy's sake' Ford had made no
    copy (*Nightingale* 151).
112 *Reader* 489–90.
113 Both appeared on 30 October 1926; Cornell University has clippings, but their source
    is lost.
114 'America came creeping in', Ford was to write in *It Was the Nightingale*, and the first
    evidence he provides of the change is a prize awarded by Monroe's magazine for a
    poem, 'A House', in 1921 (*Nightingale* 157–8).

assessing his year as a whole, it was with great understatement that he replied to her on the day following receipt, adding as a post-script 'I see your letter is dated the 13th. It only reached me yesterday as I've been moving about.'[115] Ford had begun *A Man Could Stand Up –* in January, at Toulon. It was a winter holiday from his chaotic life with Stella Bowen in Paris, where another studio move in the autumn had left them without a kitchen or a bathroom. While the necessary work was done, they travelled, and Bowen painted while Ford wrote. They visited Ezra and Dorothy Pound in Rapallo, and although at Easter they found themselves heading back to Paris, via Tarascon, he was able to write to his publisher Gerald Duckworth on 9 March saying that he was 'getting on pretty well with my novel. A month's good work will finish it.'[116] He dedicated *A Man Could Stand Up –* to Duckworth, concluding what he calls his 'Epistle Dedicatory' on 18 May, in Paris. It was considerably more than a 'month's good work' to the finish therefore. But this May date also suggests that the mention of July in the composition dates at the end of the novel (TOULON, 9th January, 1926 / PARIS, 21st July " [1926]) are when Ford completed working with the proofs, as opposed to writing the novel itself – which itself took just over four months. The composition dates do not originate on the typescript, which makes this more likely still. Less than three months after he finished with the proofs, then, the novel was out. The earliest reviews of *A Man Could Stand Up –* put the UK publication of the novel in the same month (October) as that in the US, representing a considerable condensing of the six-month gap between the UK and US publications of *Some Do Not ...*, for example. (No other reviews have been found to challenge this assumption.) The UK *Observer* reviewed the book on 10 October, and the *New York Herald Tribune* carried a review by Ford's American champion Isabel Paterson, to whom he dedicated *Last Post*, a mere week later, on the 17th.

---

115 *Reader* 491.
116 *Letters* 168–9. See the footnote to the dedicatory letter in the text for more on Duckworth.

Description of the Typescript

The typescript of *A Man Could Stand Up* – numbers 249 leaves of typing. These are mostly full pages, but in four cases inserts, representing a revision of a cancelled passage, are shorter than a full page. There are numerous deletions, additions and revisions of individual words, clauses, sentences and occasionally paragraphs. Errors are often circled, probably by Ford, though the printer has not always picked these up (see I.i note 28 for an example). Other than the sometimes quite long autograph and typed additions in the margins around the typed text, or between its lines, the most notable aspects of the typescript are the numbers usually found at the top right corner of each leaf. In most cases these consist of a typed number which is crossed through in pencil and the addition of a second handwritten number. In almost no cases do these numbers coincide (in the first instance because the handwritten sequence treats the opening page as 1, while the typed sequence begins at 1 on the second leaf).[117] Close examination of the sequences, especially when trying to ascertain the compositional history of the novel, makes them more interesting still. Both are likely to have originated with Ford, for reasons that will be discussed below.

Authorial Number Sequences

In this section I give a detailed map of the number sequences of the TS. For the conclusions I draw from it, please see the summaries at the end of each part, and the following section in this Note, 'Overall Summary'.

The Dedicatory Letter is part of neither the typed nor the handwritten sequences. Nonetheless, it has a circled and handwritten number '5' on its first page, and a typed 'b' on its second.

I.i contains typed, scored-through, sequence 1–17, but does not number the very first leaf; handwritten sequence 1–18.

I.ii contains typed, scored-through sequence 18–36 inclusive

---

117 In most later cases as Ford was writing the typed sequence he omitted the number from the first page of a chapter – standard practice – but remembered to skip a number in his sequence to compensate.

of an 18a, a 19a and a 20a.[118] There is no typed 28, but a typed 36 is in its place. Typed 20 is a half leaf, indicating revision of the text here (though this leaf ends with a full stop, leaf 20a originally began mid-sentence, which Ford then revises; see textual note 9 in II.i). Handwritten sequence 19–39, with a double 37 due to error – there is no significant revision at this point in the text.

I.iii contains typed, scored-through sequence 37–56; handwritten sequence skips 40 and begins new chapter on 41, running through to 60.

Summary: Part I of the TS is fairly straightforward, though it bears signs of revision (only as a result of one of the 'a' leaves in I.ii, however). There are a few duplications or omissions of numbers in the sequences. The sequences end up four apart.

II.i starts with a new typed sequence instead of the 57 we would be expecting. This new sequence is not signified until the third leaf ('3'), and then 4, 5, 6 and 7 follow on. The typed numbers 4–7 have been deleted and replaced with handwritten numbers that start from 57, running on to 63. On the following leaf the typed number switches to 64 and this sequence runs on to the end of the chapter, at 85, though it includes two 68s and two 85s. This is the only section of the TS, apart from a handful of separate pages, without handwritten numbers.

The second page of II.ii begins with a typed 87. This sequence then runs regularly to the end of the chapter, on 107. All these typed numbers are, however, scored through due to a resurgence of the handwritten sequence. This begins on the second page of the chapter, with 92, and runs through regularly to 112. The sequences are thus now running five apart.

II.iii contains typed and scored sequence 108–127 (though the 108 is handwritten rather than typed). The handwritten sequence skips 113, and begins with 114 on the first page of the chapter, running through to 133, meaning the two are now six apart.

II.iv contains typed and scored 128–146 inclusive, though 129 and 130 are handwritten and scored, rather than typed. There is some revision of the typed numbers on leaves 142, 143 and 144

118 As noted above, Ford generally does not type the number on the first leaf of a chapter; he did not type number 18.

– all of which seem to have had another number in the low 140s first. The handwritten sequence runs from 134–152.

II.v contains typed and scored sequence 147–163 (unusually the typed number does appear on the first leaf of the chapter); handwritten 153–169 before the chapter becomes much more interesting. Leaf 163 typed/169 handwritten is an insert, part of a revision. It contains only nine complete lines of text, plus a couple of words on line ten ('the Germans'; see note 37 in the chapter). And, more dramatically, immediately after the insert the typed sequence switches to 145, continuing from here to the end of the chapter (at 156). A half-page is inserted at typed 150 (handwritten 175), containing nearly nine lines of text (see note 48 in the chapter), and there is one other anomaly described below. The handwritten sequence, however, continues regularly after the insert at 169, to 174 and then the second insert of the chapter (175). There is then a new leaf, in very sharp type, which proves its status as a late insert to the TS, and a revision, because it bears as its sole, typed number 176, which is what it would be in the handwritten sequence. The typed sequence recommences after it at 151. The handwritten sequence runs regularly too to finish on 182.

II.vi contains typed and scored sequence 157–171 with little incident, though there is a jump from 163 to 166. (An example from this sequence is reproduced on p. lx.) Ford may have eliminated some text here, but due to some smudged type it's more likely he misread his place in the sequence. The handwritten sequence does not skip, but runs smoothly from 183 to 195 on the typed, scored 171. The typed sequence runs on from 171 smoothly to 182, though 176 (handwritten 200) is an incomplete leaf – Ford has drawn a vertical squiggle underneath the last line of text to show nothing is missing (see note 41 in the text). There are three separate leaves carrying the typed, scored number 182 and the chapter, and Part II, ends on the last of them. The hand-written sequence runs from 196 to 199, skipping two numbers. Leaf 199 is corrected, though not in Ford's hand, to 197, and the sequence continues correctly on the next leaf. It runs on to 204 (typed and scored 180), but then the next leaf, 205, is also given the handwritten number 206. The following leaf (the first of the triple typed and scored 182s) is 207, the next 207A (helping to make sense of the 182s) and the next 208, which is where Part and chapter conclude.

Summary: II.i represents the greatest challenge, overall, in determining the compositional history of TS. There is the disruption to the number sequences, but, in addition, the TS changes abruptly from a blurred copy – possibly even the bottom of three copies – to the sharpest type we have yet seen. A reading of the number sequences suggests that the final version of the chapter was revised late in the process; and it is also possible that the opening of the first draft was written out of all contact with the previous chapters – up to leaf 7. (The other most likely reason for the typed sequence starting here at 1 – though the first number given is in fact 3 – is that Ford originally began the book here, or at least thought about beginning the new Part at 1 on the typescript.) Ford may have begun typing the chapter having moved location; he is certainly managing the copies differently here as the last page of I.iii is very blurred, while the first of II.i, as noted above, is extremely sharp. Ford's letter to Bradley specified that he already had copies of the early chapters, 'to Part II.1'. Perhaps he sent these duplicates as he was editing, deciding that II.i needed substantial work. This formed a natural break, then, in some stage of the composition, as he seems not to have sent Bradley any further duplicates until he later passed on for (literally) safe keeping what was a nearly complete copy. However he managed the transition, II.i was revised and inserted into TS at a stage that post-dated the handwritten sequence, and the new version was not substantially different in length, probably only two pages or so shorter. The few handwritten numbers that appear only serve to correct the 1–7 sequence, and don't, for example, pick up on the handwritten 60 at the end of I.iii. II.v is the other chapter in the Part most worthy of comment. The shift in the typed sequence that occurs after the first 163 is carried forwards to the end of TS. Although there are autograph revisions to the typed numbers in the early 140s the text remains, in the main, tightly sequential. A new, longer version of the first half of *A Man Could Stand Up –* was almost certainly substituted here, suggesting (assuming that Ford would only have wanted to type a minimum of leaves again) that the extra material was added to II.iv/II.v. The handwritten sequence would have been added to the typescript as a result of this significant revision. Finally, II.vi deserves brief comment; the handwritten sequence uses an 'A' to help solve the riddle of those three typed 182s. In contrast to other places in which inserts or revision sheets do not disrupt the flow of text, there is a problem in the move from the first 182 to the second that TS fails to remedy. See textual note 53 for the way the witnesses took over, and did so differently from each other, in this chapter.

III.i contains typed and scored sequence 183–188; handwritten 210–215 (so 209 has been skipped). At this point there is an inserted leaf, distinguished by sharp type from the blurred leaves before and after it, and given the typed number 215 (thus adopting the handwritten sequence though possibly after it had been completed). This number is altered authorially to 216, and is preceded by 'é' – perhaps some symbol for identifying inserts.[119] On the next leaf the typed and scored sequence returns with 190 (217 handwritten) but then another insert, also with sharp type, follows with only the typed number 218 – again adopting the handwritten sequence. The typed and scored sequence moves to 192 and on to the end of the chapter, on 209. There is a duplicated 197, one of which contains a good deal of revision and is likely to be an insert (see note 33 to that chapter). The handwritten sequence moves from 219 (on typed and scored 192) to 237 at chapter's end.

III.ii contains typed, scored sequence 210–216 where there is an inserted page then another 216 in this sequence, which has been scored out authorially and corrected to 217. Then this sequence continues from 218 to the chapter's, and book's, conclusion at 222. The chapter begins with a handwritten '237A' (a second 237, with which the last chapter ended), but then proceeds without incident or irregularity to 249, which is the final leaf.

Summary: The major revision in the final Part comes in the last chapter. This results in an inserted page, which was evidently completed at the same time as the first draft was being typed, as

---

119 This may or may not be linked to the fact that the beginning of II.i has the number '60E' on the first leaf, and the subsequent three leaves as well. The old handwritten sequence stopped at the end of I.iii on 60, as we know, so '60E' may here indicate an inserted section.

Ford is able to absorb it into the typed sequence – it becomes 217. This number is of course itself scored out as the page is itself then incorporated into the handwritten sequence.

Other Number Sequences

The most regular number sequence on the TS is likely to signal the active presence of the printer and/or editor at Duckworth. This sequence appears in pencil, in the left-hand margin, and is accompanied by a slash on the adjacent line indicating a page break. The sequence moves from 2–99. The first number appears on the leaf where the text of the novel begins, suggesting, perhaps, that the Dedicatory Letter and Title page were gathered together under '1'. These numbers then occur regularly, every 2/3 TS leaves. Their regularity leads to the supposition that they represent breaks in the slip proofs. In one notable case, referred to above (in the description of II.vi), the same hand that writes these numbers appears to become involved in solving a sequence problem, correcting the handwritten sequence when it skips a number. There is also a sense of a moderate dialogue between Ford and those who were to then set his proofs in a couple of places on TS, where the printer questions or clarifies TS text (see II.v note 42 and II.vi note 55 for examples). Mostly early on in TS, there are also numbers that seem to indicate counting of unit batches of 100 words; this happens five times in total, in I.i and II.v. Finally there are a few cases, in the second half of TS only, where the Duckworth page-proof page number appears on TS. This happens eight times overall, but is not regular in occurrence.

Overall Summary of Number Sequences on TS

The typescript of *A Man Could Stand Up* – bears evidence in its dual numbering of extensive revision, compositional breaks and, probably, moving around too on Ford's part. The handwritten sequence restores near-numerical order to the typed sequence, but it too occasionally duplicates numbers and skips them. The case of the inserted 176 (in II.v) provides one of the clearest pieces of evidence that this handwritten sequence is part of Ford's editorial procedure, rather than a series added later by printers or library staff as they were cataloguing the TS. The first major revision to TS was probably the one in II.v. The typed numbers needed to be replaced because of the new extra length up to what had been 144 in the old draft, and was now 163. After this new sequence had been added, II.i was completely retyped, and revised. The whole chapter boasts consistently sharp type, in great contrast to the end of I.iii and the start of II.ii, suggesting at the very least continuity of method throughout and probably a sustained burst of attention to this particular chapter. Ford's usual practice was to type using carbon paper, and work with the duplicates, as we have seen. There is a high level of coincidence throughout between revised leaves and sharpness of type. This may indicate that Ford typed only single versions of inserts, perhaps more likely in later stages of editing, or it may mean that he treated them differently, keeping any duplicates to one side or discarding them, and inserting the top copy instead into the draft. The first few leaves after the insert and sequence shift at 163 are also in sharp type, suggesting an earlier period of revision, which perhaps then led to the wholesale rewriting of the chapter.[120] Leaf 176, which belongs as we know to the period when Ford added the handwritten sequence, acts as a bridge between this sharp type and the blurred variety that then recommences.

Further Characteristics of TS and its Relationship to UK

The most impressive characteristic of the TS, on first view, is the unpredictable nature of its punctuation. The minimum number of suspension dots in what is unquestionably Ford's favourite kind of punctuation, for example, is three, but the maximum is eight. 'If in short I were the means of bringing you together again… For I believe you have not been corresponding….. You might in return….. You can see for yourself that at this moment the sum

---

120 Confirming this sense of layered revisions dating from different periods, three leaves later the name 'McKechnie' is also spelt correctly for the only time in TS: Ford usually spells it 'Mckechnie', after, as well as up to, here.

would be absolutely crushing…….' is how chapter 1 of TS concludes. The number of dots was (mostly) standardised in UK to three (mid-sentence) or four – see the relevant textual notes. Exclamation marks also sometimes come in groups in TS, and occasional examples have been provided in a textual note. Punctuation becomes more strange than this, however, when Ford suffers what appears to be a problem with the typewriter. In one section '%' functions as a full stop, '2' appears instead of ", and '½' is given instead of !.[121] This is rectified after a few leaves of type. The TS uses in general less capitalisation than is found in UK, especially for military titles, and 'Mr' and 'Mrs' do not come with a full stop. There are fewer commas in TS as well, although the difference is not dramatic. In the spectacularly Jamesian first two sentences, the punctuation in UK matches that in TS exactly; in this later example, however, the first two commas are missing from TS: 'He said he would go mad if he thought he would be blinded, because there was a girl in the teashop at Bailleul, and a fellow called Spofforth of the Wiltshires would get her if his, Aranjuez's, beauty was spoiled' (II.i). Sometimes, therefore, when Ford adopts a loose and unpunctuated style in a long sentence, UK will break it up. Sticking with punctuation, TS uses short dashes instead of the long ones in UK, and these are used in clumps of four, or thereabouts, when Ford was doing his own censoring for swearing. 'Bleedin'', however, makes it into UK of *A Man Could Stand Up* –, and mostly occurs in some reference or other to the phrase that is the novel's title. TS cannot make its mind up (and nor can UK) about the use of 'shew' vs 'show'. Both are used. Where TS and UK differ over 'ize/ise' endings, which happens in the case of 'realise' on a few occasions (and 'surprise' once or twice), though notably not in Part I, TS adopts what would probably be described as the more modern, and Americanised, form. (US follows UK here.) There are notable differences in many of these cases in the textual history of the other volumes of *Parade's End*. TS capitalises 'They', referring to the schoolgirls, more than once in I.i. Finally, in terms of the description of TS (though this comment belongs equally in a discussion of revision and I shall refer to it at more length there),

---

121 See relevant textual notes to II.vi

there are sections of the typescript in which occasional gaps are left on the lines. In general these are filled in with handwritten words, and one must assume that this happened later. Sometimes, however, Ford must have neglected to check certain sections, and a little gap remains.

Types of Revisions

Ford revised the TS in type, and by hand, sometimes both on the same leaf. Limited conjecture as to a time-frame for these different revisions is possible; in the case of the gaps left on the line, revisions are always by hand, suggesting that here at least revision was not immediate (he forgot to attend to one or two of those gaps, as discussed above). Otherwise it makes sense to assume that the majority, anyway, of typed revisions happened earlier than handwritten ones. This is not just because typed revisions were easier if the leaf was still in the machine, but because of what we have learned about the difference between the number sequences on TS: here the typed sequence predates the handwritten series, which took place at a later stage of editing. Typed insertions are generally above the line, and accompanied by a '/' signifying their exact position in the text. Handwritten inserts receive an insert sign and happen at the end of, or above, the line if relatively short. Sometimes they are squeezed in at the end of a leaf. In longer examples, Ford tends to draw a pencil line from the insert sign to the section of text to be inserted, around which he draws a circle. This text is placed in the margins, generally written at right angles to the text, or at the top or bottom of the leaf. Ford is not dedicated, for the most part, to erasing all possible reading of those words or passages that he decides to delete. There are often two or more pencil lines through a word, but rarely a frenzied scribbling rendering the original text illegible.[122] Typed deletions happen too, but are taken similarly lightly in most cases.

---

122 Though this, I am aware, does occur in other volumes of the series.

Examples of Revisions

On the first page of TS there are two revisions that provide good examples of what was often going on when Ford decided to change his text. In the first instance Ford changes 'Valentine' to 'her' (by hand), rendering the description less stark and prioritising the sense of her interior world. It is six lines since he mentioned her name, so repetition may not be quite such a worry as it would have been in the second case, where Ford strikes out a 'probably' which would have been the second in the sentence. In most cases where repetition is most likely to have been a causal factor in revision I have said so in the textual note. Often, too, a revision is likely to be related to a verbal tangle, in which tenses need attention, or time needs to become more clearly signified. In the first part of *A Man Could Stand Up –*, Ford's more substantial revisions are often to do with extending the 'back story' relating to Valentine's relationship with Christopher, so this is, in part, him sorting out the progression from one novel in the series to the next, as well as, probably, trying to avoid alienating readers who have come to volume III first (see, for example, I.ii note 3). In I.iii there is a good example relating instead to Valentine's relationship with Sylvia (note 22), in which Ford's highly nuanced revision renders Valentine as less obviously forthright (by the deletion), but also more sure of herself and, admirably in this context, loyal. Later on, where a revision is an example of Ford going over a relationship in ways such as this (II.ii note 14, for example), or, alternatively, some aspect of the representation of the war, then the textual note includes brief discussion. It is a relatively low proportion of leaves – approximately 20 per cent – which remains completely unaltered (though every leaf is altered if one includes the number sequences), and the revisions are scattered quite regularly through the text, with the exception of those signs of more detailed attention to Valentine's and Christopher's relationship mentioned above, and two other notable examples of more intensive, localised work on the text.

The gaps on the lines of text warrant further investigation. They don't start until II.iii, and, in the same chapter, TS begins to bear witness to repeated mistakes with French place names. In II.iii and II.iv spaces are left on the line into which common words such as 'chits', 'thorn', 'oddity', 'zero', 'owlish' and 'mining' have been added, as well as the odd Latin word (e.g. 'Conticuere'), or more outlandish English offering: 'scunner'. On one occasion it's a phrase that Ford adds: 'square on her feet'. In a couple of these instances it is easy to suppose that Ford may have wanted to look something up ('scunner', perhaps), or consider a detail of character portrayal ('square on her feet'). But he rarely leaves a space to go away and look up Latin (even when it might have been a good idea to do so), and those other examples listed above are too obvious to require any further thought or research. Turning to the place names, 'Bécourt' is written twice in type as 'Bicairt', and corrected authorially above the line. 'Mametz' – a place any soldier in that war would have known well, especially one whose unit had seen heavy losses there, as Ford's had done – is given as 'Manitz', and corrected similarly.[123] All these occurrences are in the space of two chapters. In the introduction to this Note, above, I discussed Ford's autograph statement on the front page of the typescript asserting that this was his typing. I think this was true of most of TS, but, despite what he says about the practice in *It Was the Nightingale,* I suspect that somebody helped him out at certain points by typing some of it, from his dictation.[124] This was probably not a professional arrangement, because the texture of TS remains fairly constant; and if it happened it was a short-term arrangement, perhaps even stopping and starting within these specific chapters. Some of the words I list above are not rare or complicated, but they may not be that easy to hear.[125] Elsewhere in II.iv there is a page of TS on

123 Mametz Wood was finally taken by the British on 12 July 1916 as part of the Battle of the Somme. The Welch Regiment suffered heavy casualties. In *No Enemy,* Gringoire recalls passing the night in a Y.M.C.A hut, discussing Mametz Wood of the 14/7/'16 with an officer of the 38th Division (62).
124 In a section that is both serious (detailing his trouble with cramp) and funny, Ford describes how 'you become a perfect fountain of words' with a secretary, because it is so easy to 'try on any effect'. He does not like dictating because 'It is as if they waited for me to write and write I do. Whereas if I have to go to a table and face pretty considerable pain [from the cramp] I wait until I have something to say and say it in the fewest possible words' (*Nightingale* 239–40).
125 Even when all other things are equal, and Ford's voice was not very clear. Douglas Goldring gives an account of listening to Ford read aloud the first chapter of *Some Do Not ...* as he was at work on it, attributing the 'strange noises' that punctuated it, and the wheezing, to the fact that Ford had been gassed during the war (*South Lodge: Reminiscences of Violet Hunt, Ford Madox Ford and the "English Review" Circle* [London: Constable & Co, 1943], 139–40).

which two almost homophone errors occur ('and' instead of 'funds'; 'backgannon' instead of 'backgammon' – if the typist didn't know the game!); slightly later, in II.v, 'hastily built' appears in type, corrected by Ford to 'beastly bullet', in what I think is a similar case (also on the same leaf a space is left on the line for 'heavy'). If Ford had writer's cramp, his hands may not have been up to long periods of typing either. Jean Rhys, for example, could have taken over for a few pages here and there. As we have seen, Ford was heading back to Paris, which is where Rhys was (or would imminently be), when the novel was at roughly mid-point.[126] The spelling of 'neighborhood' in the TS, corrected authorially to 'neighbourhood', suggests strongly a typist with American rather than British English. Relating all this to the number sequences, the signs of dictation (which began in II.iii) seem to cease at the end of the revision in II.v that led to the switch in the typed series (where 163 replaces 144). From the typed 145 onwards there are no gaps on the lines.[127] Perhaps this typist helped Ford out for the most part with the retyping that was necessitated by this revision. It could even be that conversation with the typist, especially if s/he were also a writer, led to the revision, or encouraged Ford in its boldness, hence the much longer time-frame in the completion of the novel than the 'month' he confidently wrote about to Duckworth on 9 March.[128]

Finally, there is a notable amount of revision in III.i. Here Ford seems to find it difficult to find the exact tone to portray the relationship between Valentine and her mother. Their conversation is happening on the telephone, so this may be one, unnatural factor impeding his progress. But he doesn't have the same trouble once Christopher takes over the conversation. Over a sequence of five TS leaves there are deletions, paired deletions and additions, contractions, and on one leaf there is the

126 See discussion in the Introduction here. According to her biographer Carole Angier, while Rhys went to London to look for a publisher when Ford and Stella went south, she returned to Paris in the spring of 1926. Her affair with Ford ended in the late summer of that year, by which time *A Man Could Stand Up* – was with the publishers (*Jean Rhys* [Harmondsworth: Penguin, 1992], 152–7).

127 Though, as I say in the textual note in II.v, the signs of mechanical fault with the typewriter may possibly be of relevance here too.

128 He may also just have wanted to let his publisher know in that letter how well he was getting on, and exaggerated his progress.

remainder of five lines from an earlier draft of this passage, all crossed through but still legible. (See the textual note for the detail, but it is worth pointing out here that the struck-out text appears at the top of a leaf that bears the typed 197, the second of two with this number in this sequence. The first is an inserted page, being shorter than normal and necessitating revision at the end of the previous leaf – 196 – as well as at the start of the second 197. There was evidently a larger-scale revision here as well.) The most likely cause for this hesitation and rethinking is, apart from the 'complete exhaustion' he commented on to Bradley when posting the nearly finished typescript, the intensely challenging nature of this exchange. Valentine is, after all, talking to her mother about the fact that she intends to have an affair with Christopher. The finely weighted balance eventually struck between love and duty, convention and freedom, respect and independence, especially when two such impressive characters as these are involved, must have been extraordinarily difficult to find. Ford did rework several sections of III.ii as well, however. The final part of the novel was revised thoroughly, though not as dramatically as Part II.

Rules of Engagement

As set out above, in the Note on this Edition, our aim in the case of each of the four novels that make up *Parade's End* is to produce an edition based on the first UK edition, informed by a reading of the manuscript and any other witnesses. In the case of *A Man Could Stand Up –* these other witnesses consist of an uncorrected proof copy and the first American edition (US). US, one might suppose, is likely to have been set from the typescript of this novel, or from Duckworth page proofs, rather than from UK. There was certainly a very narrow gap between the dates of publication on either side of the Atlantic: in the section of Harvey's *Bibliography* in which he describes the appearance of Ford's books he places them at around two weeks apart from the reviews (it would have been something like 9 and 23 October on this account). This is an error, however; it was closer than that. Harvey later includes the Paterson US review from 17 October, suggesting instead a UK publication around the 9th, but an even more immediate American one around the 16th.

Though Ford did produce duplicate copies of TS, as we know, he does not mention sending such an early version of the completed novel to publishers, but only to agents for safe keeping. (And this would be unusual, especially in the case of a TS that is annotated, bearing lots of evidence of handwritten revision.) This leads us to the proofs. A bound proof copy has been consulted in the preparation of this edition, as noted above. Under normal circumstances, we might assume this represents a later state than the corrected ones, both sets of which – UK and US – are missing, as they mostly are for the other three novels in the series. However, we know Ford had adopted a particular practice with regard to proofs in the *Parade's End* novels, beginning with the second, at least: 'I usually get Duckworth to print a set or two of proofs off right away and thus save myself the bother and expense of typing', he wrote to Bradley in January 1925,[129] suggesting the copy that has been consulted may represent a relatively early post-typescript state (though after the galley proofs too), the same as that worked on by Ford, and then post-dated by his corrected version. The pattern on examination of all the witnesses suggests US must indeed have been set from a later state.

When, for example, in I.iii, UK reads 'behaved very badly indeed', US follows UK, rather than TS and the Duckworth proofs, which carry 'appeared to have behaved very badly indeed'. A sentence is inserted to II.i in UK that does not appear in TS: 'A dream!' It is also in US. In my textual note I suggest that it was a late addition, intended to clarify the text immediately before it, but it post-dated the Duckworth proof. Later, in II.iii, UK has 'the easterly winds were needed for the use of the gas without which, in the idea of the German leaders, [it] was impossible to attack'. US follows this, more or less (with an extra bit of editing), rather than the typescript version which is also preserved in the proof copy: 'The easterly winds needed for the use of the gas without which the enemy troops could not be induced to attack.' There are cases in which US appears to follow

TS and the proofs, but often these cases can equally be explained by the more professional editing that tends to characterise US, especially in punctuation – US irons out errors that exist in UK (see I.iii, notes 4 and 20, for example), though also has manifest problems dealing with cockney dialect ('was it not smashed' is the best example of a 'correction', from 'was it n smashed' in UK; see II.i note 43). For US to have been set from later, missing proofs, Ford would have had to do an incredibly thorough job of editing two sets of proofs in almost exactly the same way. One can imagine him taking care over missing words, for example, as in I.ii where 'Edith Ethel's story' (UK and US) has been only 'Edith Ethel's' in TS and uncorrected proof, necessitating an urgent insert. Likewise one can, perhaps, imagine close attention to revisions of key words, which change dramatically the sense of a passage; in II.iv 'with terror' in TS and proof becomes 'with rage' in UK and US. But is it likely that even the most careful and attentive proofreader would alter the speech marks round a paragraph exactly in two sets of proofs, as in II.ii, note 10? (The fact that this is, in the event, a punctuation error – one that is emended in the text given here in line with TS – makes it less likely that the US copy-editor emended the proofs and ended up accidentally matching UK.) And Ford was not this kind of proofreader. In fact Janice Biala, as we know from the quotation given first above in the Note on this Edition, thought him the 'worst proof reader on earth'. This kind of proofreader does not pick up on speech marks, and may well not pick up on key words, or missing ones, in exactly the same way.

The evidence suggests strongly, in the end, that US was set from UK, with the copy-editor making the corrections, as well as introducing some new errors, that are noted in the text of *A Man Could Stand Up –*. Yes, the time-frame suggested by the reviews initially makes this hard to imagine. But perhaps those American reviewers had early copies – especially Paterson, whom Ford knew. (The English edition of *Some Do Not . . .* had been selling in New York before the American publisher Seltzer got his edition out, much to 'his disgust'.)[130] The next American review

130 *Reader* 488–9; and later, on 18 November 1926, in reference to *A Man Could Stand Up –*, Ford wrote from New York to Stella Bowen: 'It also appears to have sold out the first English edition almost on publication: at any rate the American booksellers

wasn't until the 24th, giving something more like the delay between British and American first publications that we might expect to find in this case.

The Note on this Edition sets out our rules for emendation of UK. Though in *A Man Could Stand Up* – I should have liked, for example, to replace the 'dishevelled veils of murdered bodies' of UK (II.i) with the 'dishevelled veils of murdered brides' of TS, those rules – for good reason – would not permit it. The textual notes, however, record such differences in full. Emendations to UK include errors that neither Ford nor his editors corrected, especially around the issue of characters' names (see the textual notes in Part II concerning O Nine Morgan and O Nine Griffiths, for example, and the case of McKechnie throughout). Medical Officer Terence is abbreviated to Terry initially in TS and US, though US then moves to follow UK with Derry. Authority to correct UK's punctuation can often be taken from US, as suggested above, but Ford's technique causes particular problems in the case of speech marks, as can be seen from a succession of textual notes in II.i (47 ff.).[131] TS provides the most accurate version often here, as is argued in the textual notes. There are errors in the possessive of Tietjens' name in all states, and the possessive of 'Mistresses' foxes all editors each time it is used in Part I. All of these cases, however, receive a note, in line with our declared intention to signal alterations to the UK text. All diversions from UK are noted also, and US is cited when it differs from UK, even if it differs in the same way as TS. Where US is not cited, as is most often the case, it is because it carries the same version as UK.

---

complain bitterly that they can't get any first English editions' (Ford/Bowen 227). This is, of course, a slightly different point, but it suggests that the English editions of the novels had particular value in America, though the novel was published there too.

131 I discuss this aspect of Ford's technique in the Introduction.

A MAN COULD
STAND UP —[1]
A Novel

By
FORD MADOX FORD

To
GERALD DUCKWORTH[1]*

My dear Duckworth,

Permit me to address to you this Epistle Dedicatory, for without you the series of books of which this is the third and penultimate, could not have existed. We have been working together for a great number of years now and always without a cloud on our relationships. At any rate there has never been a cloud on my half of the landscape.

I fancy that you at least know how much I dislike not letting a book go merely as a book; but it appears that if one has the misfortune to be impelled to treat of public matters that is impossible. So let me here repeat: As far as I am privately concerned these books, like all my others, constitute an attempt simply to reflect—not in the least to reflect on—our own times.[†]

Nevertheless as far as this particular book is concerned I find myself ready to admit to certain public aims. That is to say that, in it, I have been trying to say to as much of humanity as I can reach, and, in particular to such members of the public as, because of age or for other reasons did not experience the shocks and anxieties of the late struggle:

"This is what the late war was like: this is how modern fighting of the organised, scientific type affects the mind. If, for reasons

---

* Ford's publisher. Ford's relationship with the firm, founded by Gerald Duckworth in 1898, began in 1902 with the appearance of *Rossetti*. In 1922, when Ford signed a contract for *The Marsden Case*, he apparently also agreed with the firm that they take over all his work, including reissues once copyrights reverted to him. Duckworth certainly published the next eleven of Ford's books that appeared in England, including all four volumes of *Parade's End*. Ford was questioning this professional relationship by 1928, along with the business of publishing in England altogether, but his friendship with Duckworth remained a significant one. *A Man Could Stand Up –* is the second of the four volumes of the tetralogy to include a dedicatory letter.

† Ford's axiomatic belief in authorial impartiality, or 'aloofness', was well-documented. See, for example, 'Literary Portraits: VIII. Mr. Joseph Conrad', *Tribune* (14 Sept. 1907), 2. He moderates his strictly held view in this dedicatory letter – though in a few lines' time he also puts great emphasis on the need to recognise the distance between his own 're-actions and reflections' and those of his fictional creation, Christopher Tietjens.

of gain or, as is still more likely out of dislike for collective types other than your own, you choose to permit your rulers to embark on another war, this—or something very accentuated along similar lines—is what you will have to put up with!"

I hope, in fact, that this series of books, for what it is worth, may make war seem undesirable. But in spite of that hope I have not exaggerated either the physical horrors or the mental distresses of that period. On the contrary I have selected for treatment less horrible episodes than I might well have rendered and I have rendered them with more equanimity than might well have been displayed. You see here the end of the war of attrition through the eyes of a fairly stolid, fairly well-instructed man. I should like to add that, like all of us, he is neither unprejudiced nor infallible. And you have here his mental re-actions and his reflections—which are not, *not*, NOT presented as those of the author.

The hostilities in which he takes part are those of a period of relative calm. For it should be remembered that great battles, taking months and months to prepare and to recover from, were of relatively rare occurrence. The heavy[2] strain of the trenches came from the waiting for long periods of inaction, in great—in mortal[3]—danger every minute of the day and night.

The fighting here projected is just fighting, as you might say at any old time: it is not specifically, say, the battle of the 21st March, 1918, or any particular one of the series of combats after the 9th of April, of that year.

Finally I have to repeat that, with the exception of the central figure—as to whose Toryism I had my say in the preface to the last-published book of this series!—I have most carefully avoided so much as adumbrating the characteristics—and certainly the vicissitudes—of any human being known to myself.*

---

* Ford refers to *No More Parades* (1925), volume II of *Parade's End*. In the dedicatory letter, to the publisher William Bird, Ford describes the 'English Tory' Tietjens as a necessary medium through which to treat the horrors of war. He says that Tietjens is based on a friend, whom he only identifies as 'X'. Later, in a memoir, Ford acknowledged that he had Arthur Pierson Marwood in mind (*Return* 281).

And, in the meantime, my dear Duckworth, let me say that I shall always describe and subscribe, myself as
Yours very gratefully,
Ford Madox Ford.

Paris, May 18th, 1926.

PART I

CHAPTER I[4]

SLOWLY, amidst intolerable noises from, on the one hand the street and, on the other, from the large and voluminously echoing playground, the depths of the telephone began, for Valentine, to assume an aspect that, years ago it had used to have—of being a part of the supernatural paraphernalia of inscrutable Destiny.[*]

The telephone, for some ingeniously torturing reason was in a corner of the great schoolroom without any protection and, called imperatively, at a moment of considerable suspense, out of the asphalte[5] playground where, under her command ranks of girls had stood electrically only just within the margin of control, Valentine with the receiver at her ear was plunged immediately into incomprehensible news uttered by a voice that she seemed half to remember.[†] Right in the middle of a sentence it hit her:

" . . . .[6] that he ought presumably to be under control, which you mightn't like!"; after that the noise burst out again and rendered the voice inaudible.

It occurred to her[7] that probably at that minute the whole population of the world[8] needed to be under control; she knew she herself did. But she had no male relative that the verdict

---

* Cf. 'blind and inscrutable destiny' in *The Good Soldier* 40; also 'blind but August destiny' in Ford's *Henry James: A Critical Study* (London: Martin Secker, 1914), 121; and '[d]estiny who is blind and implacable' at war in *No Enemy* 72. The idea of 'blind destiny' recurs later in this volume and has its roots in ancient philosophy – Epicurus (341–270 BC), for example.

† In Ford's Edwardian novel *A Call* (1910), a telephone is the device around which he conjures a plot of sexual frustration, betrayal and psychological fragility. Valentine's difficulties with the caller in this case are reminiscent of Robert Grimshaw's in *A Call*. See my Introduction, as well as Philip Horne's essay, 'Absent-mindedness: Ford on the Phone', *Ford Madox Ford's Modernity*, ed. Robert Hampson and Max Saunders, International Ford Madox Ford Studies, 2 (New York and Amsterdam: Rodopi), 17–34. Cf. Ford's *When the Wicked Man* (London: Jonathan Cape, 1932), 195–202.

could apply to in especial. Her brother? But he was on a mine-sweeper. In dock at the moment. And now ... safe for good! There was also an aged great uncle that she had never seen. Dean of somewhere ... Hereford? Exeter? ... Somewhere.... Had she just said *safe*? She[9] was shaken with joy![10]

She said into the mouthpiece:

"Valentine Wannop speaking.... Physical Instructress at this school, you know!"

She had to present an appearance of sanity ... a sane voice at the very least!

The tantalisingly half-remembered voice in the telephone now got in some more incomprehensibilities. It came as if from caverns and as if with exasperated rapidity it exaggerated its[11] "s'"s with an effect of spitting vehemence.

"His brothers.s.s got pneumonia, so his mistress.ss.ss even is unavailable to look after...."

The voice disappeared; then it emerged again with:

"They're said to be friends now!"

It was drowned then, for a long period in a sea of shrill girls' voices[12] from the playground, in an ocean of factory-hooters' ululations,[13] amongst innumerable explosions that trod upon one another's heels. From where on earth did they get explosives, the population of squalid suburban streets amidst which the school lay? For the matter of that where did they get the spirits to make such an appalling row? Pretty drab people! Inhabiting liver-coloured boxes. Not on the face of it an imperial race.

The sibilating voice in the telephone went on spitting out spitefully that the porter said he had no furniture at all; that he did not appear to recognise the porter.... Improbable sounding pieces of information half-extinguished by the external sounds but uttered in a voice that seemed to mean to give pain by what it said.

Nevertheless it was impossible not to take it gaily. The thing, out there, miles and miles away must have been signed—a few minutes ago. She imagined along an immense line sullen and disgruntled cannon sounding for a last time.

"I haven't," Valentine Wannop shouted into the mouthpiece, "the least idea of what you want or who you are."

She got back a title.... Lady someone or other.... It might

have been Blastus.* She imagined that one of the lady governoresses of the school must be wanting to order something in the
way of school sports organised to celebrate the auspicious day. A
lady governoress or other was always wanting something done by
the School to celebrate something. No doubt the Head who was
not wanting in a sense of humour—not *absolutely* wanting!—had
turned this lady of title on to Valentine Wannop after having
listened with patience to her for half an hour. The Head had
certainly sent out to where in the playground they had all stood
breathless, to tell Valentine Wannop that there was someone on
the telephone that she—Miss Wanostrocht,† the said Head—
thought that she, Miss Wannop, ought to listen to.... [14] Then:
Miss Wanostrocht must have been able to distinguish what had
been said by the now indistinguishable lady of title. But of course
that had been ten minutes ago ... [15] Before the maroons or the
sirens,[16] whichever it had been, had sounded.... "The porter said
he had no furniture at all.... He did not appear to recognise the
porter.... Ought presumably to be under control!" ... Valentine's mind thus recapitulated the information that she had from
Lady (provisionally) Blastus.[17] She imagined now that the Lady
must be concerned for the[18] superannuated drill-sergeant the
school had[19] had before it had acquired her, Valentine, as physical instructor. She figured to herself the[20] venerable, mumbling
gentleman, with several ribbons on a black commissionaire's
tunic. In an almshouse, probably.[21] Placed there by the Governors of the school. Had pawned his furniture no doubt....

Intense heat possessed Valentine Wannop. She imagined
indeed her eyes flashing. Was this the moment?

* A chamberlain, servant of Herod Agrippa, and mediator in times of war (Acts 12:20).
Contained here also is a likely Fordian reference to Wyndham Lewis and the Vorti-
cist publication, *Blast*, in which chapters of *The Good Soldier* first appeared. The
magazine famously listed those who were to be 'blessed' or 'blasted', a clue to the fact
that this is no neutral caller on the telephone.

† Max Saunders' biography of Ford mentions a Miss Wanostrocht as a cousin of the
Garnetts. She lent Ford money (*A Dual Life* I 258). She may herself have been related
to the Belgian Nicolas Wanostrocht, who revised the Book of Common Prayer in
1794. He had come to England in around 1780 and established a school near Camberwell. Camberwell was well known for its riotousness; there was a long-lasting tradition
of saturnalia at the site. Also note that there is supposed to be the potential for confusion between Valentine's name (Wannop) and the Head's (Wanostrocht). Edith
Ethel, as we soon learn, is one potential victim. In *No More Parades* (I.iii), Colonel
Levin gets the two names confused.

She didn't even know whether what they had let off had been maroons or aircraft guns or sirens. It had happened—the noise, whatever it was—whilst she had been coming through the underground passage from the playground to the schoolroom to answer this wicked telephone. So she had not heard the sound. She had missed the sound for which the ears of a world had waited for years, for a generation. For an eternity. No sound. When she had left the playground there had been dead silence. All waiting: girls rubbing one ankle with the other rubber sole. . . .

Then. . . . For the rest of her life she was never to be able to remember the greatest stab of joy that had ever been known by waiting millions. There would be no one but she who would not be able to remember that. . . . Probably a stirring of the heart that was like a stab; probably a catching of the breath that was like an inhalation of flame! . . .* It was over now; they were by now in a situation;[22] a condition, something that would affect certain things in certain ways. . . .

She remembered that the putative ex-drill sergeant had a brother who had pneumonia and thus an unavailable mistress. . . .

She was about to say to herself:

"That's just my luck!" when she remembered good-humouredly that her luck was not like that at all. On the whole she had had good luck—ups and downs. A good deal of anxiety at one time—but who hadn't had! But good health; a mother with good health; a brother safe. . . . Anxieties, yes! But nothing that had gone so very wrong. . . .

This then was an exceptional stroke of bad luck! Might it be an omen[23]—to the effect that things in future would go wrong: to the effect that she would miss other universal experiences. Never marry, say; or never know the joy of childbearing: if it was a joy! Perhaps it was; perhaps it wasn't. One said one thing, one another. At any rate might it not be an omen that she would miss some universal and necessary experience! . . . Never see Carcassonne, the French said. . . .† Perhaps she would never see the

---

*   Cf. Ford's poem 'Peace' (1918), *Selected Poems* 110.

†   Paul Skinner asks whether Carcassonne stands for all that Ford 'may not see, do, achieve?', in his essay '"Speak Up, Fordie!": How Some People Want to Go to Carcassonne', in *Ford Madox Ford and the City*, ed. Sara Haslam, International Ford Madox Ford Studies, 4 (New York and Amsterdam: Rodopi), 197–210 (207). In Ford's work, mention of the city comes most often in *Provence* (1935), but occurs in other books

Mediterranean. You could not be a proper man if you had never seen the Mediterranean: the sea of Tibullus, of the Anthologists, of Sappho, even.... Blue: incredibly blue! People would be able to travel now. It was incredible! Incredible! Incredible! But you *could*. Next week you would be able to! You could call a taxi? And go to Charing Cross!* And have a porter! A whole porter!... The wings, the wings of a dove: then would I flee away, flee away† and eat pomegranates‡ beside an infinite wash tub of Reckitt's blue.§ Incredible, but you *could*! She felt eighteen again. Cocky! She said, using the good, metallic, Cockney bottoms of her lungs that she had used for shouting back at interrupters at Suffrage meetings** before .... ²⁴ before this ... she shouted blatantly into the telephone:

"I say, whoever you are! I suppose they have *done* it; did they announce it in your parts by maroons or sirens?" She repeated it three times, she did not care for Lady Blastus or Lady Blast Anybody else. She was going to leave that old school and eat pomegranates in the shadow of the rock where Penelope, wife of

---

too, including *The Good Soldier* ('I just wanted to marry her as some people want to go to Carcassonne', writes narrator Dowell about Nancy, 84). The 'saying' quoted in *A Man Could Stand Up* – may well be a reference to a line in the first verse of a poem by Gustave Nadaud (1820–93), 'Carcassonne': 'Never have I seen Carcassonne'. The phrase recurs in *Last Post* (II.iii), in French.

* See Ford's poem 'Antwerp', written after the city surrendered to the Germans in October 1914 (*Selected Poems* 82–5). He saw Belgian refugees at Charing Cross station, and as well as provoking what T. S. Eliot called 'the only good poem I have met with on the subject of the war' (*Egoist*, 4 [Nov. 1917], 151), this experience encouraged Ford to raise money for those displaced by German aggression. Until 1923 Charing Cross was the London station that acted as the gateway to Paris and the continent.

† Psalm 55:6: 'Oh that I had wings like a dove! for then would I fly away, and be at rest.'

‡ The pomegranate was a symbol of beauty for the Greeks and the Romans and is one of the seven species enumerated in Deuteronomy 8:8 as being special products of the land of Israel. Mrs Macmaster is earlier described as having 'dark blue eyes in the shadows of her hair and bowed, pomegranate lips in a chin curved like the bow of a Greek boat' (*Some Do Not ...* II.iv).

§ Reckitt's Blue – a laundry whitener – was one of the first widely marketed laundry products manufactured by Reckitt & Sons. This laundry starch company began producing 'laundry blue' in 1852 by combining a synthetic ultramarine and sodium bicarbonate, making the product widely affordable (the active ingredient was previously made by grinding lapis lazuli).

** The campaign for votes for women in Britain began at the time of the Second Reform Bill in 1867. Supporters of the campaign held their own meetings, and drew attention to their cause through a variety of protests and actions. Some women were able to vote in the General Election of 1918 but voting equality with men did not come until 1928, the year *Last Post* was published.

Ulysses, did her washing.* With lashings of blue in the water! Was all your underlinen bluish in those parts owing to the colour of the sea? She could! She could! She *could!* Go with her mother and brother and all to where you could eat . . . Oh new potatoes! In December, the sea being blue. . . . *What songs the Sirens sang and whether. . . .* †

She was not going to show respect for any Lady anything ever again. She had had to hitherto, independent young woman of means though she were, so as not to damage the School and Miss Wanostrocht with the Governoresses. Now . . . She was never going to show respect for anyone ever again. She had been through the mill: the whole world had been through the mill! No more respect!

As she might have expected she got it in the neck immediately afterwards—for over cockiness!

The hissing, bitter voice from the telephone enunciated the one address she did not want to hear:

"Lincolnss . . s.s. . . . sInn!"‡

Sin! . . . Like the Devil!

It hurt.

The cruel voice said:

"I'm s.s.peaking from there!"

Valentine said courageously:

"Well; it's a great day. I suppose you're bothered by the cheering like me. I can't hear what you want. I don't care. Let 'em cheer!"

---

* Ford and Stella did manage something akin to the escape Valentine fantasises about in the early twenties when they based themselves in the Mediterranean. Ford began writing *Some Do Not . . .* at Cap Ferrat in 1923.

† From Chapter 5 of Thomas Browne's essay 'Hydriotaphia' (or 'Urn Burial'), published in 1658 together with 'The Garden of Cyrus'. The full sentence reads 'What song the Syrens sang, or what name Achilles assumed when he hid himself among women, though puzzling questions, are not beyond all conjecture.' Cf. Literary Portraits XXVIII. 'Mr. Morley Roberts and *Time and Thomas Waring*', *Outlook*, 33 (21 Mar. 1914), 390; 'On a Notice of *Blast*', *Outlook*, 36 (31 July 1915), 144; and *Thus to Revisit* (London: Chapman & Hall, 1921), 7. Ford's admiration of Browne also opens Chapter 4, Part 1 of Book Two ('From the Elizabethans to Modern Times') of *The March of Literature: From Confucius to Modern Times* (1939). He quotes the sirens passage, calling it 'perhaps the most famous of all passages of Browne' (*March* 470). Edgar Allan Poe (1809–49) uses it to open his tale 'The Murders in the Rue Morgue' (1841).

‡ One of the legal institutions of medieval origin situated in London and responsible for the education of barristers. Originally around twenty Inns are known to have existed, of which only four survive, Lincoln's Inn being one. Tietjens and Macmaster are living on Gray's Inn Road at the beginning of *Some Do Not . . . .*

She felt like that. She should not have.

The voice said:

"You remember your Carlyle...."

It was exactly what she did not want to hear. With the receiver hard at her ear she looked round at the great schoolroom—the Hall, made to let a thousand girls sit silent while the Head made the speeches that were the note of the School. Repressive!... The place was like a nonconformist chapel.[25] High, bare walls with Gothic windows running up to a pitch-pine varnished roof. Repression, the note of the place; the place, the very place not to be in to-day.... You *ought* to be in the streets, hitting policemen's helmets with bladders. This was Cockney London: that was how Cockney London expressed itself. Hit policemen innocuously because policemen were stiff, embarrassed at these tributes of affection, swayed in rejoicing mobs over whose heads they looked remotely, like poplar trees jostled by vulgarer vegetables!

But she was there, being reminded of the dyspepsia of Thomas Carlyle!

"*Oh!*" she exclaimed into the instrument, "You're Edith Ethel!" Edith Ethel Duchemin, now of course Lady Macmaster! But you weren't used to thinking of her as Lady Somebody.

The last person in the world: the very last! Because, long ago she had made up her mind that it was all over between herself and Edith Ethel.* She certainly could not make any advance to the ennobled personage who vindictively disapproved of all things made—with a black thought in a black shade, as you might say.† Of all things that were not being immediately useful to Edith Ethel!

And, aesthetically draped and meagre, she had sets of quotations for appropriate occasions. Rossetti for Love; Browning for optimism—not frequent that: Walter Savage Landor to show[26] acquaintance with more esoteric prose. And the unfailing quotation from Carlyle for damping off saturnalia: for New Year's Day,

---

* A reference back to *Some Do Not* ..., a scene set (probably) in 1917 so not, in fact, all that long ago. Here, Valentine realised that Edith Ethel is trying both to prise Macmaster away from his friend, and to drop her as a friend because of her attachment to Christopher (II.iv).

† Andrew Marvell's poem 'The Garden' includes a final couplet 'Annihilating all that's made / To a green Thought in a green Shade.'

Te Deums,* Victories, anniversaries, celebrations.... It was coming over the wire now, that quotation:

".... And then I remembered that it was the birthday of their Redeemer!"

How well Valentine knew it: how often with spiteful conceit had not Edith Ethel intoned that. A passage from the diary of the Sage of Chelsea who lived near the Barracks.

"To-day," the quotation ran, "I saw that the soldiers by the public house at the corner were more than usually drunk. And then I remembered that it was the birthday of their Redeemer!"†

How superior of the Sage of Chelsea not to remember till then that that had been Christmas Day! Edith Ethel, too, was trying to shew[27] how superior she was. She wanted to prove that until she, Valentine Wannop, had reminded her, Lady Macmaster, that that day had about it something of the popular[28] festival she, Lady Mac, had been unaware of the fact. Really quite unaware, you know. She lived in her rapt seclusion along with Sir Vincent—the critic, you know: their eyes fixed on the higher things, they disregarded maroons and had really a quite remark-able collection, by now, of first editions, official-titled friends and At Homes to their credit.‡

Yet Valentine remembered that once she had sat at the feet of the darkly mysterious Edith Ethel Duchemin—Where had *that* all gone?—and had sympathised with her marital martyrdoms, her impressive taste in furniture, her large rooms[29] and her spiri-tual adulteries. So she said good-humouredly to the instrument:

"Aren't you just the same, Edith Ethel? And what can I do for you?"

---

*   Te Deum Laudamus, translated into English as 'We praise thee O God', is part of the mass as celebrated in the Roman Catholic Church and is also part of the service of Morning Prayer in the Church of England. It is a hymn of praise used at times of cele-bration. (See Shakespeare's *Henry V*, IV.viii.123, 'Let there be sung *Non nobis* and *Te Deum*', after England's victory at Agincourt.)

†   By the early 1840s Thomas Carlyle (1795–1881), the noted commentator on contem-porary politics, society and morals, was known as 'the Sage of Chelsea'. Thackeray commented that 'Tom Carlyle lives in perfect dignity in a little house in Chelsea, with a snuffy Scotch maid to open the door, and the best company in England knocking at it.' See 'The Sage of Chelsea', Chapter 8 of John Morrow's book *Thomas Carlyle* (2006), in which he places the remark Ford quotes from Carlyle's *Reminiscences* in a wider context. Carlyle receives no mention in *The March of Literature*, for example, but his work is cited in some of Ford's critical essays. In *Ancient Lights*, Ford quotes this same phrase of Carlyle's, calling it a 'touching sentence' (74).

‡   'At home' was a formula for inviting company to an informal reception.

The good-natured patronage in her tone astonished her, and she was astonished, too, at the ease with which she spoke. Then she realised that the noises had been going away: silence was falling: the cries receded. They were going towards a cumulation at a distance. The girls' voices in the playground no longer existed: the Head must have let them go. Naturally, too, the local population wasn't going to go on letting off crackers in side streets. . . . She was alone: cloistered with the utterly improbable!

Lady Macmaster had sought her out and here was she, Valentine Wannop; patronising Lady Macmaster! Why? What could Lady Macmaster want her to do? She *couldn't*—But of course she jolly well could!—be thinking of being unfaithful to Macmaster and be wanting her, Valentine Wannop, to play the innocent, the virginal gooseberry or Disciple. Or alibi. Whatever it was. Goose was the most appropriate word. . . . Obviously Macmaster was the sort of person to whom any Lady Macmaster would want—would have—to be unfaithful. A little, dark-bearded, drooping, deprecatory fellow. A typical Critic! All Critics' wives[30] were probably unfaithful to them. They lacked the creative gift. What did you call it? A word unfit for a young lady to use!

Her mind ran about in this unbridled, Cockney school-girl's vein. There was no stopping it. It was in honour of the DAY! She was temporarily inhibited from bashing policemen on the head, so she was mentally disrespectful to constituted authority—to Sir Vincent Macmaster, Principal Secretary to H.M. Department of Statistics, author of Walter Savage Landor,[31] a Critical Monograph, and of twenty-two other Critical Monographs in the Eminent Bores' Series. . . . *Such* books! And she was being[32] disrespectful and patronising to Lady Macmaster, Egeria* to innumerable Scottish Men of Letters! No more respect! Was that to be a lasting effect of the cataclysm that had involved the world? The *late* cataclysm! Thank God, since ten minutes ago they could call it the late cataclysm!

She was positively tittering in front of the telephone from which Lady Macmaster's voice was now coming in earnest,

---

* Cf. *Some Do Not . . .* ('"Well, she was an Egeria!"', Tietjens said", II.i); and also Ford's description of Edith Ethel in *Last Post* (II.i). In Roman myth, Egeria was a nymph who inspired and advised Numa Pompilius, the wise and pious second king of Rome.

cajoling tones—as if she knew that Valentine was not paying very
much attention, saying:
  "Valentine! *Valentine!* *Valentine!*"
  Valentine said negligently:
  "I'm listening!"
  She wasn't really. She was really reflecting on whether there
had not been more sense in[33] the Mistresses' Conference[34] that
that morning, solemnly, had taken place in the Head's private
room. Undoubtedly what the Mistresses with the Head at their
head had feared was that if they, Headmistresses, Mistresses,
Masters, Pastors—by whom I was made etcetera!*—should cease
to be respected because saturnalia broke out on the sounding of
a maroon the whole world would go to pieces![†] An awful thought!
The Girls no longer sitting silent in the nonconformist hall while
the Head addressed repressive speeches to them. . . .
  She had addressed a speech, containing the phrase: "the Credit
of a Great Public School," in that Hall only last afternoon in
which, fair thin woman, square-elbowed, with a little of sunlight
really still in her coiled fair hair, she had seriously requested the
Girls not again to repeat the manifestations of joy of the day
before. The day before there had been a false alarm and the
School—Horribly!—had sung:
  "Hang Kaiser Bill from the hoar apple tree
  And Glory Glory Glory till it's tea-time!"[‡]

---

* 'For by him were all things created, that are in heaven, and that are in earth, visible
  and invisible, whether they be thrones, or dominions, or principalities, or powers',
  Colossians 1:16.
† On saturnalia cf. *The Good Soldier* 85.
‡ The origins of this couplet seem to lie in a verse of the American Civil War ballad,
  'John Brown's Body', which expressed Union soldiers' hatred for Confederate Presi-
  dent Jefferson Davis:

    They will hang Jeff Davis to a sour apple tree, [× 3]
    As they march along!
    Glory, glory, hallelujah

  As to the contemporary, and English, version given here, Lloyd George's slogan 'Hang
  the Kaiser' was a key theme of the 1918 general election in Britain, whereas the 'hoar
  apple tree' as a phrase has a pedigree dating back to Anglo-Saxon times. A contemporary writer reported, on what was also a popular theme in published war songs, that
  'One heard during the First World War many "communal improvisations" from groups
  of singing soldiers such as "We'll hang Kaiser Bill to a sour apple tree"...' (From 'Poetic
  Origins and the Ballad', Louise Pound, University of Nebraska, Lincoln, Department
  of English, 1921.) http://digitalcommons.unl.edu/cgi/viewcontent.cgi?article=1042&
  context=englishfacpubs (accessed 20 July 2009).

The Head, now, making her speech was certain that she had now before her a chastened School, a School that anyhow felt foolish because the rumour of the day before had turned out to be a canard. So she impressed on the Girls the nature of the joy they ought to feel: a joy repressed that should send them silent home. Blood was to cease to be shed: a fitting cause for home-joy—as it were a home-lesson. But there was to be no triumph. The very fact that you ceased hostilities precluded triumph. . . .

Valentine, to her surprise, had found herself wondering when you *might* feel triumph? . . . You couldn't whilst you were still contending: you must not when you had won! Then when? The Head told the girls that it was their province as the future mothers of England—Nay, of reunited Europe!—to—well, in fact, to go on with their home-lessons and not run about the streets with effigies of the Great Defeated! She put it that it was their function to shed further light of womanly culture—that there, Thank Heaven, they had never been allowed to forget!—athwart a re-illumined Continent. . . . As if you could light up now there was no fear of submarines or raids!*

And Valentine wondered why, for a mutinous moment, she had wanted to feel triumph . . . had wanted *someone* to feel triumph. Well, he . . . they . . . had wanted it so much. Couldn't they have it just for a moment—for the space of one Benkollerdy!† Even if it were wrong? or vulgar? Something human, someone had once said, is dearer than a wilderness of decalogues!‡

But at the Mistresses' Conference[35] that morning, Valentine had realised that what was really frightening them[36] was the other note. A quite definite fear. If, at this parting of the ways, at this crack across the table of History, the School—the World, the future mothers of Europe—got out of hand, would they ever come

---

*   Ford writes about blackouts and air raids in *Nightingale* 92–7, for example.
†   Phonetic cockney for 'Bank Holiday'.
‡   In Max Saunders' discussion of this section of the novel (*A Dual Life* II 226–7) he follows the link in Ford's thought between the 'table of History' (see the next para-graph) and the stone table on which the finger of God wrote the Ten Commandments (the decalogue). One possible root of Valentine's memory of the phrase is found in a Conrad quotation, in which he's quoting the brothers Grimm in the epigraph of *Youth* (1902).

back? The Authorities—Authority all over the world—was afraid of that; more afraid of that than of any other thing. Wasn't it a possibility that there was to be no more Respect? None for constituted Authority and consecrated Experience?

And, listening to the fears of those careworn, faded, ill-nourished gentlewomen, Valentine Wannop had found herself speculating.

"No more respect.... For the Equator! For the Metric system. For Sir Walter Scott! Or George Washington! Or Abraham Lincoln! Or the Seventh Commandment!!!!!!"*

And she had a blushing vision of fair, shy, square-elbowed Miss Wanostrocht—the Head!—succumbing to some specious-tongued beguiler!... That was where the shoe really pinched! You had to keep them—[37] the Girls, the Populace, everybody!— in hand now, for once you let go there was no knowing where They, like waters parted from the seas, mightn't carry You. Goodness knew! You might arrive anywhere—at county families taking to trade; gentlefolk selling for profit! All the unthinkable sorts of things!

And with a little inward smirk of pleasure Valentine realised that that Conference was deciding that the Girls were to be kept in the playground that morning—at Physical Jerks. She hadn't ever put up with *much* in the way of patronage from the rather untidy-haired bookish branch of the establishment. Still, accomplished Classicist as she once had been, she had had to acknowledge that the bookish branch of a School was what you might call the Senior Service.† She was there only to oblige— because her distinguished father had insisted on paying minute attention to her physique which was vital and admirable. She had been there, for some time past only to oblige—War Work and all that—but still she had always kept her place and had never hitherto raised her voice at a Mistresses' Conference.[38] So it was

---

* 'Thou shalt not commit adultery' (Exodus 20:14).
† A phrase used to denote the Royal Navy, as opposed to the Army. 'The Navy is the senior service of the Crown and has a long and distinguished history', National Archives Website (nationalarchives.gov.uk, accessed 9 November 2009). In *No More Parades*, I.ii, variations of the phrase 'nothing but His Majesty's Navy could save us...' occur more than once.

indeed the World Turned Upside Down*—already!—when Miss Wanostrocht hopefully from behind her desk decorated with two pale pink carnations said:

"The idea is, Miss Wannop, that They should be kept—that you should keep them, please—as nearly as possible—isn't it called?—at attention until the—eh—[39] noises ... announce the ... well, *you* know. Then we suppose they[40] will have to give, say, three cheers. And then perhaps you could get them—in an orderly way—back to their classrooms...."

Valentine felt that she was by no means certain that she *could*. It was not really practicable to keep every one of six hundred aligned girls under your eye. Still she was ready to have a shot. She was ready to concede that it might not be altogether—oh, expedient!—to turn six hundred girls stark mad with excitement into the streets already filled with populations that would no doubt be also stark mad with excitement. You had better keep them in if you could. She would have a shot. And she was pleased. She felt fit: amazingly fit! Fit to do the quarter in ... oh, in any time![†] And to give a clump on the jaw to any large, troublesome Jewish type of maiden—or Anglo-Teutonic—who should try to break ranks. Which was more than the Head or any one of the other worried and underfed ones could do. She was pleased that they recognised it. Still she was also generous and recognising that the world ought not really to be turned upside down at any rate until the maroons went, she said:

"Of course I will have a shot at it. But it would be a reinforcement, in the way of keeping order, if the Head—you Miss Wanostrocht—and one or two others of the Mistresses would be strolling about. In relays, of course; not all of the staff all the morning ... "

That had been two and a half hours or so ago: before the world changed, the Conference having taken place at eight-thirty. Now

---

* This phrase originates in the Bible (Acts 17:6). It became known widely and popularly as an English ballad published in the 1640s. The abiding message of the song is one of protest against Cromwell's policies relating to the celebration of Christmas in particular: chorus 'Yet let's be content, / and the times lament, / you see the world turn'd upside down.' The tune is that of another ballad, 'When the King Enjoys his Own Again'. The original is in the British Library, part of the Thomason Tracts, printed mainly between 1640 and 1661 in London. Cf. *Wicked Man* 276.

† Valentine is referring to a quarter-mile run or race.

here she was, after having kept those girls pretty exhaustingly jumping about for most of the intervening time—here she was treating with disrespect obviously constituted Authority. For whom *ought* you to respect if not the wife of the Head of a Department, with a title, a country place and most highly attended Thursday afternoons?

She was not really listening to the telephone because Edith Ethel was telling her about the condition of Sir Vincent: so over-worked, poor man, over Statistics that a nervous breakdown was imminently to be expected. Worried over money, too. Those dreadful taxes for this iniquitous affair....

Valentine took leisure to wonder why—why in the world!—Miss Wanostrocht who must know at the least the burden of Edith Ethel's story[41] had sent for her to hear this farrago? Miss Wanostrocht must know: she had obviously been talked to by Edith Ethel for long enough to form a judgment. Then the matter must be of importance. Urgent even, since the keeping of discipline in the playground was of such utter importance to Miss Wanostrocht: a crucial point in the history of the School and the mothers of Europe.

But to whom then could Lady Macmaster's communication be of life and death importance? To her, Valentine Wannop? It could not be: there were no events of importance that could affect her life outside the playground, her mother safe at home and her brother safe on a mine-sweeper in Pembroke Dock.... *

Then ... of importance to Lady Macmaster herself? But how? What could she do for Lady Macmaster? Was she wanted to teach Sir Vincent to perform physical exercises so that he might avoid his nervous breakdown and, in excess of physical health, get the mortgage taken off his country place which she gathered was proving an overwhelming burden on account of iniquitous taxes the result of a war that ought never to have been waged?

It was absurd to think that she could be wanted for that! An absurd business.... There she was, bursting with health, strength, good-humour, perfectly *full* of beans—there she was,

---

* Situated at the southern end of the Cleddau river in south-west Wales. It is an industrial town with a dockyard which had a 112-year history of ship building until it closed in 1926. A ferry service now runs from Pembroke Dock to Ireland.

ready in the cause of order to give Leah Heldenstamm, the large
girl, no end of a clump on the side of the jaw or, alternatively, for
the sake of all the beanfeastishnesses in the world to assist in the
amiable discomfiture of the police. There she was in a sort of
nonconformist cloister. Nunlike! Positively nunlike! At the
parting of the ways of the universe!

She whistled slightly to herself.

"By Jove," she exclaimed coolly, "I hope it does not mean an
omen that I'm to be—oh, nunlike—for the rest of my career in
the reconstructed world!"

She began for a moment seriously to take stock of her position—of her whole position in life. It had certainly been hitherto
rather nunlike. She was twenty-threeish: rising twenty-four. As
fit as a fiddle; as clean as a whistle. Five foot four in her gym shoes.
And no one had ever wanted to marry her. No doubt that was
because she was so clean and fit. No one even had ever tried to
seduce her. That was *certainly* because she was so clean-run.* She
didn't obviously offer—What was it the fellow called it?—
promise of pneumatic bliss† to the gentlemen with
sergeant-majors' horse-shoe moustaches and gurglish voices! She
never would. Then perhaps she would never marry. And never
be seduced!

Nunlike! She would have to stand at an attitude of attention
beside a telephone all her life; in an empty schoolroom with the
world shouting from the playground. Or not even shouting from
the playground any more. Gone to Piccadilly!‡

---

* Ford is fond of this racing-linked phrase and also uses it in *No More Parades*, I.i (as
 well as later in *A Man Could Stand Up –*), to refer to Sylvia Tietjens: immediately afterwards she is also 'thorough-bred'. In *The Good Soldier* the Powys girls strike Mrs
 Ashburnham as 'clean run' on their visit to meet Edward (94) and in this case a link
 is immediately established by Dowell between being 'clean run' and androgyny: 'they
 were indeed so clean run that, in a faint sort of way Edward seems to have regarded
 them rather as boys than as girls'. The detailed description of Sylvia in *No More
 Parades* is similar at least in its emphasis on her height, her fitness, her small bust etc.
† T. S. Eliot's 'Whispers of Immortality' appeared in *Poems 1920*. Thus as of November
 1918 in the novel Valentine's remembering 'Grishkin is nice: her Russian eye / Is
 underlined for emphasis; / Uncorseted, her friendly bust / Gives promise of pneumatic
 bliss' is anachronistic (*Selected Poems* [London: Faber & Faber, 1961], 42).
‡ For the Armistice celebrations there and elsewhere in central London. In Vera Brit-
 tain's *Testament of Youth* (London: Fontana, 1979 [1933]), she records struggling
 through the 'waving, shrieking crowds in Piccadilly and Regent Street on the over-
 loaded top of a 'bus' (462).

... But, hang it all, she wanted some fun! Now!

For years now she had been—oh, yes, nunlike!—looking after the lungs and limbs of the girls of the adenoidy,[42] nonconformistish—really undenominational or so little Established as made no difference!—Great Public Girls' School. She had had to worry about impossible but not repulsive little Cockney creatures' breathing when they had their arms extended.... You *mustn't* breathe rhythmically with your movements. No. No. No!... *Don't* breathe out with the first movement and in with the second! Breathe naturally! Look at me!... She breathed perfectly!

Well, for years that! War-work for a b—y Pro-German.[43] Or Pacifist.[*] Yes, that too she had been for years. She hadn't liked being it because it was the attitude of the superior and she did not like being superior. Like Edith Ethel!

But now! Wasn't it manifest? She could put her hand wholeheartedly into the hand of any Tom, Dick or Harry. And wish him luck! Whole-heartedly! Luck for himself and for his enterprise.[44] She came back: into the fold: into the Nation even. She could open her mouth! She could let out the good little Cockney yelps that were her birthright! She could be free, independent!

Even her dear, blessed, muddle-headed, tremendously eminent mother by now had a depressed looking Secretary. She, Valentine Wannop, didn't have to sit up all night typing after all day enjoining perfection of breathing in the playground.... By Jove they could go all, brother, mother in untidy black and mauve, secretary in untidy black without mauve, and she, Valentine, out of her imitation Girl Scout's[†] uniform and in—oh, white muslin or Harris tweeds—and with Cockney yawps discuss the cooking under the stone-pines of Amalfi.[‡] By the Mediterranean.... No

---

[*]   During the First World War pacifists who refused to fight became known as conscientious objectors. Some were prepared to work in non-combat roles but others rejected any involvement at all. After the passing of the Military Service Act in 1916, a vigorous campaign was mounted against the punishment and imprisonment of conscientious objectors but conditions continued to be very hard for them.

[†]   The British Girl Scouts organisation was founded in 1909 and was the counterpart to the British Boy Scouts, an organisation independent of Baden-Powell's scouting movement. There was controversy at the time around the encouragement of young women to engage in the general run of scouting activities, which Baden-Powell met by establishing the Girl Guides in 1910.

[‡]   The Amalfi coast is a stretch of mountainous coastline south of Naples.

one, then, would be able to say that she had never seen the sea of Penelope, the Mother of the Gracchi, Delia, Lesbia, Nausicaa, Sappho. . . .*

"*Saepe te in somnis vidi!*"†

She said:

"Good . . . *God!*"

Not in the least with a Cockney intonation but like a good Tory English gentleman confronted by an unspeakable proposition. Well: it was an unspeakable proposition. For the voice from the telephone had been saying to her inattention, rather crawlingly,[45] after no end of details as to the financial position of the house of Macmaster:

"So I thought, my dear Val, in remembrance of old times; that . . . If in short I were the means of bringing you together again. . . . For I believe you have not been corresponding. . . . You might in return. . . . You can see for yourself that at this moment the sum would be absolutely *crushing*. . . ."

CHAPTER II[1]

TEN minutes later she was putting to Miss Wanostrocht, firmly if without ferocity, the question:

"Look here, Head, what did that woman say to you. I don't like her; I don't approve of her and I didn't really listen to her. But I want to hear!"

Miss Wanostrocht, who had been taking her thin, black cloth coat from its peg behind the highly varnished pitch-pine door of her own private cell, flushed, hung up her garment again and turned from the door. She stood, thin, a little rigid, a little flushed, faded and a little as it were at bay.

"You must remember," she began, "that I am a schoolmistress." She pressed, with a gesture she constantly had, the noticeably golden plait of her dun-coloured hair with the palm of her thin left hand. None of the gentlewomen of that school had had quite enough to eat—for years now. "It's," she continued, "an instinct to accept any means of knowledge. I like you so much, Valentine—if in private you'll let me call you that. And it seemed to me that if you were in . . . ."

"In what?" Valentine asked, "Danger? . . . Trouble?"

"You understand," Miss Wanostrocht replied, "That . . . person seemed as anxious to communicate to me facts about yourself as to give you—that was her ostensible reason for ringing you up—news. About a . . . another person. With whom you once had . . . relations. And who has reappeared."

"Ah," Valentine heard herself exclaim. "He has reappeared, has he? I gathered as much." She was glad to be able to keep herself under control to that extent.[2]

Perhaps she did not have to trouble. She could not say that she felt changed from what she had been—just before ten minutes ago, by the reappearance of a man she hoped she had put out of her mind. A man who had "insulted" her. In one way or the other he had insulted her![3]

But probably all her circumstances had changed. Before Edith Ethel had uttered her impossible sentence in that instrument her complete prospects had consisted of no more than the family picnic, under fig-trees, beside an unusually blue sea—and the prospect had seemed as near—as near as kiss your finger! Mother in black and purple; mother's secretary in black without adornments. Brother? Oh, a romantic figure; slight, muscular, in white flannels with a Leghorn hat and—well, why *not* be romantic over one's brother—with a broad scarlet sash. One foot on shore and one . . . in a light skiff that gently bobbed in the lapping tide. Nice boy; nice little brother. Lately employed nautically, so up to managing a light skiff. They were going to-morrow . . . but why not that very afternoon by the 4.20?

"They'd got the ships, they'd got the men,
They'd got the money too!"*

Thank goodness they'd got the money!
The ships, Charing Cross to Vallombrosa,† would no doubt run in a fortnight.† The men—the porters—would also be released. You can't travel in any comfort with mother, mother's secretary and brother—with your whole world and its baggage—without lots of porters. . . . Talk about rationed butter! What was that to trying to get on without porters?
Once having begun it her mind went on singing the old eighteen-fiftyish, or seventy-ish, martial, British, anti-Russian patriotic song that one of her little friends had unearthed lately—to prove the historic ferocity of his countrymen:

"We've fought the Bear before,
And so we will again!

---

* This paraphrase of a line is Valentine's first mention of 'Macdermott's War Song'. She remembers more on the following page; see subsequent note.
† Vallombrosa is an area of Tuscany, in Italy. It is the location, and name, of a Benedictine monastery founded in the eleventh century by St John Gualbert. The story of his conversion is the subject of Burne-Jones's painting *The Merciful Knight* (1863). The monastery was suppressed finally by the Italian government in 1866 and by the time Valentine and her mother were planning to visit the area was a school of forestry. The place name translates literally to mean 'shady valley', and is used by Milton in Book I of *Paradise Lost* (ll. 299–303). Milton cites a brook, but otherwise there doesn't seem much obvious hope of Valentine's 'lapping tide'.

The Russians shall not have Constantino . . . '"*

She exclaimed suddenly: "*Oh!*"

She had been about to say: "Oh, *Hell!*" but the sudden recollection that the War had been over a quarter of an hour made her leave it at "*Oh!*" You would have to drop war-time phraseology! You became again a Young Lady. Peace, too, has its Defence of the Realm Acts.[†] Nevertheless, she had[5] been thinking of the man who had once insulted her as the Bear, whom she would have to fight again![6] But with warm generosity she said:

"It's a shame to call him the Bear!" Nevertheless he was—the man who was said to have "reappeared" —with his problems and all, something devouring. . . . Overwhelming, with rolling grey shoulders that with their intolerable problems pushed you and your own problems out of the road. . . .

She had been thinking all that whilst still in the School Hall, before she had gone to see the Head: immediately after Edith Ethel, Lady Macmaster had uttered the *intolerable* sentence.

She had gone on thinking there for a long time. . . . Ten minutes!

She formulated for herself summarily the first item of a period of nasty worries of a time she flattered herself she had nearly forgotten. Years ago, Edith Ethel, out of a clear sky, had accused her of having had a child by that man. But she hardly thought of him as a man. She thought of him as a[7] ponderous, grey, intel-

---

* 'Macdermott's War Song', by G. W. Hunt, dates from 1877, and was sung by Gilbert Hastings MacDermott, one of the biggest music hall stars. As is often the case with popular songs, there are different versions. Another recorded example of this verse runs: 'We don't want to fight but by jingo if we do / We've got the ships, we've got the men, and got the money too! / We've fought the Bear before and while we're Britons true / The Russians shall not have Constantinople' – and this is similar to the one Ford gives in his book on Joseph Conrad (*Joseph Conrad* 57). It gave rise to the term 'jingoism', so was arguably one of the most effective 'patriotic' songs of all. The 'Bear before' ('Rugged Russian' in the song's first line) refers to the Russian army of the Crimean War (1854–6), hence Valentine's reference to the song being 'eighteen-fiftyish, or seventy-ish'.

† On 8 August 1914, the House of Commons passed the Defence of the Realm Act (DORA). The legislation gave the government executive powers to suppress published criticism, imprison without trial and commandeer economic resources for the war effort. DORA was added to as the war progressed, and it listed every prohibited action. Ford expresses the resulting frustrations in *It Was the Nightingale*: 'Even during the Armistice Dora meddled imbecilely with the sales of cigarettes, candies, new bread, liquors.... Life became a perpetual round of petty annoyances' (99).

lectual mass who now, presumably, was mooning, obviously
dotty, since he did not recognise the porter, behind the closed
shutters of an empty house in Lincoln's Inn.... Nothing less, I
assure you! She had never been in that house, but she figured him,
with cracks of light coming between the shutters, looking back
over his shoulder at you in the doorway, grey, super-ursine....
Ready to envelop you in suffocating bothers!

   She wondered how long it had been since the egregious Edith
Ethel had made that assertion ... with, naturally, every appearance of indignation for the sake of the man's Wife with whom,
equally naturally, Edith Ethel had "sided." (Now she was trying
to "bring you together again." ... The Wife, presumably, did not
go to Edith Ethel's tea-parties often enough, or was too brilliantly
conspicuous when there. Probably the latter!) ... How many
years ago? Two? Not so much! Eighteen months, then? Surely
more!... surely, surely more!...* When you thought of Time in
those days your mind wavered impotently like eyes tired by
reading too small print.... He went out surely in the autumn of
... No, it had been the first time he went that he went in the
autumn. It was her brother's friend, Ted, that went in '16. Or the
other ... Malachi. So many goings out and returnings: and goings
out and perhaps not returning. Or only in bits: the nose gone ...
or both eyes. Or—or, Hell! oh, Hell![8] and she clenched her fists,
her nails into her palms—no mind!

   You'd think it must be that from what Edith Ethel had said. He
hadn't recognised the porter: he was reported to have no furniture. Then ... She remembered....

   She was then—ten minutes before she interviewed Miss
Wanostrocht; ten seconds after she had been blown out of the
mouth of the telephone—sitting on a varnished pitch-pine
bench that had black iron, clamped legs against the plaster wall,
non-conformishistically distempered in torpedo-grey; and she
had thought all that in ten seconds.... But that had been *really*
how it had been!

___

* There is possibly an echo here of Hamlet's 'too solid flesh' speech, from I.ii of Shakespeare's play: 'That it should come to this – / But two months dead – nay, not so much,
not two' (137–8). In the plot of *Parade's End*, Valentine is referring to *Some Do Not*
... (II.iv), when Sylvia appeared at the Macmasters' salon; after this Edith Ethel starts
to claim Sylvia as a friend and simultaneously begins the distancing process mentioned
in a note to the last chapter.

The minute Edith Ethel had finished saying the words:
"The sum would be absolutely *crushing*. . . ."[9] Valentine had
realised that[10] she had been talking about a debt owed by her
miserable husband to the one human being she, Valentine, could
not bear to think about. It had naturally at the same moment
flashed upon her that[11] Edith Ethel had been giving her his news:
He was in new troubles: broken down, broken up, broke to the
wide. . . .* Anything in the world but broken in. . . . But broken
. . . And alone. . . . And calling for her!

She could not afford—she could not bear!—to recall even his
name or to so much as bring up before her mind, into which,
nevertheless, they were continually forcing themselves, his grey-
blond face, his clumsy, square, reliable feet; his humpish bulk; his
calculatedly wooden expression; his perfectly overwhelming, but
authentic omniscience. . . . His masculinity. His . . . his Frightfulness!†

Now, through Edith Ethel—you would have thought that
even *he* would have found someone more appropriate—he was
calling to her again to enter into the suffocating web of his
imbroglios. Not even Edith Ethel would have dared to speak to
her again of him without his having taken the first step. . . .

It was unthinkable; it was intolerable; and it had been as if she
had been lifted off her feet and deposited on that bench against
the wall by the mere sound of the offer. . . . What was the offer?

"I thought that you might, if I were the means of bringing you
together . . . "[12] She might . . . what?

Intercede with that man, that[13] grey mass, not to enforce the
pecuniary claim that it had against Sir Vincent Macmaster. No
doubt she and . . . the grey mass! . . . would then be allowed the
Macmaster drawing-room to . . . to discuss the ethics of the day
in! Just like that!

She was still breathless; the telephone continued to quack. She
wished it would stop but she felt too weak to get up and hang the
receiver on its hook. She wished it would stop; it gave her the
feeling that a strand of Edith Ethel's hair, say, was penetrating
nauseously[14] to her torpedo grey cloister. Something like that!

---

*   Cf. *No More Parades*, I.iv. The phrase is a colloquialism for penniless.
†   Cf. *No Enemy*, in which the German 'Schrecklichkeiten' – 'frightfulness' – is used by
    Gringoire to describe the German policy of terrorising the civilian population (56).

The grey mass never would enforce its pecuniary claim.... Those people had sponged mercilessly on him for years and years without ever knowing the kind of object upon which they sponged. It made them the more pitiful.[15] For it *was* pitiful to clamour to be allowed to become a pimp in order to evade debts that would never be reclaimed....

Now, in the empty rooms at Lincoln's Inn—for that was probably what it came to!—that man[16] was a grey ball of mist; a grey bear rolling tenebrously about an empty room with closed shutters. A grey problem! Calling to *her!*[17]

A hell of a lot.... Beg pardon, she meant a remarkably great deal!... to have thought of in ten seconds! Eleven, by now, probably. Later she realised that that was what thought was. In ten minutes after large, impassive arms had carried you away from a telephone and deposited you on a clamped bench against a wall of the peculiar coldness of torpedo-grey distempered plaster, the sort of thing rejoiced in by Great Public (Girls') Schools ... in those ten minutes you found you thought out more than in two years. Or it was not as long ago as that.

Perhaps that was not astonishing. If you had not thought about, say, washable distemper for two years and then thought about it for ten minutes you could think a hell of a lot about it in those ten minutes. Probably all there was to think. Still, of course, washable distemper was not like the poor—always with you.[*] At least it always was in those cloisters, but not spiritually. On the other hand you always *were* with yourself!

But perhaps you were not always with yourself spiritually; you went on explaining how to breathe without thinking of how the life you were leading was influencing your ... What? Immortal soul? Aura? Personality?... Something!

Well, for two years.... Oh, *call* it two years, for goodness' sake, and get it over!... she must have been in ... well, call *that* a "state of suspended animation" and get that over too! A sort of what they called inhibition. She had been inhibiting— *prohibiting*—herself from thinking about herself. Well, hadn't

---

[*] 'For ye have the poor always with you; but me ye have not always', Matthew 26:11. See also John 12:8. In 1911 Ford wrote a letter to the editor of the *New Age*, defending his support of women's suffrage thus: 'But the poor are always with us – and so are women, because they are poor' (*Letters* 47).

she been right? What had a b—y Pro-German to think about in
an embattled, engrossed, clamouring nation: especially when she
had not much liked her brother-Pro's! A solitary state, only to be
dissolved by . . . maroons! In suspension!

But . . . Be conscientious with yourself, my good girl! *When that
telephone blew you out of its mouth you knew really that for two years
you had been avoiding wondering whether you had not been insulted!*
Avoiding wondering that. And nothing else! No other qualified
thing.

She had, of course, been, not in suspension, but in suspense.
Because, if he made a sign—"I understand," Edith Ethel had said,
"that you have not been in correspondence" . . . or had it been
"in communication" that she had said? . . . Well, they hadn't
been either. . . .

Anyhow, if that grey Problem, that ravelled ball of grey knit-
ting worsted, had made a sign she would have known that she had
not been insulted. Or was there any sense in that?

Was it really true that if a male and female of the same species
were alone in a room together and the male didn't . . . then it was
an insult? That was an idea that did not exist in a girl's head
without someone to put it there,[18] but once it had been put there
it became a luminous veracity! It had been put into her, Valentine Wannop's head, naturally by Edith Ethel, who equally
naturally said that she did not believe it, but that it was a tenet
of . . . oh, the man's wife! Of the idle, surpassing-the-Lily-and-
Solomon-too,* surprisingly svelte, tall, clean-run creature who for
ever on the shiny paper of illustrated journals advanced towards
you with improbable strides along the railings of the Row,
laughing, in company with the Honourable Somebody, second
son of Lord Some-one-or-other. . . .† Edith Ethel was more
refined. She had a title, whereas the other hadn't, but she was
pensive. She showed you that she had read Walter Savage
Landor, and had only very lately given up wearing opaque amber

---

*   'I am the rose of Sharon, and the lily of the valleys. As the lily among thorns, so is my
     love among the daughters', Song of Solomon 2:1–2. On the description of Sylvia as
     'idle' in this context, cf. Matthew 6:28–9.
†   Rotten Row runs through the south side of London's Hyde Park. It is a track broad
     enough for horses and carriages, where – as is implied by Ford's text – fashionable
     Londoners would go to be seen.

beads, as affected[19] by the later pre-Raphaelites.* She was practically never in the illustrated papers,† but she held more refined views. She held that there were some men who were not like that—and those, all of them, were the men to whom Edith Ethel accorded the *entrée* to her Afternoons. She was their Egeria! A refining influence!

The Husband of the Wife then? Once he had been allowed in Edith Ethel's drawing room: now he wasn't! ... Must have deteriorated!

She said to herself sharply, in her "No nonsense, there" mood: "Chuck it. You're in love with a married man who's a Society wife and you're upset because the Titled Lady has put into your head the idea that you might 'come together again'. After ten years!"

But immediately she protested:

"No. NO. No! It isn't that. It's all right the habit of putting things incisively, but it's misleading to put things too crudely."

What was the coming together that was offered her? Nothing, on the face of it, but being dragged again into that man's[20] intolerable worries as unfortunate machinists are dragged into wheels by belts—and all the flesh torn off their bones! Upon her word that had been her first thought. She was afraid, afraid, afraid! She suddenly appreciated the advantages of nunlike seclusion. Besides she wanted to be bashing policemen with bladders in celebration of Eleven Eleven!‡

That fellow—he had no furniture; he did not appear to recognise the hall porter.... Dotty. Dotty and too morally

---

* Elsie Hueffer, Ford's first wife, was remembered as wearing a 'great amber necklace' in the 1890s by David Garnett (see Saunders, *A Dual Life* I 99, and the portrait of her by Cathy Hueffer reproduced there – her necklace may well include some amber). In *Some Do Not ...* Tietjens muses that 'no woman should wear clouded amber' (I.v), and in the same novel Macmaster recalls an 'immense necklace of yellow polished amber' being an aspect of Mrs Duchemin's dress (I.iii). Macmaster is a Rossetti specialist of course – see Rossetti's *The Blue Bower* (1865) for an example of a Pre-Raphaelite painting in which the subject wears amber.

† Though there were many morning and evening papers published in London during this part of the century, these were far outnumbered by the weeklies. There were popular political weeklies, for example, but Ford is referring to the pictorial papers here, such as *The Illustrated London News* and *The Graphic*, which published portraits of brides and bridegrooms, and actors etc. But Ford himself also featured. In *The Sketch*, dated 1 November 1911, the 'Literary Lounger' section includes a notice, with photographs of Ford and Violet Hunt (116).

‡ In other words, Armistice Day, 11 November.

deteriorated to be admitted to drawing-room of titled lady, the frequenters of which could be trusted not to make love to you on insufficient provocation, if left alone with you....[21]

Her generous mind reacted painfully.

"Oh, that's not *fair!*" she said.

There were all sorts of sides to the unfairness. Before this War, and, of course, before he had lent all his money to Vincent Macmaster that—that grey grizzly[22] had been perfectly fit for the country-parsonage drawing-room of Edith Ethel Duchemin: he had been welcomed there with effusion!... After the War and when his money was—presumably exhausted, and his mind exhausted, for he had no furniture and did not know the porter.... After the War, then, and when his money was exhausted he was not fit for the Salon of Lady Macmaster—the only Lady to have a Salon in London.

It was what you called kicking down your ladder!*

Obviously it had to be done. There were such a lot of these bothering War heroes that if you let them all into your Salon it would cease to be a Salon, particularly if you were under an obligation to them!... That was already a pressing national problem: it was going to become an overwhelming one now—in twenty minutes'[23] time; after those maroons. The impoverished War Heroes[24] would all be coming back. Innumerable. You would have to tell your parlourmaid that you weren't at home to ... about seven million!

But wait a minute.... Where did they just stand?

He.... But she could not go on calling him just HE like a school-girl of eighteen, thinking of her favourite actor ... in the purity of her young thoughts. What was she to call him? She had never—even when they had known each other—called him anything other than Mr. So and So.... She could not bring herself to let her mental lips frame his name.... She had never used anything but his surname to this grey thing, familiar object of her mother's study, seen frequently at tea-parties.... Once she had been out with it for a whole night in a dog cart! Think of

---

* "'Oh, I've got a frock alright'" says Valentine as she confronts Edith Ethel with her snobbery in *Some Do Not* ... (II.iv), "'But there's a Jacob's ladder in my stockings and that's the sort of ladder you can't kick down".' (Incidentally, Mrs Duchemin has her amber beads on again in this scene.)

that! ... And they had spouted Tibullus one to another in moon-lit mist. And she had certainly wanted it to kiss her—in the moon-lit mists, a practically, a really completely strange bear!*

It couldn't be done, of course, but she remembered still how she had shivered. ... Ph ... Ph ... Ph. ... Shivering. She shivered.

Afterwards they had been run into by the car of General Lord Edward Campion, V.C., P.G., Heaven knows what!† Godfather of the man's[25] Society Wife, then taking the waters in Germany. ... Or perhaps not *her* Godfather. The man's rather;[26] but her especial champion, in shining armour. In those[27] days they had worn broad red stripes down the outsides of their trousers, Generals.‡ What a change! *How* significant of the times!

That had been in[28] 1912. ... Say the first of July; she could not remember exactly. Summer weather, anyhow, before haymaking or just about. The grass had been long in Hogg's Forty Acre, when they had walked through it, discussing Woman's Suffrage. She had brushed the seed-tops of the heavy grass with her hands as they walked. ... Say the 1/7/12.

Now it was Eleven Eleven. ... What? Oh, Eighteen, of course! Six years ago! What changes in the world! What cataclysms! What Revolutions! ... She heard all the newspapers, all the half-penny paper journalists in creation crying in chorus!

But hang it: it was true! If, six years ago she had kissed the ... the greyish lacuna of her mind then sitting beside her on the dog-cart seat it would have been the larkish freak of a school-girl: if she did it to-day—as per invitation presumably of Lady Macmaster, bringing them together, for, of course, it could not

---

* This episode occurs in *Some Do Not* . . . (I.vii).

† V.C. means he has been awarded the Victoria Cross, the highest British military and naval decoration, for conspicuous bravery in battle. P.G. is likely to be an abbreviation for the Latin 'persona grata'. The final chapter of *No More Parades* opens by calling him 'GENERAL LORD EDWARD CAMPION, G.C.B., K.C.M.G. (MILITARY), D.S.O., etc.'

‡ The stripe at the left of the trouser leg represents the uniform colours of a General Officer of the British Army. The dress uniform was dark blue with a broad red stripe on the trousers. Until 1914 the majority of armies still provided colourful dress uniforms for all ranks, at least for parade and off-duty wear. By 1914 drab colours were increasingly being adopted for active service and ordinary duty wear – changes were made partly because of the cost of dyeing cloth red and also because it turned officers into targets – but officers were given dispensation to wear their old dress uniforms on ceremonial and special occasions.

be performed from a distance or without correspondence—No, communication!... If, then, she did it to-day ... to-day ... to-day—the Eleven Eleven!—Oh, what a day to-day would be.... Not her sentiments those; quotation from Christina, sister of Lady Macmaster's favourite poet....* Or, perhaps, since she had had a title she would have found poets more ... more chic! The poet who was killed at Gallipoli ... Gerald Osborne, was it?† Couldn't remember the name!

But for six years then she had been a member of that ... triangle. You couldn't call it a *ménage à trois*, even if you didn't know French. They hadn't lived together!... They had d—d near died together when the general's car hit their dog-cart! D—d near! (You *must* not use those Wartime idioms. *Do* break yourself of it! Remember the maroons!)

An oafish thing to do! To take a school-girl, just ... oh, just past the age of consent, out all night in a dog-cart and then get yourself run into by the car of the V.C., P.G., champion-in-red-trouser-stripe of your Legitimate! You'd think any man who *was* a man would have avoided that!

Most men knew enough to know that the Woman Pays ...‡ the school-girl too!

But they get it both ways....§ Look here: when Edith Ethel

---

* Christina Rossetti (1830–94), sister of Dante Gabriel Rossetti, and one of Ford's favourite poets. Praise from Ford opens C. H. Sisson's introduction to her *Selected Poems* (Manchester: Carcanet, 1984): 'Christina Rossetti seems to us to be the most valuable poet that the Victorian age produced' (9). Valentine's quotation is from her poem 'If': 'If he would come to-day, to-day, to-day, / O what a day to-day would be!'

† Perhaps Rupert Brooke, who sailed with the British Mediterranean Expeditionary Force on 28 February 1915, but developed sepsis from an infected mosquito bite. He died on 23 April off the island of Lemnos.

‡ 'The Woman Pays' is the title of the fifth part (or 'phase') of Thomas Hardy's popular, notorious novel about a Victorian victim of sex and circumstance, *Tess of the D'Urbervilles* (1891). Ford admired Hardy's poetry greatly, and knew his work well, but the phrase had been circulating, proverbially, long before this. Several films adopted it as a title between 1910 and 1916, and it appears in a novel by Lucas Malee (*The History of Sir Richard Calmady*) in 1901 as well as in the Katherine Mansfield/Beatrice Hastings 'Pastiche' in *New Age* (May 1911).

§ In Ford's novel *A Call* it is the woman, Katya Lascarides, who 'get[s]' the man, Robert Grimshaw, 'both ways'. He finally agrees that he will live with her as her lover, rather than her husband, which is what she has always insisted on. But she then changes her mind and says that they must marry:

"'So that you get me both ways", Robert Grimshaw said; and his hands fell desolately open at his side.
"Every way and altogether", she answered' (158).

Duchemin, then, just—or perhaps not quite, Lady Macmaster!
At any rate, her husband was dead and she had just married that
miserable little.... (Mustn't use that word!) She, Valentine
Wannop, had been the only witness of the marriage—as of the
previous, discreet, but so praiseworthy adultery!... When, then,
Edith Ethel had.... It must have been on the very day of the
knighthood, because Edith Ethel made it an excuse not to ask her
to the resultant Party.... Edith Ethel had accused her of having
had a baby by ... oh, Mr. So and So.... And heaven was her,
Valentine Wannop's, witness that, although Mr. So and So[29] was
her mother's constant adviser, she, Valentine Wannop, was still
in such a state of acquaintance[30] with him that she still called him
by his surname.... When Lady Macmaster, spitting like the
South American beast of burden called a llama,[31] had accused her
of having had a baby by her mother's adviser—to her natural
astonishment, but, of course, it had been the result of the dog-
cart and the motor and the General, and the general's sister, Lady
Pauline Something—or perhaps it was Claudine? Yes, Lady Claudine!—who had been in the car and the Society Wife, who was
always striding along the railings of the Row.... When she had
been so accused out of the blue, her first thought—and, confound
it, her enduring thought!—had not been concern for her own
reputation but for *his*....
     That was the *quality* of his entanglements, their very essence.
He got into appalling messes, unending and unravellable—no,
she meant ununravellable!—messes and other people suffered for
him whilst he mooned on—into more messes! The General
charging the dog-cart was symbolical of him. He was perfectly on
his right side and all, but it was like him to be in a dog-cart when
flagitious automobiles carrying Generals were running a-muck!
Then ... the Woman Paid!... She really did, in this case. It had
been her mother's horse they had been driving and, although
they had got damages out of the General, the costs were twice
that.... And her, Valentine's reputation had suffered from being
in a dog-cart at dawn, alone with a man.... It made no odds that
he had—or was it hadn't?—"insulted" her in any way all through
that—oh, that delicious, delirious night.... She had to be said
to[32] have a baby by him, and then she had to be dreadfully worried
about *his* poor old reputation.... Of course it *would* have been

pretty rotten of him—she so young and innocent, daughter of so preposterously eminent, if so impoverished a man, his father's best friend and all. "He hadn't oughter'er done it!" He hadn't really oughter. . . . She heard them all saying it, still! Well, he hadn't! . . . But she?

That magic night. It was just before dawn, the mists nearly up to their necks as they drove; the sky going pale in a sort of twilight. And one immense star! She remembered only one immense star, though, historically, there had been also a dilapidated sort of moon. But the star was *her* best boy—what her wagon was hitched on to. . . .* And they had been quoting—quarrelling over, she remembered:

"*Flebis et arsuro me, Delia, lecto
Tristibus et.* . . ."†

She exclaimed suddenly:

"Twilight and evening star
    And one clear call for me
And may there be no moaning at the bar
    When I. . . . "

She said:
"Oh, but you *oughtn't* to, my dear! That's *Tennyson!*"‡ Tennyson, with a difference!

She said:
"All the same, that would have been an inexperienced schoolgirl's prank. . . . But if I let him kiss me now I should be. . . . " She would be a what was it . . . a fornicatress? . . . *trix!* Fornicatrix is

---

*   Henry Martin's father repeats a similar phrase in Ford's *The Rash Act* (1933) (Manchester: Carcanet, 1982), 34: 'My boy . . . if you want to hitch your wagon to a star you can. But not on my money!'

†   A reference to Tibullus' poem 'Delia' – 'Flebis et arsuro positum me, Delia' (I.I, l. 61). Valentine is recalling the adventure in the dog-cart from *Some Do Not* . . . once more, when she and Tietjens argued over Ovid and then the translation of the second line from Tibullus quoted in part here ('Tristibus et lacrimis oscula mixta dabis'). Translated, the lines read: 'You'll weep for me laid on my pyre, Delia, and grant me kisses mixed [Valentine's choice but Tietjens preferred 'mingled'] with sad tears.'

‡   The quotation is from Tennyson's 'Crossing the Bar', in *The Death of OEnone, and Other Poems*. The verse concludes 'When I put out to sea'.

preferable! Very preferable. Then why not adultrix? You
couldn't: you had to be a "cold-blooded adultress!" or morality
was not avenged.

Oh; but surely not cold-blooded!... Deliberate, then!...
That wasn't, either, the word for the process. Of osculation!...
Comic things, words, as applied to states of feelings!

But if she went now to Lincoln's Inn and the Problem held out
its arms.... That would be "Deliberate." It would be asking for
it in the fullest sense of the term.

She said to herself quickly:

"This way madness lies!"* And then:

"What an imbecile thing to say!"

She had had an Affair with a man, she made her mind say to
her, two years ago. That was all right. There could not be a, say,
a schoolmistress rising twenty-four or twenty-five, in the world
who hadn't had *some* affair, even if it were no more than a
gentleman in a tea-shop who every afternoon for a week had
gazed at her disrespectfully over a slice of plum-cake.... And
then disappeared.... But you had to have had at least a might-
have-been or you couldn't go on being a schoolmistress or a girl
in a ministry or a dactylographer of respectability.† You packed
that away in the bottom of your mind and on Sunday mornings
before the perfectly insufficient Sunday dinner, you took it out
and built castles in Spain in which you were a castanetted heroine
turning on wonderful hips, but casting behind you inflaming
glances.... Something like that!

Well, she had had an affair with this honest, simple creature!
So good! So unspeakably GOOD.... Like the late Albert, prince
consort! The very, helpless, immobile sort of creature that she
ought not to have tempted. It had been like shooting tame
pigeons! Because he had had a Society wife always in the illustrated papers whilst he sat at home and evolved Statistics or came
to tea with her dear, tremendous, distracted mother, whom she
helped to get her articles accurate. So a woman tempted him and
he did.... No; he didn't quite eat!

But why?... Because he was GOOD?

* 'O, That way madness lies. Let me shun that.' *King Lear*, III.iv.21.
† A 'dactylographer' is literally a 'finger-writer', usually defined as someone studying
  fingerprints, but probably here meaning 'typist'.

Very likely!

Or was it—That was the intolerable thought that she shut up within her along with the material for castles in the air!—was it because he had been really indifferent?

They had revolved round each other at tea-parties—or rather he had revolved around her, because at Edith Ethel's affairs she always sat, a fixed starlet, behind the tea-urn and dispensed cups. But he would moon round the room, looking at the backs of books; occasionally laying down the law to some guest; and always drifting in the end to her side where he would say a trifle or two.... And the beautiful—the quite excruciatingly beautiful wife—striding along the Row with the second son of the Earl of someone at her side.... Asking for it....

So it had been from the 1/7/12, say to the 4/8/14!

After that, things had become more rubbled—mixed up with alarums. Excursions on his part to unapproved places.* And trouble. He was quite damnably in trouble. With his Superiors; with, so unnecessarily, Hun projectiles, wire, mud; over Money; politics; mooning on without a good word from anyone.... Unravellable muddles that never got unravelled but that somehow got you caught up in them....

Because he needed her moral support! When, during the late Hostilities,[33] he hadn't been out there, he had drifted to the tea-table much earlier of an afternoon and stayed beside it much longer: till after everyone else had gone and they could go and sit on the tall fender side by side, and argue ... about the rights and wrongs of the War!

Because she was the only soul in the world with whom he could talk.... They had the same sort of good, bread-and-butter brains; without much of the romantic.... No doubt a touch ... in him. Otherwise he would not have always been in these muddles. He gave all he possessed to anyone who asked for it. That was all right. But that those who sponged on him should also involve him in intolerable messes.... That was not proper. One ought to

---

* 'Alarums. Excursions' was a common stage direction in Elizabethan drama (see *Henry V*, IV.iv, for example), indicating sounds of war or warlike activity, or the movement of soldiers across the stage. Henry Brereton Marriott Watson published a novel with the title *Alarums and Excursions* in 1903, and a collection of poetry with the same title by Arthur Keedwell H. James followed a few years later.

defend oneself against that!

Because ... if you do not defend yourself against that, look how you let in your nearest and dearest—those who have to sympathise with you in your confounded troubles whilst you moon on, giving away more and more and getting into more troubles! In this case it was she who was his Nearest and Dearest.... Or had been!

At that her nerves suddenly got the better of her and her mind went mad.... Supposing that that fellow, from whom she had not heard for two years, *hadn't* now communicated with her.... Like an ass she had taken it for granted that he had *asked* Lady ... Blast her!... to "bring them together again"! She had imagined that even Edith Ethel would not have had the cheek to ring her up if he hadn't asked her to!

But she had nothing to go on.... Feeble, over-sexed ass that she was, she had let her mind jump at once to the conclusion, the moment the mere mention of him seemed implied—jump to the conclusion that he was asking her again[34] to come and be his mistress.... Or nurse him through his present muddle till he should be fit to....

Mind, she did not say that she would have succumbed. But if she had not jumped at the idea that it was he, really, speaking through Edith Ethel, she would never have permitted her mind to dwell on ... on his blasted, complacent perfections!

Because she had taken it for granted that if he had had her rung up he would not have been monkeying with other girls during the two years he hadn't written to her.... Ah, but hadn't he?

Look here! *Was* it reasonable? Here was a fellow who had all but ... all BUT ... "taken advantage of her" one night just before going out to France, say, two years ago.... And not another word from him after that!... It was all very well to say that he was portentous, looming, luminous, loony: John Peel with his coat so grey,[35*] the English Country Gentleman *pur sang* and then some;

* Tietjens whistles, then sings, some of this nineteenth-century hunting song in *Some Do Not ...* (I.vii). The first lines of the song run: 'D'ye ken John Peel with his coat so grey, / D'ye ken John Peel at the break of day / D'ye ken John Peel when he's far away, / With his hounds and his horn in the morning' (words by John Woodcock Graves). The second line is often written as 'coat so gay', an error stemming from the fact that southern transcribers of the words believed all fox-hunters wore red jackets. The song also appears – parodied – in collections of trench songs, F. T. Nettleingham's *Tommy's*

saintly; Godlike, Jesus-Christ-like.... He was all that. But you don't seduce, as near as can be, a young woman and then go off to Hell, leaving her, God knows, in Hell, and not so much as send her, in two years, a picture-postcard with MIZPAH* on it. You don't. You don't!

Or if you do you have to have your character revised. You have to have it taken for granted that you were only monkeying with her and that you've been monkeying ever since with WAACS† in Rouen or some other Base....

Of course, if you ring your young woman up when you come back ... or have her rung up by a titled lady.... That might restore you in the eyes of the world, or at least in the eyes of the young woman if she was a bit of a softie....

But *had* he? *Had* he? It was absurd to think that Edith Ethel hadn't had the face to do it unasked! To save three thousand two hundred pounds, not to mention interest—which was what Vincent owed *him!*—Edith Ethel with the sweetest possible smile would beg the pillows off a whole hospital ward full of dying.... She was quite right. She had to save her man. You go to any depths of ignominy to save your man.

But that did not help her, Valentine Wannop!

She sprang off the bench; she clenched her nails into her palms; she stamped her thin-soled shoes into the coke-brise floor that was singularly unresilient. She exclaimed:

"Damn it all, he didn't ask her to ring me up.³⁶ He didn't ask her to. He didn't ask her to!" still stamping about.

She marched straight at the telephone that was by now

Tunes (London: Erskine Macdonald, 1917), for example. In *It Was the Nightingale*, Ford uses the song to symbolise the incongruities of life, his example being the way an army band might play it at a military funeral as counterpoint to the tragedy (34); cf. the final, related, lines of *No More Parades* too.

* Mizpah (or Mizpeh) is a city in Gilead, mentioned in Judges 11, for example. Here, Jephthah comes home to Mizpah to be greeted by his daughter, when he has just vowed to God that the first thing he sees on returning shall be sacrificed (v. 34). Meaning 'beacon' or 'watch tower', however, the word 'Mizpah' features first in Genesis when Laban gives the name to the pillar of stones: 'And Mizpah; for he said, The LORD watch between me and thee, when we are absent from one another' (31:49). In the novel, then, Valentine is referring back to her parting from Tietjens at the end of *Some Do Not* ... when she gives him a piece of parchment transcribed with 'God bless you and keep you: God watch over you at your goings out and at ...' in Hebrew.

† WAACS: Women's Army Auxiliary Corps.

uttering long, tinny, night-jar's calls and, with one snap, pulled the receiver right off the twisted green-blue cord.... Broke it! With incidental satisfaction!

Then she said:

"Steady the Buffs!" not out of repentance for having damaged School Property, but because she was accustomed to call her thoughts The Buffs because of their practical, unromantic character as a rule.... A fine regiment, the Buffs!*

Of course, if she had not broken the telephone she could have rung up Edith Ethel and have asked her whether he had or hadn't asked to ... to be brought together again.... It was like her, Valentine Wannop, to smash the only means of resolving a torturing doubt....

It wasn't, really, in the least like her. *She* was practical enough: none of the "under the ban of fatality" business about her. She had smashed the telephone because it had been like smashing a connection with Edith Ethel; or because she hated tinny night-jars; or because she had smashed it. For nothing in the world; for nothing, nothing, nothing in the world would she ever ring up Edith Ethel and ask her:

"Did *he* put you up to ringing me up?"

That would be to let Edith Ethel come between their intimacy.

A subconscious volition was directing her feet towards the great doors at the end of the Hall, varnished, pitch-pine doors of Gothic architecture; economically decorated as if with straps and tin-lids of Brunswick-blacked cast iron.†

She said:

"Of course if it's his wife who has removed his furniture that would be a reason for his wanting to get into communication. They would have split.... But he does not hold with a man divorcing a woman, and she won't divorce."

---

* The Royal East Kent Regiment of the British Army. This regiment has a history dating back to 1572, and became known as 'The Buffs' after being issued with buff coats. The phrase 'Steady, the Buffs' entered common parlance (see, for example, Kipling's *Soldiers Three*, 1888) from the regimental parade ground where it had been used in training. The regiment features more than once in *Some Do Not ...*, as well as in *No More Parades*.

† Brunswick-blacking was a kind of varnish, made of oil varnish, lamp black and turpentine.

As she went through the sticky postern—All that woodwork seemed sticky on account of its varnish!—beside the great doors she said:

"Who cares!"

The great thing was ... but she could not formulate what the great thing was. You had to settle the preliminaries.

CHAPTER III[1]

SHE said eventually to Miss Wanostrocht who had sat down at her table behind two pink carnations:

"I didn't consciously want to bother you but a spirit in my feet has led me who knows how.... That's Shelley, isn't it?"[*]

And indeed a quite unconscious but shrewd mind had pointed out to her whilst still in the School Hall and even before she had broken the telephone, that Miss Wanostrocht very probably would be able to tell her what she wanted to know and that if she didn't hurry she might miss her, since the Head would probably go now the girls were gone. So she had hurried through gauntish corridors whose Decorated Gothic windows positively had bits of pink glass here and there interspersed in their lattices. Nevertheless a nearly deserted, darkish, locker-lined dressing-room being a short cut, she had paused in it before the figure of a clumsyish girl, freckled, in black and, on a stool, desultorily lacing a dull black boot, an ankle on her knee. She felt an impulse to say: "Good-bye, Pettigul!" she didn't know why.

The clumsy, fifteenish, bumpy-faced girl was a symbol of that place—healthyish, but not over healthy; honestish but with no craving for intellectual honesty; big-boned in unexpected places ... and uncomelily blubbering so that her face appeared dirtyish.... It was in fact all "ishes" about that Institution. They were all healthyish, honestish, clumsyish, twelve-to-eighteenish and big-boned in unexpected places because of the late insufficient feeding.... Emotionalish, too; apt to blubber rather than to go into hysterics.

Instead of saying good-bye to the girl she said:

---

[*] From the first verse of P. B. Shelley's 'The Indian Serenade': 'I arise from dreams of thee / In the first sweet sleep of night. / When the winds are breathing low, / And the stars are shining bright: / I arise from dreams of thee, / And a spirit in my feet / Hath led me – who knows how? / To thy chamber window, Sweet!' The typescript of *A Man Could Stand Up* – originally continued to quote more of the poem – to 'thy chamber window, Sweet' – but this further line is then deleted by hand.

"Here!" and roughly, since she was exhibiting too much leg, pulled down the girl's shortish skirt and set to work to lace the unyielding boot on the unyielding shin-bone.... After a period of youthful bloom, which would certainly come and as certainly go, this girl would, normally, find herself one of the Mothers of Europe, marriage being due to the period of youthful bloom.... Normally that is to say according to a normality that that day might restore. Of course it mightn't!

A tepid drop of moisture fell on Valentine's right knuckle.

"My cousin Bob was killed the day before yesterday," the girl's voice said above her head. Valentine bent her head still lower over the boot with the patience that, in educational establishments, you must, if you want to be businesslike and shrewd, acquire and display in face of unusual mental vagaries.... This girl had never had a cousin Bob, or anything else. Pettigul and her two sisters, Pettiguls Two and Three, were all in that Institution at extremely reduced rates precisely because they had not got, apart from their widowed mother, a discoverable relative. The father, a half-pay major, had been killed early in the war. All the mistresses had had to hand in reports on the moral qualities of the Pettiguls, so all the mistresses had this information.

"He gave me his puppy to keep for him before he went out," the girl said. "It doesn't seem just!"

Valentine, straightening herself, said:

"I should wash my face if I were you, before I went out. Or you might get yourself taken for a German!" She pulled the girl's clumsyish blouse straight on her shoulders.

"Try," she added, "to imagine that you've got someone just come back! It's just as easy and it will make you look more attractive!"

Scurrying along the corridors she said to herself:

"Heaven help me, does it make *me* look more attractive?"[2]

She caught the Head, as she had anticipated, just on the point of going to her home in Fulham, an unattractive suburb but near a bishop's palace nevertheless. It seemed somehow appropriate. The lady was episcopally-minded but experienced in the vicissitudes of suburban children: very astonishing some of them unless you took them very much in the lump.

Miss Head had stood behind her table for the first three questions and answers, in an attitude of someone who is a little at bay,
but she had sat down just before Valentine had quoted her
Shelley at her, and she had now the air of one who is ready to
make a night of it. Valentine continued to stand.

"This," Miss Wanostrocht said very gently, "is a day on which
one might . . . take steps . . . that might influence one's whole
life."

"That's," Valentine answered, "exactly why I've come to you.
I want to know what that woman said to you so as to know where
I stand before I take a step."

The Head said:

"I had to let the girls go. I don't mind saying that you are very
valuable to me. The Governors—I had an express* from Lord
Boulnois—ordered them to be given a holiday to-morrow. It's
very inconsistent. But that makes it all the. . . ."

She stopped. Valentine said to herself:

"By Jove, I don't know anything about men; but how little I
know about women. What's she getting at?"

She added:

"She's nervous. She must be wanting to say something she
thinks I won't like!"

She said chivalrously:

"I don't believe anybody could have kept those girls in to-day.
It's a thing one has no experience of. There's never been a day
like this before."

Out there in Piccadilly there would be seething mobs shoulder
to shoulder: she had never seen the Nelson column stand out of
a solid mass. They might roast oxen whole in the Strand:
Whitechapel would be seething, enamelled iron advertisements
looking down on millions of bowler hats. All sordid and immense
London stretched out under her gaze. She felt herself *of* London
as the grouse feels itself of the heather, and there she was in an
emptied suburb looking at two pink carnations. Dyed probably:
offering of Lord Boulnois to Miss Wanostrocht! You never saw a
natural-grown carnation that shade!

She said:

* In the postal service, an item delivered immediately by special messenger.

"I'd be glad to know what that woman—Lady Macmaster—
told you."

Miss Wanostrocht looked down at her hands. She had the
little-fingers hooked together, the hands back to back; it was a
demoded gesture.... Girton of 1897, Valentine thought.
Indulged in by the thoughtfully blonde.... Fair girl graduates the
sympathetic comic papers of those days had called them.* It
pointed to a long sitting. Well, she, Valentine, was not going to
brusque the issue!† ... French-derived expression that. But how
would you put it otherwise?

Miss Wanostrocht said:
"I sat at the feet of your father!"

"You see!" Valentine said to herself. "But she must then have
gone to Oxford, not Newnham!" She could not remember
whether there had been women's colleges³ at Oxford as early as
1895 or 1897.‡ There must have been.

"The greatest Teacher.... The greatest influence in the
world," Miss Wanostrocht said.

It was queer, Valentine thought: This woman had known all
about her—at any rate all about her distinguished descent all the
time she, Valentine, had been Physical Instructress at that Great
Public School (Girls'). Yet except for an invariable courtesy such
as she imagined Generals might show to non-commissioned

---

*   Many women attended and gave papers to the meetings of the Social Science Asso-
     ciation, and its president, Lord Brougham, was unusual in the encouragement he gave
     to the participation of women. This was a source of heavy-handed amusement to *The
     Times*, which reported on the 'Lady's Parliament':
         The section was crowded during the whole day by a throng of ladies, who filled,
         not only the area of the court, but the jury-box and the seats for counsel, and gave
         the chamber very much the appearance of the College of the 'Princess' with its
         rows of 'fair girl graduates in their golden hair' [this phrase originates in Louisa May
         Alcott's *Jo's Boys*] [...] Some of the ladies [...] were at the first rather nervous [...]
         But they soon regained their confidence, and spoke out with a distinctness and
         animation which might put most young curates, and even some barristers, to the
         blush. (*The Times*, 12 June 1862)
     See M. Diamond, 'Henry Parkes and the Strong-Minded Women', *Australian Journal
     of Politics and History*, 38.2 (1992), 152–62.
         Girton College was founded in 1869 but women could not graduate until 1947.
†   She would not treat it in an off-handed way.
‡   University of Cambridge women's colleges (and date of foundation): Girton (1869);
     Newnham (1873); New Hall (1954). University of Oxford: Lady Margaret Hall
     (1878); Somerville (1879); St Anne's (1879); St Hugh's Hall (1886); St Hilda's Hall
     (1893).

officers, Miss Wanostrocht had hitherto taken no more notice of her than she might have taken of a superior parlourmaid. On the other hand she had let Valentine arrange her physical training exactly as she liked: without any interference.

"We used to hear," Miss Wanostrocht[4] said, "how he spoke Latin with you and your brother from the day of your births. . . . He used to be regarded as eccentric, but how *right!* . . . Miss Hall says that you are the most remarkable Latinist she has ever so much as imagined."

"It's not true," Valentine said, "I can't *think* in Latin. You cannot be a real Latinist unless you do that. He did of course."

"It was the last thing you would think of him as doing," the Head answered with a pale gleam of youth. "He was such a thorough man of the world. So awake!"

"We ought to be a queer lot, my brother and I," Valentine said. "With such a father . . .[5] And mother of course!"

Miss Wanostrocht said:

"Oh . . . your *mother*. . . ."

And immediately Valentine conjured up the little, adoring female clique of Miss Wanostrocht's youth, all spying on her father and mother in their walks under the Oxford Sunday trees, the father so jaunty and awake, the mother so trailing, large, generous, unobservant. And all the little clique saying: If only he had *us* to look after him. . . . She said with a little malice:

"You don't read my mother's novels, I suppose. . . . It was she who did all my father's writing for him. He couldn't write, he was too impatient!"

Miss Wanostrocht exclaimed:

"Oh, you *shouldn't* say that!" with almost the pain of someone defending her own personal reputation.

"I don't see why I shouldn't," Valentine said. "He was the first person to say it about himself."

"He shouldn't have said it either," Miss Wanostrocht answered with a sort of soft unction. "He should have taken care more of his own reputation for the sake of his Work!"*

---

* *Work* is the title of one of Ford Madox Brown's most famous paintings (1856–63). It allegorises artists' labour, and was particularly important to Ford. A little later in this chapter, Valentine bemoans the 'brilliant Victorians' who talked 'through their hats', imitating to a significant degree Ford's own feelings about the Victorian Great Figures,

Valentine considered this thin, ecstatic spinster with ironic curiosity.

"Of course, if you've sat . . . if you're still sitting at father's feet as much as all that," she conceded, "it gives you a certain right to be careful about his reputation. . . . All the same I wish you would tell me what that person said on the phone!"

The bust of Miss Wanostrocht moved with a sudden eagerness further towards the edge of her table.

"It's precisely because of that," she said, "that I want to speak to you first. . . . That I want you to consider. . . . "

Valentine said:

"Because of my father's reputation. . . . Look here, did that person—Lady Macmaster!—speak to you as if you were me? Our names are near enough to make it possible."

"You're," Miss Wanostrocht said, "as one might say, the fine fruit of the product of his views on the education of women. And if you . . . [6] It's been such a satisfaction to me to observe in you such a . . . a sound, instructed head on such a . . . oh, you know, sane body. . . . * And then. . . . An earning capacity. A commercial value. Your father, of course, never minced words. . . . " She added:

"I'm bound to say that my interview with Lady Macmaster . . . Who surely isn't a lady of whom you could say that you disapprove. I've read her husband's work. It surely—you'd say, wouldn't you?—conserves some of the ancient fire."

"He,"[7] Valentine said, "hasn't a word of Latin to his tail. He makes his quotations out, if he uses them, by means of school-cribs. . . . I know his methods of work, you know."

It occurred to Valentine to think that if Edith Ethel really *had* at first taken Miss Wanostrocht for herself there might pretty obviously be some cause for Miss Wanostrocht's concern for her father's reputation as an intimate trainer of young women. She figured Edith Ethel suddenly bursting into a description of the circumstances of that man who was without furniture and did not

---

some of them known to his grandfather, and the ways in which they overshadowed his life and development. See the opening pages of Ford's first memoir, *Ancient Lights and Certain New Reflections* (1911).

* Juvenal's phrase is 'Orandum est ut sit mens sana in corpore sano' [You should pray to have a sound mind in a sound body], *Satires*, 10.

appear to recognise the porter. The relations she might have described as having existed between her and him[8] might well worry the Head of a Great Public School for Middle Class Girls. She had no doubt been described as having had a baby.[9] A disagreeable and outraged current invaded her feelings. . . .

It was suddenly obscured by a recrudescence of the thought that had come to her only incidentally[10] in the hall. It rushed over her with extraordinary vividness now, like a wave of warm liquid. . . . If it *had* really been that fellow's wife who had removed his furniture what *was* there to keep them apart? He couldn't have pawned or sold or burnt his furniture whilst he had been with the British Expeditionary Force in the Low Countries! He couldn't have without extraordinary difficulty! Then . . . What *should* keep them apart? . . . Middle Class Morality? A pretty gory carnival that had been for the last four years! Was this then Lent, pressing hard on the heels of Saturnalia? Not so hard as that, surely! So that if one hurried. . . . What on earth did she want, unknown to herself?

She heard herself saying, almost with a sob, so that she was evidently in a state of emotion:

"Look here: I disapprove of this whole thing: of what my father has brought me to! Those people. . . . [11] the brilliant Victorians[12] talked all the time through their hats. They evolved a theory from anywhere and then went brilliantly mad over it. Perfectly reck- lessly. . . . Have you noticed Pettigul One? . . . Hasn't it occurred to you that you *can't* carry on violent physical jerks and mental work side by side? I ought not to be in this school and I ought not to be what I am!"

At Miss Wanostrocht's perturbed expression she said to herself:

"What on earth am I saying all this for? You'd think I was trying to cut loose from this school! Am I?"

Nevertheless her voice was going on:

"There's too much oxygenation of the lungs, here. It's unnat- ural. It affects the brain, deleteriously. Pettigul One is an example of it. She's earnest with me and earnest with her books. Now she's gone dotty. Most of them it only stupefies."*

---

* There had been a significant debate in Victorian Britain about whether exercise was good for girls and women or not. Exercise was clearly thought good for men but views

It was incredible to her that the mere imagination that that fellow's wife had left him should make her spout out like this—for all the world like her father spouting out one of his ingenious theories! . . . It had really occurred to her once or twice to think that you could not run a dual physical and mental existence without some risk. The military physical developments of the last four years had been responsible for a real exaggeration of physical values. She was aware that in that Institution, for the last four years, she had been regarded as supplementing if not as actually replacing both the doctor and the priest. . . . But from that to evolving a complete theory that the Pettigul's lie was the product of an over-oxygenated brain was going pretty far. . . .

Still, she was prevented from taking part in national rejoicings; pretty certainly Edith Ethel had been talking scandal about her to Miss Wanostrocht. She had the right to take it out in some sort of exaggerated declamation!

"It appears," Miss Wanostrocht said, "for we can't now go into the question of the whole curriculum of the school, though I am inclined to agree with you. What by the bye[13] is the matter with Pettigul One? I thought her rather a solid sort of girl. But it appears that the wife of a friend. . . .[14] perhaps it's only a former friend of yours, is in a nursing home."

Valentine exclaimed:

"Oh, He. . . . But that's too ghastly!"

"It appears," Miss Wanostrocht said, "to be rather a mess." She added: "That appears to be the only expression to use."

---

about girls taking exercise were mixed. The legacy of this debate can be seen in Valentine's outburst as to Pettigul One, in which – despite being a fitness instructor and in many ways a prototypical feminist – she reproduces a conservative line on both physical and mental exercise in women. Valentine admits immediately that she's been guilty of 'exaggerated declamation' here, but also indicates the ways in which the debate has moved on: in her school her role as fitness instructor has been related to that of both doctor and priest.

See for a fuller discussion of the nineteenth-century context Molly Engelhardt, 'Seeds of Discontent: Dancing Manias and Medical Inquiry in Nineteenth-Century British Literature and Culture', *Victorian Literature and Culture*, 35 (2007), 135–56. She points out that 'since exercise was celebrated as a disease deterrent at the same time as some medical professionals were instructing women to stay home and be still, we see female pathology being constructed as a by-product of gendered difference. The discourses about health thus engender disease at the same time as they ensured its prophetic fulfilment' (143).

For Valentine, that piece of news threw a blinding light upon herself. She was overwhelmingly appalled because that woman was in a nursing home. Because in that case it would not be sporting to go and see the husband!

Miss Wanostrocht went on:

"Lady Macmaster was anxious for your advice.... It appears that the only other person that could look after the interests of ... of your friend: his brother ..."

Valentine missed something out of that sentence. Miss Wanostrocht talked too fluently. If people wanted you to appreciate items of sledge-hammering news they should not use long sentences. They should say:

"He's mad and penniless. His brother's dying: his wife's just been operated on." Like that! Then you could take it in; even if your mind was rioting about like a cat in a barrel.

"The brother's ... female companion," Miss Wanostrocht was wandering on, "though it appears that she would have been willing is therefore not available.... The theory is that he—he himself, your friend, has been considerably unhinged by his experiences in the war. Then.... Who in your opinion should take the responsibility of looking after his interests?"

Valentine heard herself say:

"Me!"

She added:

"Him! Looking after him. I don't know that he has any ... interests!"

He didn't appear to have any furniture, so how could he have the other things? She wished Miss Wanostrocht would leave off using the word "appear." It was irritating.... [15] and infectious. Could the lady not make a direct statement? But then, no one ever made clear statements, and this no doubt appeared to that anaemic spinster a singularly tenebrous affair.

As for clear statements.... If there had ever been any in precisely this tenebrous mess she, Valentine, would know how she stood with that man's wife. For it was part of the preposterous way in which she herself and all her friends behaved that they never made clear statements—except for Edith Ethel who had the nature of a female costermonger and could not tell the truth, though she could be clear enough. But even Edith Ethel had never hitherto said anything about the way the wife in this case treated the husband. She had given Valentine very clearly to understand that she "sided" with the wife—but she had never gone as far as to say that the wife was a good wife. If she—Valentine—could only know that.

Miss Wanostrocht was asking:

"When you say 'Me,' do you mean that you would propose to look after that man yourself? I trust not."

. . . . Because, obviously, if she were a good wife, she, Valentine, couldn't butt in . . . not generously. As her father's and still more her mother's daughter. . . . On the face of it you would say that a wife who was always striding along the palings of the Row, or the paths of other resorts of the fashionable could not be a good—a domestic—wife for a Statistician. On the other hand he was a pretty smart man, Governing class, county family and the rest of it—so he might like his wife to figure in Society: he might even exact it. He was quite capable of that. Why, for all she knew, the wife might be a retiring, shy person whom he thrust out into the hard world. It was not likely: but it was as possible as anything else.

Miss Wanostrocht was asking:

"Aren't there Institutions . . . Military Sanatoria. . . .[16] for cases precisely like that of this Captain Tietjens. It appears to be the war[17] that has broken him down, not merely evil living."

"It's precisely," Valentine said, "because of that that one should want . . . shouldn't one. . . . Because it's because of the War . . . "[18]

The sentence would not finish itself.

Miss Wanostrocht said:

"I thought. . . . It has been represented to me . . . that you were a Pacifist. Of an extreme type!"

It had given Valentine a turn—like the breaking out of sweat in a case of fever—to hear the name, coldly: "Captain Tietjens," for it was like a release. She had been irrationally determined that hers should not be the first tongue to utter that name.

And apparently from her tone Miss Wanostrocht was prepared to detest that Captain Tietjens. Perhaps she detested him already.

She was beginning to say:

"If one is an extreme Pacifist because one cannot bear to think

of the sufferings of men, isn't that a precise reason why one should
wish that a poor devil, all broken up ... "

But Miss Wanostrocht had begun one of her own long
sentences. Their voices went on together, like trains dragging
along ballast—disagreeably. Miss Wanostrocht's organ, however,
won out with the words:

" .... behaved very badly indeed."[19]

Valentine said hotly:

"You ought not to believe anything of the sort—on the
strength of anything said by a woman like Lady Macmaster."

Miss Wanostrocht appeared to have been brought to a
complete stop: she leaned forward in her chair; her mouth was a
little open. And Valentine said: "Thank Goodness!" to herself.

She had to have a moment to herself to digest what had the
air of being new evidence of the baseness of Edith Ethel; she felt
herself to be infuriated in regions of her own being that she hardly
knew. That seemed to her to be a littleness in herself. She had
not thought that she had been as little as that. It ought not to
matter what people said of you. She was perfectly accustomed to
think of Edith Ethel as telling whole crowds of people very bad
things about her, Valentine Wannop. But there was about this a
recklessness that was hardly believable. To tell an unknown
person, encountered by chance on the telephone, derogatory
facts about a third party who might be expected to come to the
telephone herself in a minute or two—and, not only that—who
must in all probability hear what had been said very soon after,
from the first listener.... That was surely a recklessness of evil-
speaking that almost outpassed sanity.... Or else it betrayed a
contempt for her, Valentine Wannop, and what she could do in
the way of reprisals that was extremely hard to bear!

She said suddenly to Miss Wanostrocht:

"Look here! Are you speaking to me as a friend to my father's
daughter or as a Headmistress to a Physical Instructor?"

A certain amount of blood came into the lady's pinkish
features. She had certainly been ruffled when Valentine had
permitted her voice to sound so long alongside her own; for,
although Valentine knew next to nothing about the Head's likes
or dislikes she had once or twice before seen her evince marked
distaste on being interrupted in one of her formal sentences.

Miss Wanostrocht said with a certain coldness:

"I'm speaking at present. . . . I'm allowing myself the liberty—as a much older woman—in the capacity of a friend of your father. I have been, in short, trying to recall to you all that you owe to yourself as being an example of his training!"

Involuntarily Valentine's lips formed themselves for a low whistle of incredulity. She said to herself:

"By Jove! I am in the middle of a nasty affair. . . . This is a sort of professional cross-examination."

"I am in a way glad," the lady was now continuing, "that[20] you take that line. . . . I mean of defending Mrs. Tietjens with such heat against Lady Macmaster. Lady Macmaster appears to dislike Mrs. Tietjens, but I am bound to say that she appears to be in the right of it. I mean of her dislike. Lady Macmaster is a serious personality and, even on her public record Mrs. Tietjens appears to be very much the reverse. No doubt you wish to be loyal to your . . . friends, but . . ."

"We appear," Valentine said, "to be getting into an extraordinary muddle."

She added:

"I haven't, as you seem[21] to think, been defending Mrs. Tietjens. I would have. I would at any time. I have always thought of her as beautiful and kind. But I heard you say the words: '*has been behaving very badly*,' and I thought you meant that Captain Tietjens had. I denied it. If you meant that his wife has, I deny it, too.[22] She's an admirable wife . . . and mother . . . that sort of thing, for all I know. . . ."

She said to herself:

"Now why do I say that? What's Hecuba to me?"* and then:

"It's to defend *his* honour, of course . . . I'm trying to present Captain Tietjens as English Country Gentleman complete with admirably arranged establishment, stables, kennels, spouse, offspring . . .[23] That's a queer thing to want to do!"

Miss Wanostrocht who had breathed deeply said now:

---

*   In Greek mythology Hecuba is the wife of Priam and the mother of Hector. Valentine is probably making a reference to *Hamlet* here: 'What's Hecuba to him or he to Hecuba, / That he should weep for her?' (II.ii.561–2). Hamlet is wondering at the 'fiction', the 'dream of passion', of the players, in comparison with his own feelings and the causes of them.

"I'm extremely glad to hear that. Lady Macmaster certainly said that Mrs. Tietjens was—let us say—at least a neglectful wife.... Vain, you know; idle; overdressed.... All that ...[24] And you appeared to defend Mrs. Tietjens."

"She's a smart woman in smart Society," Valentine said, "but it's with her husband's concurrence. She has a right to be...."

"We shouldn't," Miss Wanostrocht said, "be in the extraordinary muddle to which you referred if you did not so continually interrupt me. I was trying to say that, for you, an inexperienced girl, brought up in a sheltered home, no pitfall could be more dangerous than a man with a wife who neglected her duties!"

Valentine said:

"You will have to excuse my interrupting you. It *is*, you know, rather more my funeral than yours."

Miss Wanostrocht said quickly:

"You can't say that. You don't know how ardently...."

Valentine said:

"Yes, yes.... Your *schwaerm*[*] for my father's memory and all.... But my father[25] couldn't bring it about that I should lead[26] a sheltered life.... I'm about as experienced as any girl of the lower classes.... No doubt it was his doing, but don't make any mistakes."

She added:

"Still, it's I that's the corpse. You're conducting the inquest. So it's more fun for you."

Miss Wanostrocht had grown slightly pale:

"I; if...." she stammered slightly, "by 'experience' you mean...."

"I don't," Valentine exclaimed, "and you have no right to infer that I do on the strength of a conversation you've had, but shouldn't have had, with one of the worst tongues in London.... I mean that my father left us so that I had to earn my and my mother's living as a servant for some months after his death. That was what his training came to. But I can look after myself ... In consequence...."

Miss Wanostrocht had thrown herself back in her chair.

---

[*] In colloquial German, 'schwarm' means idol, hero or crush. 'Schwärmen' means to dream of, also colloquial.

"But . . ." she exclaimed: she had grown completely pale—like discoloured wax. "There was a subscription. . . . We. . . ." She began again: "We[27] knew that he hadn't. . . ."

"You subscribed," Valentine said, "to purchase his library and presented it to his wife . . . who had nothing to eat but what my wages as a tweeny maid* got for her." But before the pallor of the other lady she tried to add a touch of generosity: "Of course the subscribers wanted, very naturally, to preserve as much as they could of his personality. A man's books are very much himself. That was all right": She added: "All the same I had that training: in a suburban basement. So you cannot teach me a great deal about the shady in life. I was in the family of a Middlesex County Councillor. In Ealing."

Miss Wanostrocht said faintly:

"This is very dreadful!"

"It isn't really!" Valentine said. "I wasn't badly treated as tweeny maids go. It would have been better if the Mistress hadn't been a constant invalid and the cook constantly drunk. . . . After that I did a little office work. For the suffragettes. That was after old Mr. Tietjens came back from abroad and gave mother some work on a paper he owned. We scrambled along then, somehow. Old Mr. Tietjens was father's greatest friend, so father's side, as you might say, turned up trumps—If you like to think that to console you. . . ."

Miss Wanostrocht was bending her face down over her table, presumably to hide a little of it from Valentine or to avoid the girl's eyes.

Valentine went on:

"One knows all about the conflict between a man's private duties and his public achievements. But with a very little less of the flamboyant in his life my father might have left us very much better off. It isn't what I *want*—to be a cross between a sergeant in the army and an upper housemaid. Any more than I wanted to be an under one."

---

* A shortened form of 'between maid', a maid-servant who assisted both the cook (in the kitchens) and the housemaid (in the rest of the house). The 'lady novelist' with whom a recently demobilised Ford shares a taxi in *It Was the Nightingale* points out that, in those times, 'housemaids were unattainable' – 'They had all gone into armaments.' She continues, 'if you could find as much as a tweeny you were lucky' (86).

Miss Wanostrocht uttered an "Oh!" of pain. She exclaimed rapidly:

"It was your moral rather than your mere athletic influence that made me so glad to have you here.... It was because I felt that you did not set such a high value on the physical...."

"Well, you aren't going to have me here much longer," Valentine said. "Not an instant more than I can in decency help. I'm going to...."

She said to herself:

"What on earth am I going to do?... What do I want?"

She wanted to lie in a hammock beside a blue, tideless sea and think about Tibullus ... There was no nonsense about her. She did not want to engage in intellectual pursuits herself. She had not the training. But she intended to enjoy the more luxurious forms of the intellectual products of others.... That appeared to be the moral of the day!

And, looking rather minutely at Miss Wanostrocht's inclined face, she wondered if, in the history of the world, there had ever been such another day. Had Miss Wanostrocht, for instance, ever known what it was to have a man come back? Ah, but amid the tumult of a million other men coming back! A collective impulse to slacken off! Immense! Softening!

Miss Wanostrocht had apparently loved her father. No doubt in company with fifty damsels. Did they ever get a collective kick out of that affair? It was even possible that she had spoken as she had ... *pour cause.* Warning her, Valentine, against the deleterious effect of being connected with a man whose wife was unsatisfactory.... Because the fifty damsels had all, in duty bound, thought that her mother was an unsatisfactory wife for the brilliant, grey-black haired Eminence with the figure of a stripling that her father had been....[28] They had probably thought that, without the untidy figure of Mrs. Wannop as a weight upon him, he might have become.... Well, with one of *them!*... Anything! Any sort of figure in the councils of the nation. Why not Prime Minister? For along with his pedagogic theories he had had political occupations. He had certainly had the friendship of Disraeli. He supplied—it was historic!—materials for eternally famous, meretricious speeches. He would have been head-trainer of the Empire's pro-consuls if the other fellow, at Balliol, had not got in first. . . .* As it was he had had to specialise in the Education of Women. Building up Primrose Dames. . . .†

So Miss Wanostrocht warned her against the deleterious effect of neglected wives upon young, attached virgins! It probably *was* deleterious. Where would she, Valentine Wannop have been by now if she had thought that Sylvia Tietjens was really a bad one! Miss Wanostrocht said, as if with sudden anxiety:

"You are going to do what? You propose to do what?"

Valentine said:

"Obviously after your conversation with Edith Ethel you won't be so glad to have me here. My moral influence has not been brightened in aspect!" A wave of passionate resentment swept over her.

"Look here," she said, "if you think that I am prepared to. . . ." She stopped, however. "No," she said, "I am not going to introduce the housemaid note. But you will probably see that this is irritating." She added: "I would have the case of Pettigul One looked into, if I were you. It might become epidemic in a big school like this. And we've no means of knowing where we stand nowadays!"

---

*   Among the list of notable alumni of Balliol for the period is Benjamin Jowett, Master of Balliol from 1870 to 1893. 'Pro-consuls' are defined as 'governors of a modern colony', and the *DNB* entry for Jowett states that in the 1850s he was 'consulted about the reform of the Indian Civil Service and the manner in which its recruits were trained'. It continues: '[Jowett] acquired the reputation of being a great picker, trainer, and placer of able young men, whom he sent from the college into positions of influence in government and civil service.'

†   Primrose Day is 19 April, the anniversary of the death of Benjamin Disraeli (and, roughly speaking, the peak of the primrose season). The Primrose League was founded in 1883, and given the name in what Brewer's *Dictionary of Phrase and Fable* calls the mistaken belief that this was his favourite flower. The aims of the League were 'the maintenance of religion, of the estates of the realm, and of the imperial ascendancy'. A distinct women's branch was founded in 1885. The League adopted some quasi-Masonic nomenclature: 'The League offered one class of membership at a guinea a year for "Knights" and "Dames"', writes Martin Pugh, 'and another for associate members whose much lower dues went to their local branches' (*The Making of Modern British Politics* [Oxford: Blackwell, 2002], 52). The Primrose League was wound up in 2004. In *No More Parades* (I.ii), the thought of Valentine makes Tietjens smell primroses, 'Primroses, like Miss Wannop'.

PART II

CHAPTER I[1]

MONTHS and months before[2] Christopher Tietjens had stood extremely wishing that his head were level with a particular splash of purposeless whitewash. Something behind his mind forced him to the conviction that, if his head—and of course the rest of his trunk and lower limbs—were suspended by a process of levitation to that distance above the duckboard on which, now, his feet were, he would be in an inviolable sphere.* These waves of conviction recurred continually: he was constantly glancing aside and upwards at that splash: it was[3] in the shape of the comb of a healthy rooster;† it gleamed, with[4] five serrations, in the just beginning light that shone along the thin, unroofed channel in the gravel slope. Wet half-light, just filtering;[5] more visible there than in the surrounding desolation[6] because the deep, narrow channel framed a section of just-illuminated rift[7] in the watery eastwards!

Twice he had stood up on a rifleman's step enforced by a bully-beef case to look over—in the last few minutes. Each time, on

---

* Like Gringoire's magical experience of the 'utterly secure and inviolable' English country in *No Enemy* (23) perhaps, and cf. also *The Marsden Case* (London: Duckworth, 1923), 304. Less poetically, this common phrase – especially so in legal circles – goes back as far as Plato and Socrates. It is used often in connection with liberty or privacy or rights (personal or property).

† The shape of a coxcomb does not seem to be a particular indication of healthiness (though a droop is not good), but a bright red one is clearly to be prized. See Chaucer's 'Nun's Priest's Tale': 'His coomb was redder than the fyn coral / And batailled as it were a castel wal' (l. 2859). The name of Chaucer's cock is Chauntecleer. Aesop's 'Milord Chantecler' makes an appearance in *Last Post* (l.ii), and 'chanticleer' provides Ford with an effective simile in *No Enemy*, as Gringoire describes a 'very fat old gendarme' surrounded by four market women: 'they were grouped around the gendarme like pullets around chanticleer' (27–8).

stepping down again, he had been struck by that phenomenon: the light seen from the trench seemed if not brighter, then more definite. So, from the bottom of a pit-shaft in broad day you can see the stars. The wind was light, but from the North West. They had there the weariness of a beaten army: the weariness of having to begin always new days again. . . .

He glanced aside and upwards: that cockscomb of phosphorescence. . . . He felt waves of some X force* propelling his temples towards it. He wondered if perhaps the night before he had not observed that that was a patch of reinforced concrete, therefore more resistant. He might of course have observed that and then forgotten it. He hadn't! It was therefore irrational.

If you are lying down under fire—flat under pretty smart fire— and you have only a paper bag in front of your head for cover you feel immeasurably safer than you do without it. You have a mind at rest. This must be the same thing.

It remained dark and quiet. It was forty-five minutes: it became forty-four . . . forty-three . . . forty-two minutes and thirty seconds before a crucial moment and the slate grey cases of miniature metal pineapples had not come from the bothering place. . . . Who knew if there was anyone in charge there?

Twice that night he had sent runners back. No results yet. That bothering fellow might quite well have forgotten to leave a substitute. That was not likely. A careful man. But a man with a mania might forget. Still it was not likely! . . .

Thoughts menaced him as clouds threaten the heads of mountains but for the moment they kept away. It was quiet; the wet cool air was agreeable. They had autumn mornings that felt like that in Yorkshire. The wheels of his physique moved smoothly; he was more free in the chest than he had been for months.

A single immense cannon, at a tremendous distance, said something. Something sulky. Aroused in its sleep and protesting. But it was not a signal to begin anything. Too heavy. Firing at something at a tremendous distance. At Paris, may be: or the

---

* The letter 'x' signifies an 'incalculable or mysterious force or influence' (along with 'y' and 'z' since Descartes introduced them as symbols of unknown quantities in his book *Géométrie*, 1637). By 1930, in the US at least, 'X factor' was used to denote 'an indefinable but important element', according to the OED. In 'A Haughty and Proud Generation', from the *Yale Review* in 1922, Ford noted that '[i]t is not enough to say that every man is homo duplex; every man is homo x-plex' (*Critical Essays* 217).

North Pole: or the moon! They were capable of that, those fellows! It would be a tremendous piece of frightfulness to hit the moon. Great gain in prestige. And useless. There was no knowing what they would not be up to, as long as it was stupid and useless. And, naturally, boring.... And it was a mistake to be boring. One went on fighting to get rid of those bores—as you would to get rid of a bore in a club.

It was more descriptive to call what had spoken a cannon than a gun—though it was not done in the best local circles. It was all right to call 75's* or the implements of the horse artillery 'guns'; they were mobile and toy-like. But those immense things were cannons; the sullen muzzles always elevated. Sullen, like cathedral dignitaries or butlers. The thickness of barrel compared to the bore appeared enormous as they pointed at the moon, or Paris, or Nova Scotia.

Well, that cannon had not announced anything except itself! It was not the beginning of any barrage; our own fellows were not pooping off to shut it up. It had just announced itself, saying protestingly, "CAN ... NON," and its shell soaring away to an enormous height caught the reflection of the unrisen sun on its base. A shining disc, like a halo in flight.... Pretty! A pretty motive[8] for a decoration, tiny pretty planes up on a blue sky amongst shiny, flying haloes! Dragon flies amongst saints.... No, "with angels and archangels!"† ... Well, one had seen it!

Cannon.... Yes, that was the right thing to call them. Like the up-ended, rusted things that stuck up out of parades when one had been a child.

No, not the signal for a barrage! A good thing! One might as well say "Thank Goodness," for the later they began the less long it lasted.... Less long it lasted was ugly alliteration. Sooner it was

---

* The famous 75mm French artillery cannon/gun. Tietjens discusses '75's with General Campion in *Some Do Not* ... (I.iv): 'your eighteen pounders are better than the French seventy-fives. They tell us so in the House [...]' says Tietjens, before questioning the truth of this 'fact'. The gun was light and manoeuvrable (hence Tietjens' description here); the British Army relied more on heavy and relatively immobile cannons.

† Taken from the hymn of praise in the service of Holy Communion (Book of Common Prayer): 'Therefore with Angels and Archangels and all the company of heaven, we laud and magnify thy glorious name.' It also appears in verse 4 of 'In the bleak midwinter' by Christina Rossetti, written before 1872 but not published until 1904.

over was better.... No doubt about half-past eight[9] or at half-past eight to the stroke those boring fellows would let off their usual offering, probably plump, right on top of that spot.... As far as one could tell three salvoes of a dozen shells each at half minute intervals between the salvoes. Perhaps salvoes was not the right word. Damn all artillery, anyhow!

Why did those fellows do it? Every morning at half-past eight; every afternoon at half-past two. Presumably just to shew[10] that they were still alive, and still boring. They were methodical. That[11] was their secret. The secret of their boredom. Trying to kill them was like trying to shut up Liberals who would talk party politics in a non-political club ... had to be done, though! Otherwise the world was no place for ... Oh, post-prandial naps!... Simple philosophy of the contest!... Forty minutes! And he glanced aside and upwards at the phosphorescent cockscomb! Within his mind something said that if he were only suspended up there....

He stepped once more on to the rifle-step and on to the bully-beef-case. He elevated his head cautiously: grey desolation sloped down and away.[12] F.R.R.R.r.r.r.! A gentle purring sound!

He was automatically back, on the duckboard, his breakfast hurting his chest. He said:

"By Jove! I got the fright of my life!" A laugh was called for: he managed it, his whole stomach shaking. And cold!

A head in a metal pudding-basin—a Suffolk type of blonde head, pushed itself from a withdrawn curtain of sacking in the gravel wall beside him, at his back. A voice said with concern:

"There ain't no beastly snipers, is there, sir. I did 'ope[13] there would'n be[14] henny beastly snipers 'ere. It gives such a beastly lot of extra trouble warning the men."

Tietjens said it was a beastly skylark that almost walked into his mouth. The Acting Sergeant-Major[15] said with enthusiasm that them 'ere skylarks could fair scare the guts out of you. He remembered a raid in the dark, crawling on 'is 'ands 'n knees wen 'e put 'is 'and on a skylark on its nest. Never left 'is nest till 'is 'and was on 'im! Then it went up and fair scared the wind out of 'im. Cor! Never would 'e fergit that!

With an air of carefully pulling parcels out of a carrier's cart he produced from the cavern behind the sacking two blinking

assemblages of tubular khaki-clad limbs. They wavered to erect-
ness, pink cheeses of faces yawning beside tall rifles and bayonets.
The Sergeant[16] said:
"Keep yer 'eds down as you go along. You never knows!"
Tietjens told the Lance-Corporal of that party of two that his
confounded gas-mask nozzle was broken. Hadn't he seen that for
himself? The dismembered object bobbed on the man's chest. He
was to go and borrow another from another man and see the other
drew a new one at once.
Tietjens' eyes were drawn aside and upwards. His knees were
still weak. If he were levitated to the level of that thing he would
not have to use his legs for support.
The elderly Sergeant went on with enthusiasm about skylarks.
Wonderful the trust they showed in hus 'uman beens! Never left
ther nesteses till you trod on them tho hall 'ell was rockin' around
them. . . . An appropriate skylark from above and before the
parapet made its shrill and heartless noise heard. No doubt the
skylark that Tietjens[17] had frightened—that had frightened him.*
Therd bin, the Sergeant went on still enthusiastically,
pointing a hand in the direction of the noise, skylarks singin' on
the mornin' of every straf 'e'd ever bin in! Won'erful trust in
yumanity! Won'erful hinstinck set in the fethered brest by the
Halmighty! For oo was goin' to 'it a skylark on a battlefield!
The solitary Man drooped beside his long, bayoneted rifle that
was muddied from stock to bayonet[18] attachment. Tietjens said
mildly that he thought the Sergeant had got his natural history
wrong. He must divide the males from the females. The females
sat on the nest through obstinate attachment to their eggs; the
males obstinately soared above the nests in order to pour out
abuse at other male skylarks in the vicinity.

---

* Duff Cooper wrote home to his girlfriend in 1918 from the trenches saying that larks
were shot by 'Français sportifs' elsewhere in France but that the front line had become
a 'regular bird refuge' due to the fact that 'neither the English nor the Germans can
ever hit anything' (quoted in Nicolson, *The Great Silence 1918–1920*, 147). Lark song
traditionally symbolises daybreak, as in *Romeo and Juliet* (III.v.1–3). Ford's volume of
reminiscence covering the inter-war years is called *It Was the Nightingale*, of course,
and the lines from Shakespeare serve as its epigraph. Skylarks nest on the ground, and
are renowned for their display flight, vertically up in the air – hence the fright they
cause Tietjens and his sergeant. Cf. also Ford's earlier, uncompleted, novel, *True Love
& a GCM* [General Court Martial], *War Prose* 109. See my Introduction here for a
longer discussion of larks in writing about the war.

He said to himself that he must get the doctor to give him a bromide. A filthy state his nerves had got into unknown to himself. The agitation communicated to him by that bird was still turning his stomach round. . . .

"Gilbert White of Selbourne," he said to the Sergeant, "called the behaviour of the female STORGE: a good word for it."* But, as for trust in humanity, the Sergeant might take it that larks never gave us a thought. We were part of the landscape and if what destroyed their nests whilst they sat on them was a bit of H.E. shell† or the coulter of a plough it was all one to them.

The Sergeant said to the re-joined Lance-Corporal whose box now hung correctly on his muddied chest:

"Now it's HAY post you gotter wait at!" They were to go along the trench and wait where another trench ran into it and there was a great A in whitewash on a bit of corrugated iron that was half-buried. "You can tell a great HAY from a bull's foot as well as another, can't you Corporal?" patiently.

Wen they Mills bombs‡ come 'e was to send 'is Man into Hay Cumpny§ dugout fer a fatigue to bring 'em along 'ere, but Hay Cumpny could keep 'is little lot fer 'isself.

An if they Mills Bomb did'n'[19] come the Corporal'd better manufacture them on is own. An not make no mistakes![20]

The Lance-Corporal said "Yes sargint, no sargint!"[21] and the two went desultorily wavering along the duckboards, grey silhouettes against the wet bar of light,** equilibrating themselves with hands on the walls of the trench.

---

*   Revd Gilbert White (1720–93) wrote *The Natural History of Selborne* (1787), and is described by Tietjens in *Some Do Not . . .* as 'the last English writer that could write' (I.vii). He features, too, in *No Enemy*, as in this current example immediately after a section on birdlife (25) which itself is reworked into a later section of *A Man Could Stand Up* – (see the relevant note in II.vi). White's *Natural History* is a deceptively simple, and much republished, account of wildlife through the seasons. He is often referred to as the founding father of the ecology movement. 'Storge': from the Greek, 'natural affection', usually of parents for their offspring, and a word White uses often, in his letters for example.
†   High explosive shell; consisting of a strong steel case, bursting charge and a fuse. Most of the damage to soft targets is caused by the blast rather than by fragments and splinters.
‡   The standard British hand grenade in the First World War, and until its withdrawal in the 1960s.
§   Phonetic cockney for 'A' Company.
** Ford had used a similar formulation before, in *The Portrait* (London: Methuen, 1910), when a backdrop is formed by a 'transluscent and liquid bar of light in the sky' (134).

"Ju 'eer what the orfcer said, Corporal," the one said to the other. "Wottever'll 'e say next! Skylarks not trust 'uman beens in battles! Cor!" The other grunted and, mournfully, the voices died out.

The cockscomb-shaped splash became of overwhelming interest momentarily to Tietjens; at the same time his mind began upon abstruse calculation of chances! Of his chances! A bad sign when the mind takes to doing that. Chances of direct hits by shells, by rifle bullets, by grenades, by fragments of shells or grenades. By any fragment of metal impinging on soft flesh. He was aware that he was going to be hit in the soft spot behind the collar-bone. He was conscious of that spot—the right hand one; he felt none of the rest of his body. It is bad when the mind takes charge like that. A bromide was needed. The doctor must give him one. His mind felt pleasure at the thought of the M.O. A pleasant little fellow of the no account order that knows his job. And carried liquor cheerfully. Confoundedly cheerfully!

He saw the doctor—plainly! It was one of the plainest things he could see of this whole show.... The doctor, a slight figure, vault on to the parapet, like a vaulting horse for height; stand up in the early morning sun.... Blind to the world, but humming *Father O'Flynn.** And stroll in the sunlight, a swagger cane of all things in the world, under his arms, right straight over to the German trench.... Then throw his cap down into that trench. And walk back! Delicately avoiding the strands in the cut apron of wire that he had to walk through!

The doctor[22] said he had seen a Hun—probably an officer's batman—cleaning a top-boot with an apron over his knees. The

* An example of a 'broadside ballad', i.e. a ballad printed on a broadside (a large sheet of paper printed on one side); a dramatic/humorous narrative song derived from folk culture. Musical notation is rarely given as tunes were usually established favourites. This one begins:

'Of praists we can offer a charmin' variety / Far renowned for lernin' and piety / Still I'd advance ye, widout impropriety / Father O'Flynn as the flower of them all.'

Published between 1890 and 1900 [?] by Poet's Box of Dundee. Tune: Top O'Cork. James Joyce had a version about Ford that he sent to Harriet Weaver in 1931, soon after meeting Ford with Janice Biala:

'O Father O'Ford, you've a masterful way with you, / Maid, wife and widow are wild to make hay with you, / Blonde and brunette turn-about run away with you, / You've such a way with you Father O'Ford.'

The second verse is also quoted by Richard Ellmann in his biography of Joyce (*James Joyce* [Oxford: Oxford University Press, 1983], 635–6 n).

Hun had shied a boot brush at him and he had shied his cap at the Hun. The blinking Hun, he called him! No doubt the fellow had blinked!

No doubt you could do the unthinkable with impunity!

No manner of doubt: if you were blind drunk and all! . . . And however you strained, in an army you fell into routine. Of a quiet morning you do not expect drunken doctors strolling along your parapet. Besides, the German front lines were very thinly held. Amazingly! There might not have been a Hun with a gun within half a mile of that boot-black!

If he, Tietjens, stood in space, his head level with that cockscomb, he would be in an inviolable vacuum—as far as projectiles were concerned!

He was asking desultorily of the Sergeant whether he often shocked the men by what he said and the Sergeant was answering with blushes: Well, you do *say* things, sir! Not believing in sky-larks now! If there was one thing the men believed hit was in the hinstincks of them little creatures!

"So that," Tietjens said, "they look at me as a sort of an atheist."

He forced himself to look over the parapet again, climbing heavily to his place of observation. It was sheer impatience and purely culpable technically. But he was in command of the regiment, of an establishment of a thousand and eighteen men, or that used to be the Establishment of a battalion; of a strength of three hundred and thirty three. Say seventy-five per company. And two companies in command of second lieutenants, one just out. . . . The last four days. . . . There ought to be, say, eighty pairs of eyes surveying what he was going to survey. If there were fifteen it was as much as there were! . . . Figures were clean and comforting things. The chance against being struck by a shell-fragment that day, if the Germans came in any force, was fourteen to one against. There were battalions worse off than they. The sixth had only one one six left!

The tortured ground sloped down into mists. Say a quarter of a mile away. The German front lines were just shadows, like the corrugations of photographs of the moon: the paradoses of our own trenches two nights[23] ago! The Germans did not seem to have troubled to chuck up much in the way of parapets. They didn't. They were coming on. Anyhow they held their front lines always very sparsely.... Was that the phrase? Was it even English? Above the shadows the mist behaved tortuously: mounting up into umbrella shapes. Like snow-covered umbrella pines. Disagreeable to force the eye to examine that mist. His stomach turned over.... That was the sacks. A flat, slightly disordered pile of wet sacks, half-right at two hundred yards. No doubt a shell had hit a G.S. wagon coming up with sacks for trenching. Or the bearers had bolted, chucking the sacks down. His eyes had fallen on that scattered pile four times already that morning. Each time his stomach had turned over. The resemblance to prostrate men was appalling. The enemy creeping up.... Christ! Within two hundred yards. So his stomach said. Each time, in spite of the preparation.

Otherwise the ground had been so smashed up that it was flat: went down into holes but did not rise up into mounds. That made it look gentle. It sloped down. To the untidiness. They appeared mostly to lie on their faces; Why?[24] Presumably they were mostly Germans pushed back in the last counter-attack. Anyhow you saw mostly the seats of their trousers. When you did not, how profound was their repose! You must phrase it a little like that—rhetorically. There was no other way to get the effect of that profoundness. Call it profundity!

It was different from sleep. Flatter. No doubt when the appalled soul left the weary body, the panting lungs.... Well, you can't go on with a sentence like that.... But you collapsed inwards.[25] Like the dying pig they sold on trays in the street.*

---

* A 'dying pig' was a toy. In the preface to the 1921 edition of his *Letters from an Ocean Tramp* (New York: Doubleday, Page & Co. [1908]), William McFee offers a vivid description of a dying pig for (he says) the benefit of readers who are not Londoners:

> Down below, a gentleman who sold studs, shoe-laces and dying pigs on the curb, and who kept his stock in a cupboard under the arch, was preparing to start out for the day. A dying pig, it may be mentioned, was a toy much in demand among stock-broking clerks and other frivolous young gentlemen in the City, and consisted of a bladder shaped like a pig whose snout contained a whistle which gave out on deflation an almost human note of anguish. (ix)

In I.i Valentine likes the idea of policemen being hit over the head 'with bladders' on Armistice Day. In *Adventures in London* (London: Cassell, 1909), by James Douglas, the more sinister description of the toy also conjures up a history of pig selling on the street (going back as far as Elizabethan times), and the buying of fresh brawn chronicled by writers such as Henry Mayhew in the 1850s (252–5).

Painter fellows doing battlefields never got that *intimate* effect.
Intimate to them there. Unknown to the corridors in Whitehall. . . . Probably because they—the painters—drew from living
models or had ideas as to the human form. . . . But these were not
limbs, muscles, torsi. . . . Collections of tubular shapes in field-
grey or mud-colour they were.[26] Chucked about by Almighty
God! As if He had dropped them from on high to make them
flatten into the earth. . . . Good gravel soil, that slope and relatively dry. No dew to speak of. The night had been covered. . . .

Dawn on the battlefield. . . . Damn it all, why sneer? It *was*
dawn on the battlefield. . . . The trouble was that *this* battle was
not over. By no means over. There would be a hundred and[27]
eleven years, nine months and twenty-seven days of it still. . . .
No, you could not get the effect of that endless monotony of effort
by numbers. Nor yet by saying "Endless monotony of effort". . . .[28]
It was like bending down to look into darkness of corridors under
dark curtains. Under clouds. . . . Mist. . . .

At that, with dreadful reluctance his eyes went back to the
spectral mists over the photographic shadows. He forced himself
to put his glasses on the mists. They mopped and mowed,* fantas-
tically; grey, with black shadows; drooping like the dishevelled
veils of murdered bodies.[29] They were engaged in fantastic and
horrifying layings out of corpses of vast dimensions;[30] in silence
but in accord they performed unthinkable tasks. They were the
Germans. This was fear. This was the intimate fear of black quiet
nights, in dugouts where you heard the obscene suggestions of the
miners' picks below you; tranquil, engrossed. Infinitely threat-
ening. . . . But not FEAR.

It was in effect the desire for privacy. What he dreaded at those
normal times when fear visited him at lunch; whilst seeing that
the men got their baths or when writing, in a trench, in support,

---

* 'Mops and mows' appears in Brewer's *Dictionary of Phrase and Fable* and is defined as
'grimaces' ('la moue' means pout in French). Ford uses 'miching and mowing' in
Mightier than the Sword (1938 – published first in the US as *Portraits from Life*, 1937)
and in *Provence* 85: 'On the 9.40 from the Gare du Lyon, around Montélimar, you will
find all sorts of Beings peeping, leering, ironically smiling, miching and mowing at you
on the banks that fly by.' Miching (meaning 'sneaking' or 'skulking') appears in *Hamlet*
('Marry, this is miching malhecho. That means mischief', III.ii.131–2). In *Lear*, in
Edgar's Poor Tom speech (Quarto text, xv.56–60), there's something more similar to
Ford's 'mopped and mowed'. Christina Rossetti uses 'mopping and mowing' in her
description of the triumphant goblins too, in 'Goblin Market' (*Selected Poems* 90).

a letter to his bank-manager, was finding himself unhurt, surrounded by figures like the brothers of the Misericordia,* going unconcerned about their tasks, noticing him hardly at all.... Whole hillsides, whole stretches of territory, alive with myriads of whitish-grey, long cagoules, with slits for eyeholes. Occasionally one would look at him through the eye-slits in the hoods.... The prisoner!

He would be the prisoner: liable to physical contacts—to being handled and being questioned. An invasion of his privacy!

As a matter of fact that wasn't so far out; not so dotty as it sounded. If the Huns got him—as they precious near had the night before last!—they would be—they had then been—in gas-masks of various patterns. They must be short of these things: but they looked, certainly, like goblin pigs with sore eyes, the hood with the askew, blind-looking[31] eyeholes and the mouthpiece or the other nose attachment going down into a box, astonishingly like snouts!... Mopping and mowing—no doubt shouting through the masks!

They had appeared with startling suddenness and as if with a supernatural silence, beneath a din[32] so overwhelming that you could not any longer bother to notice it. They were there, as it were, under a glass dome of silence that sheltered beneath that dark tumult,[33] in the white illumination of Verey lights that went on.† They were there, those of them that had already emerged from holes—astonishingly alert hooded figures with the long rifles that always looked rather amateurish—though, Hell, they weren't. The hoods and the white light gave them the aspects of Canadian trappers in snow; made them no doubt look still more husky fellows as against our poor rats of Derby men. The heads of goblin pigs were emerging from shell-holes, from rifts in the torn earth, from old trenches.... This ground had been fought over again and again.... Then the counter-attack had come through his, Tietjens', own crowd. One disorderly mob, as you might

---

* The Misericordia is considered a most prestigious, active charitable network in Italy, as well as being the most highly esteemed Florentine institution. It is also the most long-lived (established more than 760 years ago). Brothers wore a black cowl to make them anonymous as they gave aid, especially to victims of plague.
† Named after their inventor, Edward Very (1847–1910), these were chemical flares used in night-signalling or for illuminating the enemy's position.

think, going through a disordered crowd that was damn glad to
let them through, realising slowly, in the midst of a general not
knowing what was going to happen, that the fellows were reliefs.[34]
They shot past you clumsily in a darkness spangled with shafts of
light coming from God knows where and appeared going forward,
whilst you at least had the satisfaction that, by order, you were
going back. In an atmosphere of questioning. What was
happening? What was going to happen?... What the bloody
hell.... What....

Tidy-sized shells began to drop among them saying: "Wee ...
ee ... ry.... Whack!" Some fellow shewed Tietjens the way
through an immense apron of wire that was beginning to fly
about. He, Tietjens, was carrying a hell of a lot of paper folders
and books. They ought to have evacuated an hour ago; or the
Huns ought not to have got out of their holes for an hour.... But
the Colonel had been too ... too exalted. Call it too exalted. He
was not going to evacuate for a pack of ...[35] Damn orders!...
The fellow, McKechnie,[36] had at last had to beg Tietjens to give
the order.... Not that the order mattered. The men could not
have held ten minutes longer. The ghostly Huns would have been
in the trenches.[37] But the Company Commanders knew that
there was a Divisional Order to retire, and no doubt they had
passed it on to their subalterns before getting killed.[38] Still, that
Bn. H.Q. should have given the order made it better even if there
was no one to take it to the companies. It turned a practical
expulsion into an officially strategic retreat.... And damn good
divisional staff work at that. They had been fitted into beautiful,
clean, new trenches, all ready for them—like chessmen fitting
into their boxes. Damn good for a beaten army that was being
forced off the face of the earth. Into the English Channel....
What made them stick it? What the devil made the men stick it?
They were unbelievable.*

There was a stroking on his leg. A gentle, timid, stroking!
Well, he *ought* to get down: it was setting a bad example. The
admirable trenches were perfectly efficiently fitted up with spy-

---

* Cf. Ford's war poem, 'Antwerp': 'In the name of God how could they do it?' (*Selected Poems* 82). Also of note here is the fact that 'Stick it, the Welch!' was the motto of Ford's regiment (see the essay 'Pon... ti... pri... ith', from 1918, republished in *War Prose* 30–5).

holes. For himself he always disliked them. You thought of a rifle
bullet coming smack through them and guided by the telescope
into your right eye. Or perhaps you would not have a telescope.
Anyhow you wouldn't know. . . .

There were still the three wheels, a-tilt, attached to slanting
axles: in a haze of disintegrated wire, that, bedewed, made profuse
patterns like frost on a window. There was their own apron—a
perfect village!—of wire over which he looked. Fairly intact. The
Germans had put up some of their own in front of the lost
trenches, a quarter of a mile off: over the reposing untidinesses.
In between there was a perfect maze: their own of the night before
last. How the deuce had it not been *all* mashed to pieces by the
last Hun barrage? Yet there were three frosty erections—like fairy
sheds, half-way between the two lines. And, suspended in them,
as there would have to be, three bundles of rags and what
appeared to be a very large, squashed crow. How the devil had
that fellow managed to get smashed into that shape? It was
improbable. There was also—suspended, too, a tall melodramatic
object, the head cast back to the sky. One arm raised in the attitude of, say, a Walter Scott Highland officer waving his men on.
Waving a sword that wasn't there. . . . That was what wire did for
you. Supported you in grotesque attitudes, even in death! The
beastly stuff! The men said that was Lieutenant Constantine.* It
might well be. The night before last he, Tietjens, had looked
round at all the officers that were in H.Q. dug-out, come for a last
moment conference. He had speculated on which of them would
be killed. Ghostly! Well, they had all been killed: and more on
to that. But his premonition hadn't run to thinking that
Constantine would get caught up in the wire. But perhaps it was
not Constantine. Probably they would never know. The Huns
would be where he stood by lunch-time. If the attack of which
Brigade H.Q. had warned them came off. But it mightn't. . . .

As a final salute to the, on the whole not thrilling landscape,
he wetted his forefinger by inserting it in his mouth and held it
in the air. It was comfortingly chilly on the exterior, towards his

* Possibly a reference to the men's sacrifice here in the name Ford chooses – although
  it is important too that he's an 'everyman' character. Emperor Constantine converted
  to Christianity some time around AD 310. In 313 he issued the edict of Milan, which,
  among other things, granted religious freedom throughout the Roman Empire.

back. Light airs were going right in the other fellows' faces. It might only be the dawn wind. But if it stiffened a very little or even held, those blessed Wurtembergers* would never that day[39] get out of their trenches. They couldn't come without gas. They were probably pretty well weakened, too. . . . You were not traditionally[40] supposed to think much of Wurtembergers. Mild, dull creatures they were supposed to be. With funny hats. Good Lord! Traditions were going by the board!

He dropped down into the trench. The rather reddish soil with flakes of flint and little, pinkish nodules of pebbles was a friendly thing to face closely.

That sergeant was saying:

"You hadn't ought to do it, sir. Give me the creeps." He added rather lachrymosely that they couldn't do without superior officers altogether. Odd creatures these Derby N.C.O.'s! They tried to get the tone of the old, time-serving N.C.O. They couldn't; all the same you couldn't say they weren't creditable achievements.

Yes, it was friendly, the trench face. And singularly unbellicose. When you looked at it you hardly believed that it was part of this affair. . . . Friendly! You felt at peace looking at its flints and pebbles. Like being in the butts up above Groby on the moor, waiting for the grouse to come over. The soil was not of course like those butts which were built[41] of turfs. . . .

He asked, not so much for information, as to get the note of this fellow:

Why? What difference did it make whether there were senior officers or not? Anyone above eighteen would do, wouldn't they? They would keep going on. It was a young man's war![42]

"It hasn't got that comfortable feeling, sir!" the Sergeant expressed it. The young officers were very well for keeping you going through wire and barrages. But when you looked at them you didn't feel they knew so well what you were doing it for, if he might put it that way.

Tietjens said:

"Why? What are you doing it for?"

---

* Albrecht, Duke of Württemberg, was a successful German army general on the Western Front. Before the Battle of the Somme (1916), Thiepval was in German hands, garrisoned by the 160th Regiment of Württembergers.

It wanted thirty-two minutes to the crucial moment. He said: "Where are those bloody bombs?"

A trench cut in gravel wasn't, for all its friendly reddish-orange coloration, the ideal trench. Particularly against rifle-fire. There were rifts, presumably alongside flakes of flint, that a rifle-bullet would get along. Still, the chances against a hit by a rifle-bullet were eighty thousand to one in a deep gravel trench like that. And he had had poor Jimmy Johns killed beside him by a bullet like that. So that gave him, say, 140,000 chances to one against. He wished his mind would not go on and on figuring. It did it whilst you weren't looking. As a well-trained dog will do when you tell it to stay in one part of a room and it prefers another. It prefers to do figuring. Creeps from the rug by the door to the hearth-rug, its eyes on your unconscious face. . . . That was what your mind was like. Like a dog!

The Sergeant said:

"They do say the first consignment of bombs was it n smashed.[43] H in a gully; well beind[44] the line. Another was coming down."

"Then you'd better whistle," Tietjens said, "Whistle for all you're worth."

The Sergeant said:

"Fer a wind, sir? Keep the 'Uns beck,[45] sir?"

Looking up at the whitewash cockscomb Tietjens lectured the sergeant on Gas. He always *had* said, and he said now, that the Germans had ruined themselves with their gas. . . .

He went on lecturing that Sergeant on gas. . . .

He considered his mind: it was alarming him. All through the war he had had one dread—that a wound, the physical shock of a wound, would cause his mind to fail. He was going to be hit behind the collar-bone. He could feel the spot; not itching but the blood pulsing just a little warmer. Just as you can become conscious of the end of your nose if you think about it![46]

The Sergeant said that 'e wished 'e could *feel* the Germans 'ad ruined theirselves: they seemed to be drivin' us into the Channel.[47] Tietjens gave his reasons. They were driving us. But not fast enough. Not fast enough. It was a race between our disappearance and their endurance. They had been hung up yesterday by the wind: they were as like as not going to be held up to-day.... They were not going fast enough. They could not keep it up.

The Sergeant said 'e wished, sir, you'd tell the men that. That was what the men ought to be told: not the stuff that was hin Divisional Comic Cuts* and the 'ome pipers.... [48][†]

A key-bugle[‡] of singular sweetness—at least Tietjens supposed it to be a key-bugle, for he knew the identities of practically no wind-instruments; it was certainly not a cavalry bugle, for there were no cavalry and even no Army Service Corps at all near—a bugle, then, of astounding sweetness made some remarks to the cool, wet dawn. It induced an astonishingly melting mood. He remarked:

"Do you mean to say, then, that your men, Sergeant, are really damned heroes? I suppose they are!"

He said "your men," instead of "our" or even "the" men, because he had been till the day before yesterday merely the second-in-command—and was likely to be to-morrow again merely the perfectly inactive second-in-command of what was called a rag-time collection that was astonishingly a clique and mutely combined to regard him as an outsider. So he really regarded himself as rather a spectator; as if a railway passenger had taken charge of a locomotive whilst the engine-driver had gone to have a drink.

The Sergeant flushed with pleasure. Hit was, he said, good to 'ave prise from Regular officers.[49] Tietjens said that he was not a Regular. The Sergeant stammered:

"*Hain't* you, sir, a Ranker. The men all thinks you are a promoted Ranker."

No, Tietjens said, he was not a promoted Ranker.[§] He added,

---

* Colloquialism for 'reports from Divisional Headquarters (*Corps Intelligence Summaries*)' containing morale-boosting (and often false) information. *Comic Cuts* was a humorous paper of the time for children.
† Or 'home papers'.
‡ Musical instrument, a type of bugle with side holes covered with keys similar to those used on woodwind instruments. It was invented in the early nineteenth century.
§ There are many sources of information devoted to the subjects of 'gentlemen' and 'rankers' and their inter-relationships. These make it clear that the issue had caused contention as far back as the Crimean War and beyond. One could be (1) a gentleman and commissioned as an officer, (2) a gentleman but in the ranks, or (3) a regular soldier promoted to officer through the ranks. All three of these categories have their own mythologies and while some regular soldiers seem to prefer an officer with experience of the ranks, others seemed to take confidence from a gentleman officer.

after consideration, that he was a militiaman. The men would have, by the will of chance, to put up with his leadership for at least[50] that day. They might as well feel as good about it as they could—as settled in their stomachs! It certainly made a difference that the men should feel assured about their officers: what exact difference there was no knowing. This crowd was not going to get any satisfaction out of being led by a "gentleman". They did not know what a gentleman was: a quite un-feudal crowd. Mostly Derby men.[51]* Small drapers, rate-collectors' clerks, gas-inspectors. There were even three music-hall performers, two scene shifters and several milkmen.

It was another tradition that was gone. Still, they desired the companionship of elder, heavier men who had certain knowledges. A militiaman probably filled the bill! Well, he was that, officially![52]

He glanced aside and upwards at the whitewash cockscomb. He regarded it carefully. And with amusement. He knew what it was that had made his mind take the particular turn it had insisted on taking. . . . The picks going in the dark under the H.Q. dugout in the Cassenoisette section. The men called it Cracker-jack.†

He had been all his life familiar with the idea of picks going in the dark, underground. There is no North Country man who is not. All through that country, if you awake at night you hear the sound, and always it appears supernatural. You know it is the miners, at the pit-face,[53] hundreds and hundreds of feet down.

But just because it was familiar it was familiarly rather dreadful.

---

* With popular and mainstream political opposition to mandatory military service, Britain was the sole major European power not to have in place a policy of conscription when war began in August 1914. Individual politicians advocated a form of conscription in 1914, but there was broad agreement that Britain could maintain its European policy with a volunteer army. However, growing battlefront demand soon outstripped volunteer numbers and in May 1915 Prime Minister Asquith appointed Lord Edward Derby – himself an opponent of conscription – as Director General of Recruitment, tasked with rapidly boosting Britain's volunteer army. His solution was the 'Derby scheme', which encouraged men to voluntarily register their name on the principle that once registered they would be called up only when necessary. As an added incentive married men would be called up only when the supply of single men was exhausted. The scheme proved unsuccessful, and was abandoned in December 1915 – excluding men exempted from military service on grounds of their occupation, just 350,000 had volunteered.

† *Cassenoisette* means nutcracker in French.

Haunting. And the silence had come at a bad moment. After a perfect hell of noise; after so much of noise that he had been forced to ascend the slippery clay stairs of the dug-out.... And heaven knew if there was one thing that on account of his heavy-breathing chest he loathed, it was slippery clay ... he had been forced to pant up those slippery stairs.... His chest had been much worse, then ... two months ago!

Curiosity had forced him up. And no doubt FEAR. The large battle fear; not the constant little, haunting misgivings. God knew! Curiosity or fear. In terrific noise; noise like the rushing up of innumerable noises determined not to be late, whilst the earth rocks or bumps or quakes or protests, you cannot be very coherent about your thoughts. So it might have been cool curiosity or it might have been sheer panic at the thought of being buried alive in that dug-out, its mouth sealed up. Anyhow, he had gone up from the dug-out where in his capacity of second-in-command, detested as an interloper by his C.O., he had sat ignominiously in that idleness of the second-in-command that it is in the power of the C.O. to inflict. He was to sit there till the C.O. dropped dead: then, however much the C.O. might detest him, to step into his shoes. Nothing the C.O. could do could stop that. In the meantime, as long as the C.O. existed the second-in-command must be idle; he would be given nothing to do. For fear he got kudos!

Tietjens flattered himself that he cared nothing about kudos. He was still Tietjens of Groby: no man could give him anything, no man could take anything from him. He flattered himself that he in no way feared death, pain, dishonour, the after-death, feared very little disease—except for choking sensations!... But his Colonel got in on him.

He had no disagreeable feelings,[54] thinking of the Colonel. A good boy, as boys go: perfectly warranted in hating his second-in-command.... There are positions like that! But the fellow got in on him. He shut him up in that reeling cellar. And, of course, you might lose control of your mind in a reeling cellar where you cannot hear your thoughts. If you cannot hear your thoughts how the hell are you going to tell what your thoughts are doing?

You couldn't hear. There was an orderly with fever or shell-shock or something—a rather favourite orderly of the orderly room—asleep on a pile of rugs. Earlier in the night Orderly Room had asked permission to dump the boy in there because he was making such a beastly row in his sleep that they could not hear themselves speak and they had a lot of paper work to do. They could not tell what had happened to the boy, whom they liked. The acting Sergeant-Major thought he must have got at some methylated spirits.

Immediately, that *strafe*[55] had begun. The boy had lain, his face to the light of the lamp, on his pile of rugs—army blankets, that is to say.... A very blond boy's face, contorted in the strong light, shrieking—positively shrieking obscenities at the flame. But with his eyes shut. And two minutes after that *strafe* had begun you could see his lips move, that was all.

Well, he, Tietjens, had gone up. Curiosity or fear? In the trench you could see nothing and noise rushed like black angels gone mad; solid noise that swept you off your feet.... Swept your brain off its feet. Someone else took control of it. You became second-in-command of your own soul. Waiting for its C.O. to be squashed flat by the direct hit of a four point two before you got control again.

There was nothing to see; mad lights whirled over the black heavens. He moved along the mud of the trench. It amazed him to find that it was raining. In torrents. You imagined that the heavenly powers in decency suspended their activities at such moments.[56] But there was positively lightning. They didn't![57] A Verey light or something extinguished *that*: not very efficient lightning, really. Just at that moment he fell on his nose at an angle of forty-five degrees against some squashed earth where, as he remembered, the parapet had been revetted. The trench had been squashed in. Level with the outside ground. A pair of boots emerged from the pile of mud. How the deuce did the fellow get into that position?

Broadside on to the hostilities in progress!... But, naturally, he had been running along the trench when that stuff buried him. Clean buried, anyhow. The obliging Verey light showed to Tietjens,[58] just level with his left hand, a number of small smoking fragments. The white smoke ran level with the ground in a stiff breeze. Other little patches of smoke added themselves quickly. The Verey light went out. Things were coming over. Something hit his foot; the heel of his boot. Not unpleasantly, a smarting feeling as if his sole had been slapped.

It suggested itself to him, under all the noise, that there being no parapet there ... [59] He got back into the trench towards the dug-out, skating in the sticky mud. The duckboards were completely sunk in it. In the whole affair it was the slippery mud he hated most.* Again a Verey light obliged, but the trench being deep there was nothing to see except the backside of a man. Tietjens said:

"If he's wounded ... Even if he's dead one ought to pull him down.... And get the Victoria Cross!"

The figure slid down into the trench. Speedily, with drill-movements, engrossed, it crammed two clips of cartridges into a rifle correctly held at the loading angle. In a rift of the noise, like a crack in the wall of a house, it remarked:

"Can't reload lying up there, sir. Mud gets into your magazine."

He became again merely the sitting portion of a man, presenting to view the only part of him that was not caked with mud. The Verey light faded. Another reinforced the blinking effect. From just overhead.

Round the next traverse after the mouth of their dug-out a rapt face of a tiny subaltern, gazing upwards at a Verey illumination, with an elbow on an inequality of the trench and the forearm pointing upwards suggested—the rapt face suggested The Soul's Awakening! ... † In another rift in the sound the voice of the tiny subaltern stated[60] that he had to economise the Verey cartridges. The battalion was very short. At the same time it was difficult to time them so as to keep the lights going.... This seemed

---

*   When in *No More Parades* Tietjens hears he is going up the line his fears are immediately focused on the mud (I.iv; III.ii). He was not alone, and many soldier-writers recreate this exhausting and filthy aspect of trench life. The first chapter of Dan Todman's *The Great War: Myth and Memory* (London and New York: Hambledon, 2005) is titled 'Mud', and he details some of its constituents: 'excrement, dead soldiers and animals, shrapnel, barbed wire and the remnants of poison gas' (1).

†   Possibly Tietjens has in mind William Holman Hunt's famous Pre-Raphaelite painting *The Awakening Conscience* (1854). There may be a further Hunt allusion in the opening half of the sentence – to *Rienzi* (1849), in which there is indeed a raised forearm as the subject is politically converted (post-1848) to the cause of the oppressed. But Tietjens may also be thinking of a painting of that name by the British artist James Sant, RA (1820–1916), which featured in other writing about the war as an example of the idealism those who fought could not sustain for long (see, for example, H. M. Tomlinson's *Waiting for Daylight* [1922]).

fantastic! The Huns were just coming over.

With the finger of his upward pointing hand the tiny subaltern pulled the trigger of his upward pointing pistol. A second later more brilliant illumination descended from above. The subaltern pointed the clumsy pistol to the ground in the considerable physical effort—for such a tiny person!—to reload the large implement. A very gallant child—name of Aranjuez. Maltese, or Portuguese, or Levantine—in origin.

The pointing of the pistol downwards revealed that he had practically coiled around his little feet, a collection of tubular, dead, khaki limbs. It didn't need any rift in the sound to make you understand that his loader had been killed on him.... By signs and[61] removing his pistol from his grasp Tietjens made the subaltern—he was only two days out from England—understand that he had better go and get a drink and some bearers for the man who might not be dead.

He was, however. When they removed him a little to make room for Tietjens' immensely larger boots his arms just flopped in the mud, the tin hat that covered the[62] face, to the sky. Like a lay figure, but a little less stiff. Not yet cold.

Tietjens became like a solitary statue of the Bard of Avon, the shelf for his elbow being rather low. Noise increased. The orchestra was bringing in *all* the brass, *all* the strings, *all* the wood-wind, all the percussion instruments. The performers[63] threw about biscuit tins filled with horse-shoes; they emptied sacks of coal on cracked gongs, they threw down forty-storey iron houses. It was comic to the extent that an operatic orchestra's crescendo is comic. Crescendo!.... Crescendo! CRRRRRESC.... The Hero *must* be coming! He didn't!

Still like Shakespeare contemplating the creation of, say, Cordelia, Tietjens leaned against his shelf. From time to time he pulled the trigger[64] of the horse-pistol; from time to time he rested the butt on his ledge and rammed a charge home. When one jammed he took another. He found himself keeping up a fairly steady illumination.

The Hero arrived. Naturally, he was a Hun. He came over, all legs and arms going, like a catamount; struck the face of the parados, fell into the trench on the dead body, with his hands to his eyes, sprang up again and danced. With heavy deliberation

Tietjens drew his great trench-knife rather than his revolver. Why? The butcher-instinct? Or trying to think himself with the Exmoor stag-hounds? The man's shoulders had come down heavily on him as he had rebounded from the parados-face. He felt outraged. Watching that performing Hun he held the knife pointed and tried to think of the German for *Hands Up*. He imagined it to be *Hoch die Haende!* He looked for a nice spot in the Hun's side.

His excursion into a foreign tongue proved supererogatory. The German threw his arms abroad, his—considerably mashed!—face to the sky.

Always dramatic, Cousin Fritz! Too dramatic, really.

He fell, crumpling, into his untidy boots. Nasty boots, all crumpled too, up the calves! But he didn't say *Hoch der Kaiser*, or *Deutschland über*[65] *alles,* * or anything valedictory.

Tietjens fired another light upwards and filled in another charge, then, down on his hams in the mud he squatted over the German's head, the fingers of both hands under the head. He could feel the great groans thrill his fingers. He let go and felt tentatively for his brandy flask.

But there was a muddy group round the traverse end. The noise reduced itself to half. It was bearers for the corpse.[66] And the absurdly wee Aranjuez and a new loader.... In those days they had not been so short of men! Shouts were coming along the trench. No doubt other Huns were in.

Noise reduced itself to a third. A bumpy diminuendo. Bumpy! Sacks of coal continued to fall down the stairs with a regular cadence; more irregularly, Bloody Mary,† who was just behind the trench, or seemed like it, shook the whole house as you might say and there were other naval howitzers or something, somewhere. Tietjens said to the bearers:

"Take the Hun first. He's alive. Our man's dead." He was quite

---

* Translated as 'Long live the Kaiser' or 'Up with the Kaiser', and 'Germany before/ beyond all'. The latter phrase is the first line of 'The Germany Song', a poem of aspiration for the unity of German peoples written before the 1848 revolutions. It was the national anthem of the German Republic from 1922 to 1945, with music by Haydn.

† Records at the Royal Artillery Museum show that a navy gun was known as 'Bloody Mary' as early as the Boer Wars (1880–1, 1899–1902). In *No Enemy* Ford describes the way in which 'Bloody Mary and two of her lady friends let off, enormous and august, breaking the quiet night' (53).

remarkably dead. He hadn't, Tietjens had observed, when he bent over the German, really got what you might call a head, though there was something in its place. What had done that? Aranjuez, taking his place beside the trench-face, said: "Damn cool you were, sir. Damn cool. I never saw a knife drawn so slow!" They had watched the Hun do the *danse du ventre!*[*] The poor beggar had had rifles and the young feller's revolver turned on him all the time. They would probably have shot him some more but for the fear of hitting Tietjens. Half-a-dozen Germans[67] had jumped into that sector of trenches in various places. As mad as march hares! . . .[†] That fellow had been shot through both eyes, a fact that seemed to fill the little Aranjuez with singular horror. He said he would go mad if he thought he would be blinded, because there was a girl in the teashop at Bailleul, and a fellow called Spofforth of the Wiltshires would get her if his, Aranjuez's, beauty was spoiled. He positively whimpered at the thought and then gave the information that this was considered to be a false alarm: he meant a feigned attack to draw off troops from somewhere else where the real attempt was being made. There must be pretty good hell going on somewhere else, then.

It looked like that. For almost immediately all the guns had fallen silent except for one or two that bumped and grumped. . . . It had all been just for fun, then![68]

Well, they were damn near Bailleul now. They would be driven past it in a day or two. On the way to the Channel. Aranjuez would have to hurry to see his girl. The little devil! He had overdrawn his confounded little account over his girl, and Tietjens had had to guarantee his overdraft—which he could not afford to do. Now the little wretch would probably overdraw still

---

[*] Belly dancing. The French version was common in England until around 1899 when 'belly dancing' was coined.

[†] Hares are unusually shy and wild in March, which is their rutting season. Directed by the Cheshire Cat to either the Mad Hatter or the March Hare ('they're both mad'), Alice chooses the Hare, because 'the March Hare will be much the most interesting, and perhaps because this is May it won't be raving mad – at least not so mad as it was in March' (*Alice's Adventures in Wonderland* [London: Arcturus, 2008 (1865)], 63–4). There is a cancelled passage in *Some Do Not . . .* in which Wilhem II calls the English 'as mad as March hares'. See that volume for details.

more—and Tietjens would have to guarantee still more of an overdraft.

But that night, when Tietjens had gone down into the black silence of his own particular branch of a cellar—they really had been in wine-cellars at that date, cellars stretching for hundreds of yards under chalk with strata of clay which made the mud so particularly sticky and offensive—he had found the sound of the pickaxes beneath his flea-bag almost unbearable. They were probably our own men. Obviously they were our own men. But it had not made much difference, for, of course, if they were there they would be an attraction, and the Germans might just as well be below them, countermining.

His nerves had been put in a bad way by that rotten *strafe* that had been just for fun. He knew his nerves were in a bad way because he had a ghostly[69] visit from O9 Morgan,[70] a fellow whose head had been smashed, as it were, on his, Tietjens', own hands, just after Tietjens had refused him home leave to go and get killed by a prize-fighter who had taken up with his, O9 Morgan's,[71] wife. It was complicated, but Tietjens wished that fellows who wished to fall on him when they were stopping things would choose to stop things with something else than their heads. That wretched Hun dropping on his shoulder, when, by the laws of war, he ought to have been running back to his own lines, had given him, Tietjens, a jar that still shook his whole body. And, of course, a shock. The fellow had looked something positively Apocalyptic, his whitey-grey arms and legs spread abroad.... And it had been an imbecile affair, with no basis of real fighting....

That thin surge of whitey-grey objects of whom not more than a dozen had reached the line—Tietjens knew that, because, with a melodramatically drawn revolver and the fellows who would have been really better employed carrying away the unfortunate Hun who had had in consequence to wait half an hour before being attended to—with those fellows loaded up with Mills bombs like people carrying pears, he had dodged, revolver first, round half-a-dozen traverses, and in quite enough of remains of gas to make his lungs unpleasant ...[72] Like a child playing a game of "I spy!" Just like that.... But only to come on several lots of Tommies standing round unfortunate objects who were either trembling with fear and wet and sweat, or panting with their nice little run. . . .

This surge then of whitey-grey objects, sacrificed for fun, was intended . . . was intended ulti . . . ultim . . . then . . .

A voice, just under his camp-bed, said: "*Bringt dem Hauptmann eine Kerze.* . . ."As who should say: "Bring a candle for the Captain. . . ." Just like that! A dream![73] It hadn't been as considerable of a shock as you might have thought to a man just dozing off. Not really as bad as the falling dream: but quite as awakening. . . .[74] His mind had resumed that sentence.

The handful of Germans who had reached the trench, had been sacrificed for the stupid sort of fun called Strategy. Probably. Stupid! . . . It was, of course, just like German spooks to go mining by candle-light. Obsoletely Nibelungen-like.* Dwarfs probably! . . . They had sent over that thin waft of men under a blessed lot of barrage and stuff. . . . A lot! A *whole* lot! It had been quite an artillery *strafe*. Ten thousand shells as like as not. Then, somewhere up the line they had probably made a demonstration in force. *Great* bodies of men, an immense surge. And twenty to thirty thousand shells. Very likely some miles of esplanade, as it were, with the sea battering against it. And only a demonstration in force. . . .

It could not be real fighting. They had not been ready for their spring advance.

It had been meant to impress somebody imbecile. . . . Somebody imbecile in Wallachia, or Sofia, or Asia Minor. Or Whitehall, very likely. Or the White House! . . . Perhaps they had killed a lot of Yankees—to make themselves Transatlantically popular. There were no doubt, by then, whole American Army Corps in the line somewhere. By then! Poor devils, coming so late into such an accentuated hell. Damnably accentuated. . . . The sound of even that little bit of fun had been portentously

---

*   The Nibelungen appear in German mythology from the twelfth/thirteenth centuries onwards (see, for example, the medieval epic poem *The Nibelungenlied*). In Wagner's four-opera *Ring* cycle, first performed in its entirety at Bayreuth in 1876, they are dwarts who have forged a magic ring from gold stolen from the Rhinemaidens. Ford's father, Francis Hueffer (music critic of *The Times* from 1879) was an early supporter of Wagner's music, and author of a biography of the composer in 1874. Ford wrote to Conrad in 1916: 'You are a blooming old Titan, really – or do I mean Nibelung?' (*Letters* 79).

more awful than even quite a big show say in '15. It was better to
have been in then and got used to it. . . . If it hadn't broken you,
just by duration. . . .

Might be to impress anybody. . . . But who was going to be
impressed? Of course, our legislators with the stewed-pear brains
running about the ignoble corridors with coke-brize floors and
mahogany doors . . . might be impressed. . . . You must not
rhyme! . . . Or, of course, our own legislators might have been
trying a nice little demonstration in force, equally idiotic somewhere else, to impress someone just as unlikely to be
impressed. . . . This, then, would be the answer! But no one ever
would be impressed again. We all had each other's measures. So
it was just wearisome. . . .

It was remarkably quiet in that thick darkness. Down below,[75]
the picks continued their sinister confidences in each other's
ears. . . . It was really like that. Like children in the corner of a
schoolroom whispering nasty comments about their masters, one
to the other. . . . Girls, for choice. . . . Chop, chop, chop, a pick
whispered. Chop? another asked in an undertone. The first said
Chopchopchop. Then *Chup*. . . . And a silence of irregular duration. . . . Like what happens when you listen to typewriting and
the young woman has to stop to put in another page. . . . *

Nice young women with typewriters in Whitehall had very
likely taken from dictation, on hot-pressed, square sheets with
embossed royal arms, the plan for that very *strafe*. . . . Because,
obviously it might have been dictated from Whitehall almost as
directly as from Unter den Linden.† We might have been making
a demonstration in force on the Dwolologda in order to get the
Huns to make a counter-demonstration in Flanders. Hoping poor
old Puffles‡ would get it in the neck. For they were trying still to
smash poor old General Puffles and stop the single command. . . .
They might very well be hoping that our losses through the
counter-demonstration would be so heavy that the Country
would cry out for the evacuation of the Western Front. . . . If they

---

* Cf. *Nightingale* 239.
† This is a boulevard in the heart of Berlin's historic district lined with lime trees. Signif-
 icant buildings along the road include the State Library and the State Opera. The
 Kaiser's Hohenzollern palace, the Stadtschloss, was also here.
‡ The nickname for General Perry, in command of the regiment to which Tietjens is
 promoted in *No More Parades*, and apparently the victim of a Whitehall conspiracy.

could get half-a-million of us killed perhaps the Country[76]
might.... They, no doubt, thought it worth trying. But it was
wearisome: those fellows in Whitehall never learned. Any more
than Brother Boshe....*
Nice to be in poor old Puffles' army. Nice but wearisome....
Nice girls with typewriters in well-ventilated offices. Did they
still put paper cuffs on to keep their sleeves from ink? He would
ask Valen ... Valen.... It was warm and still.... On such a
night....
"*Bringt dem Hauptmann eine Kerze!*" A voice from under his
camp bed! He imagined that the Hauptmann spook must be
myopic: short-sightedly examining a tamping fuse.... If they
used tamping fuses or if that was what they called them in the
army!
He could not see the face or the spectacles of the Hauptmann
any more than he could see the faces of his men. Not through his
flea-bag and shins! They were packed in the tunnel; whitish-grey,
tubular agglomerations.... Large! Like the maggots that are
eaten by Australian natives.... Fear possessed him!
He sat up in his flea-bag, dripping with icy sweat.
"By Jove, I'm for it!" he said. He imagined that his brain was
going: he was mad and seeing himself go mad. He cast about in
his mind for some subject about which to think so that he could
prove to himself that he had not gone mad.

---

*   This was a 1914 coining, a French soldiers' word for a German. Held to be a shortening of 'tête (de) boche', where 'boche' itself is short for 'caboche' – hard skull, or,
colloquially, 'cabbage head'.

CHAPTER II[1]

THE key-bugle remarked with singular distinctness to the dawn:

dy

I know a la   *fair*   *kind*

and

Was never face

so   *mind*

pleased my

y

A sudden waft of pleasure at the seventeenth century air that the tones gave to the landscape went all over Tietjens.... Herrick and Purcell!* ... Or it was perhaps a modern imitation. Good enough. He asked:

"What the devil's that row, Sergeant?"[2]

The Sergeant disappeared behind the muddied sacking curtain. There was a guard-room in there. The key-bugle said:

Fair   *kind*....

and

Fair   *Fair*   *Fair*

kind....

and ...   *and* ...   *and*

---

* A version of this song, titled 'Passing By' (published in 1875), is attributed to Robert Herrick (1591?–1674), with music by Edward Purcell. Other attributions are to Barnabe Googe, Thomas Ford and Anon. Quiller-Couch's *Oxford Book of English Verse* (1919) opts for Anonymous, and prints it along with a reference to Thomas Ford's *Music of Sundry Kinds*, published in 1607. In this collection, the first stanza is as follows (Tietjens himself soon says 'perhaps he had not got [the words] quite right'):

> There is a lady sweet and kind,
> Was never face so pleased my mind;
> I did but see her passing by,
> And yet I love her till I die.

'Fair and kind' is a repeated description of Alcestis in Ford's translation of Euripides' play; see my Introduction.

It might be two hundred yards off along the trenches. Astonishing pleasure came to him from that seventeenth century air and the remembrance of those exact, quiet words.... Or perhaps he had not got them right. Nevertheless, they were exact and quiet. As efficient working beneath[3] the soul as the picks of miners in the dark.

The Sergeant returned with the obvious information that it was O9 Griffiths practising on the cornet. Captain McKechnie[4] ad promised to ear im after breakfast n recommend im to the Divisional Follies* to play at the concert to-night, if e likes im.[5]

Tietjens said:

"Well, I hope Captain McKechnie likes him!"

He hoped McKechnie, with his mad eyes and his pestilential accent, would like that fellow. That fellow spread seventeenth-century atmosphere across the landscape over which the sun's rays were beginning to flood a yellow wash. Then, might the seventeenth century save the fellow's life, for his good taste! For his life would probably be saved. He, Tietjens, would give him a pass back to Division to get ready for the concert. So he would be out of the *strafe*.... Probably none of them would be alive after the *strafe* that Brigade reported to be coming in.... Twenty-seven minutes, by now! Three hundred and twenty-eight fighting men against.... Say a Division. Any preposterous number....

Well, the seventeenth century might as well save one man!

What had become of the seventeenth century? And Herbert and Donne and Crashaw and Vaughan, the silurist?†... Sweet day so cool, so calm, so bright, the bridal of the earth and sky!‡

---

*   Entertainments for the troops, performed by other soldiers. Cf. Ford's story 'The Colonel's Shoes' (*War Prose* 168).

†   George Herbert (1593–1633), John Donne (1572–1631), Richard Crashaw (1612–49) and Henry Vaughan (1621/2–95) form part of the loose group of seventeenth-century poets later known as the 'metaphysical poets'. For more details as to individual poets and the characteristics of the group, who were never self-consciously a school, see, for example, Helen Gardner's anthology, *The Metaphysical Poets* (London: Penguin, 1985). Vaughan assumed the title 'the Silurist' due to the fact his native county (Brecknockshire) had once been inhabited by a tribe known as the Silures.

‡   The first two lines of George Herbert's poem, 'Vertue' The verse continues, 'The dew shall weep thy fall tonight; / For thou must die.' In a much earlier essay in *Outlook* (1914) Ford writes about an un-named 'Anglican friend' who very much liked Herbert's 'Vertue'; in this instance it is used as a symbol of the distance Ford feels from his friend's 'High Church' religion, and he talks himself into a position where he writes that he 'hates' it (*Critical Essays* 130–1).

... By Jove, it was that!... Old Campion, flashing like a popinjay in the scarlet and gilt of the Major-General, had quoted that in the base camp, years ago.* Or was it months? Or wasn't it: "But at my back I always hear Time's winged chariots hurrying near,"† that he had quoted?

Anyhow, not bad for an old General!

He wondered what had become of that elegant collection of light yellow, scarlet and gilt.... Somehow he always thought of Campion as in light yellow, rather than khaki, so much did he radiate light.... Campion and his, Tietjens',[6] wife, radiating light together—she in a golden gown!

Campion was about due in these latitudes. It was astonishing that he had not turned up before. But poor old Puffles with his abominably weakened Army had done too jolly well to be replaced. Even at the request of the Minister who hated him. Good for him!

It occurred to him that if he ... call it "stopped one" that day, Campion would probably marry his, Tietjens',[7] widow.... Sylvia in crêpe. With perhaps a little white about it!

The cornet—obviously it was not a key-bugle—remarked:

> : *her pass   by* ...
>   *ing*
>   *I did but view*

and then stopped to reflect. After a moment it added meditatively:

> . *her* ...
>   *And*   .   .
>   *now*   .   .
>   *I*   .   .
>   *love*   . *till*
>   *I die!*‡

---

* See the detail in that volume as to a deleted passage in *No More Parades* (III.ii).
† From Andrew Marvell's poem 'To his Coy Mistress' (ll. 21–2), though 'chariot' is singular here. Campion quotes it too in *No More Parades* (III.ii).
‡ These extracts are both reworkings of lines from the poem at the head of the chapter.

That would scarcely refer to[8] Sylvia. . . . Still, perhaps in crêpe, with a touch of white, passing by, very tall. . . . Say, in a seventeenth-century street. . . .

The only satisfactory age in England! . . . Yet what chance had it to-day? Or,[9] still more, to-morrow? In the sense that the age of, say, Shakespeare had a chance. Or Pericles! or Augustus! Heaven knew, we did not want a preposterous drum-beating such as the Elizabethans produced—and received. Like lions at a fair. . . . But what chance had quiet fields, Anglican sainthood, accuracy of thought, heavy-leaved, timbered hedgerows, slowly creeping plough-lands moving up the slopes? . . . Still, the land remains. . . .

The land remains. . . . It remains! . . .* At that same moment the dawn was wetly revealing; over there in George Herbert's parish. . . . What was it called? . . . What the devil was its name? Oh, Hell! . . . Between Salisbury and Wilton. . . . The tiny church. . . . But he refused to consider the plough-lands, the heavy groves, the slow highroad above the church that the dawn was at that moment wetly revealing—until he could remember that name. . . . He refused to consider that, probably even to-day, that land ran to . . . produced the stock of . . . Anglican sainthood.† The quiet thing!

But until he could remember the name he would consider nothing. . . .

He said:

"Are those damned Mills bombs coming?"

The Sergeant said:

"In ten minutes they'll be ere, sir." HAY Cumpny had just telephoned that they were coming in now.[10]

It was almost a disappointment: in an hour or so, without bombs,[11] they might all have been done with. As quiet as the seventeenth century: in heaven. . . . The beastly bombs would have to explode before that, now! They might, in consequence,

---

*   'The fields remain', writes Ford in an essay in 1924 praising the 'minute observers' Herbert, Herrick and Walton (*Critical Essays* 261). Also a possible allusion to Ecclesiastes 1:4: 'One generation passeth away, and another generation cometh: but the earth abideth forever.'

†   Such sainthood is a recurrent theme in *Some Do Not . . .*, particularly with reference to Tietjens' mother.

survive.... Then what was he, Tietjens, going to do! Take
orders![12]* It was thinkable....

He said:

"Those bloody imbeciles of Huns are coming over in an hour's
time, brigade says. Get the beastly bombs served out, but keep
enough in store to serve as an emergency ration if we should want
to advance.... Say a third. For C. and D. Companies....[13] Tell
the Adjutant I'm going along all the trenches and I want the
Assistant-Adjutant, Mr. Aranjuez, and Orderly-Corporal Colley
to come with me.... As soon as the bombs come for certain!...
I don't want the men to think they've got to stop a Hun rush
without bombs.... They're due to begin their barrage in fourteen
minutes, but they won't really come over without a hell of a lot
of preparation.... I don't know how brigade knows all this!"

The name *Bemerton* suddenly came on to his tongue. Yes,
Bemerton, Bemerton, Bemerton was George Herbert's
parsonage. Bemerton, outside Salisbury....† The cradle of the
race as far as our race was worth thinking about. He imagined
himself standing up on a little hill, a lean contemplative parson,
looking at the land sloping down to Salisbury spire. A large, clumsily bound seventeenth century testament, Greek, beneath his
elbow.... Imagine standing up on a hill! It was the unthinkable
thing there!

The Sergeant was lamenting, a little wearily, that the Huns
were coming.

"Hi did think them bleeding 'uns, 'xcuse me, sir, wasn' per'aps
coming this morning.... Giv us a rest an' a chance to clear up a
bit...." He had the tone of a resigned schoolboy saying that the
Head *might* have given the school a holiday on the Queen's
birthday. But what the devil did that man think about his
approaching dissolution?

That was the unanswerable question. He, Tietjens, had been

---

* A probable pun in the context on taking military, versus holy, orders.
† Herbert, who wrote no secular verse, took holy orders in 1626. This was an unusual
  step for a man of education and family (his stepfather was Sir John Danvers; he was
  educated at Westminster and Cambridge, becoming Public Orator from 1620–7).
  Gardner (*Metaphysical Poets* 313) writes that it was 'only with the death of his "Court
  hopes"' that he took Orders, and 'decided to lose himself in a humble way'. He was
  presented with the living of Bemerton, Wiltshire, in April 1630, but died less than
  three years later. On Salisbury, Bemerton and Herbert, cf. *No More Parades* III.ii.

asked several times what death was like.... Once, in a cattle truck under a bridge, near a Red-Cross Clearing Station, by a miserable fellow called Perowne. In the presence of the troublesome lunatic called McKechnie. You would have thought that even a Movement Order Officer would have managed to send up the line that triangle differently arranged. Perowne was known to have been his wife's lover; he, Tietjens, against his will, had been given the job, as second-in-command of the battalion, that McKechnie wanted madly. And indeed he had a right to it. They *ought* not to have been sent up together.[14]

But there they had been—Perowne broken down, principally at the thought that he was not[15] going to see his, Tietjens', wife ever again in a golden gown.... Unless, perhaps, with a golden harp on a cloud, for he looked at things like that.... And, positively, as soon as that baggage-car—it had been a baggage-car, not a cattle-truck!—had discharged the deserter with escort and the three wounded Cochin-Chinese* platelayers whom the French authorities had palmed off on them.... And where the devil had they all been going? Obviously up into the line, and already pretty near it: near Division Headquarters. But where?... God knew? Or when? God knew too!... A fine-ish day with a scanty remains of not quite melted snow in the cutting and the robins singing in the coppice above. Say February.... Say St. Valentine's Day: which, of course, would agitate Perowne some more.... Well, positively as soon as the baggage-car had discharged the wounded who had groaned, and the sheepish escort who did not know whether they ought to be civil to the deserter in the presence of the orfcers, and the deserter who kept on defiantly—or if you like brokenheartedly, for there was no telling the difference—asking the escort questions as to the nature of their girls, or volunteering information as to the intimate behaviour of *his*.... The deserter a gipsyfied, black-eyed fellow with an immense jeering mouth; the escort a Corporal and two Tommies, blond[16] and blushing East Kents, remarkably

---

* Cochin-China is the former name for the southern region of what is now Vietnam. Part of French Indo-China from 1862, it became a French overseas territory in 1946 before merging officially with Vietnam in 1949 – nearly twenty years after Ford was writing *A Man Could Stand Up –*. Cf. the similar description of a wartime bombardment in *No Enemy* 133.

polished about the buttons and brass numerals, with beautifully neatly put on puttees: obviously Regulars, coming from behind the lines: the Cochin-Chinese, with indistinguishable broad yellow faces, brown poetic eyes, furred top-boots and blue furred hoods over their bandaged heads and swathed faces. Seated, leaning back against the side of the box-truck and groaning now and then and shivering all the time. . . .

Well, the moment they had been cleared out at the Deputy Sub. R.T.O.'s* tin shed by the railway bridge, the fellow Perowne with his well-padded presence and his dark babu-Hindooish† aspect had bubbled out with questions as to the hereafter according to Tietjens and as to the nature of Death; the immediate process of dissolution: dying. . . . And in between Perowne's questions McKechnie, with his unspeakable intonation and his dark eyes as mad as a cat's, had asked Tietjens how he dared get himself appointed second-in-command of his, McKechnie's, own battalion. . . . "You're no soldier," he would burst out, "Do you think you are a b—y infantryman? You're a mealsack, and what the devil's to become of *my* battalion. . . . Mine. . . . My battalion! *Our* battalion of pals!"

That had been in, presumably, February, and, presumably, it was now April. The way the dawn came up looked like April. . . . What did it matter? . . . That damned truck had stayed under that bridge for two hours and a half . . . in the process of the eternal waiting that is War.‡ You hung about and you hung about, and you kicked your heels and you kicked your heels: waiting for Mills bombs to come, or for jam, or for generals, or for the tanks, or transport, or the clearance of the road ahead. You waited in offices under the eyes of somnolent orderlies, under fire on the banks of canals, you waited in hotels, dug-outs, tin sheds, ruined

---

* Most likely in this context is Railway Transport Officer.
† 'babu' is a Hindi word, borrowed into, but not 'naturalised' in, English. It is roughly equivalent to 'Mr' or 'Esquire' and is a term of respect. A more nuanced reading of the phrase is reached on examining the way in which it is also applied to Hindus who write and speak English (often in the context of the civil service) and it features in Kipling, for example, and Anthony Burgess more recently. See also Donald Davie's analysis of Ezra Pound's 'Homage to Sextus Propertius' in which he describes as 'babu English' Pound's deliberately pompous and polysyllabic English – used to suggest servants of the Empire (*Ezra Pound* [New York, 1975]).
‡ In *No Enemy* Ford employs a similar phrase: it is the 'eternal "waiting to report" that takes up 112/113ths of one's time during war' (33).

houses. There will be no man who survives of His Majesty's Armed Forces that shall not remember those eternal hours when Time itself stayed still as the true image of bloody War! . . .

Well, in that case Providence seemed to have decreed a waiting just long enough to allow Tietjens to[17] persuade the unhappy mortal called Perowne that death was not a very dreadful affair. . . . He had enough intellectual authority to persuade the fellow with his glued-down black hair that Death supplied His own anaesthetics. That was the argument. On the approach of Death all the faculties are so numbed that you feel neither pain nor apprehension. . . . He could still hear the heavy, authoritative words that, on that occasion, he had used.[18]

The Providence of Perowne! For, when he was dug out after, next night having been buried in going up into the trenches, they said, he had a smile like a young baby's on his face. He didn't have long to wait and died with a smile on his face . . . nothing having so much become him during the life as . . .* Well, a becoming smile! During life he had seemed a worried, fussing sort of chap.

Bully for Perowne. . . . But what about him, Tietjens? Was that the sort of thing that Providence ought to do to one? . . . That's TEMPTING GOD!

The Sergeant beside him said:

"Then a man could stand hup on an ill. . . . You really mean to say, sir, that you think a man will be able to stand up on a bleedin' ill. . . ."

Presumably Tietjens had been putting heart into that acting temporary Sergeant-Major. He could not remember what he had been saying to the N.C.O. because his mind had been so deeply occupied with the image[19] of Perowne. . . . He said:

"You're a Lincolnshire man, aren't you? You come from a Fen country. What do you want to stand up on a hill for?"

The man said:

"Ah, but you do, sir!"

He added:

"You want to stand up! Take a look around. . . ." He struggled

---

* Malcolm's famous speech from Act I of *Macbeth* relates to the death of the Thane of Cawdor – whose title will now pass to Macbeth: 'Nothing in his life / Became him like the leaving it. He died / As one that had been studied in his death / To throw away the dearest thing he owed / As 'twere a careless trifle' (iv.7–11).

for expression: "Like as if you wanted to breathe deep after bein in a stoopin posture for a long time!"

Tietjens said:

"Well, you can do that here. With discretion. I did it just now...."

The man said:

"You, sir.... You're a law hunto yourself!"

It was the most considerable shock that Tietjens received in the course of his military career. And the most considerable reward.

There were all these inscrutable beings: the Other Ranks, a brownish mass, spreading underground, like clay strata in the gravel, beneath all this waving country that the sun would soon be warming: they were in holes, in tunnels, behind sackcloth curtains, carrying on ... carrying on some sort of life: conversing, breathing, desiring. But completely mysterious, in the mass. Now and then you got a glimpse of a passionate desire: "A man could stand up on a bleedin' ill!"; now and then you got—though you knew that they watched you eternally and knew the minutest gestures of your sleep—you got some sort of indication as to how they regarded you: "You are a law unto yourself!"

That must be hero-worship: an acting temporary regimental Sergeant-Major, without any real knowledge of his job, extemporising, not so long ago a carrier in an eastern county of remarkable flatness, does not tell his Acting[20] Commanding Officer that he is a law unto himself without meaning it to be a flattering testimony: a certificate, as far as it went, of trustworthiness....

They were now crawling out into the light of day; ... from behind the sacking: six files that he had last night transferred from C to D Coy., D having been reduced to forty-three rank and file. They shuffled out, an extraordinary Falstaff's battalion* of muddy[21] odd-come shorts; fell into some sort of alignment in the trench; shuffled an inch further this way, an inch further that; pushed up their chin-straps and pulled them down; humped up their packs by hunching their shoulders and jerking; adjusted

---

* A reference to Sir John Falstaff, Henry, Prince of Wales' 'boon companion' in Shakespeare's *Henry IV* Part I. In III.iii, for example, set in the Boar's Head, Falstaff 'marches' to meet Hal on his arrival.

their water bottles and fell into some sort of immobility, their rifles, more or less aligned, poked out before them. In that small company they were men[22] of all sorts of sizes, of all sorts of disparities and grotesquenesses of physique. Two of them were music-hall comedians and the whole lot looked as if they made up a knock-about turn.... The Rag Time Army: at its vocation: living and breathing.*

The Sergeant called them to attention and they wavered back and forward. The Sergeant said:

"The Commandin' Officer's lookin' at you. FIX ... B'ts!"

And, positively, a dwarf concealed under a pudding basin shuffled a foot length and a half forward in the mud, protruded his rifle-muzzle between his bent knees, jerked his head swiftly to strain his sight along the minute line.... It was like a blurred fairy-tale! Why did that dwarf behave in a smart and soldierly manner? Through despair? It wasn't likely!

The men wavered like the edge of a field of tall grass with the wind running along it; they felt round themselves for their bayonet-handles, like women attempting difficult feats with their skirts.... The dwarf cut his hand smartly away to his side, as the saying is;† the men pulled their rifles up into line. Tietjens exclaimed:

"Stand at ease: stand easy," negligently enough, then he burst out in uncontrollable irritation: "For God's sake, put your beastly hats straight!" The men shuffled uneasily, this being no order

---

* One version of a popular trench song went as follows: 'We are Fred Karno's Army / The ragtime infantry. / We cannot fight / We cannot shoot / What bleeding use are we? / And when we get to Berlin / We'll hear the Kaiser say / "Hoch, hoch! Mein Gott / What a fucking rotton lot / Are the ragtime infantry".' 'Ragtime' was originally (from about 1901) an American musical term, referring to tunes with frequent syncopation. By 1917 it was employed regularly in trench songs, indicating shambolic disorganisation; for more examples, including 'The Ragtime Navy', see F. T. Nettleingham's *Tommy's Tunes* (1917). Fred Karno (1866–1941) was a well-known music-hall impresario with a London base, the 'fun factory' in Camberwell. Ford apparently lost to him at poker on board the *Minnetonka* in 1906, referring to him as an 'amazing impresario' in his story about it (*Nightingale* 125–6). Karno's acts (comedians including Charlie Chaplin and Stan Laurel) were together known as 'Fred Karno's Army'. The song detailed above is sometimes recorded with the first line 'We are Kitchener's Army', and there are numerous other variants too.

† Ford's 'saying' relates to a military movement, a particular kind of salute. The *Infantry Drill* (1914) gives details, and the Training Notes for the (Australian) Light Horse Association are as follows (Section 100): 'Step One: "Bring the right hand smartly, with a circular motion to the head, palm to the front, fingers extended and close together [...]"; Step Two: "Cut away the arm smartly to the side by the shortest way".'

known to them, and Tietjens explained: "No, this isn't drill. It's only that your hats all at sixes and sevens give me the pip!"* And the whispers of the men went down the little line:

"You 'eer the orfcer.... Gives 'im the pip, we do!... Goin' for a wawk in the pawk wiv our gels, we are...." They glanced nevertheless aside and upwards at each other's tin-hat rims and said: "Shove 'im a shade forward, 'Orace.... You tighten your martingale, Erb!" They were gaily rueful and impenitently profane: they had had thirty-six hours of let-off. A fellow louder-than-hummed:

"As²³ I wawk erlong ther Bor dee Berlong
Wiv an indipendent air....
W'ere's me swegger-kine, you fellers!"†

Tietjens addressed him:

"Did you ever hear Coborn sing that, Runt?"‡ and Runt replied:

"Yes, sir. I was the hind legs of the elephant when he sung it in the Old Drury panto!"§ ... A little, dark, beady-eyed Cockney, his enormous mouth moved lip on lip as if he were chewing a pebble in pride at the reminiscence. The men's voices went on: "'Ind legs 'f the elephink!... good ol' Helefink.... I'll go n see 'n elephink first thing I do in Blighty!"

Tietjens said:

"I'll give every man of you a ticket for Drury Lane next Boxing Day. We'll all be in London for the next Boxing Day. Or Berlin!"

They exclaimed polyphonically and low:

---

* According to Brewer's *Dictionary of Phrase and Fable*, 'to have' or 'to get the pip' is to be thoroughly fed up, downhearted and miserable. It suggests a probable connection with the poultry disease, 'pip', which causes fowls to pine away. In *The Good Soldier*, Ashburnham would have been 'pipped' a 'good deal' Dowell tells us, in finding all the money necessary to have one of his affairs (44).

† A phonetic cockney reworking of the first line of a music-hall song, 'As I walk along the Bois de Boulogne with an independent air...' The song's title is 'The Man Who Broke the Bank at Monte Carlo' and it was offered to the singer Charles Coborn (see below) in 1891 by its writer Fred Gilbert. The 'swegger-kine' (or 'swagger cane', also featured here, in mock patrician accent) was an item of commissioned rank equipment introduced at the time of Charles I for punishing minor offences; by 1914 they were purely decorative.

‡ Charles Coborn's real name was Charles Whitton McCallum (1852–1945). The song that Ford refers to here transformed Coborn's stage act and he used it for many years, recording it several times up to the 1920s.

§ This is another name for the Middlesex, a music hall established in 1851 in Drury Lane. There is likely to be a link between Charles Coborn and the 'Old Mo', as it was also known, given his career in London at the time.

"Oo-er! Djee 'eer 'im? Di'djee 'eer the orfcer? The noo C.O.?"
A hidden man said:
"Mike it the old Shoreditch Empire,* sir, n we'll thenk you!"
Another:
"I never keered fer the Lane meself! Give me the old Balham†
for Boxing Day." The Sergeant made the sounds for them to move
off.

They shuffled off up the trench. An unseen man said:
"Better'n a bleedin' dipso!" Lips said "S.h.h.h!"

The Sergeant shouted—with an astonishing brutal panic:
"You shut your bleedin' mouth, you man, or I'll shove you in
the b—y clink!" He looked nevertheless at Tietjens with calm
satisfaction a second later.

"A good lot of chaps, sir," he said. "The best!" He was anxious
to wipe out the remembrance of the last spoken word.[24] "Give 'em
the right sort of officers n they'll beat the world!"

"Do you think it makes any difference to them what officers
they have?" Tietjens asked. "Wouldn't it be all the same if they
had just anyone?"

The Sergeant said:
"No, sir. They bin frightened these last few days. Now they're
better."

This was just exactly what Tietjens did not want to hear. He
hardly knew why. Or he did. . . . He said:
"I should have thought these men knew their job so well—for
this sort of thing—that they hardly needed orders. It cannot
make much difference whether they receive orders or not."

The Sergeant said:
"It *does* make a difference, sir," in a tone as near that of cold
obstinacy as he dare attain to; the feeling of the approaching
strafe was growing on them. It hung over them.

---

* The Shoreditch Empire opened in 1856. By 1894 it had been enlarged to a capacity
of about 2,300. In 1895 it was given the name of the London Theatre of Varieties (a
name that hasn't taken on among Ford's soldiers) and was later known as the Griffin
Music Hall and the London Music Hall. It was demolished in 1935.

† The Empire Theatre Balham originally opened as a music hall in 1907. It was the first
theatre in London to be converted into a full-time cinema and in 1909 it became
known as the Theatre de Luxe. By 1915 it had been renamed the Olympia, and again
as the Pavilion in 1920. Perhaps Ford's character in this instance decides he'd rather
see a film on Boxing Day.

McKechnie stuck his head out from behind the sacking. The sacking had the lettering P X L* in red and the word Minn† in black. McKechnie's eyes were blazing maniacally. Jumping maniacally in his head. They always were jumping maniacally in his head. He was a tiring fellow. He was wearing not a tin hat, but an officer's helmet. The gilt dragon on it glittered. The sun was practically up, somewhere. As soon as its disc cleared the horizon, the Huns, according to Brigade, were to begin sending over their wearisome stuff. In thirteen and a half minutes.

McKechnie gripped Tietjens by the arm, a familiarity that Tietjens detested. He hissed—he really hissed because he was trying to speak under his breath:

"Come past the next traverse. I want to speak to you."

In correctly prepared trenches, made according to order as these had been to receive them in retreat, by a regular battalion acting under the orders of the Royal Engineers, you go along a straight ditch of trench for some yards, then you find a square block of earth protruding inwards from the parapet round which you must walk; then you come to another straight piece, then to another traverse, and so on to the end of the line, the lengths and dimensions varying to suit the nature of the terrain or the character of the soil. These outjuttings were designed to prevent the lateral spreading of fragments of shell bursting in the trench which would otherwise serve as a funnel, like the barrel of a gun to direct those parts of missiles into men's bodies. It was also exciting—as Tietjens expected to be doing before the setting of the not quite risen sun—to crouch rapidly along past one of them, the heart moving very disagreeably, the revolver protruded well in advance, with half a dozen careless fellows with grenades of sorts just behind you. And you not knowing whether, crouching against the side that was just round the corner, you would or would not find a whitish, pallid, dangerous object that you would have no time to scrutinise closely.

Past the nearest of these McKechnie led Tietjens. He was portentous and agitated.

At the end of the next stretch of trench, leaning as it were

---

* PX was an American military abbreviation for 'Post Exchange'. 'L' is less clear, though a guess might be hazarded, as to 'large', for example.
† 'Minn' was the old-style abbreviation for the state of Minnesota (now MN).

against a buttress in an attitude of intense fatigue was a mud-coloured, very thin, tall fellow; squatting dozing on his heels in the mud just beside that one's foot was another, a proper Glamorganshire man of whom not many more than ten were left in the battalion. The standing man was leaning like that to look through a loophole that had been placed very close to the buttress of raw earth. He grunted something to his companion and continued looking intently. The other man grunted too.

McKechnie withdrew precipitately into the recessed pathway. The column of earth in their faces gave a sense of oppression. He said:

"Did you put that fellow up to saying that damnable thing?...."

He repeated: "That perfectly damnable thing! Damnable!" Besides hating Tietjens he was shocked, pained, femininely lachrymose. He gazed into Tietjens' eyes like a forsaken mistress fit to do a murder, with a sort of wistful incredulity of despair.

To that Tietjens was accustomed. For the last two months McKechnie whispering in the ear of the C.O. wherever Battalion Headquarters might happen to be—McKechnie,[25] with his arms spread abroad on the table and his chin nearly on the cloth that they had always managed to retain in spite of three precipitate moves, McKechnie, with his mad eyes every now and then moving in the direction of Tietjens, had been almost the most familiar object of Tietjens' night landscapes. They wanted him gone so that McKechnie might once again become Second in Command of that body of pals.... That indeed was what they were ... with the addition of a great deal too much of what they called Ooch.*

Tietjens obviously could not go. There was no way of managing it: he had been put there by old Campion and there he

---

* Or 'hooch', American slang for alcohol since the turn of the twentieth century, widely used by soldiers. Niall Ferguson states that 'without alcohol, the First World War could not have been fought'. He quotes a medical officer emphasising the job the rum ration did in enabling men to sleep in otherwise impossible circumstances. When men weren't in the front line, Ferguson continues, 'ordinary soldiers would get drunk at every opportunity', and morale fell catastrophically when alcohol wasn't available (*The Pity of War* [Harmondsworth: Penguin, 1998], 351). In Stanley Weintraub's *A Stillness Heard Round the World: The End of the Great War: November 1918* (New York: Oxford University Press, 1987), he writes of how a rum ration would be issued when brigade commanders certified that the weather was inclement; this had the effect of ensuring that '[o]fficially it rained every day in 1918' (69).

must remain. So that by the agreeable irony of Providence there was Tietjens, who had[26] wanted above all McKechnie's present[27] relatively bucolic job, hated to hell by half a dozen quite decent if trying young squits—the pals—because Tietjens was in his, McKechnie's, desired position. It seemed to make it all the worse that they were all, with the exception of the Commanding Officer himself, of the little, dark, Cockney type and had the Cockney's voice, gesture and intonation, so that Tietjens felt himself like a blond Gulliver with hair very silver in patches, rising up amongst a lot of Lilliputian brown creatures. . . . Portentous and unreasonably noticeable.

A large cannon, nearer than the one that had lately spoken, but as it were with a larger but softer voice, remarked: "Phoh.h.h.h.h.h.h.h.," the sound wandering round the landscape for a long while. After a time about four coupled railway-trains hurtled jovially amongst the clouds and went a long way away.—Four in one. They were probably trying to impress the North Sea.

It might of course be the signal for the German barrage to begin. Tietjens' heart stopped; his skin on the nape of the neck began to prickle: his hands were cold. That was fear:[28] the BATTLE FEAR, experienced in *strafes*. He might not again be able to hear himself think. Not ever. What did he want of life? . . . Well, just not to lose his reason. One would pray:* Not that. . . . Otherwise, perhaps a nice parsonage might do. It was just thinkable. A place in which for ever to work at the theory of waves. . . . But of course it was not thinkable. . . .

He was saying to McKechnie:

"You ought not to be here without a tin hat. You will have to put a tin hat on if you mean to stop here. I can give you[29] four minutes if that is not the *strafe* beginning. Who's been saying what?"

McKechnie said:

"I'm not stopping here. I'm going back, after I've given you a piece of my mind, to the beastly job you have got me defiled with."

Tietjens said:

* As Ford himself did; see the Introduction here.

"Well, you'll put on a tin hat to go there, please. And don't ride your horse, if you've got it here, till after you're a hundred yards at least down a communication trench."

McKechnie asked how Tietjens dared give him orders and Tietjens said: Fine he would look with Divisional Transport dead in his lines at five in the morning in a parade hat. McKechnie with objurgations said that the Transport Officer had the right to consult the C.O. of a battalion he supplied. Tietjens said:

"I'm commanding here. You've not consulted me!"

It appeared to him queer that they should be behaving like that when you could hear ... oh, say: the wings of the angel of death.... You can "almost hear the very rustling of his wings" was the quotation.* Good enough rhetoric.... But of course that was how armed men would behave.... At all times!

He had been trying the old trick of the military, clipped voice on the half-dotty subject. It had before then reduced McKechnie to some sort of military behaviour.

It reduced him in this case to a maudlin state. He exclaimed with a sort of lachrymose agony:

"This is what it has come to with the old battalion ... the b—y, b—y, b—y old battalion of b—rs!"[30] Each imprecation was a sob. "How we worked at it.... And now ... you've got it!"

Tietjens said:

"Well, you were Vice-Chancellor's Latin Prize-man once. It's what we get reduced to." He added: "*Vos mellificatis apes!*"†

McKechnie said with gloomy contempt:

"You.... You're no Latinist!"

By now Tietjens had counted two hundred and eighty since the big cannon had said "Pho.o.o.o.h." Perhaps then it was not the signal for the barrage to begin.... Had it been it would have begun before now; it would have come thumping along on the

---

*   A (near) quotation from John Bright (1811–89), English Liberal politician and reformer: 'The angel of death has been abroad throughout the land; you may almost hear the beating of his wings', as Hansard has it. Bright was talking on 23 February 1855 about the effects of war in the Crimea (*Oxford Dictionary of Quotations*)

†   An extract from a longer line of Virgil's: 'Sic vos non vobis Mellificatis apes', translated as 'Thus [or so] do you bees make honey, not for yourselves'. The shorter form Ford uses translates as 'you bees make honey'. The lines are only attributed to Virgil, and the *Oxford Dictionary of Quotations* writes that they were in response to Bathyllus claiming authorship of certain other lines by the poet.

heels of the "Pho.o.o.h." His hands and the nape of his neck were preparing to become normal.

Perhaps the *strafe* would not come at all that day. There was the wind. If anything it was strengthening. Yesterday he had suspected that the Germans hadn't got any tanks handy. Perhaps the ugly, senseless armadillos*—and incapable at that! Under-engined!—had all got stuck in the marshes in front of G section. Perhaps the heavy artillery fire of ours that had gone on most of yesterday had been meant to pound the beastly things to pieces. Moving, they looked like slow rats, their noses to the ground, snouting crumbs of garbage. When they were still they looked merely pensive.

Perhaps the *strafe* would not come. He hoped it would not. He did not want a *strafe* with himself in command of the battalion. He did not know what to do: what he ought to do by the book. He knew what he would do. He would stroll about along those deep trenches. Stroll. With his hands in his pockets. Like General Gordon in pictures.† He would say contemplative things as the time dragged on.... A rather abominable sort of Time really.... But that would introduce into the Battalion a spirit of calm that it had lately lacked ... The night before last the C.O., with a bottle in each hand had hurled them both at Huns who did not materialise for an hour and a half. Even the Pals had omitted to laugh. After that he, Tietjens, had taken command. With lots of the Orderly Room papers under both arms. They had had to be in a hurry. At night. With men suggesting pale grey Canadian trappers coming out of holes!

He did not want to command in a *strafe*: or at any other time! He hoped the unfortunate C.O. would get over his trouble by the evening.... But he supposed that he, Tietjens, would get through it all right if he had to. Like the man who had never tried playing the violin!

---

* On the subject of tanks see, for example, Trudi Tate's article 'The Culture of the Tank 1916–18', *Modernism/modernity*, 4.1 (January 1997), 69–87. Also Patrick White, *Tank* (2002).

† Major General Charles George Gordon (1833–85) was an army officer and adminis-trator, renowned in Victorian times for his campaigns in China and Africa. His reputation was for great bravery and composure at times of crisis. One famous portrait of him (*General Gordon's Last Stand* by George William Joy, 1885, Leeds Art Gallery) shows him standing at the top of a flight of steps surrounded by those about to murder him. He looks composed, though his hands are not in his pockets.

McKechnie had suddenly become lachrymosely feminine: like a woman pleading, large-eyed, for her lover, his eyes explored Tietjens' face for signs of treachery: for signs that what he said was not what he meant in his heart. He said:

"What are you going to do about Bill? Poor old Bill that has sweated for his Battalion as you never...." He began again:

"Think of poor old Bill! You can't be *thinking* of doing the dirty on him.... *No* man could be such a swine!"

It was curious how those circumstances brought out the feminine that was in man. What was that ass of a German Professor's theory ... formula? M^y *plus* W^x equals Man?...* Well, if God hadn't invented woman men would have had to do so. In that sort of place. You grew sentimental. He, Tietjens was growing sentimental. He said:

"What does Terence say about him this morning?"

The nice thing to have said would have been:

"Of course, old man, I'll do all I can to keep it dark!" Terence was the M.O.—the man who had chucked his cap at the Hun orderly.

McKechnie said:

"That's the damnable thing! Terence is ratty with him. He won't take a pill!"

Tietjens said:

"What's that? What's that?"

McKechnie wavered: his desire for comfort became overpowering.

He said:

"Look here! *Do* the decent thing! You know how poor Bill has worked for us! Get Terence not to report him to Brigade!"

This was wearisome: but it had to be faced.

A very minute subaltern—Aranjuez—in a perfectly impossible tin hat peered round the side of the bank. Tietjens sent him away for a moment.... These tin hats were probably all right: but they were the curse of the army. They bred distrust! How could you trust a man whose incapable hat tumbled forward on his nose? Or

---

* Ford read Otto Weininger's populist *Geschlecht und Charakter* (1903) (*Sex and Character* [New York: AMS Press, 1975]), in which the writer suggested that the sexes are not, in fact, polar opposites, but are rather like 'two substances combined in different proportions' (8). Ford mentions the work disparagingly in *Women and Men* (1923).

another, with his hat on the back of his head, giving him the air of a ruined gambler! Or a fellow who had put on a soap-dish. To amuse the children: not a serious proceeding.... The German things were better—coming down over the nape of the neck and rising over the brows. When you saw a Hun sideways he looked something: a serious proposition. Full of ferocity. A Hun against a Tommie looked like a Holbein *lansknecht* fighting a music-hall turn.* It made you feel that you were indeed a rag-time army. Rubbed it in!

McKechnie was reporting that the C.O. had refused to take a pill ordered him by the M.O. Unfortunately the M.O. was ratty that morning—too much hooch overnight! So he said he should report the C.O. to Brigade. Not as being unfit for further service, for he wasn't. But for refusing to take the pill. It was damnable. Because if Bill wouldn't take a pill he wouldn't... The M.O. said that if he took a pill, and stayed in bed that day—without hooch of course!—he would be perfectly fit on the morrow. He had been like that often enough before. The C.O. had always been given the dose before as a drench. He swore he would not take it as a ball. Sheer contrariety!

Tietjens was accustomed to think of the C.O. as a lad—a good lad, but young. They were, all the same, much of an age, and, for the matter of that, because of his deeply-lined forehead the Colonel looked the older often enough. But when he was fit he was fine. He had a hooked nose, a forcible, grey moustache, like two badger-haired paintbrushes joined beneath the nose, pink skin as polished as the surface of a billiard ball, a noticeably narrow but high forehead, an extremely piercing glance from rather colourless eyes; his hair was black and most polished in slight waves. He was the[31] soldier.

He was, that is to say, the ranker. Of soldiering in the English sense—the real soldiering of peace-time, parades, social events,

---

* 'Lansknecht' or 'landsknecht' were European, most often German, mercenary pikesmen and foot soldiers from the late fifteenth century to the early seventeenth century. They had a formidable reputation as effective fighting troops during the Euro- pean renaissance, and were known in addition for their outlandish dress, characterised by 'puff and slash' decoration. Aspects of the dress caught on after Henry VIII employed some of these soldiers, and in the famous Holbein portrait of the monarch (1537) he is wearing a doublet decorated in this way. In Ford's book about Holbein (1905) he includes a plate of this portrait, and another work, 'The Fighting Lanzknechts'.

spit and polish, hard worked summers, leisurely winters, India, the Bahamas, Cairo seasons and the rest he only knew the outside, having looked at it from the barrack windows, the parade ground and, luckily for him, from his Colonel's house. He had been a most admirable batman to that Colonel, had—in Simla— married the Colonel[32] memsahib's lady's maid, had been promoted to the orderly-room, to the Corporals' and Sergeants'[33] messes, had become a Musketry-Colour Sergeant and, two months before the war had been given a commission. He would have gained this before but for a slight—a very slight—tendency to overdrinking, which had given on occasion a similarly slight tone of insolence to his answers to Field-Officers. Elderly Field-Officers on parade are apt to make slight mistakes in their drill, giving the command to move to the right when technically, though troops are moving to the right, the command should be: "Move to the left!"; and the officer's left being the troops' right, on a field-day, after lunch, Field-Officers of a little rustiness are apt to grow confused. It then becomes the duty of warrant-officers present if possible to rectify, or if not, to accept the responsibility for the resultant commotion. On two occasions during his brilliant career, being slightly elated, this war-time C.O. had neglected this military duty, the result being subsequent Orderly Room *Strafes* which remained as black patches when he looked back on his past life and which constantly embittered his remembrances. Professional soldiers are like that.

In spite of an exceptionally fine service record he remained bitter, and upon occasion he became unreasonable. Being what the men—and for the matter of that the officers of the battalion, too—called a b—y h-ll of a pusher, he had brought his battalion up to a great state of efficiency; he had earned a double string of ribbons and by pushing his battalion into extremely tight places, by volunteering it for difficult services which, even during trench warfare did present themselves, and by extricating what remained of it with singular skill during the first battle of the Somme on an occasion—perhaps the most lamentable of the whole war—when an entire division commanded by a political rather than a military general had been wiped out, he had earned for his battalion a French decoration called a *Fourragère** which is seldom given to

* A military award recognising military units as a whole rather than individuals.

other than French regiments. These exploits and the spirit which dictated them were perhaps less appreciated by the men under his command than was imagined by the C.O. and his bosom friend Captain McKechnie who had loyally aided him, but they *did* justify the two in attaching to the battalion the sort of almost maudlin sentimentality that certain parents will bestow upon their children.

In spite, however, of the appreciation that his services had received the C.O. remained embittered. He considered that, by this time, he ought at least to³⁴ have been given a brigade, if not a division, and he considered that, if that was not the case, it was largely due to the two black marks against him as well as to the fact of his low social origin. And when he had a little liquor taken these obsessions exaggerated themselves very quickly to a degree that very nearly endangered his career. It was not that he soaked—but there were occasions during that period of warfare when the consumption of a certain amount of alcohol was a necessity if the human being were to keep on carrying on and through rough places. Then, happy was the man who carried his liquor well.

Unfortunately the C.O. was not one of these. Worn out by continual attention to papers—at which he was no great hand—and by fighting that would continue for days on end, he would fortify himself with whiskey and immediately his bitterness would overwhelm his mentality, the aspect of the world would change and he would rail at his superiors in the army and sometimes would completely refuse to obey orders, as had been the occasion a few nights before, when he had refused to let his battalion take part in the concerted retreat of the Army Corps. Tietjens had had to see to this.

Now, exasperated by the after effects of several days' great anxieties and alcoholisms he was refusing to take a pill. This was a token of his contempt for his superiors, the outcome of his obsession of bitterness.

CHAPTER III[1]

AN army—especially in peace time!—is a very complex and nicely adjusted affair, and though active operations against an enemy force are apt to blunt nicenesses and upset[2] compensations—as they might for a chronometer!*—and although this of ours, according to its own computation was only a rag-time aggregation, certain customs[3] of times when this force was also Regular had an enormous power of survival.

It may seem a comic affair that a Colonel[4] commanding a regiment in the midst of the most breathless period of hostilities, should refuse to take a pill. But the refusal, precisely like a grain of sand in the works of a chronometer, may cause the most singular perturbations. It was so in this case.

A sick officer of the very highest rank is the subordinate of his doctor the moment he puts himself into the M.O.'s hands: he must obey orders as if he were a Tommy. A Colonel whole and in his senses may obviously order his M.O. to go here and there and to perform this or that duty; the moment he becomes sick the fact that his body is the property of His Majesty the King, comes forcibly into operation and the M.O. is the representative of the sovereign in so far as bodies are concerned. This is very reasonable and proper, because sick bodies are not only of no use to the King, but are enormously detrimental to the army that has to cart them about.

In the case that Tietjens had perforce to worry over, the matter was very much complicated in the first place by the fact of the great personal dislike that the C.O. had manifested—though always with a sort of Field-Officer's monumental courtesy[5]—towards himself, and then because Tietjens had a very great respect for the abilities of the Commanding Officer as Commanding Officer. His rag-time battalion of a rag-time army

---

* A compensation in a chronometer (a highly accurate clock originally used only on ships) is a device to counter the side-effects of factors such as heat and cold on the timekeeping of the watch.

was as nearly on the level of an impeccable regular battalion as
such a unit with its constantly changing personnel could possibly
be. Nothing had much more impressed Tietjens in the course of
even the whole war, than the demeanour of the soldier whom the
other night he had seen firing engrossedly into invisibility. The
man had fired with care, had come down to re-load with exact
drill movements—which are the quickest possible. He had
muttered some words which showed that his[6] mind was entirely
on his job like a mathematician engrossed in an abstruse calculation. He had climbed back on to the parapet; continued to fire
engrossedly into invisibility; had returned and re-loaded and had
again climbed back. He might have been firing off a tie at the
butts!*

It[7] was a very great achievement to have got men to fire at
moments of such stress with such complete tranquillity. For discipline works in two ways: In the first place it enables the soldier
in action to get through his movements in the shortest possible
time; and then the engrossment in the exact performance begets
a great indifference to danger. When, with various sized pieces of
metal flying all round you, you go composedly through efficient
bodily movements, you are not only wrapped up in your task, but
you have the knowledge that that exact performance is every
minute decreasing your personal danger.† In addition you have
the feeling that Providence ought to[8]—and very frequently
does—specially protect you.‡ It would not be right that a man
exactly and scrupulously performing his duty to his sovereign, his
native land and those it holds dear, should not be protected by a
special Providence. And he is!

It is not only that that engrossed marksman might—and very
probably did—pick off an advancing enemy with every second

---

* To 'fire off a tie' is to have a re-match.
† Cf. 'Stocktaking', 'I', *transatlantic review*, 1.1 (January 1924), 75–6:

> During the late war, for instance, the aggressive and Intellectual classes used to ask
> unceasingly what purpose was served in 'trench' warfare by jumping to it on parade
> at home. The effect is psychological [. . .].
>
> And the effect of imaginative culture on the natural mind engaged in human
> affairs is much that of drill on troops afterwards to be engaged in warfare. It affords
> and inspires confidence; it furnishes you with illustration in argument, knowledge
> of human nature, vicarious experience.

‡ Ford's story 'The Miracle', *Yale Review*, 18 (winter 1928), 320–31, exemplifies this
view.

shot, and thus diminish his personal danger to that extent, it is that the regular and as if mechanical falling of comrades spreads disproportionate dismay in advancing or halted troops. It is no doubt terrible to you to have large numbers of your comrades instantaneously annihilated by the explosion of some huge engine, but huge engines are blind and thus accidental; a slow, regular picking off of the man beside you is evidence that human terribleness that is not blind or accidental is cold-bloodedly and unshakably[9] turning its attention to a spot very near you. It[10] may very shortly turn its attention to yourself.

Of course, it is disagreeable when artillery is bracketting across your line: a shell falls a hundred yards in front of you, another a hundred yards behind you: the next will be half-way between, and you are half-way between. The waiting wrings your soul; but it does not induce panic or the desire to run—at any rate to nearly the same extent. Where, in any event, could you run to?

But from coldly and mechanically advancing and firing troops you *can* run. And the C.O. was accustomed to boast that on the several occasions when imitating the second battalion of the regiment he had been able to line[11] his men up on tapes before letting them go in an attack and had insisted that they should advance at a very slow double indeed, and in exact alignment, his losses had been not only less than those of every other battalion in the Division, but they had been almost farcically negligible. Faced with troops advancing remorselessly and with complete equanimity the good Wurtembergers had fired so wildly and so high that you could hear their bullets overhead like a flock of wild-geese at night. The effect of panic is to make men fire high. They pull too sharply on their triggers.[12]

These boasts of their Old Man naturally reached the men: they would be uttered before warrant officers and the orderly room staff; and the men—than whom in this matter none are keener mathematicians—were quick to see that the losses of their battalion until lately, at any rate, had been remarkably[13] smaller than those of other units engaged in the same places. So that hitherto, though the men had regarded their Colonel with mixed feelings, he had certainly come out on top. That he was a b—y h-ll of a pusher did not elate them; they would have preferred to be reserved for less dangerous enterprises than those by which the battalion gained its remarkable prestige. On the other hand, though they were constantly being pushed into nasty scrapes, they lost less than units in quieter positions, and that pleased them. But they still asked themselves: "If the Old Man let us be quiet shouldn't we lose proportionately still less? No one at all?"[14]

That had been the position until very lately: until a week or so, or even a day or so before.

But for more than a fortnight this Army had been what amounted to on the run. It retreated with some personal[15] stubbornness and upon prepared positions, but these prepared positions were taken with such[16] great speed and method by the enormous forces attacking it, that hostilities had assumed the aspect almost of a war of movement. For this these troops were singularly ill-adapted, their training having been almost purely that suited for the process of attrition known as trench-warfare. In fact, though good with bombs and even with the bayonet, and though courageous and composed when not in motion, these troops were singularly inept when it was a matter of keeping in communication with the units on either side of them, or even within their own unit and they had practically no experience in the use of the rifle when in motion. To both these branches the Enemy had devoted untiring attention all through the period of relative inaction of the winter that had now closed and in both particulars their troops though by now apparently inferior in moral[17] were remarkably superior. So it appeared to be merely a matter of waiting for a period of easterly winds for this Army to be pushed into the North Sea. The easterly winds were needed for the use of the gas without which, in the idea of the German leaders, it was impossible to attack.[18]

The position, nevertheless,[19] had been desperate and remained desperate, and standing there in the complete tranquillity and inaction of an April morning with a slight westerly breeze, Tietjens[20] realised that he was experiencing what were the emotions of an army practically in flight. So at least he saw it. The use of Gas had always been extremely disliked by the enemy's men, and its employment in cylinders had long since been abandoned. But the German Higher Staff persisted in preparing their attacks by dense screens of gas put over by huge plasterings of shells. These screens the enemy forces refused to enter if the wind blew in their direction.[21]

There had come in, then, the factor which caused him himself to feel particular discomfort.

The fact that the battalion was remarkably ably commanded and unusually well-disciplined had not, of course, been overlooked by either brigade or division. And the brigade, too, happened to be admirable. Thus—these things did happen even in the confused periods that preceded the final breaking up of trench warfare—the brigade was selected to occupy positions where the enemy divisions might be expected to be hottest in attack, the battalion was selected to occupy the hottest points in that hottest sector of the line. The chickens of the C.O.'s efficiency had come home to roost.

It had been, as Tietjens felt all over his body, nearly more than flesh and blood could stand. Do what the C.O. had been able to do to husband his men, and, do what discipline could do to aid in the process, the battalion was reduced to not more than a third of what would have been a reasonable strength for the position it had had to occupy—and to abandon. And it was small comfort to the men that the Wiltshires on their right and the Cheshires on their left were in far worse case. So the aspect of the Old Man as a b—y h-ll of a pusher became foremost in their considerations.

To a sensitive officer—and all good officers in this respect are sensitive—the psychology of the men makes itself felt in innumerable ways. He can afford to be blind to the feelings of his officers, for officers have to stand so much at the hands of their seniors before the rules of the service give them a chance to retaliate, that it takes a really bad Colonel to put his own mess in a bad way. As officer you *have* to jump to your C.O.'s orders, to applaud his sentiments, to smile at his lighter witticisms and to guffaw at those that are more gross. That is the Service. With the Other Ranks it is different. A discreet warrant-officer will discreetly applaud his officer's eccentricities and good humours, as will a Sergeant desirous of promotion; but the rank and file are under no such compulsion. As long as a man comes to attention when spoken to that is all that can be expected of him. He is under no obligation to understand his officer's witticisms so he can still less be expected to laugh at or to repeat them with gusto. He need not even come very smartly to attention. . . .

And for some days the rank and file of the battalion had gone dead, and the C.O. was aware that it had gone dead. Of the various types of Field-Officer upon whom he could have modelled himself as regards the men he had chosen that of the genial, rubicund, slightly whiskeyfied C.O. who finishes every sentence with the words: "Eh, what?" . . . In him it was a perfectly cold-blooded game for the benefit of the senior non-commissioned[22] officers and the Other Ranks, but it had gradually become automatic.

For[23] some days now, this mannerism had refused to work. It was as if Napoleon the Great had suddenly found that the device of pinching the ear of a grenadier on parade, had suddenly become ineffective. After the "Eh, what!" like a pistol shot the man to whom it was addressed had not all but shuffled, nor had any other men within earshot tittered and whispered to their pals. They had all remained just loutish. And it is a considerable test of courage to remain loutish under the Old Man's eyes!

All this the C.O. knew by the book, having been through it. And Tietjens knew that the C.O. knew it; and he half suspected that the C.O. knew that he, Tietjens, knew it. . . . And that the Pals and the Other Ranks also knew: that, in fact, everyone knew that everyone knew. It was like a nightmare game of bridge with all hands exposed and all the players ready to snatch pistols from their hip-pockets. . . .

And Tietjens, for his sins, now held the trump card and was in play!

It was a loathsome position. He loathed having to decide the fate of the C.O. as he loathed the prospect of having to restore the *moral*[24] of the men—if they survived.

And he was faced now by the conviction that he could do it. If he hadn't felt himself get his hand in with that dozen of disreputable tramps he would not have felt that he could do it. Then he must have used his moral authority with the doctor to get the Old Man patched up, drugged up, bucked up,[25] sufficiently to carry the battalion at least to the end of the retreat of the next few days. It was obvious that that must be done if there was no one else to take command—no one else that was pretty well certain to handle the men all right. But if there *was* anyone else to take over, didn't the C.O.'s condition make it too risky to let him remain in authority? Did it, or didn't it? Did it, or didn't it?

Looking at McKechnie[26] coolly as if to see where next he should plant his fist he had thus speculated. And he was aware that, at the most dreadful moment of his whole life his besetting sin, as the saying is, was getting back on him. With the dreadful dread of the approaching *strafe* all over him, with a weight on his forehead, his eyebrows, his heavily labouring chest, he had to take ... Responsibility. And to realise[27] that he was a fit person to take responsibility.

He said to McKechnie:

"The M.O. is the person who has to dispose of the Colonel."

McKechnie exclaimed:

"By God, if that drunken little squit[28] dares...."

Tietjens said:

"Terry[29] will act along the lines of my suggestions. He doesn't have to take orders from me. But he has said that he will act along the lines of my suggestions. I shall accept the moral responsibility."

He felt the desire to pant: as if he had just drunk at a draft a too great quantity of liquid. He did not pant. He looked at his wrist-watch. Of the time he had decided to give McKechnie thirty seconds remained.

McKechnie made wonderful use of the time. The Germans sent over several shells. Not such very long distance shells either. For ten seconds McKechnie went mad. He was always going mad. He was a bore. If that were only the German customary pooping off....[30] But it was heavier. Unusual obscenities dropped from the lips of McKechnie. There was no knowing where the German projectiles were going. Or aimed at. A steam laundry in Bailleul as like as not. He said:

"Yes! Yes! Aranjuez!"

The tiny subaltern had peeped again, with his comic hat, round the corner of the pinkish gravel buttress.... A good, nervous boy. Imagining that the fact that he had reported had not been noticed! The gravel certainly looked more pink now the sun was come up ... It was rising on Bemerton![31] Or perhaps not so far to the west yet. The parsonage of George Herbert, author of *Sweet day so cool, so calm, so bright, the bridal of the earth and sky!* It was odd where McKechnie who was still shouting got his

words for unnatural vice. He had been Latin Prize Man. But he
was probably quite pure. The words very likely meant nothing to
him. . . . As to the Tommies! . . . Then, why did they use them?
The German artillery thumped on! Heavier than the usual
salvoes with which methodically they saluted the dawn. But
there were no shells falling in[32] that neighbourhood.[33] So it might
not be the barrage opening the Great *Strafe!* Very likely they were
being visited by some little German Prince and wanted to show
him what shooting was. Or by Field-Marshal Count von Brunk-
ersdorf! Who had ordered them to shoot down the chimney of
the Bailleul steam laundry. Or it might be sheer irresponsibility
such as distinguished all gunners. Few Germans were imaginative
enough to be irresponsible, but no doubt their gunners were more
imaginative than other Germans.

He remembered being up in the artillery O.P.—what the devil
was its name?—before Albert. On the Albert-Bécourt-Bécordel[34]
Road! What the *devil* was its name? A gunner had been looking
through his glasses. He had said to Tietjens: "Look at that fat. . . !"
And through the glasses lent him, Tietjens had seen, on a hillside in the direction of Martinpuich, a fat Hun, in shirt and
trousers, carrying in his right hand a food tin from which he was
feeding himself with his left. A fat, lousy object: suggesting an
angler on a quiet day.* The gunner had said to Tietjens:

"Keep your glass on him!"

And they had chased that miserable German about that naked
hillside, with shells, for ten minutes. Whichever way he bolted,
they put a shell in front of him. Then they let him go. His action,
when he had realised[35] that they were really attending to him,
had been exactly that of a rabbit dodging out of the wheat the
reapers have just reached. At last he just lay down. He wasn't
killed. They had seen him get up and walk off later. Still carrying

---

* The road Ford mentions was a well-known route in and through the war zone. Nowadays the D938 is known as the Route d'Albert for at least some of its length and runs
from Albert to Péronne. The villages that Ford mentions were behind the lines for the
Battle of the Somme in 1916. Bécordel-Bécourt was fairly sheltered and was used by
various army medical facilities. It was also the location of a large artillery depot, and
many troops bivouacked here as they made their way up to the lines. In *It Was the
Nightingale*, Ford recalls travelling from headquarters behind the wood there in 'order
to give instructions to a fellow officer in charge of a detachment by an artillery observation post on the ridge facing Martinpuich' (113). There is no mention in his memoir
of a 'fat Hun'.

his bait can!

His antics had afforded those gunners infinite amusement. It afforded them almost more when[36] all the German artillery on that front, imagining that God knew what was the matter, had awakened and plastered heaven and earth and everything between for a quarter of an hour with every imaginable kind of missile. And had then, abruptly, shut up.... Yes.... Irresponsible people, gunners!

The incident had really occurred because Tietjens had happened to ask that gunner how much he imagined it had cost in shells to smash to pieces an indescribably smashed field of about twenty acres that lay between Bazentin-le-petit and Mametz[37] Wood. The field was unimaginably smashed, pulverised, powdered.... The gunner had replied that with shells from all the forces employed it might have cost three million sterling. Tietjens asked how many men the gunner imagined might have been killed there. The gunner said he didn't begin to know. None at all, as like as not![38] No one was very likely to have been strolling about there for pleasure, and it hadn't contained any trenches. It was just a field. Nevertheless, when Tietjens had remarked that in that case two Italian labourers with a steam plough could have pulverised that field about as completely for, say, thirty shillings, the gunner had taken it quite badly. He had made his men poop[39] off after that inoffensive Hun with the bait can, just to show what artillery *can* do.[40]

.... At that point Tietjens had remarked to McKechnie:

"For my part, I shall advise the M.O. to recommend that the Colonel should be sent back on sick leave for a couple of months. It is within his power to do that."

McKechnie had exhausted all his obscene expletives. He was thus sane. His jaw dropped:

"Send the C.O. back!" he exclaimed lamentably. "At the very moment when ... "

Tietjens exclaimed:

"Don't be an ass. Or don't imagine that I'm an ass. No one is going to reap any glory. In this Army. Here and now!"

McKechnie said:

"But what price the money? Command pay! Nearly four quid a day. You could do with two-fifty quid at the end of his two months!"

Not so very long ago it would have seemed impossible that any man *could* speak to him about either his private financial affairs or his intimate motives.

He said:

"I have obvious responsibilities. . . ."

"Some say," McKechnie went on, "that you're a b—y million-aire. One of the richest men in England. Giving coal mines to duchesses. So they say. Some say you're such a pauper that you hire your wife out to generals. . . . Any generals. That's how you get your jobs."

To that Tietjens had had to listen before. . . .

Max Redoubt. . . . It had come suddenly on to his tongue—just as, before, the name of Bemerton had come, belatedly. The name of the artillery observation post between Albert and Bécourt-Bécordel[41] had been Max Redoubt! During the intolerable waitings of that half-forgotten July and August the name had been as familiar on his lips as . . . say, as Bemerton itself. . . . When I forget thee, oh, my Bemerton . . . or, oh, my Max Redoubt . . . may my right hand forget its cunning! . . .* The unforgettables! . . . Yet he had forgotten them! . . .

If only for a time he had forgotten them. Then, his right hand might forget its cunning. If only for a time. . . . But even that might be disastrous: might come at a disastrous moment. . . . The Germans had suppressed themselves. Perhaps they had knocked down the laundry chimney. Or hit some G.S. wagons loaded with coal. . . . At any rate, that was not the usual morning *strafe*. That was to come. Sweet day so cool—began again.

McKechnie hadn't suppressed himself. He was going to get suppressed. He had just been declaring that Tietjens had not displayed any chivalry in not reporting the C.O. if he, Tietjens, considered him to be drunk—or even chronically alcoholic. No chivalry. . . .

This was like a nightmare! . . . No it wasn't. It was like fever when things appear stiffly unreal. . . . And exaggeratedly real! Stereoscopic, you might say!

McKechnie with an accent of sardonic hate begged to remind

---

* Psalm 137, which begins 'By the rivers of Babylon, there we sat down, yea, we wept.' The allusion is to verse 5: 'If I forget thee, O Jerusalem: let my right hand forget her cunning.'

Tietjens that if he considered the C.O. to be a drunkard he ought to have him put under arrest. King's Regs. exacted that. But Tietjens was too cunning. He meant to have that two-fifty quid. He might be a poor man and need it. Or a millionaire, and mean. They said that was how millionaires became millionaires: by snapping up trifles of money that, God knows, would be godsends to people like himself, McKechnie.

It occurred to Tietjens that two hundred and fifty pounds after this was over, might be a godsend to himself in a manner of speaking. And then he thought:

"Why the devil shouldn't I earn it?"

What was he going to do? After this was over.

And it was going over. Every minute the Germans were not advancing they were losing. Losing the power to advance.... Now, this minute! It was exciting.

"No!" McKechnie said. "You're too cunning. If you got poor Bill cashiered for drunkenness you'd have no chance of commanding. They'd put in another pukka colonel. As a stop-gap, whilst Bill's on sick leave, you're pretty certain to get it. That's why you're doing the damnable thing you're doing."

Tietjens had a desire to go and wash himself. He felt physically dirty.

Yet what McKechnie said was true enough! It was true!... The mechanical impulse to divest himself of money was so strong that he began to say:

"In that case ..." He was going to finish: "I'll *get* the damned fellow cashiered." But he didn't.

He was in a beastly hole. But decency demanded that he shouldn't act in panic. He had a mechanical, normal panic that made him divest himself of money. Gentlemen don't earn money. Gentlemen, as a matter of fact, don't do anything. They exist. Perfuming the air like Madonna lilies. Money comes into them as air through petals and foliage. Thus the world is made better and brighter. And, of course, thus political life can be kept clean!... So you can't make money.

But look here: This Unit was the critical spot of the whole affair. The weak spots of Brigade, Division, Army, British Expeditionary Force, Allied Forces.... If the Hun went through there.... *Fuit Ilium et magna gloria....* * Not much glory!

He was bound to do his best for that unit. That poor b—y unit. And for the poor b—y knockabout comedians to whom he had lately promised tickets for Drury Lane at Christmas.... The poor devils had said they preferred the Shoreditch Empire or the old Balham.... That was typical of England. The Lane was the *locus classicus* of the race, but these rag-time ... heroes, call them heroes!—preferred Shoreditch and Balham!

An immense sense of those grimy, shuffling, grouching, dirty-nosed pantomime-supers[42] came over him and an intense desire to give them a bit of luck, and he said:

"Captain McKechnie, you can fall out. And you will return to duty. Your own duty. In proper head-dress."

McKechnie, who had been talking, stopped with his head on one side like a listening magpie. He said:

"What's this? What's this?" stupidly. Then he remarked:

"Oh, well, I suppose if you're in command ..."

Tietjens said:

"It's usual to say 'sir,' when addressing a senior officer on parade. Even if you don't belong to his unit."

McKechnie said:

"Don't belong!... *I* don't.... To the poor b—y old pals!..."

Tietjens said:

"You're attached to Division Headquarters, and you'll get back to it. Now! At once!... And you won't come[43] back here. Not while I'm in command.... Fall out...."

That was really a duty—a feudal duty!—performed for the sake of the rag-time fellows. They wanted to be rid—and at once!—of dipsomaniacs in command of that unit and having the disposal of their lives.... Well, the moment McKechnie had uttered the words: "To the poor b—y old pals," an illuminating flash had presented Tietjens with the conviction that, alone, the C.O. was too damn good an officer to appear a dipsomaniac, even if he were observably drunk quite often. But, seen together with his fellow McKechnie, the two of them must present a formidable appearance of being alcoholic lunatics!

---

* Possibly a version of a line from Virgil (*Aeneid* II): 'fuit Ilium et ingens / gloria Teucrorum': 'Troy is past, Ilium is past, and the great glory of the Trojans.'

The rest of the poor b—y old pals didn't really any more exist. They were a tradition—of ghosts![44] Four of them were dead: four in hospital: two awaiting court-martial for giving stumer[45]* cheques. The last of them, practically, if you excepted McKechnie, was the collection of putrescence and rags at that moment hanging in the wire apron.... The whole complexion of Headquarters would change with the going of McKechnie.

He considered with satisfaction that he would command a very decent lot. The Adjutant was so inconspicuous you did not even notice him. Beady-eyed, like a bird! Always preoccupied. And little Aranjuez, the signalling officer![46] And a fat fellow called Dunne, who had represented Intelligence since the Night Before Last! "A" Company Commander was fifty, thin as a pipe-stem and bald; "B" was a good, fair boy: of good family; "C" and "D" were subalterns, just out. But clean.... Satisfactory!

What[47] a handful of frail grass with which to stop an aperture in the dam of—of the Empire! Damn the Empire! It was England! It was Bemerton Parsonage that mattered![48] What did we want with an Empire! It was only a jerry-building Jew like Disraeli that could have provided us with that jerry-built name! The Tories said they had to have someone to do their dirty work.... Well: they'd had[49] it!

He said to McKechnie:

"There's a fellow called Bemer—I mean Griffiths, O Nine Griffiths,[50] I understand you're interested in for the Divisional Follies. I'll send him along to you as soon as he's had his breakfast. He's first-rate with the cornet."

McKechnie said:

"Yes, sir," saluted rather limply and took a step.

That was McKechnie all over. He never brought his mad fits to a crisis. That made him still more of a bore. His face would be distorted like that of a wild-cat in front of its kittens' hole in a stone wall. But he became the submissive subordinate. Suddenly! Without rhyme or reason!

Tiring people! Without manners!... They would presumably run the world now. It would be a tiresome world.

---

* Slang dating from c.1890, of unknown origin, meaning worthless. The phrase also appears in Robert Graves' memoir *Goodbye to All That* (1929).

McKechnie, however, was saluting. He held a sealed envelope, rather small and crumpled, as if from long carrying. He was talking in a controlled voice after permission asked. He desired Tietjens to observe that the seal on the envelope was unbroken. The envelope contained "The Sonnet".

McKechnie must, then, have gone mad! His eyes, if his voice was quiet, though with an Oxford-Cockney accent—his prune-coloured eyes were certainly mad.... Hot prunes!

Men shuffled along the trenches, carrying by rope-handles very heavy, lead-coloured wooden cases: two men to each case. Tietjens said:

"You're "D" Company?... Get a move on!...."

McKechnie, however, wasn't mad. He was only pointing out that he could pit his Intellect and his Latinity against those of Tietjens: that he could do it when the great day came!

The envelope, in fact, contained a sonnet. A sonnet Tietjens, for distraction, had written to rhymes dictated by McKechnie ... for distraction in a moment of stress....

Several moments of stress they had been in together. It ought to have formed a bond between them. It hadn't.... Imagine having a bond with a Highland-Oxford-Cockney!

Or perhaps it had! There was certainly the sonnet. Tietjens had written it in two and a half minutes, he remembered, to stave off the thought of his wife who was then being a nuisance.... Two and a half minutes of forgetting Sylvia! A bit of luck!... But McKechnie had insisted on regarding it as a challenge. A challenge to his Latinity. He had then and there undertaken to turn that sonnet into Latin hexameters in two minutes. Or perhaps four....

But things had got in the way. A fellow called O9 Morgan[51] had got himself killed over their feet. In the hut. Then they had been busy: with the Draft!*

Apparently McKechnie had sealed up that sonnet in an envelope. In *that* envelope. Then and there. Apparently McKechnie had been inspired with a blind, Celtic, snorting rage to prove that he was better as a Latinist than Tietjens as a sonnetteer. Appar-

---

* Cf. *No More Parades* I.ii. These lines represent an unusually clear summary of previous action in the series, but they do not occur at a point of detailed revision of the text in the typescript (one possible reason for Ford covering earlier ground in this way).

ently he was still so inspired. He was mad to engage in competition with Tietjens.

It was perhaps that that made him not quite mad. He kept sane in order to be fit for this competition. He was now repeating, holding out the envelope, seal upwards:

"I suppose you believe I have not read your sonnet, sir. I suppose you believe I have not read your sonnet, sir.... To prepare myself to translate it more quickly."

Tietjens said:

"Yes! No!... I don't care."

He couldn't tell the fellow that the idea of a competition was loathsome to him. Any sort of competition was loathsome to Tietjens. Even competitive games. He liked playing tennis. Real tennis.[*] But he very rarely played because he couldn't get fellows to play[52] with, that beating would not be disagreeable.... And it would be loathsome to be drawn into any sort of competition with this Prizeman.... They were moving very slowly along the trench, McKechnie retreating sideways and holding out the seal.

"It's your seal, sir!" he was repeating. "Your own seal. You see, it isn't broken.... You don't perhaps imagine that I read the sonnet quickly and made a copy from memory?"

.... The fellow wasn't even a decent Latinist. Or verse-maker, though he was always boasting about it to the impossible, adenoidy, Cockney subalterns who made up the battalion's mess. He would translate their chits[53] into Latin verse.... But it was always into tags. Generally from the Aeneid. Like:

"*Conticuere*[54] *omnes*, or *Vino somnoque sepultum!*"[†]

That was, presumably, what Oxford of just before the War was doing.

He said:

"I'm not a beastly detective.... Yes, of course, I quite believe it."

He thought of emerging into the society of little Aranjuez who was some sort of gentle earnest Levantine with pleasure. Think of thinking of a Levantine with pleasure! He said:

---

[*]   Or the ancestor of lawn tennis, a mark, perhaps, 'of the upper class' (*OED*).
[†]   Another reference to Book II of the *Aeneid*. 'Conticuere omnes' are the first words of this Book, and translate as 'They all fell silent...': Aeneas was about to tell his story. The second phrase ('buried in wine and sleep') comes from stanza 35.

"Yes. It's all right, McKechnie."

He felt himself solid. He was really in a competition with this fellow. It was deterioration. He, Tietjens, was crumpling up morally. He had accepted responsibility: he had thought of two hundred and fifty pounds with pleasure: now he was competing with a Cockney-Celtic-Prizeman. He was reduced to that level. . . . Well, as like as not he would be dead before the afternoon. And no one would know.

Think of thinking about whether any one would know or no! . . . But it was Valentine Wannop that wasn't to know. That he had deteriorated under the strain! . . . That enormously surprised[55] him. He said to his subconscious self:

"What! Is *that* still there?"

That girl was at least an admirable Latinist. He remarked, with a sort of sardonic glee that, years before, in a dog-cart, emerging from mist, somewhere in Sussex—Udimore!*—she had made him look silly. Over Catullus! Him, Tietjens! . . . Shortly afterwards old Campion had run into them with his motor that he couldn't drive but *would* drive.

McKechnie, apparently assuaged, said:

"I don't know if you know, sir, that General Campion is to take over this Army the day after to-morrow. . . . But, of course, you would know."

Tietjens said:

"No. I didn't. . . . You fellows in touch with Headquarters get to hear of things long before us." He added:

"It means that we shall be getting reinforcements. . . . It means the Single Command."

---

* Tietjens is again remembering his experience with Valentine in *Some Do Not* . . . (I.vii). The village of Udimore lies about four miles to the west of Rye; it receives several mentions in *The Cinque Ports* (1900).

CHAPTER IV[1]

IT meant that the end of the war was in sight.

In the next sector, in front of the Headquarters' dug-out sacking they found only Second-Lieutenant Aranjuez and Lance-Corporal Duckett of the Orderly Room. Both good boys, the Lance-Corporal[2] with very long graceful legs. He picked up his feet well, but continually rubbed his ankles with his shoe when he talked earnestly.[3]* Somebody's bastard.

McKechnie[4] plunged at once into the story of the sonnet. The Lance-Corporal had, of course, a large number of papers for Tietjens to sign. An untidy, buff and white sheaf, so McKechnie had time to talk. He wished to establish himself as on a level with the temporary C.O. At least intellectually.[5]

He didn't. Aranjuez kept on exclaiming:

"The Major wrote a sonnet in two and a half minutes! The Major! Who would have thought it!" Ingenuous boy!

Tietjens looked at the papers with some attention. He had been so[6] kept out of contact with the affairs of the battalion, that he wanted to know. As he had suspected, the paper business of the unit was in a shocking state. Brigade, Division, even Army and, positively, Whitehall were *strafing* for information about everything imaginable from jam, toothbrushes and braces, to religions, vaccination and barrack damages.... This was interesting matter. A relief to contemplate.... You would almost think all-wise Authority snowed under and broke the backs of Commanding Officers with papers in order to relieve their minds by[7] affording alternative interests ... alternative to the exigencies of active hostilities! It was certainly a relief whilst waiting for a *strafe* to come to the right stage—to have to read a violent enquiry about P.R.I.† funds,[8] whilst the battalion had been resting

---

* Duckett does this throughout this novel and the habit is discussed in the Introduction. Cf. *No More Parades* II.ii.

† The letters stand for President of the Regimental Institute. The Regimental Institute was a body set up to support the improvement of the soldiers in a variety of ways (often

near a place called Béhencourt. . . . *

It appeared that Tietjens might well be thankful that he had
not been allowed to handle the P.R.I. funds.

The second-in-command is the titular administrator of the
Regimental Institute: he is the President, supposed to attend to
the men's billiard tables, almanacks, backgammon[9] boards, foot-
ball boots. . . . But the C.O. had preferred to keep these books in
his own hands. Tietjens regarded that as a slight. Perhaps it had
not been!

It went quickly through his head that the C.O. perhaps had
financial difficulties—though that was no real affair of his. . . . The
Horse Guards[10] was pressingly interested in the pre-enlistment
affairs of a private called 64 Smith. They asked violently and for
the third time for particulars of his religion, previous address and
real name. . . . That was no doubt the espionage branch at
work. . . . But Whitehall was[11] also more violently interested in
answers to queries about the disposal of regimental funds of a
training camp in January, 1915. . . . As long ago as that! The mills
of God grind slowly. . . . That query was covered by a private note
from the Brigadier saying that he wished for goodness' sake the
C.O. would answer these queries or there would have to be a
Court of Enquiry.†

---

by seeking to reduce excessive drinking). The President was responsible for the distri-
bution of funds.

*   A town about 15 kilometres west of Albert.

†   The confusion in the textual witnesses in this section (see relevant textual notes) may
be partly explained by the fact that the headquarters of the army, which had been in
the Horse Guards, had moved to Whitehall in 1906. The reforms that led to this
change were highly contentious – especially the creation of the first full-time secretary of state for military affairs, to whom the Commander-in-Chief was to be
subservient. They resulted in the war department being divided into three sections of
which the Commander-in-Chief, the surveyor-general of the ordnance and the financial secretary were the respective heads. The War Office Act of 1870 consolidated the
War Office and Horse Guards and required the Commander-in-Chief to physically
move from Horse Guards. 'Even though the British Army Commander-in-Chief and
his staff moved to the War Office in Pall Mall' (where it was before shifting again to
Whitehall), writes Harold E. Raugh in *The Victorians at War, 1815–1914* (Santa
Barbara, CA: ABC-CLIO, 2004), 'the term "Horse Guards" was still frequently used
to refer to the military component of the War Office' (168). These developments may
be one reason why, in *No More Parades* (I.iv), a communication from the War Office
is said to have come from Whitehall, but the colonel remarks that '"You never know
where these things come from nowadays. I call them the arrow that flieth by night!"'
    Despite the textual confusion (replicated in II.v), Ford's aim at this point is to
distinguish between aspects of the army hierarchy (and bureaucracy).

These particular two papers ought not to have been brought to Tietjens. He held them between the thumb and forefinger of his left hand and the query upon 64 Smith S.—which seemed rather urgent—between the first and second, and so handed them to Lance-Corporal Duckett.[12] That nice, clean, fair boy was, at the moment, talking in intimate undertones to Second Lieutenant Aranjuez about the resemblances between the Petrarchan and the Shakespearean sonnet form. . . .

This was what His Majesty's Expeditionary Force had come to. You had four of its warriors, four minutes before the zero[13] of a complete advance of the whole German line, all interested in sonnets. . . . Drake and his game of bowls—in[14] fact repeated itself! . . .* Differently, of course! But times change.

He handed the two selected papers to Duckett.[15]

"Give this one to the Commanding Officer," he said, "and tell the Sergeant-Major to find what Company 64 Smith is in and have him brought to me, wherever I am. . . . I'm going right along the trenches now. Come after me when you've been to the C.O. and the Sergeant-Major. Aranjuez will make notes of what I want done about revetting, you can put down anything about the personnel of the companies. . . . Get a move on!"

He told McKechnie amiably[16] to be out of those lines forth-with. He didn't want him killed on his hands.

The sun was now shining into the trench.

He looked again through Brigade's that morning communication concerning dispositions the unit was to make in the event of the expected German attack. . . . Due to begin—the preparatory artillery at least—in three minutes' time.

Don't we say prayers before battle? . . . He could not imagine himself doing it. . . . He just hoped that nothing would happen that would make him lose control of his mind. . . . Otherwise he found that he was meditating on how to get the paper affairs[17] of the unit into a better state. . . . *"Who sweeps a room as for Thy*

---

* The myth has it that Francis Drake was playing a game of bowls on Plymouth Hoe when the Spanish Armada was sighted. In a characteristic display of bravado he finished the game before taking to sea. There is in fact no evidence that he was playing this game, but he may well have been able to finish it if he were, as the English fleet was trapped for some hours in the harbour by a south-westerly wind and an incoming tide.

cause ... "* It was the equivalent of prayer probably. ...

He noted that Brigade's injunctions about the coming fight were not only endorsed[18] with earnestness by Division but also by very serious exhortations from Army. The chit from Brigade was in handwriting, that from Division in fairly clear type-script, that from Army in very pale typed characters. ... It amounted to this: that they were that day to stick it till they burst. ... That meant that there was nothing behind their backs—from there to the North Sea! ... The French were hurrying along probably. ... He imagined a lot of little blue fellows in red breeches trotting along pink, sunlit plains.

(You cannot control your imagination's pictures. Of course the French no longer wore red trousers.†) He saw the line breaking just where the blue section came to: the rest, swept back into the sea. He saw the whole of the terrain behind them. On the horizon was a glistening haze. That was where they were going to be swept to. Or of course they would not be swept. They would be lying on their faces, exposing the seats of their breeches. Too negligible for the large dust-pan and broom. ... What was death like: the immediate process of dissolution? He stuffed the papers into his tunic pocket.

He remembered with grimmish amusement that one chit promised him reinforcements. Sixteen men! Sixteen! Worcesters! From a Worcester training camp. ... Why the deuce weren't they sent to the Worcester battalion just next door? Good fellows, no doubt. But they hadn't got the drill quiffs of our lot:‡

---

* A Herbert reference once more, this time to a line from 'The Elixir', part of 'The Temple' (1634). The verse runs:

> A servant with this clause
> Makes drudgery divine:
> Who sweeps a room, as for thy laws,
> Makes that and the action fine.

In context, the first verse may help to explain its relevance for Ford as an 'equivalent of prayer':

> Teach me, my God and King,
> In all things thee to see,
> And what I do in any thing,
> To do it as for thee.

† The French army began the war wearing red trousers, but they made a perfect target, and very quickly changes began in this aspect of the uniform.

‡ Drill quiffs: in the army used of any drill method peculiar to a battalion. Where the wording of the Drill Book is vague, units often read different meanings into the phraseology and invent their own 'quiffs' (OED).

they were not pals with our men: they did not know the officers by name. There would be no welcome to cheer them. . . . It was a queer idea, the deliberate destruction of regimental esprit de corps that the Home Authorities now insisted on. It was said to be imitated at the suggestion of a civilian of advanced social views from the French who in turn had imitated it from the Germans.* It is of course lawful to learn of the Enemy: but is it sensible? Perhaps it is. The Feudal Spirit was broken. Perhaps it would therefore be harmful to Trench Warfare. It used to be comfortable and cosy. You fought beside men from your own hamlet under the leadership of the parson's son. Perhaps that was not good for you?

At any rate, as at present arranged, dying was a lonely[19] affair.

He, Tietjens, and little Aranjuez[20] there, if something hit them would die—a Yorkshire territorial magnate's son and the son of, positively, an Oporto† Protestant[21] minister, if you can imagine such a thing!—the dissimilar souls winging their way to heaven side by side. You'd think God would find it more appropriate if Yorkshiremen went with other North Country fellows, and Dagoes with other Papists. For Aranjuez, though the son of a Nonconformist of sorts, had reverted to the faith of his fathers.

He said:

"Come along, Aranjuez. . . . I want to see that wet bit of trench before the Hun shells hit it."

Well. . . . They were getting reinforcements. The Home Authorities had awakened to their prayers. They sent them sixteen Worcesters. They would be three hundred and forty-four—no, forty-three, because he had sent back O-Nine Griffiths,[22] the fellow with the cornet—three hundred and forty-three lonely souls against. . . .[23] say two Divisions! Against about eighteen thousand, very likely. And they were to stick it till they burst. Reinforced!

---

* Niall Ferguson writes that heavy casualties had depleted ranks of 'pals' by the spring of 1915, meaning that 'men had to accustom themselves to fighting alongside strangers' (*The Pity of War* 206). On 30 July 1916, 500 of the 2,500-strong Liverpool Pals Battalion were killed, plunging Liverpool into mourning (Martin Gilbert, *First World War* [London: Weidenfeld and Nicolson, 1993], 272). 'Pals' battalions did survive until the end of the war, however, suggesting that there was not, in fact, a deliberate policy of destroying *esprit de corps*, as suggested by Tietjens here. Pragmatism, and casualties, were more likely to be the cause if 'strangers' were drafted in.

† A Protestant would still be a very rare thing in Oporto according to this site, accessed in May 2009: http://www.catholicity.com/encyclopedia/o/oporto.html

Reinforced. Good God!... Sixteen Worcesters!
What was at the bottom of it all?

Campion was going to command that Army. That meant that
real reinforcements had been promised from the millions of men
that filled the base camps. And it meant the Single Command!
Campion would not have consented to take the command of that
Army if he had not had those very definite promises.

But it would take time. Months! Anything like adequate reinforcements would take months.

And at that moment, in the most crucial point of the line of
the Army, of the Expeditionary Force, the Allied Forces, the
Empire, the Universe, the Solar-system, they had three hundred
and sixty-six[24] men commanded by the last surviving Tory. To
face wave on wave of the Enemy.

In one minute the German barrage was due.

Aranjuez said to him:

"You can write a sonnet in two and a half minutes, sir.... And
your syphon works like anything in that damp trench.... It took
my mother's great-uncle, the canon of Oporto, fifteen weeks to
finish his celebrated sonnet. I know because my mother told
me.... But you oughtn't to be here, sir."

Aranjuez then was the nephew of the author of the *Sonnet to
Night.** He could be. You had to have that sort of oddity[25] to make
up this world. So naturally he was interested in sonnets.

And, having got hold of a battalion with a stretch of damp
trench, Tietjens had had the opportunity of trying a thing he had
often thought of—of drying[26] out vertically cut, damp soil by
means of a syphon of soil-pipes put in, not horizontally but vertically. Fortunately Hackett, the commander of B Company, that
had the wet trench, had been an engineer in civil life. Aranjuez
had been along, out of sheer hero-worship, to B trenches to see

---

* Joseph Blanco White (1775–1841) was a friend of Coleridge and Southey, and the
  author of, among other poems, a sonnet, 'To Night'. The first lines are as follows:

  Mysterious Night! when our first parent knew
  Thee from report divine, and heard thy name,
  Did he not tremble for this lovely frame,
  This glorious canopy of light and blue?

  Its author was Spanish/English, not Portuguese like Aranjuez, but Aranjuez does
  mention just previously that he is referring to his mother's great uncle. The sonnet
  was well thought-of (Coleridge praised it particularly highly) and it was included in
  Quiller-Couch's *Oxford Book of English Verse* (1919).

how his hero's syphons had worked. He reported that they worked like a dream.

Little Aranjuez said:

"These trenches are like Pompeii, sir."

Tietjens had never seen Pompeii, but he understood that Aranjuez was referring to the empty square-cut excavations in the earth.* Particularly to their emptiness. And to the deadly stillness in the sunlight.... Admirable trenches. Made to hold an[27] establishment of several thousand men. To bustle with Cockney life. Now dead empty. They passed three sentries in the pinkish gravel passage and two men, one with a pick, the other with a shovel. They were exactly squaring the juncture of the wall and the path, as they might have done in Pompeii. Or in Hyde Park! A perfect devil for tidiness, "A" Company Commander. But the men seemed to like it. They were sniggering, though they stopped that, of course, when Tietjens passed....

A nice, dark, tiny boy, Aranjuez: his adoration was charming. From the very first—and naturally, frightened out of his little life, he had clung to Tietjens as a child clings to an omnipotent father. Tietjens, all-wise, could direct the awful courses of war and decree safety for the frightened! Tietjens needed that sort of worship. The boy said it would be awful to have anything happen to your eyes. Your girl naturally would not look at you. Not more than three miles away, Nancy Truefitt was now. Unless they had evacuated her. Nancy was his flame. In a tea-shop at Bailleul.

A man was sitting outside the mouth of "A" dugout, just after they passed the mouth of the communication trench.... Comforting that channel in the soil looked, running uphill. You could saunter away up there, out of all this.... But you couldn't![28] There was no turning here either to the right or to the left!

The man writing in a copy-book had his tin hat right over his eyes. Engrossed, he sat on a gravel-step, his copy-book on his knees. His name was Slocombe and he was a dramatist. Like Shakespeare. He made fifty pounds a time[29] writing music-hall sketches for the outer halls. The outer halls were the cheap music-halls that go in a ring round the suburbs of London.

* Methods for excavation at Pompeii did indeed become more systematic during the pre-war period.

Slocombe never missed a second, writing in his copy-books. If you fell the men out for a rest when marching, Slocombe would sit by the roadside—and out would come his copy-book and his pencil. His wife would type out what he sent home. And write him grumbling letters if the supply of copy failed. How was she to keep up the Sunday best of George and Flossie if he did not keep on writing one-act sketches? Tietjens had this information through censoring one of the man's letters containing manuscript.... Slocombe was slovenly as a soldier, but he kept the other men in a good humour, his mind being a perfect repertoire of Cockney jests at the expense of Big and Little Willy and Brother Fritz. Slocombe wrote on, wetting his pencil with his tongue.

The Sergeant in the mouth of "A" Company headquarters dugout started to turn out some sort of a guard, but Tietjens stopped him. "A" Company ran itself on the lines of regulars in the depôt. The O.C. had a conduct sheet book as neat as a ledger! The old, bald, grim fellow. Tietjens asked the Sergeant questions. Had they their Mills bombs all right? They weren't short of rifles—first-class order?... But how could they be! Were there any sick?... Two!... Well, it was a healthy life!... Keep the men under cover until the Hun barrage began. It was due now.

It was due now. The second-hand of Tietjens' watch,[30] like an animated pointer of hair, kicked a little on the stroke of the minute.... "Crumb!" said the punctual, distant sound.

Tietjens said to Aranjuez:

"It's presumably coming[31] now!" Aranjuez pulled at the chin strap of his tin hat.

Tietjens' mouth[32] filled itself with a dreadful salty flavour, the back of his tongue being dry. His chest and heart laboured heavily. Aranjuez said:

"If I stop one, sir, you'll tell Nancy Truefitt that . . ."

Tietjens said:

"Little nippers like you don't stop things.... Besides, feel the wind!"[33]

They were at the highest point of the trenches that ran along a hillside. So they were exposed. The wind had undoubtedly freshened, coming down the hill. In front and behind, along the trench, they could see views. Land, some green, greyish trees.

Aranjuez said:

"You think the wind will stop them, sir," appealingly.

Tietjens exclaimed with gruffness:

"Of course it will stop them. They won't work without gas. Yet their men hate to have to face the gas-screens.[34] It's our great advantage. It saps their *moral*.[35] Nothing else would. They can't put up smoke-screens either."

Aranjuez said:

"I know you think their gas has ruined them, sir.... It was wicked of them to use it. You can't do a wicked thing without suffering for it, can you, sir?"

It remained indecently quiet. Like Sunday in a village with the people in church. But it was not pleasurable.

Tietjens wondered how long physical irregularities would inconvenience his mind. You cannot think well with a parched back to your tongue. This was practically his first day in the open during a *strafe*. His first whole day for quite a time. Since Noircourt!...[36] How long ago?... Two years?... Maybe!...* Then he had nothing to go on to tell him how long he would be inconvenienced!

It remained indecently quiet! Running footsteps, at first on duckboards, then on the dry path of trench! They made Tietjens start violently, inside himself. The house must be on fire!

He said to Aranjuez:

"Some one is in a hurry!"

The lad's teeth chattered. They must have made him feel bad too, the footsteps.... The knocking on the gate in "Macbeth"!†

They began. It had come. Pam ... Pamperi ... Pam! Pam!.... Pa ... Pamperi ... Pam! Pam!... Pampamperipampampam ... Pam .... They were the ones that sound like drums. They continued incessantly. Immensely big drums. The ones that go at it with real zest ... You know how it is, looking at an opera orchestra when the fellow with the big drum-sticks really begins.

---

* This time-frame takes us back to action that we do not have details for in *Some Do Not* .... Part II of that novel begins with Tietjens at home in London, suffering from shell-shock. He is about to return to the Front.

† In Act II of the play, the drunken porter opens a scene with '[h]ere's a knocking indeed!' (ii.1). Ford may also have known Thomas de Quincey's essay, 'On the Knocking at the Gate' (1823), in which he discusses the strength of feeling this section of Shakespeare's play provokes in him.

Your own heart beats like hell. Tietjens' heart did. The drummer appears to go mad.

Tietjens was never much good at identifying artillery by the sound. He would have said that these were anti-aircraft guns. And he remembered that, for some minutes, the drone of plane engines had pervaded the indecent silence.... But that drone was so normal it was part of the silence. Like your own thoughts. A filtered and engrossed sound, drifting down from overhead. More like fine dust than noise.

A familiar noise said: "We ... e ... e ... ry!" Shells always appeared tired of life. As if after a long, long journey they said: "Weary!" Very much prolonging the "e" sound. Then "Whack!" when they burst.*

This was the beginning of the *strafe*.... Though he had been convinced the *strafe* was coming he had hoped for a prolongation of the ... say Bemerton!... conditions. The life Peaceful. And Contemplative. But here it was beginning. "Oh well ..."

This shell appeared heavier and to be more than usually tired. Desultory. It seemed to pass within six feet over the heads of Aranjuez and himself. Then, just twenty yards up the hill it said, invisibly, "Dud!" ... And it *was* a dud!

It had not, very likely, been aimed at their trench at all. It was probably just an aircraft shrapnel shell that had not exploded. The Germans were firing a great number of duds—these days.

So it might not be a sign of the beginning! It was tantalising.[37] But as long as it ended the right way one could bear it.

Lance-Corporal Duckett, the fair boy, ran to within two foot of Tietjens' feet and pulled up with a Guardee's stamp and a terrific salute. There was life in the old dog yet. Meaning that a zest for spit and polish survived in places in these ragtime days.

The boy said, panting—it might have been agitation, or that he had run so fast.... But why had he run so fast if he were not agitated:

"If you please, sir," ... Pant.... "Will you come to the Colonel?" ... Pant. "With as little delay as possible!" He remained panting.

It went through Tietjens' mind that he was going to spend the

*   Cf. *No Enemy* 67.

rest of that day in a comfortable, dark hole. Not in the blinding daylight.... Let us be thankful!

Leaving Lance-Corporal Duckett ... it came suddenly into his head that he liked that boy because he suggested Valentine Wannop!... to converse in intimate tones with Aranjuez and so to distract him from the fear of imminent death or blindness that would mean the loss of his girl, Tietjens went smartly back along the trenches. He didn't hurry. He was determined that the men should not see him hurry. Even if the Colonel should refuse to be relieved of the command, Tietjens was determined that the men should have the consolation of knowing that Headquarters numbered one cool, sauntering soul amongst its members.

They had had, when they took over the Trasna Valley[38] trenches before the Mametz Wood[39] affair, a rather good Major who wore an eyeglass and was of good family. He had something the matter with him for he committed suicide later.... But, as they went in, the Huns, say fifty yards away, began to shout various national battle-cries of the Allies or the melodies of regimental quicksteps of British regiments. The idea was that if they heard, say: "*Some talk of Alexander....*"* resounding from an opposite trench, H.M. Second Grenadier Guards would burst into cheers and Brother Hun would know what he had before him.

Well, this Major Grosvenor shut his men[40] up, naturally, and stood listening with his eyeglass screwed into his face and the air of a connoisseur at a quartette party.† At last he took his eyeglass out, threw it in the air and caught it again.

"Shout *Banzai!* men," he said.

That, on the off-chance, might give the Enemy a scunner[41]†‡ at the thought that we had Japanese troops in the line in front of

---

* The first line of a famous marching song, 'The British Grenadiers'. The verse continues, '... and some of Hercules / Of Hector and Lysander / And such great names as these / But of all of these great heroes / There's none that can compare / With a to-ro-ro-ro-ro-ro / With the British Grenadier.' One of the most recognisable regimental marches, the first known performance was by the Redcoats during the battle at Brandywine in 1777. The tune originates from a piece entitled 'The New Bath' which can be found in one of John Playford's dance books dating from the 1600s.

† Ford is using an alternative spelling of 'quartet', and this seems to be an image of someone listening to music. Cf. *The Critical Attitude* (London: Duckworth, 1911), 44.

‡ There's a Middle English verb that is close to Ford's meaning and spelling: 'skunner', to shrink back in disgust. This comes from 'scurnen', to flinch. A dictionary definition is 'strong aversion or dislike'. Chambers' dictionary specifies it as Scots in origin.

them, or it would show them that we were making game of them,
a form of offensive that sent these owlish[42] fellows mad with
rage.... [43] So the Huns shut up!

That was the sort of humour in an officer that the men still
liked.... The sort of humour Tietjens himself had not got: but
he could appear unconcernedly reflective and all there—and he
could tell them, at trying moments, that, say, their ideas about
skylarks were all wrong.... That was tranquillising.

Once he had heard a Papist Padre preaching in a barn, under
shell-fire. At any rate shells were going overhead and pigs underfoot. The Padre had preached about very difficult points in the
doctrine of the Immaculate Conception, and the men had
listened raptly. He said that was common sense. They didn't want
lachrymose or mortuary orations. They wanted their minds taken
off.... So did the Padre!

Thus you talk to the men, just before the event, about skylarks,
or the hind-legs of the elephant at the old Lane! And you don't
hurry when the Colonel sends for you.

He walked along, for a moment or two, thinking nothing. The
pebbles in the gravel of the trench grew clear and individual.
Some one had dropped a letter. Slocombe, the dramatist, was
closing his copy-book. Sighing, apparently, he reached for his
rifle. "A" Company Sergeant-Major was turning out some men of
sorts. He said: "Get a move on!" Tietjens said as he passed: "Keep
them under cover as much as you can, Sergeant-Major."

It occurred to him suddenly that he had committed a military
misdemeanour in leaving Lance-Corporal Duckett with Aranjuez. An officer should not walk along a stretch of lonely trench
without escort. Some Hun offering might hit him and there
would be loss of property to His Majesty. No one to fetch a doctor
or stretcher-bearers while you bled to death. That was the
Army....

Well, he had left Duckett with Aranjuez to comfort him. That
minute subaltern was suffering. God knew what little agonies ran
about in his little mind, like mice! He was as brave as a lion when
strafes were on: when they weren't, his little, blackamoor, nobbly
face quivered as the thoughts[44] visited him....

He had really left Valentine Wannop with Aranjuez! That, he
realised,[45] was what he had done. The boy Duckett *was* Valen-

tine Wannop. Clean, blonde, small: with the ordinary face,[46] the courageous eyes, the obstinately, slightly peaked nose.... It was just as if, Valentine Wannop being in his possession, they had been walking along a road and seen someone in distress. And he, Tietjens, had said: "I've got to get along. You stop and see what you can do!"

And, amazingly, he was walking along a country road beside Valentine Wannop, silent, with the quiet intimacy that comes with possession. She belonged to him.... Not a mountain road: not Yorkshire. Not a valley road: not Bemerton. A country parsonage was not for him. So he wouldn't take orders!

A dawn-land road, with some old thorn[47] trees. They only grew really in Kent. And the sky coming down on all sides. The flat top of a down!

Amazing! He had not thought of that girl for over a fortnight now, except in moments of great *strafes*, when he had hoped she would not be too worried if she knew where he was. Because he had the sense that, all the time she knew where he was.

He had thought of her less and less. At longer intervals.... As with his nightmare of the mining Germans[48] who desired that a candle should be brought to the Captain. At first, every night, three or four times every night, it had visited him.... Now it came only[49] once every night....

The physical semblance of that boy had brought the girl back to his mind. That was accidental, so[50] it was not part of any psychological rhythm. It did not show him, that is to say, whether, in the natural course of events and without accidents she was ceasing to obsess him.

She was certainly now obsessing him! Beyond bearing or belief. His whole being was overwhelmed by her ... by her mentality really. For of course the physical resemblance of the Lance-Corporal was mere subterfuge. Lance-Corporals do not resemble young ladies.... And, as a matter of fact, he did not remember exactly what Valentine Wannop looked like. Not vividly. He had not that sort of mind. It was words that his mind found that let him know that she was fair, snub-nosed, rather broad-faced and square on her feet.[51] As if he had made a note of it and referred to it when he wanted to think of her. His mind didn't make any mental picture: it brought up a sort of blur of sunlight.

It was the mentality that obsessed him: the exact mind, the impatience of solecisms and facile generalisations!... A queer catalogue of the charms of one's lady love!... But he wanted to hear her say: "Oh, chuck it, Edith Ethel!" when Edith Ethel[52] Duchemin, now of course Lady Macmaster, quoted some of the opinions expressed in Macmaster's critical monograph about the late Mr. Rossetti.... How *very* late now!

It would rest him to hear that. She was, in effect, the only person in the world that he wanted to hear speak. Certainly the only person in the world that he wanted to talk to. The only clear intelligence!... The repose that his mind needed from the crackling of thorns under all the pots of the world....* From the eternal, imbecile "Pampamperipam Pam Pamperi Pam Pam!" of the German guns that all the while continued....

Why couldn't they chuck that? What good did it do them to keep that mad drummer incessantly thundering on his stupid instrument?... Possibly they might bring down some of our planes, but they generally didn't. You saw the black ball of their shells exploding and slowly expand like[53] pocket-handkerchiefs about the unconcerned planes, like black peas aimed at dragon-flies, against the blue: the illuminated, pinkish, pretty things!... But his dislike of those guns was just dislike—a Tory prejudice. They were probably worth while. Just....

You naturally tried every argument in the unseen contest of wills that went on across the firmament.[54]

"Ho!" says our Staff, "they are going to attack in force at such an hour ackemma," because naturally the staff thought in terms of ackemma years after the twenty-four-hour day[55] had been established.† "Well, we'll send out a million machine gun planes to wipe out any men they've got moving up into support!"

It was of course unusual to move bodies of men by daylight. But this game had only two resources: you used the usual. Or the unusual. *Usually* you didn't begin your barrage after dawn and launch your attack at ten-thirty or so. So you might do it—the

---

* 'It is better to hear the rebuke of the wise, than for a man to hear the song of fools. For as the crackling of thorns under a pot, so is the laughter of the fool: this also is vanity' (Ecclesiastes 7:5–6).

† 'Ack emma' and 'pip emma' were military usages for a.m. and p.m. In fact, the 24-hour clock was not adopted by the British military until late 1917. Now 'military time' is a synonym for the 24-hour clock. Cf. *True Love & a GCM, War Prose* 101.

Huns might be trying it on—as a surprise measure.

On the other hand, our people might be sending over the planes, whose immense droning was then making your very bones vibrate, in order to tell the Huns that we were ready to be surprised: that the time had now about come round when we might be expecting the Hun brain to think out a surprise. So we sent out those deathly, dreadful things to run along just over the tops of the hedgerows, in spite of all the guns! For there was nothing more terrifying in the whole war than that span of lightness, swaying, approaching a few feet above the heads of your column of men: instinct with wrath: dispensing the dreadful rain! So we had sent them. In a moment they would be tearing down. . . .

Of course if this were[56] merely a demonstration: if, say, there were no reinforcements moving, no troops detraining at the distant railhead, the correct Hun answer would be to hammer some of our trenches to hell with all the heavy stuff they could put on to them. That was like saying sardonically:

"God, if you interfere with our peace and quiet on a fine day we'll interfere with yours!" And . . . Kerumph . . . the wagons of coal would[57] fly over until we recalled our planes and all went to sleep again over the chess-board. . . . You would probably be just as well off if you refrained from either demonstration or counter-demonstration. But Great General Staff liked to exchange these witticisms in iron. And a little blood![*]

A Sergeant of sorts approached him from Bn. H.Q. way, shepherding[58] a man with a head wound. His tin hat, that is to say, was perched jauntily forward over a bandage. He was Jewish-nosed, appeared not to have shaved, though he had, and appeared as if he ought to have worn pince-nez to complete his style of Oriental manhood. Private Smith. Tietjens said:

"Look here, what was your confounded occupation before the war?"

---

[*] Cf. Bismarck's speech to the Prussian House of Deputies, 28 January 1886: 'Place in the hands of the King of Prussia the strongest possible military power, then he will be able to carry out the policy you wish; this policy cannot succeed through speeches, and shooting-matches, and songs; it can only be carried out through blood and iron [Blut und Eisen].' Bismarck had used 'Eisen und Blut' (the way round that Ford has the words) previously (Oxford Dictionary of Quotations).

The man replied with an agreeable, cultured throaty intonation:

"I was a journalist, sir. On a Socialist paper. Extreme Left!"

"And what," Tietjens asked, "was your agreeable name?. . . I'm obliged to ask you that question. I don't want to insult you."

In the old regular army it was an insult to ask a private if he was not going under his real name. Most men enlisted under false names.

The man said:

"Eisenstein, sir!"

Tietjens asked if the man were a Derby recruit or compulsorily[59] enlisted. He said he had enlisted voluntarily. Tietjens said: "Why?" If the fellow was a capable journalist and on the right side he would be more useful outside the army. The man said he had been foreign correspondent of a Left paper. Being correspondent of a Left paper with a name like Eisenstein deprived one of one's chance of usefulness. Besides he wanted to have a whack at the Prussians. He was of Polish extraction. Tietjens asked the Sergeant if the man had a good record. The Sergeant said: "First-class man. First-class soldier." He had been recommended for the D.C.M., Tietjens said:

"I shall apply to have you transferred to the Jewish regiment. In the meantime you can go back to the First Line Transport. You shouldn't have been a Left journalist and have a name like Eisenstein. One or the other. Not both." The man said the name had been inflicted on his ancestry in the Middle Ages. He would prefer to be called Esau, as a son of that tribe. He pleaded not to be sent to the Jewish regiment, which was believed to be in Mesopotamia, just when the fighting there was at its most interesting.

"You're probably thinking of writing a book," Tietjens said. "Well, there are all Abana and Pharpar to write about.* I'm sorry. But you're intelligent enough to see that I can't take . . ." He stopped, fearing that if the Sergeant heard any more the men might make it hot for the fellow as a suspect. He was annoyed at having asked his name before the Sergeant. He appeared to be a

* See 2 Kings 5:12: 'Are not Abana and Pharpar, rivers of Damascus, better than all the waters of Israel?'

good man. Jews could fight.... And hunt!... But he wasn't going to take any risks. The man, dark-eyed and erect, flinched a little, gazing into Tietjens' eyes.

"I suppose you can't, sir," he said. "It's a disappointment. I'm not writing anything. I want to go on in the Army. I like the life."

Tietjens said:

"I'm sorry, Smith. I can't help it. Fall out!" He was sorry. He believed the fellow. But responsibility hardens the heart. It must. A very short time ago he would have taken trouble over that fellow. A great deal of trouble, very likely. Now he wasn't going to....

A large capital "A" in whitewash decorated the piece of corrugated iron that was derelictly propped against a channel at right angles to the trench. To Tietjens' astonishment a strong impulse like a wave of passion influenced his being towards the left—up that channel. It wasn't funk: it wasn't any sort of funk. He had been rather irritatedly wrapped up in the case of Private Smith-Eisenstein. It had undeniably irritated him to have to break the chances of a Jew and Red Socialist. It was the sort of thing one did not do if one were omnipotent—as he was. Then ... this strong impulse?... It was a passionate desire to go where you could find exact intellect: rest.

He thought he suddenly understood. For the Lincolnshire Sergeant-Major the word Peace meant that a man could stand up on a hill. For him it meant some one to talk to.

CHAPTER V[1]

THE Colonel said:

"Look here, Tietjens, lend me two hundred and fifty quid.
They say you're a damn beastly rich fellow. My accounts are all
out. I've got a loathsome complaint. My friends have all gone
back on me. I shall have to face a Court of Enquiry if I go home.
But my nerve's gone. I've got to go home."

He added:

"I daresay you knew all that."

From the sudden fierce hatred that he felt at the thought of
giving money to this man, Tietjens knew that his inner mind
based all its calculations on the idea of living with Valentine
Wannop ... when men could stand up on hills.

He had found the Colonel in his cellar—it really, actually was
a cellar, the remains of a farm—sitting on the edge of his camp-
bed, in his shorts, his khaki shirt very open at the neck. His eyes
were a little bloodshot, but his cropped, silver-grey hair was accurately waved, his grey moustache beautifully pointed. His
silver-backed hair-brushes and a small mirror were indeed on the
table in front of him. By the rays of the lamp that, hung overhead,
rendered that damp stone place faintly nauseating, he looked
keen, clean and resolute. Tietjens wondered how he would look
by daylight. He had remarkably seldom seen the fellow by
daylight. Beside the mirror and the brushes lay, limply, an
unfilled pipe, a red pencil and the white buff papers from Whitehall[2]* that Tietjens had already read.

He had begun by looking at Tietjens with a keen, hard, bloodshot glance. He had said:

"You think you can command this battalion? Have you had

---

* This perpetuates the textual problem of Whitehall vs the Horse Guards that began in
the last chapter (see the beginning of II.iv). In that chapter, we were introduced to
two sets of papers that had been sent, one concerning Private Smith and spying, the
other concerning regimental funds. The Brigadier expressly asked for information
from the C.O. concerning training funds going missing in January 1915.

any experience? It appears you suggest that I take two months' leave."

Tietjens had expected a violent outbreak. Threats even. None had come. The Colonel had continued to regard him with intentness, nothing more. He sat motionless, his long arms, bare to the elbow, dependent over each of his knees which were far apart. He said that if he decided to go he didn't want to leave his battalion to a man that would knock it about. He continued staring hard at Tietjens. The phrase was singular in that place and at that hour, but Tietjens understood it to mean that he did not want his battalion discipline to go to pieces.

Tietjens answered that he did not think he would let the discipline go to pieces. The Colonel had said:

"How do you know? You're no soldier, are you?"

Tietjens said he had commanded in the line a Company[3] at full strength—nearly as large as the battalion and, out of it, a unit of exactly eight times its present strength. He did not think any complaints had been made of him. The Colonel said, frostily:

"Well! I know nothing about you." He had added:

"You seem to have moved the battalion all right the night before last. I wasn't in a condition to do it myself. I'm not well. I'm obliged to you. The men appear to like you. They're tired of me."

Tietjens felt himself on tenterhooks. He had, now, a passionate desire to command that battalion. It was the last thing he would have expected of himself. He said:

"If it becomes a question of a war of motion, sir, I don't know that I should have much experience."

The Colonel answered:

"It won't become a war of motion before I come back. If I ever do come back."

Tietjens said:

"Isn't it rather like a war of motion now, sir?"[4] It was perhaps the first time in his life he had ever asked for information from a superior in rank—with an implicit belief that he would get an exact answer. The Colonel said:

"No. This is only falling back on prepared positions. There will be positions prepared for us right back to the sea. If the Staff has done its work properly. If it hasn't, the war's over. We're done, finished, smashed, annihilated, non-existent."

Tietjens said:

"But if the great *strafe*[5] that, according to Division, is due now
..."

The Colonel said: "What?" Tietjens repeated his words and
added:

"We might get pushed beyond the next prepared position."

The Colonel appeared to withdraw his thoughts from a great
distance.

"There isn't going to be any great *strafe*," he said. He was beginning to add: "Division has got...." A considerable thump shook
the hill behind their backs. The Colonel sat listening without
much attention. His eyes gloomily rested on the papers before
him. He said, without looking up:

"Yes: I don't want my battalion knocked about!" He went on
reading again—the communication from Whitehall.[6] He said:
"You've read this?" and then:

"Falling back on prepared positions isn't the same as moving
in the open. You don't have to do more than you do in a trench-
to-trench attack. I suppose you can get your direction by compass
all right. Or get someone to, for you."

Another considerable Crump of sound shook the earth but
from a little further away. The Colonel turned the sheet of paper[7]
over. Pinned to the back of it was the private note of the
Brigadier. He perused this also with gloomy and unsurprised[8]
eyes.

"Pretty stiff, all this," he said, "you've read it? I shall have to go
back and see about this."

He exclaimed:

"It's rough luck. I should have liked to leave my battalion to
someone that knew it. I don't suppose you do. Perhaps you do,
though."

An immense collection of fire-irons: all the fire-irons in the
world fell just above their heads. The sound seemed to prolong
itself in echoes, though of course it could not have.[9] It was
repeated.

The Colonel looked upwards negligently. Tietjens proposed to
go to see. The Colonel said:

"No, don't. Notting will tell us if anything's wanted...."

Though nothing can be wanted!" Notting was the beady-eyed Adjutant in the adjoining cellar. "How could they expect us to keep accounts straight in August 1914?* How can they expect me to remember what happened? At the Depôt. Then!" He appeared listless, but without resentment. "Rotten luck . . ." he said. "In the battalion and . . . with this!" He rapped the back of his hand on the papers. He looked up at Tietjens.

"I suppose I could get rid of you; with a bad report," he said. "Or perhaps I couldn't . . . General Campion put you here. You're said to be his bastard."

"He's my god-father," Tietjens said. "If you put in a bad report of me I should not protest. That is, if it were on the grounds of lack of experience. I should go to the Brigadier over anything else."

"It's the same thing," the Colonel said. "I mean a god-son. If I had thought you were General Campion's bastard, I should not have said it. . . . No; I don't want to put in a bad report of you. It's my own fault if you don't know the battalion. I've kept you out of it. I didn't want you to see what a rotten state the papers are in. They say you're the devil of a paper soldier. You used to be in a Government office, didn't you?"

Heavy blows were being delivered to the earth with some regularity on each side of the cellar. It was as if a boxer of the size of a mountain were delivering rights and lefts in heavy alternation. And it made hearing rather difficult.

"Rotten luck," the Colonel said. "And McKechnie's[10] dotty. Clean dotty." Tietjens missed some words. He said that he would probably be able to get the paper work of the battalion straight before the Colonel came back.

The noise rolled down hill like a heavy cloud. The Colonel continued talking and Tietjens, not being very accustomed to his voice, lost a good deal of what he said but, as if in a rift, he did hear:

"I'm not going to burn my fingers with a bad report on you that may bring a General on my back—to get back McKechnie who's dotty. . . . Not fit to. . . . "

---

* In II.iv the issue Tietjens is musing on is to do with training camp funds in January 1915. Here, the C.O. quotes a different point of order. It is possible of course that more than one irregularity is specified in the papers – this would make it more likely that the Colonel would need to travel back to clear his name.

The noise rolled in again. Once the Colonel listened to it, turning his head on one side and looking upwards. But he appeared satisfied with what he heard and recommenced his perusal of the Horse Guards[11] letter. He took the pencil, under-lined words and then sat idly stabbing the paper with the point.

With every minute Tietjens' respect for him increased. This man at least knew his job—as an engine-dresser does, or the captain of a steam tramp. His nerves might have gone to pieces. They probably had; probably he could not go very far without stimulants: he was probably under bromides now.*

And, all things considered, his treatment of Tietjens had been admirable and Tietjens had to revise his view of it. He realised[12] that it was McKechnie who had given him the idea that the Colonel hated him: but he would not have said anything. He was too old a hand in the Army to give Tietjens a handle by saying anything definite.... And he had always treated Tietjens with the sort of monumental deference that, in a Mess, the Colonel should bestow on his chief assistant. Going through a door[13] at meal-times, for instance, if they happened to be side by side, he would motion with his hand for Tietjens to go first, naturally though, taking his proper precedence when Tietjens halted. And here he was, perfectly calm. And quite ready to be instructive.

Tietjens was not calm: he was too much bothered by Valen-tine Wannop and by the thought that, if the *strafe* was on, he ought to be seeing about his battalion. And of course by the bombardment. But the Colonel said, when Tietjens with the aid of signs again made proposals to take a look around:

"No. Stop where you are. This isn't the *strafe*. There is not going to be a *strafe*. This is only a little extra Morning Hate.† You

---

*   In the second half of the nineteenth century, bromides were used to reduce the frequency and intensity of seizures associated with leprosy. Later, in the inter-war period, their sedative action was also used to calm highly disturbed patients. Bromides were a frequent feature of anecdotes during the First World War (hence Tietjens' refer-ence); one persistent theory had it that they were added to soldiers' tea to reduce libido. More recent research has failed to establish the truth of this and other related notions (see, for example, the letter from Professor Alan Dronsfield to *The Times*, 23 April 2004, www.timesonline.co.uk, accessed 4 June 2009).

†   This phrase, later made notorious by George Orwell in *1984* (1949), became the favoured term for the morning and evening 'stand to' (or, more formally, 'stand to arms'), observed by both sides in the trenches, notably on the Western Front. Cf. also the 'Hymn of Hate' in, for example, *No Enemy* 58–9.

can tell by the noise. That's only four point twos.* There's
nothing really heavy. The really heavies don't come so fast.
They'll be turning on to the Worcesters now and only giving us
one every half minute.... That's their game. If you don't know
that, what are you doing here?" He added:[14] "You hear?" pointing
his forefinger to the roof. The noise shifted. It went away to the
right as a slow coal-wagon might. He went on:

"This is your place. Not doing things up above. They'll come
and tell you if they want things. And you've got a first-rate Adjutant in Notting and Dunne's a good man.... The men are all
under cover: that's an advantage in having your strength down
to three hundred. There's dugouts for all and to spare.... All the
same, this is no place for you. Nor for me. This is a young man's
war. We're old uns. Three and a half years of it have done for me.
Three and a half months will do for you."

He looked gloomily at his reflection in the mirror that stood
before him.

"You're a gone coon!"† he said to it. Then he took it and,
holding it for a moment poised at the end of a bare white arm,
flung it violently at the rough stones of the wall behind Tietjens.
The fragments tinkled to the ground.

"There's seven years' bad luck," he said. "God take 'em, if they
can give me seven years worse than this last I'd find it instructive!"

He looked at Tietjens with infuriated eyes.

"Look here you!" he said. "You're an educated man ... What's
the worst thing about this war? What's the *worst* thing? Tell me
that!" His chest began to heave. "It's that they won't let us alone.
Never! Not one of us! If they'd let us alone we could fight. But
never.... No one! It's not only the beastly papers of the
battalion, though I'm no good with papers. Never was and never
shall be.... But it's the people at home. One's own people. God
help us, you'd think that when a poor devil was in the trenches
they'd let him alone.... Damn it: I've had solicitors' letters[15]
about family quarrels when I was in hospital. Imagine that!...
Imagine it! I don't mean tradesmen's dunnings.‡ But one's own

---

* A German 4.2 inch artillery shell.
† Or a person on the edge of ruin – the raccoon, being hunted for its fur, is a 'gone coon'
  once it has no escape.
‡ A dunning is a demand for payment, a 'dunning' letter.

people. I haven't even got a bad wife as McKechnie has and they say you have. My wife's a bit extravagant and the children are expensive. That's worry enough.... But my father died eighteen months ago. He was in partnership with my uncle. A builder. And they tried to do his estate out of his share of the business and leave my old mother with nothing. And my brother and sister threw the estate into Chancery in order to get back the little bit my father spent on my wife and children. My wife and children lived with my father whilst I was in India.... And out here.... My solicitor says they can get it out of my share: the cost of their keep. He calls it the doctrine of ademption.... * Ademption ... Doctrine of ... I was better off as a Sergeant," he added gloomily. "But Sergeants don't get let alone. They've always got women after them. Or their wives take up with Belgians and they get written to about it. Sergeant Cutts of "D" Company gets an anonymous letter every week about his wife. How's he to do his duty! But he does. So have I till now...." He added with renewed violence:

"Look here. You're an educated man, aren't you? The sort of man that could write a book. You write a book about that. You write to the papers about it. You'd be more use to the Army doing that than being here. I daresay you're a good enough officer. Old Campion is too keen a commander to stick a rotten officer into this job, god-son or no god-son.... Besides, I don't believe the whole story about you. If a General wanted to give a soft god-son's job to a fellow, it would be a soft job and a fat one. He wouldn't send him here. So take the battalion with my blessing. You won't worry over it more than I have: the poor bloody Glamorgans."[16]

So he had his battalion! He drew an immense breath. The bumps began to come back along the line. He figured those shells as being like sparrow-hawks beating along a hedge. They were probably pretty accurate. The Germans were pretty accurate. The trenches were probably being knocked about a good deal, the pretty, pinkish gravel falling about in heaps as it would lie in a park, ready to be spread on paths. He remembered how he had

---

* A still-current legal term used in the law of wills to determine what happens when property bequeathed under a will is no longer in the testator's estate when the testator dies.

been up on the Montagne Noire, still, thank God, behind where they were now. Why did he thank God? Did he really care where the Army was. Probably! But enough to say "thank God" about? Probably too.... But as long as they kept on at the job did anything matter? Anything else? It was keeping on that mattered. From the Montagne Noire he had seen our shells bursting on a thinnish line in the distance, in shining weather. Each shell existing in a white puff, beautifully. Forward and backward along the line.... Under Messines village.[17] He had felt exhilaration to think that our gunners were making such good practice. Now some Hun on a hill was feeling exhilaration over puffs of smoke in our line!... But he, Tietjens was ... Damn it, he was going to make two hundred and fifty quid towards living with Valentine Wannop—when you really *could* stand up on a hill ... anywhere!

The Adjutant, Notting, looked in and said:

"Brigade wants to know if we're suffering any, sir?"

The Colonel surveyed Tietjens with irony:

"Well, what are you going to report?" he asked.... "This officer is taking over from me," he said to Notting. Notting's beady eyes and red-varnished cheeks expressed no emotions.

"Oh, tell Brigade," the Colonel said, "that we're all as happy as sand-boys. We could stand this till Kingdom come." He asked: "We *aren't* suffering any, are we?"

Notting said: "No, not in particular. "C" Company was grumbling that all its beautiful revetments had been knocked to pieces. The sentry near their own dugout complained that the pebbles in the gravel were nearly as bad as shrapnel."

"Well, tell Brigade what I said. With Major[18] Tietjens' compliments, not mine. He's in command."

" ... You may as well make a cheerful impression to begin with," he added to Tietjens.

It was then that, suddenly, he burst out with:

"Look here! Lend me two hundred and fifty quid!"

He remained staring fixedly at Tietjens with an odd air of a man who has just asked a teasing, jocular conundrum. ...

Tietjens had recoiled—really half an inch. The man said he was suffering from a loathsome disease: it was being near something dirty. You don't contract loathsome diseases except

from the cheapest kind of women[19] or through being untidy-
minded.... The man's pals had gone back on him. That sort of
man's pals do go back on him! His accounts were all out.... He
was in short the sort of swindling, unclean[20] scoundrel to whom
one lent money.... Irresistibly!

A crash of the sort you couldn't ignore, as is the case with
certain claps in thunderstorms, sent a good deal of gravel down
their cellar steps. It crashed against their shaky door. They heard
Notting come out of his cellar and tell someone to shovel the
beastly stuff back again where it had come from.

The Colonel looked up at the roof. He said that had knocked
their parapet about a bit. Then he resumed his fixed gaze at Tietjens.

Tietjens said to himself.

"I'm losing my nerve.... It's the damned news that Campion
is coming ... I'm becoming a wretched, irresolute Johnny."

The Colonel said:

"I'm not a beastly sponger. I never borrowed before!" His chest
heaved.... It really expanded and then got smaller again, the
orifice in the khaki at his throat contracting.... Perhaps he
never had borrowed before....

After all, it didn't matter what kind of man this was, it was a
question of what sort of a man Tietjens was becoming. He said:

"I can't lend you the money. I'll guarantee an overdraft to your
agents. For two hundred and fifty."

Well, then, he remained the sort of man who automatically
lent money. He was glad.

The Colonel's face fell. His martially erect shoulders indeed[21]
collapsed. He exclaimed ruefully:

"Oh, I say, I thought you were the sort one could go to."

Tietjens said:

"It's the same thing. You can draw a cheque[22] on your bank
exactly as if I paid the money in."

The Colonel said:

"I *can?* It's the same thing? You're *sure?*" His questions were
like the pleas of a young woman asking you not to murder her.

... He obviously was not a sponger. He was a financial virgin.
There could not be a subaltern of eighteen in the whole army who
did not know what it meant to have an overdraft guaranteed after

a fortnight's leave. . . . Tietjens only wished they didn't. He said:

"You've practically got the money in your hand as you sit there. I've only to write the letter. It's impossible your agents should refuse my guarantee. If they do, I'll raise the money and send it to you."

He wondered why he didn't do that last in any case. A year or so ago he would have had no hesitation about overdrawing his account to any extent. Now he had an insupportable objection. Like a hatred!

He said:

"You'd better let me have your address." He added, for his mind was really wandering a little. There was too much talk! "I suppose you'll go to No. IX Red Cross at Rouen for a bit."*

The Colonel sprang to his feet:

"My God, what's that?" he cried out. "Me . . . to No. IX."

Tietjens exclaimed:

"I don't know the procedure. You said you had. . . ."

The other cried out:

"I've got cancer. A big swelling under the armpit." He passed his hand over his bare flesh through the opening of his shirt, the long arm disappearing to the elbow. "Good God . . . I suppose when I said my pals had gone back on me you thought I'd asked them for help and been refused. I haven't. . . . They're all killed. That's the worst way you can go back on a pal, isn't it? Don't you understand men's language?"

He sat heavily down on his bed again.

He said:

"By Jove:[23] if you hadn't promised to let me have the money there would have been nothing for me but to make a hole in the water."

Tietjens said:

"Well, don't contemplate it now. Get yourself well looked after. What does Terry[24] say?"

The Colonel again started violently:

"Terry! The M.O. . . . Do you think I'd tell him! Or little squits of subalterns? Or any man! You understand now why I wouldn't

---

* Ford was sent to Rouen's No. 11 Red Cross Hospital in 1916 with a respiratory illness and a recurrence of shell-shock.

take Terry's beastly pill. How do I know what it mightn't do
to. . . ."

Again he passed his hand under his armpit, his eyes taking on
a yearning and calculating expression. He added:

"I thought it a duty to tell you as I was asking you for a loan.
You might not get repaid. I suppose your offer still holds good?"

Drops of moisture had hitherto made beads on his forehead; it
now shone, uniformly wet.

"If you haven't consulted anybody," Tietjens said, "you mayn't
have got it. I should have yourself seen to right away. My offer
still holds good!"[25]

"Oh, I've got it, all right," the Colonel answered with an air of
infinite sapience. "My old man—my governor—had it. Just like
that. And he never told a soul till three days before his death.
Neither shall I."

"I should get it seen to," Tietjens maintained. "It's a duty to
your children. And the King. You're too damn good a soldier for
the Army to lose."

"Nice of you to say so," the Colonel said. "But I've stood too
much. I couldn't face waiting for the verdict."

. . . It was no good saying he had faced worse things. He very
likely hadn't, being the man he was.

The Colonel said:

"Now if I could be any good!"

Tietjens said:

"I suppose I may go along the trenches now. There's a wet
place. . . ."

He was determined to go along the trenches. He had to . . .
what was it . . . "find a place to be alone with Heaven."* He maintained also his conviction that he must show the men his
mealsack of a body, mooning along; but attentive.

A problem worried him. He did not like putting it since it might
seem[26] to question the Colonel's military efficiency. He wrapped
it up: Had the Colonel any special advice as to keeping in touch
with units on the right and left? And as to passing messages.

. . . That was a mania with Tietjens. If he had had his way he
would keep the battalion day and night at communication drill.

---

* From the final stanza of George Meredith's 'Love in the Valley' (1851; 1878).

He had not been able to discover that any precautions of that sort were taken in that unit at all. Or in the others alongside. . . .
He had hit on the Colonel's heel of Achilles.

In the open it became evident: more and more and more and always more evident! The news that General Campion was taking[27] over that command had changed Tietjens' whole view of the world. The trenches were much as he had expected. They conformed indeed exactly to the image he had had in the cellar. They resembled heaps of reddish gravel laid out ready to distribute over the roads of parks. Getting out of the dugout had been like climbing into a trolley that had just been inverted for the purposes of discharging its load. It was a nasty job for the men, cleaving a passage and keeping under cover. Naturally the German sharp-shooters were on the lookout. Our problem was to get as much of the trench as you could set up by daylight. The German problem was to get as many of our men as possible. Tietjens would see that our men stayed[28] under cover until nightfall; the commander of the unit opposite would attend to the sniping of as many men as he could. Tietjens himself had three first-class snipers left: they would attempt to get as many of the German snipers as they could. That was self-defence.[29]

In addition a great many Enemy attentions would direct themselves to Tietjens' stretch of the line. The artillery would continue to plunk in a shell or so from time to time. They would not do this very often because it would invite the attention of our artillery and that might prove too costly. More or less heavy masses[30] of High Explosives would be thrown on to the line: what the Germans called *Minenwerfer** might project what our people called sausages. These being visible coming through the air you posted lookouts who gave you warning in time to get under cover. So the Germans had rather abandoned the use of these, probably as being costly in explosives and not so very effective. They made, that is to say, good holes but accounted for few men.

* Translated as 'mine launcher', this is the German name for a class of short-range mortars used extensively in this war by the German army. Their engineers intended they would clear obstacles – bunkers and barbed wire, for example – but Tietjens seems to suggest here that their success was limited.

Airplanes with their beastly bullet-distributing[31] hoppers—
that is what they seemed like—would now and then duck along
the trench, but not very often. The proceeding was, again, too
costly: they would limit themselves as a rule to circling leisurely
overhead and dropping things whilst the shrapnel burst round
them—and spattered bullets over the trench. Flying pigs,* aerial
torpedoes, and other floating missiles, pretty, shining, silvery[32]
things with fins, would come through the air and would explode
on striking the ground or after burying themselves. There was
practically no end to their devices and the Huns had a new one
every other week or so. They perhaps wasted themselves on new
devices. A good many of them turned out to be duds. And a good
many of their usually successful missiles turned out to be duds.
They were undoubtedly beginning to feel the strain—mental and
in their materials. So that if you had to be in these beastly[33] places
it was probably better to be in our trenches than theirs. Our war
material was pretty good!

This was the war of attrition. . . . A mug's game! A mug's game
as far as killing men was concerned, but not an uninteresting
occupation if you considered it as a struggle of various minds[34]
spread all over the broad landscape in the sunlight. They did not
kill many men and they expended an infinite number of missiles
and a vast amount of thought. If you took six million men armed[35]
with loaded canes and stockings containing bricks or knives and
set them against another six million men similarly armed, at the
end of three hours four million on the one side and the entire six
million on the other would be dead. So, as far as killing went, it
really was a mug's game. That was what happened if you let yourself get into the hands of the applied scientist. For all these things
were the products not of the soldier but of hirsute, bespectacled
creatures who peered through magnifying glasses. Or of course,
on our[36] side, they would be shaven-cheeked and less abstracted.
They were efficient as slaughterers in that they enabled the
millions of men to be moved. When you had only knives you
could not move very fast. On the other hand, your knife killed at
every stroke: you would set a million men firing at each other
with rifles from eighteen hundred yards. But few rifles ever regis-

* Mortar bombs.

tered a hit. So the invention was relatively inefficient. And it dragged things out!

And suddenly it had become boring.

They were probably going to spend a whole day during which the Germans[37] would strain themselves, their intelligences flickering across the world, to kill a couple of Tietjens' men, and Tietjens would exercise all his care in the effort not to have even one casualty. And at the end of the day they would all be very tired and the poor b—y men would have to set to work to repair the trenches in earnest. That was the ordinary day's work.

He was going about it.... He had got "A" Company Commander to come up and talk to him about his fatigues. To the right of Headquarters the trenches appeared to have suffered less than to the left and it was possible to move quite a number of men without risk. "A" Company Commander was an astonishingly thin, bald man of fifty. He was so bald that his tin hat slid about all over his skull. He had been a small shipowner and must have married very late in life, for he spoke of having two children, one of five, one of seven. A pigeon pair. His business was now making fifty thousand a year for him. It pleased Tietjens to think that his children would be well provided for if he were killed. A nice, silent, capable man who usually looked into the distance rather abstractedly when he talked. He was killed two months[38] later, cleanly, by a bullet.

He was impatient that things had not got a move on. What had become of the big Hun *strafe*?

Tietjens said:

"You remember the Hun company-sergeant-major that surrendered to your crowd the night before last? The fellow who said he was going to open a little sweet-stuff shop in the Tottenham Court Road with the company money he had stolen?... Or perhaps you did not hear?"

The remembrance of that shifty-looking N.C.O. in blue-grey that was rather smart for a man coming in during a big fight stirred up intensely disagreeable feelings from the bottom of Tietjens' mind. It was detestable to him to be in control of the person of another human being—as detestable as it would have been to be himself a prisoner ... that thing that he dreaded most in the world. It was indeed almost more detestable, since to be taken prisoner was at least a thing outside your own volition, whereas to control a prisoner, even under the compulsion of discipline on yourself, implies a certain free-will of your own. And this had been an especially loathsome affair. Even normally, though it was irrational enough, prisoners affected him with the sense that they were unclean. As if they were maggots. It was not sensible; but he knew that if he had had to touch a prisoner he would have felt nausea. It was no doubt the product of his passionate Tory sense of freedom. What distinguished man from the brutes was his freedom. When then a man was deprived of freedom he became like a brute. To exist in his society was to live with brutes: like Gulliver amongst the Houynhms!*

And this unclean fellow had been a deserter in addition!

He had been brought in to the H.Q. dugout at three in the morning after the *strafe* had completely died out. It appeared that he had come over, ostensibly in the ordinary course of the attack. But he had lain all night in a shell hole, creeping in to our lines only when things were quiet. Previously to starting he had crammed his pockets with all the company money and even the papers that he could lay his hands on. He had been brought to H.Q. at that disagreeable hour because of the money and the papers, "A" Company judging that such things ought to be put in the hands at least of the Adjutant as quickly as possible.

The C.O., McKechnie,[39] the Intelligence[40] Officer and the doctor had all, in addition to Tietjens himself, just settled in there, and the air of the smallish place was already fetid and reeking with service rum and whiskey. The appearance of the German had caused Tietjens almost to vomit, and he was already in a state of enervation from having had to bring the battalion in. His temples were racked with a sort of neuralgia that he believed to be caused by eyestrain.

---

* Part IV of *Gulliver's Travels* (1726), by Jonathan Swift, is called 'A Voyage to the Country of the Houyhnhnms'. The notes to the Penguin Classics edition (1985) state that this word 'has been variously pronounced but may be taken to echo the whinny of a horse' (360). The Houyhnhnms are pronounced 'orderly and rational', 'acute and judicious' (272) by Gulliver, while he, taken to be a 'yahoo', is considered at first to be more-or-less a brute. (But the comparison might be more effective in context if it was between Gulliver and the Yahoos.) Cf. *March* 602 and *The English Novel* (1930), chapters 2 and 3, for more on Swift. In *The English Novel* Ford writes, 'but Lilliput is as real to us as the Slough of Despond and the Yahoos are the figures of the most horrible experience of every man who has come across them' (86).

Normally, the questioning of prisoners before they reached Division was strongly discountenanced, but a deserter excites more interest than an ordinary prisoner, and the C.O. who was by then in a state of hilarious mutiny absolutely ordered Tietjens to get all he could out of the prisoner. Tietjens knew a little German: the Intelligence Officer who knew that language well had been killed. Dunne, replacing him, had no German.[41]

The shifty, upright, thin, dark fellow with even unusually uneasy eyes, had answered questions readily enough: Yes, the Huns were fed-up with the war; discipline had become so difficult to maintain that one of his reasons for deserting had been sheer[42] weariness over the effort to keep the men under him in order. They had no food. It was impossible to get the men, in an advance, past any kind of food dumps.[43] He was continually being unjustly reprimanded for his want of success, and standing there he cursed his late officers! Nevertheless, when the C.O. made Tietjens ask him some questions about an Austrian gun that the Germans had lately introduced to that front and that threw a self-burying shell containing an incredible quantity of H.E.,[44] the fellow had clicked his heels together and had answered:

"*Nein, Herr Offizier, das waere Landesverratung!*"... to answer that would be to betray one's country. His psychology had been difficult to grasp. He had explained as well as he could, using a few words of English, the papers that he had brought over. They were mostly exhortations to the German soldiers,[45] circulars containing news of disasters to and the demoralisation of the Allied troops; there were also a few returns of no great interest—mostly statistics of influenza cases.[46] But when Tietjens had held before the fellow's eyes a type-written page with a heading that he had now forgotten, the Sergeant had exclaimed: "*Ach, nicht das!*" ... and had made as if to snatch the paper from Tietjens' fingers. Then he had desisted, realising that he was risking his life, no doubt. But he had become as pale as death, and had refused to translate the phrases that Tietjens did not understand; and indeed Tietjens understood practically none of the words, which were all technical.

He knew the paper contained some sort of movement orders; but he was by that time heartily sick of the affair and he knew that that was just the sort of paper that the staff did not wish men in the line to meddle with. So he dropped the matter, and the Colonel and the Pals being by that time tired of listening and not grasping what was happening, Tietjens had sent the fellow at the double back to Brigade under the charge of the Intelligence Officer and a heavier escort than was usual.

What remained to Tietjens of the affair was the expression that the fellow had used when asked what he was going to do with the Company money he had stolen. He was going to open a little sweet shop in the Tottenham Court Road. He had, of course, been a waiter: in Old Compton Street. Tietjens wondered vaguely what would become of him. What did they do with deserters? Perhaps they interned them: perhaps they made them N.C.O.s[47] in prisoners' units. He could never go back to Germany.... That remained to him—and the horror and loathing he had felt at the episode: as if it had caused him personal deterioration. He had put the matter out of his mind.

It occurred to him now that, very likely, the urgent announcements from Staff of all sorts had been inspired by that very paper! The paper that loathsome fellow had tried to grab at. He remembered that he had been feeling so sick that he hadn't bothered to have the man handcuffed.... It raised a number of questions: Does a man desert and at the same time refuse to betray his country? Well, he might. There was no end to the contradictions in men's characters. Look at the C.O. An efficient officer and a muddled ass in one: even in soldiering matters!

On the other hand, the whole thing might be a plant of the Huns. The paper—the movement order—might have been meant to reach our Army Headquarters. On the face of it, important movement orders do not lie about in Company offices. Not usually. The Huns might be trying to call our attention to this part of the line whilst their real attack might be coming somewhere else. That again was unlikely because that particular part of the line was so weak owing to poor[48] General Puffles' unpopularity with the great ones at home that the Huns would be mad if they attacked anywhere else. And the French were hurrying up straight to that spot in terrific force. He might then be a hero!...[49] But he didn't look like a hero!

This sort of complication was wearisome nowadays, though once it would have delighted him to dwell on it and work it out with nice figures and calculations of stresses. Now his only emotion about the matter was that, thank God, it was none of his job. The Huns didn't appear to be coming.

He found himself regretting that the *strafe* was not coming after all. That was incredible. How could he regret not being put into immediate[50] danger of death?

Long, thin, scrawny and mournful, with his tin hat now tilted forward over his nose, the O.C. "A" Company gazed into futurity and remarked:

"I'm sorry the Huns aren't coming!"

He was sorry the Huns were not coming. Because if they came they might as well come according to the information supplied by that prisoner. He had captured that fellow. He might as well therefore get the credit. It might get him remembered if he put in for leave. He wanted leave. He wanted to see his children. He had not seen them for two years now. Children of five and seven change a good deal in two years. He grumbled on. Without any shame at the revelation of his intimate motives. The quite ordinary man! But he was perfectly to be respected. He had a rather grating chest voice. It occurred to Tietjens that that man would never see his children.

He wished these intimations would not come to him. He found himself at times looking at the faces of several men and thinking that this or that man would shortly be killed. He wished he could get rid of the habit. It seemed indecent. As a rule he was right. But then, almost every man you looked at there was certain to get killed.... Himself excepted. He himself was going to be wounded in the soft place behind the right collar-bone.

He regretted that the *strafe* was not that morning coming! Because if they came they might as well come according to the information supplied by the prisoner he had examined in the stinking dug-out. His unit had captured the fellow. He would now be signing its H.Q. chits as Acting O.C. Ninth Glamorganshires. So he, Tietjens, had captured that fellow. And his perspicacity in having him sent immediately back to brigade with his precious paper might get him, Tietjens, remembered favourably at Brigade H.Q. Then they would leave him in temporary command of his battalion. And if they did that he might do well enough to get a battalion of his own!

He astounded himself.... His mentality was that of O.C. "A" Company!

He said:

"It was damn smart of you to see that fellow was of importance and have him sent at the double to me." O.C. "A" Coy. grew red over all his grim face. So, one day, he, Tietjens, might flush with pleasure at the words of some squit with a red band round his hat!

He said:

"Even if the Germans don't come it might have been helpful. It might have been even more helpful. It might have been the means of keeping them back." Because of course if the Germans knew that we had got hold of their Movement Order they might change their plans. That would inconvenience them.[51] It was not likely. There was perhaps not time for the news that we knew to have got through to their Important Ones. But it was possible. Such things had happened.

Aranjuez and the Lance-Corporal stood still and so silent in the sunlight that they resembled fragments of the reddish trench. The red gravel of the trenches began here, however, to be smirched with more agricultural marl.[52] Later the trenches became pure alluvial soil and then ran down more smartly into stuff so wet that it was like a quicksand. A bog. It was there he had tried revetting with a syphon-drain. The thought of that extreme of his line reminded him. He said:

"You know all about keeping in communication with immediately neighbouring units?"

The grim fellow said:

"Only what they taught in the training camps[53] at the beginning of the war, sir. When I joined up. It was fairly thorough but it's[54] all forgotten now."

Tietjens said to Aranjuez:

"You're Signalling Officer. What do you know about keeping in communication with units on your right and left?"

Aranjuez, blushing and stammering, knew all about buzzers and signals. Tietjens said:

"That's only for trenches, all that. But, in motion. At your O.T.C. Didn't they practise you in keeping communication between troops in motion?"

They hadn't at the O.T.C.... At first it had been in the

programme. But it had always been crowded out by some stunt.
Rifle-grenade drill. Bomb-throwing. Stokes-gun drill. Any sort of
machine drill as long as it was not moving bodies of men over
difficult country—sand-hills, say[55]—and hammering into them
that they must keep in touch unit with unit or drop connecting
files if a unit itself divided up.

It was perhaps the dominant idea of Tietjens, perhaps the main
idea that he got out of warfare—that at all costs you must keep
in touch with your neighbouring troops. When, later, he had to
command the escorts over immense bodies of German prisoners
on the march it several times occurred to him to drop so many
connecting files for the benefit of the men or N.C.O.'s—or even
the officers, of his escort who had fallen out through sheer fatigue
or disease, that he would arrive in a new camp at the day's end
with hardly any escort left at all—say thirty for three thousand
prisoners. The business of an escort being to prevent the escape
of prisoners it might have been thought better to retain the
connecting files for that purpose. But, on the other hand, he
never lost a prisoner except by German bombs, and he never lost
any of his stragglers at all.

. . . He said to O.C. "A" Company:

"Please look after this matter in your Company. I shall arrange
as soon as I can to transfer you to the outside right of the unit. If
the men are doing nothing lecture them, please, yourself on this
subject and talk very seriously to all lance-corporals, section
leaders and oldest privates of platoons.[56] And be good enough to
get into communication at once with the Company Commander
of the Wiltshires immediately on our right. In one of two ways
the war is over. The war of trenches. Either the Germans will
immediately drive us into the North Sea or we shall drive them
back. They will then be in a state of demoralisation and we shall
need to move fast. Lieutenant Aranjuez, you will arrange to be
present when Captain Gibbs talks to his Company and you will
repeat what he says in the other Companies."

He was talking quickly and distinctly, as he did when he was
well, and he was talking stiltedly on purpose. He could not obviously call an officers' conference with a German attack possibly
impending; but he was pretty certain that something of what he
said would penetrate to nearly every ear of the Battalion if he said

it before a Company Commander, a Signalling Lieutenant and an Orderly-room Lance-Corporal. It would go through that the Old Man was dotty on this joke, and Sergeants would see that some attention was paid to the matter. So would the officers. It was all that could be done at the moment.

He walked behind Gibbs along the trench which at this point was perfectly intact and satisfactory, the red gravel giving place to marl.[57] He remarked to the good fellow that in that way they would do something to checkmate the blasted civilians whose meddling with the processes of war had put them where they were. Gibbs agreed gloomily that civilian interference had lost the war. They so hated the regular army that whenever a civilian saw a trace of regular training remaining in this mud-fighting that they liked us to indulge in, he wrote a hundred letters under different names to the papers, and the War Secretary at once took steps to retain that hundred votes; Gibbs had been reading a home newspaper that morning.

Tietjens surprised himself by saying:

"Oh, we'll beat them yet!" It was an expression of impracticable optimism. He sought to justify his words by saying that their Army Commanders[58] having put up such a damn good fight in spite of the most criminal form of civilian interference had begun to put a stopper on their games. Campion's coming was a proof that soldiers were going to be allowed to have some say in the conduct of the war. It meant the single command.... Gibbs expressed a muted satisfaction. If the French took over those lines as they certainly would if they had the Single Command he would no doubt be able to go home and see his children. All their divisions would have to be taken out of the lines to be reorganised and brought up to strength.

Tietjens said:

"As to what we were talking about.... Supposing you detailed outside section leaders and another file to keep in touch with the Wiltshires and they did the same. Supposing that for purpose of recognition they wore handkerchiefs round their right and left arms respectively.... It has been done...."

"The Huns," Captain Gibbs said grimly, "would probably pick them off specially. They'd probably pick off specially any one who had any sort of badge. So you would be worse off."

They were going at his request to look at a section of his trench. Orderly Room had ordered him to make arrangements for machine-gun performances there. He couldn't. It didn't exist. Nothing existed. He supposed that to have been the new Austrian gun. New probably, but why Austrian? The Austrians did not usually interest themselves much in High Explosives. This one, whatever it was, threw something that buried itself and then blew up half the universe. With astonishingly little noise and commotion. Just lifted up. Like a hippopotamus. He, Gibbs, had hardly noticed anything as you would have if it had been say a mine. When they came and told him that a mine had gone off there he would not believe them. . . . But you could see for yourself that it looked exactly as if a mine had been chucking things about. A small mine. But still a mine. . . .

In the shelter of the broken end of the trench a fatigue of six men worked with pick and shovel, patiently, two at a time. They threw up mud and stones and patted them and, stepping down into the thus created vacancy, threw up more mud and stones. Water oozed about, uncertain where to go. There must be a spring there. That hillside was honeycombed with springs. . . .

You would certainly have said there had been a mine there. If we had been advancing it would have been a small mine left by the Huns to cheer us up. But we had retreated on to ground we had always held. So it couldn't have been a mine.

Also it kicked the ground forward and backward and relatively little laterally, so that the deep hole it had created more resembled the entry into a rudimentary shaft than the usually circular shell hole. A mound existed between Tietjens and "B" Company trench, considerably higher than you could see over. A vast mound; a miniature Primrose Hill.* But much bigger than anything they had seen created by flying pigs or other aerial missiles as yet. Anyhow the mound was high enough to give Tietjens a chance to get round it in cover and shuffle down into "B" Company's line. He said to Gibbs:

---

* Now in the London Borough of Camden, Primrose Hill stands at a height of 256 feet. Long fashionable, it is situated on the north side of Regents Park and commands a view over central London to the south-east and Hampstead to the north. Hampstead Heath is higher (440 feet), but less central.

"We shall have to see about that machine gun place. Don't come any further with me. Make those fellows keep their heads down and send them back if the[59] Huns seem like sending over any more dirt."

CHAPTER VI[1]

TIETJENS reclined on the reverse slope of the considerable mound. In the sunlight. He had to be alone. To reflect on his sentimental situation and his machine guns. He had been kept so out of the affairs of the unit that he had[2] suddenly remembered[3] that he knew nothing whatever about his machine guns,[4] or even about the fellow who had to look after him. A new fellow called Cobbe, who looked rather vacant, with an immense sunburnt nose and an open mouth. Not, on the face of him, alert enough for his job. But you never knew.

He was hungry. He had eaten practically[5] nothing since seven the night before, and had been on his feet the greater part of the time.

He sent Lance-Corporal Duckett to "A" Company dugout, to ask if they could favour him with a sandwich and some coffee with rum in it: he sent Second-Lieutenant Aranjuez to "B" Company to tell them that he was coming to take a look round on their men and quarters. "B" Company Commander for the moment was a very young boy just out from an O.T.C. It was annoying that he had an outside Company. But Constantine, the former Commander,[6] had been killed the night before last. He was, in fact, said to be the gentleman whose remains hung in the barbed wire which was what made Tietjens doubtful whether it could be he. He should not have been so far to the left if he had been bringing his Company in. Anyhow, there had been no one to replace him but this boy—Bennett. A good boy. So shy that he could hardly give a word of command on parade, but yet with all his wits about him. And blessed with an uncommonly experienced Company Sergeant-Major. One of the original old Glamorganshires. Well, beggars could not be choosers![7] The Company had reported that morning five cases of the influenza that was said to be ravaging the outside world. Here then was another thing for which they had to thank the outside world— this band of rag-time solitaries! They let the outside world severely alone; they were, truly, hermits. Then the outside world did this to them. Why not leave them to their monastic engrossedness?[8]

Even the rotten and detestable Huns had it! They were said by the Divisional news-sheets to have it so badly that whole Divisions were incapable of effective action. That might be a lie, invented for the purpose of heartening us; but it was probably true. The German[9] men were apparently beastly underfed, and, at that, only on substitute-foods of relatively small percentage of nutritive value. The papers brought over by that N.C.O. had certainly spoken urgently of the necessity of taking every precaution against the spread of this flail.[10] Another circular violently and lachrymosely assured the troops that they were as well fed as the civilian populations and the Corps of Officers. Apparently there had been some sort of scandal. A circular of which he had not had time to read the whole ended up with an assertion something like: "Thus the honour of the Corps of Officers has been triumphantly vindicated."

It was a ghastly thought, that of that whole vast territory that confronted them, filled with millions of half-empty stomachs that bred disorders in the miserable brains. Those fellows must be the most miserable human beings that had ever existed. God knows, the life of our own Tommies must be Hell. But those fellows. . . . It would not bear thinking of.

And it was curious to consider how the hatred that one felt for the inhabitants of those regions seemed to skip in a wide trajectory over the embattled ground. It was the civilian populations and their rulers that one hated with real hatred. Now the swine were starving the poor devils in the trenches![11]

They were detestable. The German fighters and their Intelligence and staffs were merely boring and grotesque. Unending nuisances. For he was confoundedly irritated to think of the mess they had made of his nice clean trenches. It was like when you go out for an hour and leave your dog in the drawing-room.[12] You come back and find that it has torn to pieces all your sofa-cushions. You would like to knock its head off. . . . So you would like to knock the German soldiers' heads off. But you did not wish them much real harm. Nothing like having to live in that hell on perpetually half empty, windy stomachs with the nightmares they set up! Naturally influenza was decimating them.[13]

Anyhow, Germans were the sort of people that influen
bowl over. They were bores because they came for ever
type. You read their confounded circulars and they made yo
whilst a little puking. They were like continual caricatur of
themselves and they were continually hysterical.... Hypochon-
driacal.... Corps of Officers.... Proud German Army.... His
Glorious Majesty.... Mighty Deeds.... Not much of the Rag-
time Army about that, and that was welling out continuously all
the time.... Hypochondria!

A rag-time army was not likely to have influenza so badly. It
felt neither its moral nor its physical pulse.... Still, here was
influenza in "B" Company. They must have got it from the Huns
the night before last. "B" Company had had them jump in on top
of them; then and there had been hand-to-hand fighting. It was
a nuisance. "B" Company was a nuisance. It had naturally been
stuck into the dampest and lowest part of their line. Their
company dugout was reported to be like a well with a dripping
roof. It would take "B" Company to be afflicted with such quarters.... It was difficult to see what to do—not to drain their
quarters, but to exorcise their ill-luck. Still, it would have to be
done. He was going into their quarters to make a *strafe*, but he
sent Aranjuez to announce his coming so as to give the decent
young Company Commander a chance to redd[14] up his
house....*

The beastly Huns! They stood between him and Valentine
Wannop. If they would go home he could be sitting talking to her
for whole afternoons. That was what a young woman was for. You
seduced a young woman in order to be able to finish your talks
with her. You could not do that without living with her. You
could not live with her without seducing her; but that was the by-
product. The point is that you can't otherwise[15] talk. You can't
finish talks at street corners; in museums; even in drawing-rooms.
You mayn't be in the mood when she is in the mood—for the
intimate conversation that means the final communion of your
souls. You have to wait together—for a week, for a year, for a life-

---

* The *OED* gives 'redd' as a late Middle English verb, meaning to clear, to put in order.
The references to the phrase 'to redd up' that I have found are American rather than
English.

time, before the final intimate conversation may be attained . . . and exhausted. So that. . . .

That in effect was love. It struck him as astonishing. The word was so little in his vocabulary. . . . Love, ambition, the desire for wealth. They were things he had never known of as existing—as capable of existing within him. He had been the Younger Son, loafing, contemptuous, capable, idly contemplating life, but ready to take up the position of the Head of the Family if Death so arranged matters. He had been a sort of eternal Second-in-Command.

Now: what the Hell was he? A sort of Hamlet of the Trenches? No, by God he was not. . . . [16] He was[17] perfectly ready for action. Ready to command a battalion. He was presumably a lover. They did things like commanding battalions. And worse!

He ought to write her a letter. What in the world would she think of this gentleman who had once[18] made improper proposals to her; balked; said "So long!" or perhaps not even "So long!" And then walked off. With never a letter! Not even a picture postcard! For two years! A sort of a Hamlet all right! Or a swine![19]

Well, then, he ought to write her a letter. He ought to say: "This is to tell you that I propose to live with you as soon as this show is over. You will be prepared immediately on cessation of active hostilities to put yourself at my disposal. Please. Signed, Xtopher Tietjens, Acting O.C. 9th Glams."[20] A proper military communication. She would be pleased to see that he was commanding[21] a battalion. Or perhaps she would not be pleased. She was a Pro-German.[22] She loved these tiresome fellows who tore his, Tietjens', sofa-cushions to pieces.

That was not fair. She was a Pacifist. She thought these proceedings pestilential and purposeless. Well,[23] there were times when they appeared purposeless enough. Look at what had happened to his neat gravel walks. And to the marl[24] too. Though that served the purpose of letting him sit sheltered. In the sunlight. With any number of larks. Someone once wrote:

"A myriad larks in unison sang o'er her, soaring out of sight!"*

* The line is taken from Mathilde Blind's poem 'Love-Trilogy I'. Blind (1841–96) was a British poet born in Mannheim. She was known personally to Ford, and had been since he was a child; his grandparents, the Madox Browns, had more-or-less adopted

That was imbecile really. Larks cannot sing in unison. They make a heartless noise like that produced by the rubbing of two corks one on the other.... There came into his mind an image. Years ago: years and years ago: probably after having watched that gunner torment the fat Hun, because it had been below Max Redoubt.... The sun was now for certain shining on Bemerton! Well, he could never be a country parson. He was going to live with Valentine Wannop!... he had been coming down the reverse side of the range, feeling good. Probably because he had got out of that O.P. which the Germans guns had been trying to find. He went down with long strides, the tops of thistles brushing his hips. Obviously the thistles contained things that attracted flies. They are apt to after a famous victory. So myriads of swal-lows pursued him, swirling round and round him, their wings touching; for a matter of twenty yards all round and their wings brushing him and the tops of the thistles. And as the blue sky was reflected in the blue of their backs—for their backs were below his eyes—he had felt like a Greek God striding through the sea....*

The larks were less inspiring. Really, they were abusing the German guns. Imbecilely and continuously, they were screaming imprecations and threats. They had been relatively sparse until just now. Now that the shells were coming back from a mile or so off the sky was thick with larks. A myriad—two myriad[25]—corks at once. Not in unison. Sang o'er him, soaring out of sight!... You might almost say that it was a sign that the Germans were going to shell you again. Wonderful "hinstinck"[26]† set by the Almighty in their little bosoms! It was perhaps also accurate. No doubt the shells as they approached more and more shook the earth and disturbed the little bosoms on their nests. So they got up and shouted; perhaps warning each other; perhaps mere defiance of the artillery.

He was going to write to Valentine Wannop. It was a clumsy swine's trick not to have written to her before. He had proposed

---

her. She was stern to the child and made a forbidding impression, which is perhaps why she features in Ford's account of Ford Madox Brown's death in 1893 (*Ford Madox Brown* [London: Longmans, Green, 1896]). Recent (as yet unpublished) research by Angela Thirlwell shows that Blind was Madox Brown's mistress for many years.
* Cf. *No Enemy* 23.
† 'hinstinck' – cockney dialect for 'instinct'. See similar phrase in II.i.

to seduce her; hadn't done it and had gone off without a word. . . .
Considering himself rather a swell, too![27]
    He said:
    "Did you get a bit to eat, Corporal!"
    The Corporal balanced himself before Tietjens on the slope of
the mound. He blushed, rubbing his right sole on his left instep,[28]
holding in his right hand[29] a small tin can and a cup, in his left
an immaculate towel containing a small cube.
    Tietjens debated whether he should first drink of the coffee
and army rum to increase his zest for the sandwiches, or whether
he should first eat the sandwiches and so acquire more thirst for
the coffee. . . . It would be reprehensible to write to Valentine
Wannop. The act of the cold-blooded seducer. Reprehensible! . . .
It depended on what was in the sandwiches. It would be agreeable to fill the void below and inwards from his breastbone. But
whether do it first with a solid or warm moisture?
    The Lance-Corporal was deft. . . . He set the coffee tin, cup
and towel on a flat stone that stuck out of that heap; the towel
unfolded, served as a tablecloth; there appeared three heaps of
ethereal sandwiches. He said he had eaten half a tin of warm
mutton and haricot beans, whilst he was cutting the sandwiches.
The meat in the sandwiches consisted of *foie gras*, that pile: bully
beef reduced to a paste with butter that was margarine, anchovy
paste out of a tin and minced onion out of pickles; the third pile
was bully beef *nature*, seasoned with Worcester sauce. . . . All the
materials he had at disposal!
    Tietjens smiled on the boy at his work. He said this must be a
regular *chef*. The boy said:
    "Not a *chef*, yet, sir!" He had a camp stool hung on his
trenching tool behind his hip. He had been chief assistant to one
of the chief cooks in the Savoy. He had been going to go to Paris.
"What you call a marmiton,* sir!" he said. With his trenching tool
he was scooping out a level place in front of the flat rock. He set
the camp stool on the flattened platform.
    Tietjens said:
    "You used to wear a white cap and white overalls?"
    He liked to think of the blond boy resembling Valentine

---

* Cassell's Dictionary translates this as 'scullion, cook's boy'.

Wannop dressed all in slim white. The Lance-Corporal said: "It's different now, sir!" He stood at Tietjens' side, always caressing his instep. He regarded cooking as an Art. He would have preferred to be a painter, but Mother hadn't enough money. The source of supply dried up during the War.... [30] If the C.O. would say a word for him after the War.... He understood it was going to be difficult to get jobs after the War. All the blighters who had got out of serving, all the R.A.S.C., all the Lines of Communication men would get first chance. As the saying was, the further from the Line the better the pay. And the chance, too!

Tietjens said:

"Certainly I shall recommend you. You'll get a job all right. I shall never forget your sandwiches." He would never forget the keen, clean flavour of the sandwiches or the warm generosity of the sweet, be-rummed coffee! In the blue air of that April hillside. All the objects on that white towel were defined: with iridescent edges. The boy's face, too! Perhaps not physically iridescent. His breath, too, was very easy. Pure air! He was going to write to Valentine Wannop: "Hold yourself at my disposal. Please. Signed...." Reprehensible! Worse than reprehensible! You do not seduce the child of your father's oldest friend. He said: "I shall find it difficult enough to get a job after the War!"

Not only to seduce the young woman, but to invite her to live a remarkably precarious life with him. It isn't done!

The Lance-Corporal said:

"Oh, sir; no, sir! ... You're Mr. Tietjens, of Groby!"

He had often been to Groby of a Sunday afternoon. His mother was a Middlesbrough woman. Southbank, rather.[*] He had been to the Grammar School and was going to Durham University when ... Supplies stopped. On the eight nine fourteen....[†]

They oughtn't to put North Riding, Yorkshire, boys in Welsh-traditioned units. It was wrong. But for that he would not have run against this boy of disagreeable reminiscences.

---

* Southbank is east of Middlesbrough, next to Eston, which is where Ford was posted briefly just after the Armistice.

† 8 September 1914. One country declared war on another country on many dates in August (13 in all); most declarations had been made by 8 September. This is more likely to be a reference back to the lance-corporal's discussion of his mother's money, above.

"They say," the boy said, "that the well at Groby is three hundred and twenty feet deep, and the cedar at the corner of the house a hundred and sixty. The depth of the well twice the height of the tree!" He had often dropped stones down the well and listened: they made an astonishingly loud noise. Long: like echoes gone mad! His mother knew the cook at Groby. Mrs. Harmsworth. He had often seen ... he rubbed his ankles more furiously, in a paroxysm ... Mr. Tietjens, the father, and him, and Mr. Mark and Mr. John and Miss Eleanor. He once handed Miss Eleanor her riding crop when she dropped it....

Tietjens was never going to live at Groby. No more feudal atmosphere! He was going to live, he figured, in a four-room attic-flat, on the top of one of the Inns of Court. With Valentine Wannop. *Because* of Valentine Wannop!

He said to the boy:

"Those German shells seem to be coming back. Go and request Captain Gibbs as soon as they get near to take his fatigues under cover until they have passed."

He wanted to be alone with Heaven.... He drank his last cup of warm, sweetened coffee, laced with rum.... He drew a deep breath. Fancy drawing a deep breath of satisfaction after a deep draught of warm coffee, sweetened with condensed milk and laced with rum!... Reprehensible! Gastronomically reprehensible!... What would they say at the Club?... Well, he was never going to be at the Club! The Club claret was to be regretted! Admirable claret. And the cold sideboard!

But, for the matter of that, fancy drawing deep breaths of satisfaction over the mere fact of lying—in command of a battalion!—on a slope, in the clear air, with twenty thousand—two myriad!—corks making noises overhead and the German guns directing their projectiles so that they were slowly approaching! Fancy!

They were, presumably, trying out their new Austrian gun. Methodically, with an infinite thoroughness. If, that is to say, there really was a new Austrian gun. Perhaps there wasn't. Division had been in a great state of excitement over such a weapon. It stood in Orders that every one was to try to obtain every kind of information about it, and it was said to throw a projectile of a remarkable, High Explosive efficiency. So Gibbs had jumped to the conclusion that the thing that had knocked to pieces his projected machine-gun emplacement, had been the new gun. In that case they were trying it out very thoroughly.

The actual report of the gun or guns—they fired every three minutes, so that might mean that there was only one and that it took about three minutes to re-load—was very loud and rather high in tone. He had not yet heard the actual noise made by the projectile, but the reports from a distance had been singularly dulled. When, presumably, the projectile had effected its landing, it bored extraordinarily into the ground and then[31] exploded with a time-fuse. Very likely it would not be very dangerous to life, but, if they had enough of the guns and the H.E. to plaster the things all along the Line, and if the projectiles worked as efficiently as they had done on poor Gibbs's[32] trench, there would be an end of trench warfare on the Allied side. But, of course, they probably had not either enough guns or enough High Explosive and the thing would very likely act less efficiently in other sorts of soils. They were very likely trying that out. Or, if they were firing with only one gun they might be trying how many rounds could be fired before the gun became ineffective. Or they might be trying only the attrition game: smashing up the trenches which was always useful and then sniping the men who tried to repair them. You could bag a few men in that way, now and then. Or, naturally, with planes.... There was no end to these tiresome alternatives! Presumably, again, our planes might spot that gun or battery. Then it would stop!

Reprehensible!... He snorted! If you don't obey the rules of your club you get hoofed out, and that's that! If you retire from the post of Second-in-Command of Groby, you don't have to ... oh, attend battalion parades! He had refused to take any money from Brother[33] Mark on the ground of a fantastic quarrel. But he had not any quarrel with Brother Mark. The sardonic pair of them were just matching obstinacies. On the other hand you had to set to the tenantry an example of chastity, sobriety, probity, or you could not take their beastly money. You provided them[34] with the best Canadian seed corn; with agricultural experiments suited to their soils; you sat on the head of your agent; you kept their buildings in repair; you apprenticed their sons; you looked after their daughters when they got into trouble and after their bastards, your own or another man's. But you must reside on the estate. *You must reside on the estate.* The money that comes out of those poor devils'[35] pockets must go back into the land so that the estate and all on it, down to the licensed beggars, may grow richer and richer and richer. So he had invented his fantastic quarrel with Brother Mark: because he was going to take Valentine to live with him. You could not have a Valentine Wannop having with you in a Groby the infinite and necessary communings. You could have a painted doxy from the servants' hall, quarrelling with the other maids, who would want her job, and scandalising the parsons for miles round. In their sardonic way the tenants appreciated that: it was in the tradition and all over the Riding they did it themselves. But not a lady: the daughter of your father's best friend! They wanted Quality women to *be* Quality and they themselves would go to ruin, spend their dung-and-seed-money[36]* on whores and wreck the fortunes of the Estate, sooner than that you should indulge in infinite conversations. . . . So he hadn't taken a penny of their[37] money from his brother, and he wouldn't take a penny when he in turn became Groby. Fortunately, there was the heir. . . . Otherwise he could not have gone with that girl!

Two pangs went through him. His son had never written to him: the girl might have married a War Office clerk! On the rebound! That was what it would be: a civilian War Office clerk would be the most exact contrast to himself! . . . But the son's letters would have been stopped by the mother. That was what they did to people who were where *he* was. As the C.O. had said! And Valentine Wannop, who had listened to his conversation, would never want to mingle intimately in another's! Their communion[38] was immutable and not to be shaken!

So he was going to write to her: freckled, down-right, standing square on feet rather widely planted apart, just ready to say: "Oh, *chuck* it, Edith Ethel!" . . . She made the sunlight!

Or no: by Heavens, he could not write to her! If he stopped one or went dotty. . . . Wouldn't it make it infinitely worse for her to know that his love for her had been profound and immutable? It would make it far worse, for by now the edges of

* An expressive phrase referring to the basic necessities for those who earn their living from the land.

passion had probably worn less painful. Or there was the chance
of it! ... But impenitently he would go on willing her to submit
to his will: through mounds thrown up by Austrian projectiles
and across the seas. They would do what they wanted and take
what they got for it!*

He reclined, on his right shoulder, feeling like some immense
and absurd statue: a collection of meal-sacks done in mud: with
grotesque shorts revealing his muddy knees.... The figure on
one of Michael Angelo's Medici tombs. Or perhaps his *Adam*† ...
He felt the earth move a little beneath him. The last projectile
must have been pretty near. He would not have noticed the
sound, it had become such a regular sequence. But he noticed the
quiver in the earth....

Reprehensible! He said. For God's sake *let* us be reprehensible!
And have done with it! We aren't Hun strategists for ever
balancing pros and cons of militant morality!

He took, with his left hand the cup from the rock. Little Aranjuez came round the mound. Tietjens threw the cup downhill at
a large bit of rock. He said to Aranjuez's wistful enquiring eyes:

"So that no toast more ignoble may ever be drunk out of it!"‡

The boy gasped and blushed:

"Then you've got some one that you love, sir!" he said in his
tone of hero-worship. "Is she like Nancy, in Bailleul?"

Tietjens said:

"No, not like Nancy.... Or, perhaps, yes, a little like Nancy!"
He did not want to hurt the boy's feelings by the suggestion that
any one unlike Nancy could be loved. He felt a premonition that
that child was going to be hurt. Or, perhaps, it was only that he
was already so suffering.

---

* A Ford credo, which recurs in *A Call*, and appears in *English Novel* (93) too. Cf. *No
More Parades* (I.iii) and *Last Post* (I.iv) for more variations on the theme. In Alan
Judd's biography of Ford, he quotes it in relation to Ford's affair with Jean Rhys (*Ford
Madox Ford* 364–5).

† Michelangelo's work *The Creation of Adam* (1508–12) is found on the Sistine Chapel
ceiling and is based on the creation story in Genesis. Only two of his tombs in the
Medici funerary chapel (San Lorenzo, Florence) were completed. 'Day' and 'Night'
are reclining figures, as are 'Dawn' and 'Evening', signifying, according to the *Blooms-
bury Guide to Art* (1996) 'mortality through the passage of time' (629). In Ford's time,
the painter/sculptor's name usually appeared as here in the novel: Sir Charles Holroyd
published a biography in 1903 called *Michael Angelo Buonarroti*.

‡ Cf. Ford's retelling of the story of Bérangère des Baux's suicide in *Provence* 82.

The boy said:

"Then you'll get her, sir. You'll certainly get her!"

"Yes, I shall probably get her!" Tietjens said.

The Lance-Corporal came, too, round the mound. He said that "A" Company were all under cover. They went all together round the heap in the direction of "B" Company's trench down into which they slid. It descended sharply. It was certainly wet. It ended practically in a little swamp. The next battalion had even some yards of sand-bag parapet before entering the slope again with its trench. This was Flanders. Duck country. The bit of swamp would make personal keeping in communication difficult. Where Tietjens had put in his tile-syphons a great deal of water had exuded. The young O.C. Company said that they had had to bale the trench out, until they had made a little drain down into the bog. They baled out with shovels. Two of the shovels still stood against the brushwood revetments of the parapet.

"Well, you should not leave your shovels about!" Tietjens shouted.³⁹ He was feeling considerable satisfaction at the working of his syphon. In the meantime we had begun a considerable artillery demonstration. It became overwhelming. There was some sort of Bloody Mary somewhere a few yards off or so it seemed. She pooped off. The planes had perhaps reported the position of the Austrian gun. Or we might be *strafing* their trenches to make them shut up that weapon. It was like being a dwarf at a conversation, a conflict—of mastodons. There was so much noise it seemed to grow dark. It was a mental darkness. You could not think. A Dark Age! The earth moved.

He was looking at Aranjuez from a considerable height. He was enjoying a considerable view. Aranjuez's face had a rapt expression—like that of a man composing poetry. Long dollops of liquid mud surrounded them in the air. Like black pancakes being tossed. He thought: "Thank God I did not write to her. We are being blown up!" The earth turned like a weary hippopotamus. It settled down slowly over the face of Lance-Corporal Duckett who lay on his side, and went on in a slow wave.

It was slow, slow, slow . . . like a slowed down movie. The earth manœuvred for an infinite time. He remained suspended in space. As if he were suspended as he had wanted to be in front of that cockscomb in whitewash. Coincidence!

The earth sucked slowly and composedly at his feet.
It assimilated his calves, his thighs. It imprisoned him above
the waist. His arms being free, he resembled a man in a life-buoy.
The earth moved him slowly. It was solidish.

Below him, down a mound, the face of little Aranjuez, brown,
with immense black eyes in bluish whites, looked at him. Out of
viscous mud. A head on a charger! He could see the imploring
lips form the words: "Save me, Captain!" He said: "I've got to save
myself first!" He could not hear his own words. The noise was
incredible.

A man stood over him. He appeared immensely tall because
Tietjens' face was on a level with his belt. But he was a small
Cockney Tommy really. Name of Cockshott. He pulled at Tietjens' two arms. Tietjens tried to kick with his feet. Then he
realised it was better not to kick with his feet. He was pulled out.
Satisfactorily. There had been two men at it. A second, a
Corporal had come. They were all three of them grinning. He slid
down with the sliding earth towards Aranjuez. He smiled at the
pallid face. He slipped a lot. He felt a frightful burning on his
neck, below and behind the ear. His hand came down from
feeling the place. The finger tips had no end of[40] mud and a little
pinkishness on them. A pimple had perhaps burst. He had at least
two men not killed. He signed agitatedly to the Tommies. He
made gestures of digging. They were to get shovels.

He stood over Aranjuez, on the edge of liquid mud. Perhaps he
would sink in. He did not sink in. Not above his boot tops. He
felt his feet to be enormous and sustaining. He knew what had
happened. Aranjuez was sunk in the issuing hole of the spring
that made that bog. It was like being on Exmoor. He bent down
over an ineffable, small face. He bent lower and his hands entered
the slime. He had to get on his hand and knees.

Fury entered his mind. He had been sniped at.[*] Before he had
had that pain he had heard, he realised, an intimate drone under
the hellish tumult. There was reason for furious haste. Or, no. . . .
They were low. In a wide hole. There was no reason for furious
haste. Especially on your hands and knees.

---

[*] Ford knew what this experience was like; see 'War and the Mind: II: The Enemy'
(written in 1917) in *War Prose* 46.

His hands were under the slime, and his forearms. He battled his hands down greasy cloth; under greasy cloth. *Slimy*, not greasy! He pushed outwards. The boy's hands and arms appeared. It was going to be easier. His face was now quite close to the boy's, but it was impossible to hear what he said. Possibly he was unconscious. Tietjens said: "Thank God for my enormous physical strength!" It was the first time that he had ever had to be thankful for great physical strength. He lifted the boy's arms over his own shoulders so that his hands might clasp themselves behind his neck. They were slimy and disagreeable. He was short in the wind. He heaved back. The boy came up a little. He was certainly fainting. He gave no assistance. The slime was filthy. It was a condemnation of a civilisation that he, Tietjens, possessed of enormous physical strength, should never have needed to use it before. He looked like a collection of meal-sacks; but, at least, he could tear a pack of cards in half. If only his lungs weren't . . .

Cockshott, the Tommie, and the Corporal were beside him. Grinning. With the two shovels that ought not to have stood against the parapet of their trench. He was intensely irritated. He had tried to indicate with his signs that it was Lance-Corporal Duckett that they were to dig out. It was probably no longer Lance-Corporal Duckett. It was probably by now "it." The body! He had probably lost a man, after all![41]

Cockshott and the Corporal pulled Aranjuez out of the slime.[42] He came out reluctantly, like a lugworm out of sand. He could not stand. His legs gave way. He drooped like a flower done in slime. His lips moved, but you could not hear him. Tietjens took him from the two men who supported him between the arms and laid him a little way up the mound. He shouted in the ear of the Corporal: "Duckett! Go and dig out Duckett! At the double!"

He knelt and felt along the boy's back. His spine might have been damaged. The boy did not wince. His spine might be damaged all the same. He could not be left there. Bearers could be sent with a stretcher if one was to be found. But they might be sniped coming. Probably, he, Tietjens, could carry that boy: if his lungs held out. If not, he could drag him. He felt tender, like a mother, and enormous.[43] It might be better to leave the boy there. There was no knowing. He said: "Are you wounded?" The guns had mostly stopped. Tietjens could not see any blood flowing.

The boy whispered "No, sir!"[44] He was, then, probably just faint. Shell shock, very likely. There was no knowing what shell shock was or what it did to you. Or the mere vapour of the projectile. He could not stop there.

He took the boy under his arm as you might do a roll of blankets. If he took him on his shoulders he might get high enough to be sniped. He did not go very fast, his legs were so heavy. He bundled down several steps in the direction of the spring in which the boy had been. There was more water. The spring was filling up that hollow. He could not have left the boy there. You could only imagine that his body had corked up the spring-hole before. This had been like being at home where they had springs like that. On the moors, digging out badgers. Digging earth drains, rather. Badgers have dry lairs. On the moors above Groby. April sunlight. Lots of sunlight and skylarks.

He was mounting the mound. For some feet there was no other way. They had been in the shaft made by that projectile. He inclined to the left. To the right would take them quicker to the trench, but he wanted to get the mound between them and the sniper. His breathing was tremendous. There was more light falling on them. Exactly! . . . Snap! Snap! Snap! . . . Clear sounds from a quarter of a mile away. . . . Bullets whined. Overhead. Long sounds, going away. Not snipers. The men of a battalion. A chance! Snap! Snap! Snap! Bullets whined overhead. Men of a battalion get excited when shooting at anything running. They fire high. Trigger pressure. *He* was now a fat, running object. Did they fire with a sense of hatred or fun![45] Hatred probably. Huns have not much sense of fun.[46]

His breathing was unbearable. Both his legs were like painful bolsters. He would be on the relatively level in two steps if he made them. . . . Well, make them! . . . He was on the level. He had been climbing: up clods. He *had* to take an immense breath. The ground under his left foot gave way. He had been holding Aranjuez in front of his own body as much as he could, under his right arm. As his left foot sank in, the boy's body came right on top of him. Naturally this stiffish earth in huge clods had fissures in it. Apertures. It was not like regular digging.

The boy kicked, screamed, tore himself loose. . . . Well, if he wanted to go! The scream was like a horse's in a stable on fire.

Bullets had gone overhead. The boy rushed off, his hands to his face. He disappeared round the mound. It was a conical mound. He, Tietjens, could now crawl on his belly. It was satisfactory.

He crawled. Shuffling himself along with his hips and elbows. There was probably a text-book way of crawling. He did not know it. The clods of earth appeared friendly. For bottom soil thrown to the top they did not feel or smell so very sour. Still, it would take a long time to get them into cultivation or under grass. Probably, agriculturally speaking that country would be in a pretty poor condition for a long time. . . .

He felt pleased with his body. It had had no exercise to speak of for two months—as second-in-command. He could not have expected to be in even the condition he was in. But the mind had probably had a good deal to do with that! He had, no doubt, been in a devil of a funk. It was only reasonable. It was disagreeable to think of those Hun devils hunting down the unfortunate. A disagreeable business. Still, we did the same. . . . That boy must have been in a devil of a funk. Suddenly. He had held his hands in front of his face. Afraid to see. Well, you couldn't blame him. They ought not to send out schoolgirls. He was like a girl. Still, he ought to have stayed to see that he, Tietjens, was not pipped. He might have thought he was hit from the way his left leg had gone down. He would have to be *strafed*. Gently.

Cockshott and the Corporal were on their hands and knees digging with the short-handled shovels that are known as trenching-tools. They were on the rear side of the mound.

"We've found im, sir," the Corporal said. "Regular buried. Just seed his foot. Dursen't use a shovel. Might cut im in arf!"

Tietjens said:

"You're probably right. Give me the shovel!"

Cockshott was a draper's assistant, the Corporal a milkman. Very likely they were not good with shovels.

He had had the advantage of a boyhood crowded with digging of all sorts. Duckett was buried horizontally, running into the side of a conical mound. His feet at least stuck out like that, but you could not tell how the body was disposed. It might turn to either side or upwards. He said:

"Go on with your tools above! But give me room."

The toes being to the sky, the trunk could hardly bend downwards. He stood below the feet and aimed terrific blows with the shovel eighteen inches below. He liked digging. This earth was luckily dryish. It ran down the hill conveniently. This man had been buried probably ten minutes. It seemed longer but it was probably less. He ought to have a chance. Probably earth was less suffocating than water. He said to the Corporal:

"Do you know how to apply artificial respiration? To the drowned?"[47]

Cockshott said:

"I do, sir. I was swimming champion of Islington baths!" A rather remarkable man, Cockshott. His father had knocked up the arm of a man who had tried to shoot Mr. Gladstone in 1866 or thereabouts.[*]

A lot of earth falling away, obligingly, after one withdrawal of the shovel Lance-Corporal Duckett's thin legs appeared to the fork, the knees drooping.

Cockshott said:

"E ain't rubbin' 'is ankles[48] this journey!"

The Corporal said:

"Company Cmander is[49] killed, sir. Bullet clean thru the ed!"

It annoyed Tietjens that here was another head wound. He could not apparently get away from them. It was silly to be annoyed, because in trenches a majority of wounds had to be head wounds.[†] But Providence might just as well be a little more imaginative. To oblige one. It annoyed him, too, to think that he had *strafed* that boy just before he was killed. For leaving his shovels about. A *strafe* leaves a disagreeable impression on young boys for quite half an hour. It was probably the last incident in his life. So

---

[*]   There was no attempt on the life of Gladstone in 1866, though the politician seemed much on Ford's mind at this point in his composition (he features in the subsequent chapter too). One possible source for Ford's thoughts of politically motivated crime was the attempted assassination of Tsar Alexander II of Russia in 1866. On 4 April of that year Dmitry Karakozov tried to shoot the Tsar, but was thwarted when Osip Komissarov jostled his elbow just as the shot was fired. Closer to home was Mathilde Blind's family of revolutionaries. One of her brothers tried to assassinate Bismarck, Ford says elsewhere (*Ancient Lights* 50). Ferdinand Cohen-Blind was indeed guilty of such an attempt, in May 1866, which failed when Bismarck himself grabbed hold of him. Cohen-Blind committed suicide the next day, while in custody. See Angela Thirlwell, *Into the Frame: The Four Loves of Ford Madox Brown* (London: Chatto & Windus, 2010), 184.

[†]   Tietjens is right of course because of the way trench warfare is conducted. In the Introduction I discuss the related relevance of his choice of title for this novel.

he died depressed. . . . Might God be making it up to him!

He said to the Corporal:

"Let me come." Duckett's left hand and wrist had appeared, the hand drooping and improbably clean, level with the thigh. It gave the line of the body; you could clear away beside him.

"'E wasn't on'y twenty-two," the Corporal said.

Cockshott said: "Same age as me. Very particular e was about your rifle pull-throughs."

A minute later they pulled Duckett out, by the legs. A stone might have been resting on his face, in that case his face would have been damaged. It wasn't, though you had had to chance it. It was black but asleep. . . . As if Valentine Wannop had been reposing in an ash-bin. Tietjens left Cockshott applying artificial respiration very methodically and efficiently to the prostrate form.

[handwritten margin note: Valerie finally]

It was to him a certain satisfaction that, at any rate, in that minute affair he hadn't lost one of the men but only an officer.[50] As satisfaction it was not militarily correct, though as it harmed no one there was no harm in it. But for his men he always felt a certain greater[51] responsibility; they seemed to him to be there infinitely less of their own volition. It was akin to the feeling that made him regard cruelty to an animal as a more loathsome crime than cruelty to a human being, other than a child. It was no doubt irrational.

Leaning, in the communication trench, against the corrugated iron that boasted a great whitewashed A, in a very clean thin Burberry boasting half a bushel of badges of rank—worsted crowns and things!—and in a small[52] tin hat that looked elegant, was a slight figure. How the *devil* can you make a tin hat look elegant! It carried a hunting switch and wore spurs. An Inspecting General. The General said benevolently:

"Who are you?" and then with irritation: "Where the devil is the officer commanding this Battalion? Why can't he be found?" He added: "You're disgustingly dirty. Like a blackamoor. I suppose you've an explanation."

Tietjens was being spoken to by General Campion. In a hell of a temper. He stood to attention like a scarecrow.

He said:

"I am in command of this Battalion, sir. I am Tietjens, second-in-command. Now in command temporarily. I could not be found because I was buried. Temporarily."

The General said:

"You.... Good God!" and fell back a step, his jaw dropping. He said: "I've just come from London!" And then: "By God, you don't stop in command of a Battalion of mine a second after I take over!" He said: "They said this was the smartest battalion in my unit!" and snorted with passion. He added: "Neither my galloper nor Levin can find you or get you found. And there you come strolling along with your hands in your pockets!"

In the complete stillness, for, the guns having stopped, the skylarks, too, were taking a spell, Tietjens could hear his heart beat, little dry scraping sounds out of his lungs.[53] The heavy beats were very accelerated. It gave an effect of terror. He said to himself:

"What the devil has his having been in London to do with it?" And then: "He wants to marry Sylvia! I'll bet he wants to marry Sylvia!" That was what his having been to London had to do with it. It was an obsession with him: the first thing he said when surprised and passionate.

They always arranged these periods of complete silence for the visits of Inspecting Generals. Perhaps the Great General Staffs of both sides arrange that for each other. More probably our guns had split themselves in the successful attempt to let the Huns know that we wanted them to shut up—that we were firing with what Papists call a special intention. That would be as effective as a telephone message. The Huns would know there was something up. Never put the other side in a temper when you can help it.

He said:

"I've just had a scratch, sir. I was feeling in my pockets for my field-dressing."

The General said:

"A fellow like you has no right to be where he can be wounded. Your place is the lines of communication. I was mad when I sent you here. I shall send you back."

He added:

"You can fall out. I want neither your assistance nor your information. They said there was a damn smart officer in command here. I wanted to see him.... Of the name of ... Of the name of.... It does not matter. Fall out...."

Tietjens went heavily along the trench. It came into his head to say to himself:

"It *is* a land of Hope and Glory!"* Then he exclaimed: "By God! I'll take the thing before the Commander-in-Chief. I'll take the thing before the King in Council if necessary. By God I will!" The old fellow had no business to speak to him like that. It was importing personal enmity into service matters. He stood still reflecting on the terms of his letter to Brigade. The Adjutant Notting came along the trench. He said:

"General Campion wants to see you, sir. He takes over this Army on Monday." He added: "You've been in a nasty place, sir. Not hurt, I trust!" It was a most unusual piece of loquacity for Notting.

Tietjens said to himself:

"Then I've got five days in command of this unit. He can't kick me out before he's in command." The Huns would be through them before then. Five days' fighting! Thank God!

He said:

"Thanks. I've seen him. No, I'm all right. Beastly dirty!"

Notting's beady eyes had a tinge of agony in them. He said:

"When they said you had stopped one, sir, I thought I should go mad.[54] We *can't* get through the work!"

Tietjens was wondering whether he should write his letter to Brigade before or after the old fellow took over.[55] Notting was saying:

"The doctor says Aranjuez will get through all right."

It would be better, if he were going to base his appeal on the grounds of personal prejudice. Notting was saying:

"Of course he will lose his eye. In fact it ... it is not practically there. But he'll get through."

---

* This phrase is a crucial one in Ford's telling of the story of beginning to write *Parade's End*. In *It Was the Nightingale*, he puts an unplanned meeting with Elgar in Sussex alongside his daydreams about leaving England. Immediately afterwards he writes 'There came into my mind suddenly the words: "The band will play: 'Land of Hope and Glory' ... The adjutant will say: 'There will be no more parades ...'"' (161–2). See also the relevant textual note at the beginning of III.i here.

PART III

CHAPTER I[1]

COMING into the Square was like being suddenly dead, it was so silent and so still to one so lately jostled by the innumerable crowd and deafened by unceasing shouts. The shouting had continued for so long that it had assumed the appearance of being a solid and unvarying thing: like life. So the silence appeared like Death; and now she had death in her heart. She was going to confront a madman in a stripped house. And the empty house stood in an empty square all of whose houses were so eighteenth century and silver-grey and[2] rigid and serene that they ought all to be empty too and contain dead, mad men. And was this the errand? For to-day[3] when all the world was mad with joy? To become bear-ward* to a man who had got rid of all his furniture and did not know the porter—mad without joy!

It turned out to be worse than she expected. She had expected to turn the handle of a door of a tall empty room;[4] in a space made dim with shutters she would see him, looking suspiciously round over his shoulder, a grey badger or a bear taken at its dim occupations. And in uniform. But she was not given time even to be ready. In the last moment she was to steel herself incredibly. She was to become the cold nurse of a shell-shock case.

But there was not any last moment. He charged upon her. There in the open. More like a lion. He came, grey all over, his grey hair—or the grey patches of his hair—shining, charging down the steps, having slammed the hall door. And lopsided. He was carrying under his arm a diminutive piece of furniture. A cabinet.

---

* Valentine's phrase, meaning 'keeper of the bear', refers to the old custom (only made illegal in 1925) of leading muzzled bears about the streets to attract notice and money. It relates to her earlier descriptions of Tietjens in the novel as being like a bear.

It was so quick. It was like having a fit. The houses tottered. He regarded her. He had presumably checked violently in his clumsy stride. She hadn't seen because of the tottering of the houses. His stone-blue eyes came fishily into place in his wooden countenance—pink and white. *Too* pink where it was pink and too white where it was white. Too much so for health. He was in grey homespuns. He should not wear homespuns or grey. It increased his bulk. He could be made to look ... Oh, a fine figure of a man, let us say!

What was he doing? Fumbling in the pocket of his clumsy trousers. He exclaimed—she shook at the sound of his slightly grating, slightly gasping voice:—

"I'm going to sell this thing.... Stay here." He had produced a latchkey. He was panting fiercely beside her. Up the steps. He was beside her. Beside her. Beside her. It was infinitely sad to be beside this madman.⁵ It was infinitely glad. Because if he had been sane she would not have been beside him. She could be beside him for long spaces of time if he were mad. Perhaps he did not recognise her! She might be beside him for long spaces of time with him not recognising her. Like tending your baby!

He was stabbing furiously at the latchhole with his little key. He *would*: that was normal. He was a stab-the-keyhole sort of clumsy man. She would not want that altered. But she would see about his clothes. She said: "I am deliberately preparing to live with him for a long time!" Think of that! She said to him:

"Did you send for me?"

He had the door open: he said, panting—His *poor* lungs!:

"No." Then: "Go in!" and then: "I was just going...."

She was in his house. Like a child.... He had not sent for her.... Like a child faltering on the sill of a vast black cave.

It *was* black. Stone flags. Pompeian red walls scarred pale-pink where fixed hall-furniture had been removed. Was it *here* she was going to live?

He said, panting, from behind her back:

"Wait here!" A little more light fell into the hall. That was because he was gone from the doorway.

He was charging down the steps. His boots were immense. He lolloped all over on one side because of the piece of furniture he had under his arm. He was grotesque, really. But joy radiated from his homespuns when you walked beside him. It welled out; it enveloped you.... Like the warmth from an electric heater, only that did not make you want to cry and say your prayers—the haughty oaf.

No, but he was not haughty. Gauche, then! No, but he was not gauche.... She could not run after him. He was a bright patch, with his pink ears and silver hair. Gallumphing along the rails in front of the eighteenth century houses. *He* was eighteenth century all right.... But then the eighteenth century never went mad. The only century that never went mad. Until the French Revolution: and that was either not mad or not eighteenth century.[6]

She stepped irresolutely into the shadows;[7] she returned irresolutely to the light.... A long hollow sound existed: the sea saying: Ow, Ow, Ow along miles and miles. It was the armistice. It was Armistice Day.[8*] She had forgotten it. She was to be cloistered on Armistice Day! Ah, not cloistered! Not cloistered there. My beloved is mine and I am his! But she might as well close the door!

She closed the door as delicately as if she were kissing him on the lips. It was a symbol. It was Armistice Day. She ought to go away; instead she had shut the door on . . . Not on Armistice Day! What was it like to be . . . changed!

No! She ought not to go away! She ought not to go away! She ought *not!* He had told her to wait. She was not cloistered. This was the most exciting spot on the earth. It was not her fate to live nun-like. She was going to pass her day beside a madman; her night; too....[9] Armistice Night! That night would be remembered down unnumbered generations. Whilst one lived that had seen it the question would be asked: What did you do on Armistice Night? My beloved is mine and I am his!

The great stone stairs were carpetless: to mount them would be like taking part in a procession. The hall came in straight from the front door. You had to turn a corner to the right before you

* 11 November 1918. London went 'wild with delight', wrote the *Daily Mirror*, 'when it heard the news. Bells burst forth into joyful chimes [...] bands paraded the streets followed by cheering crowds of soldiers and civilians and London generally gave itself up wholeheartedly to rejoicing [...] There was a scene of wonderful loyalty at Buckingham Palace, dense crowds were shouting "We want the King".'

came to the entrance of a room. A queer arrangement. Perhaps
the eighteenth century was afraid of draughts and did not like the
dining-room door near the front entrance.... My beloved is ...
Why does one go on repeating that ridiculous thing. Besides it's
from the *Song of Solomon*, isn't it?* The *Canticle of Canticles!* Then
to quote it is blasphemy when one is ... No, the essence of prayer
is volition, so the essence of blasphemy is volition. She did not
want to quote the thing. It was jumped out of her by sheer nerves.
She was afraid. She was waiting for a madman in an empty house.
Noises whispered up the empty stairway!

She was like Fatima.† Pushing open the door of the empty
room.[10] He might come back to murder her. A madness caused
by sex obsessions is not infrequently homicidal.... What did you
do on Armistice Night? "I was murdered in an empty house!" For,
no doubt he would let her live till midnight.

But perhaps he had not got sex-obsessions. She had not the
shadow of a proof that he had; rather that he hadn't! Certainly,
rather that he hadn't.[11] Always the gentleman.

They had left the telephone! The windows were duly shuttered
but in the dim light from[12] between cracks the nickel gleamed on
white marble. The mantel-shelf. Pure Parian marble,‡ the shelf
supported by rams' heads. Singularly chaste. The ceilings and
rectilinear mouldings in an intricate symmetry. Chaste, too.
Eighteenth century. But the eighteenth century was not
chaste.... *He* was eighteenth century.

She ought to telephone to her mother to inform that
Eminence in untidy black with violet tabs here and there of the
grave step that her daughter was ...

What was her daughter going to do?

She ought to rush out of the empty house. She ought to be

---

* Song of Solomon 2:16.
† Fatima was the seventh, final, wife of the murderous Bluebeard, a character from
   Charles Perrault's *Contes du Temps* (1697) – though found in similar form in many
   other folk traditions. Fatima yields to curiosity when her new husband is away, opens
   a forbidden locked door and discovers the bodies of her predecessors. She is saved from
   death by the timely arrival of her brothers, who then murder Bluebeard. In context,
   this suggests the height of the stakes for Valentine, the strength of her feelings, but I
   think the fact that Fatima is Bluebeard's last wife is significant too.
‡ 'Parian' – belonging to the island of Paros in the Cyclades, famed for its white stat-
   uary marble.

trembling with fear at the thought that he was coming home very likely to murder her. But she wasn't. What was she? Trembling with ecstasy? Probably. At the thought that he was coming. If he murdered her.... Can't be helped! She was trembling with ecstasy all the same. She must telephone to her mother. Her mother might want to know where she was. But her mother never *did* want to know where she was. She had her head too screwed on to get into mischief!... Think of *that*!

Still, on such a day her mother might like to. They ought to exchange gladnesses that her brother was safe for good now. And[13] others, too. Normally her mother was irritated when she rang up. She would be at her work. It was amazing to see her at work. Perhaps she never would again. Such untidiness of papers. In a little room. Quite a little room. She never would work in a big room because a big room tempted her to walk about and she could not afford the time to walk about.

She was writing at two books at once now. A novel.... Valentine did not know what it was about. Her mother never let them know what her novels were about till they were finished. And a woman's history of the War.[14] A history by a woman for women.* And there she would be sitting at a large table that hardly left room for more than getting round it. Grey, large, generous-featured and tired she would be poking over one set of papers on one side of the table or just getting up from over the novel, her loose pince-nez falling off; pushing round the table between its edge and the wall to peer at the sheets of the woman's history that were spread all over that region. She would work for ten minutes or twenty-five or an hour at the one and then for an hour and a

---

* This idea as to the subject of Mrs Wannop's writing is evidently linked to the contemporary rise in feminism, and the suffrage movement in particular, in which Valentine plays a part (though Mrs Wannop is, herself, described as an 'Anti' in *Some Do Not . . .*). In terms of a 'woman's history of the war', Ford may have in mind *Fields of Victory* (1919) by Mrs Humphry [Mary Augusta] Ward, whom he knew (she was president of Britain's anti-suffrage movement). The book is certainly a history, written with the active assistance of senior British Army officials in France and at the War Office. Chapters include 'France Under the Armistice' and 'Tanks and the Hindenburg Line'. It is also the kind of history towards which Ford would have been sympathetic; in her Introduction the author talks of the book as being based on her 'impressions' and her 'personal journeys' in France in 1916, 1917 and after the Armistice. However, there is no indication that she intends the book as particularly for women, though she mentions the 'daughter-secretary' with whom she is travelling; the book is written in a personal style.

half or half an hour or three-quarters at the other. What a muddle her dear old head must be in!

With a little trepidation she took the telephone. It had got to be done. She could not live with Christopher Tietjens without first telling her mother. Her mother ought to be given the chance of dissuading. They say you ought to give a lover a chance of a final scene before leaving him or her for good. Still more your mother. That was jannock.*

It broke the word of promise to the ear, the telephone!...†
Was it blasphemy to quote Shakespeare when one was going to.... Perhaps bad taste. Shakespeare, however, was not spotless. So they said.... Waiting! Waiting! How much of one's life wasn't spent waiting, with one's weight boring one's heels into the ground.... But *this* thing was dead. No roar came from its mouth and when you jabbed the little gadget at the side up and down no bell tinked.... It had probably been disconnected. They had perhaps cut him off for not paying. Or he had cut it off so that she might not scream for the police through it whilst he was strangling her. Anyhow they were cut off. They would be cut off from the world on Armistice Night.... Well, they would probably be cut off for good!

What nonsense. He had not known that she was coming. He had not asked her to come.

So, slowly, slowly she went up the great stone staircase, the noises all a-whispering up before her ... "So, slowly, slowly she went up and slowly looked about her. Henceforth take warning by the fall...." Well, she did not need to take warning: she was not going to fall in the way Barbara Allen did.‡ Contrariwise!

---

*   Lancashire dialect meaning straightforward, honest.
†   A reference to Macbeth's words to Macduff in the final scene of Shakespeare's play, on discovering Macduff had been born by caesarean section ('from his mother's womb untimely ripped', V.x.15–16). Macbeth answers: 'Accursèd be that tongue that tells me so, / For it hath cowed my better part of man; / And be these juggling fiends no more believed, / That palter with us in a double sense, / That keep the word of promise to our ear / And break it to our hope. I'll not fight with thee' (V.x.17–22). Ford's exclamation mark may be an acknowledgement of the anachronous telephone, and/or his rewrite.
‡   The heroine of an old ballad. Barbara Allen died of remorse after showing no pity for the young man who was dying of love for her. There are many versions, but one verse given in Brewer's *Dictionary of Phrase and Fable* runs thus: 'Fare well, she sayd, ye virgins all, / And shun the fault I fell in: / Henceforth take warning by the fall / Of cruel Barbara Allen.'

He had not sent for her. He had not asked Edith Ethel to ring her up. Then presumably she felt humiliated. But she did not feel humiliated! It was in effect fairly natural. He *was* quite notice-ably mad, rushing out, lopsided, with bits of furniture under his arm and no hat on his noticeable hair. Noticeable! That was what he was. He[15] would never pass in a crowd!... He *had* got rid of all his furniture as Edith Ethel had alleged. Very likely he had not recognised the porter, too. She, Valentine Wannop, had seen him going to sell his furniture. Madly! Running to do it. You do not run when you are selling furniture if you are sane. Perhaps Edith Ethel had seen him running along with a table on his head. And she was by no means certain that he had recognised her, Valentine Wannop!

So Edith Ethel might have been almost justified in ringing her up. Normally it would have been an offence, considering the terms on which they had parted. Considering that Edith Ethel had accused her of having had a child by this very man! It was pretty strong, even if she had seen him running about the Square with furniture, and even if there had been no one else who could help.... But she ought to have sent her miserable rat of a husband. There was no excuse!

Still, there had been nothing else for her, Valentine, to do. So there was no call for her to feel humiliated. Even if she had not felt for this man as she did she would have come, and, if he had been very bad, would have stayed.

He had not sent for her! This man who had once proposed love to her and then had gone away without a word and who had never so much as sent her a picture-postcard! Gauche! Haughty! Was there any other word for him? There could not be. Then she ought to feel humiliated. But she did not.

She felt frightened, creeping up the great staircase, and entering a great room. A very great room. All white; again with stains on the walls from which things had been removed. From over the way the houses confronted her, eighteenth-centuryishly. But with a touch of gaiety from their red chimney-pots.... And now she was spying: with her heart in her mouth. She was terribly frightened. This room was inhabited. As if set down in a field, the room being so large, there camped.... A camp-bed for the use of

officers, G.S. one,* as the saying is. And implements of green
canvas, supported on crossed white-wood staves: a chair, a bucket
with a rope handle, a washing-basin, a table. The bed was covered
over with a flea-bag of brown wool.† She was terribly frightened.
The further she penetrated the house the more she was at his
mercy. She ought to have stayed down-stairs. She was spying on
him.

These things looked terribly sordid and forlorn. Why did he
place them in the centre of the room? Why not against a wall? It
is usual to stand the head of a bed against a wall when there is no
support for the pillows. Then the pillows do not slip off. She
would change.... No, she would not. He had put the bed in the
centre of the room because he did not want it to touch walls that
had been brushed by the dress of.... You must not think bad
things about that woman!

They did not look sordid and forlorn. They looked frugal. And
glorious! She bent down and drawing down the flea bag at the
top, kissed the pillows. She would get him linen pillows. You
would be able to get linen now.‡ The war was over. All along that
immense line men could stand up!

At the head of the room was a dais. A box of square boarding,
like the model-throne artists have in studios. Surely she did not
receive her guests on a dais: like Royalty. She was capable.... [16]
You must not.... It was perhaps for a piano. Perhaps she gave
concerts. It was used as a library now. A row of calf-bound books
stood against the wall on the back edge of the platform. She
approached them to see what books he had selected. They must be
the books he had read in France. If she could know what books he
had read in France she would know what some of his thoughts there
had been. She knew he slept between very cheap cotton sheets.

---

*   General Service, so referring to any officially issued item.
†   Cf. the point at which the text of *True Love & a GCM* breaks off (*War Prose* 139).
‡   The long-term general decline in the flax/linen industry before 1914 was exacerbated
    by the Russian Revolution of 1917. (Russia had provided 80 per cent of the linen
    consumed in Western Europe.) Linen was used for a wide range of military goods:
    canvas covers, tent materials, sailcloth, machine gun belts as well as aircraft wings and
    fuselages. 'The military value of linen required restriction of civilian consumption and
    exports', writes Philip Ollerenshaw, 'and brought the state, usually for the first time,
    into direct negotiations with individual firms and their representative trade associa-
    tions' ('Textile Business in Europe During the First World War: The Linen Industry,
    1914–18', *Business History*, 41.1 [1999], 63–87 [65]).

Frugal and glorious. That was he! And he had designed this room to love her in. It was the room she would have asked.... The furnishing ... Alcestis never had....* For she, Valentine Wannop, was of frugal mind, too. And his worshipper. Having reflected glory.... Damn it, she was getting soppy. But it was curious how their tastes marched together. He had been neither haughty nor gauche. He had paid her the real compliment. He had said: "Her mind so marches with mine that she will understand."

The books were indeed a job lot. Their tops ran along against the wall like an[17] ill-arranged range of hills; one was a great folio in calf, the title indented deep and very dim. The others were French novels and little red military text books. She leaned over the dais to read the title of the tall book. She expected it to be Herbert's Poems or his *Country Parson*....† *He ought to be a Country Parson. He never would be now. She was depriving the church of.... Of a Higher Mathematician, really. The title of the book was *Vir. Obscur*.‡

Why did she take it that they were going to live together? She had no official knowledge that he wanted to. But *they* wanted to TALK. You can't talk unless you live together. Her eye, travelling downwards along the dais caught words on paper. They threw themselves up at her from among a disorder of half a dozen typed pages;[18] they were in big, firm, pencilled letters. They stood out because they were pencilled; they were:

A man could stand up on a bleedin' 'ill!

Her heart stopped. She must be out of condition. She could not stand very well, but there was nothing to lean on to. She had—she didn't know she had—read also the typed words:

"*Mrs. Tietjens is leaving the model cabinet by Barker of Bath*§ *which she believes you claim....*"[19]

She looked desperately away from the letter. She did not want to read the letter. She could not move away. She believed she was

---

dying. Joy never kills.... But it.... "fait peur". "Makes afraid."[*]
Afraid! Afraid! Afraid! There was nothing now between them.
It was as if they were already in each others' arms. For surely the
rest of the letter must say that Mrs. Tietjens had removed the
furniture. And his comment—amazingly echoing the words she
had just thought—was that he could stand up. But it wasn't in
the least amazing. My beloved is mine.... Their thoughts
marched together; not in the least amazing. They could now
stand on a hill together. Or get into a little hole. For good. And
talk. For ever. She must not read the rest of the letter. She must
not be certain. If she were certain she would have no hope of
preserving her.... Of remaining.... Afraid and unable to move.
She would be forced to read the letter because she was unable to
move. Then she would be lost. She looked beseechingly out of
the window at the house-fronts[20] over the way. They were
friendly. They would help her. Eighteenth century. Cynical, but
not malignant. She sprang right off her feet. She could move
then. She hadn't had a fit.

Idiot. It was only the telephone. It went on and on. Drrinn;
drinnnn; d.r.R.I.n.n. It came from just under her feet. No, from
under the dais. The receiver was on the dais. She hadn't
consciously noticed it because she had believed the telephone
was dead. Who notices a dead telephone?

She said—It was as if she were talking into his ear, he so
pervaded her—she said:

"Who are you?"

One ought not to answer all telephone calls, but one does so
mechanically. She ought not to have answered this. She was in
a compromising position. Her voice might be recognised. Let it
be recognised. She desired to be known to be in a compromising
position! What did you do on Armistice Day!

A voice, heavy and old said:

"You *are* there, Valentine.... "

She cried out:

"Oh, poor *mother*.... But he's not here." She added "He's not
been here with me. I'm still only waiting." She added again: "The
house is empty!" She seemed to be stealthy, the house whispering

---

[*]   'La joie fait peur' ('joy engenders fear') is a French adage.

round her. She seemed to be whispering to her mother to save her and not wanting the house to hear her. The house was eighteenth century. Cynical. But not malignant. It wanted her undoing but it knew that women liked being. . . . [21] ruined.

Her mother said, after a long time:

"Have you *got* to do this thing? . . . My little Valentine . . . My little Valentine!" She wasn't sobbing.

Valentine said:

"Yes, I've got to do it!" She sobbed. Suddenly she stopped sobbing.

She said quickly:

"Listen, mother. I've had no conversation with him.[22] I don't know even whether he's sane.[23] He appears to be mad." She wanted to give her mother hope. Quickly. She had been speaking quickly to get hope to her mother as quickly as possible. But she added: "I believe that I shall die if I cannot live with him."

She said that slowly. She wanted to be like a little child trying to get truth home to its mother.

She said:

"I have waited too long. All these years." She did not know that she had such desolate tones in her voice. She could see her mother looking into the distance with every statement that came to her, thinking. Old and grey. And majestic and kind. . . . Her mother's voice came:

"I have sometimes suspected. . . . My poor child. . . . It has been for a long time?" They were both silent. Thinking. Her mother said:

"There isn't any practical way out?" She pondered for a long time.[24] "I take it you have thought it all out. I know you have a good head and you are good." A rustling sound.[25] "But I am not level with these times. I should be glad if there were a way out. I should be glad if you could wait for each other. Or perhaps find a legal. . . . "

Valentine said:

"Oh, mother, don't cry!" . . . . "Oh mother I can't. . . . " . . . "Oh, I will come. . . . Mother, I will come back to you if you order it." With each phrase her body was thrown about as if by a wave. She thought they only did that on the stage. Her eyes said to her: . . . "*Dear Sir,*

"*Our client, Mrs. Christopher Tietjens of Groby-in-Cleveland. . . .*"
They said:
"*After the occurrence at the Base-Camp at. . . .*"
They said:
"*Thinks it useless. . . .*"
She was agonised for her mother's voice. The telephone
hummed in E flat. It tried B. Then it went back to E flat. Her eyes
said:
"*Proposes when occasion offers to remove to Groby . . .*" in fat,
blue typescript. She cried agonisedly:
"Mother. Order me to come back or it will be too late . . . "
She had looked down, unthinkingly . . . as one does[26] when
standing at the telephone. If she looked down again and read to
the end of the sentence that contained the words: "It is useless,"
it would be too late! She would know that his wife had given him
up!
Her mother's voice came,[27] turned by the means of its
conveyance into the voice of a machine of Destiny.
"No I can't.[28] I am thinking."
Valentine placed her foot on the dais at which she stood.
When she looked down it covered the letter. She thanked God.
Her mother's voice said:
"I cannot[29] order you to come back if it would kill you not to
be with him." Valentine could feel her late-Victorian advanced
mind, desperately seeking for the right plea—for any plea that
would let her do without seeming to employ maternal authority.
She began to talk like a book:* an august Victorian book; Morley's
Life of Gladstone.† That was reasonable: she wrote books like
that.[30]
She said they were both good creatures of good stock. If their
consciences let them commit themselves to a certain course of
action they were probably in the right. But she begged them, in
God's name to assure themselves that their consciences *did* urge
that course. She *had* to talk like a book!

---

* Cf. *Joseph Conrad* 209, and Stella Bowen, *Drawn from Life* 210.
† When John Morley's *Life of Gladstone* was published in three volumes in 1903
Macmillan staff struggled to keep up with demand. The book was 'widely regarded as
a standard work', a status that it has largely retained. See *Contemporary Review*, May
1993.

Valentine said:
"It is nothing to do with conscience." That seemed harsh. Her mind was troubled with a quotation. She could not find it. Quotations ease strain; she said: "One is urged by blind destiny!" A Greek quotation, then! "Like a victim upon an altar. I am afraid; but I consent!"* . . . Probably Euripides; the *Alkestis* very likely!† If it had been a Latin author the phrases would have occurred to her in Latin. Being with her mother made her talk like a book. Her mother talked like a book: then *she* did. They *must*; if they did not they would scream. . . . But they were English ladies. Of scholarly habits of mind. It was horrible. Her mother said: "That is probably the same as conscience—race conscience!"

She could not urge on them the folly and disastrousness of the course they appeared to propose. She had, she said, known too many irregular unions that had been worthy of emulation and too many regular ones that were miserable and a cause of demoralisation by their examples. . . . She was a gallant soul. She could not in conscience[31] go back on the teachings of her whole life. She wanted to. Desperately! Valentine could feel the almost physical strainings of her poor, tired brain. But she could not recant. She was not Cranmer!‡ She was not even Joan of Arc.§

So she went on repeating:

"I can only beg and pray you to assure yourself that not to live with that man will cause you to die or to be seriously mentally injured. If you think you can live without him or wait for him, if you think there is any hope of later union without serious mental injury I beg and pray. . . ."

She could not finish the sentence. . . . It was fine to behave

---

* Possibly an allusion to the speech in which Alcestis says farewell to her marriage bed – a key speech for Ford, as discussed in the Introduction.
† A further reference to Euripides' play.
‡ Under the Catholic Queen Mary Archbishop Thomas Cranmer (1489–1556) was tried for treason, and recanted in public his support of Protestantism. He was still sentenced to be burned in Oxford on 21 March 1556. He dramatically stuck his right hand, with which he had signed his recantation, into the fire first.
§ Jeanne d'Arc (1412–31) is the patron saint of France, and a national heroine for her leading of the resistance to the English in the Hundred Years War. Like Cranmer, she was also burned at the stake, in Rouen. She was said to have recanted when shown the flames, but then retracted her signing of the recantation paper. Bernard Shaw's play *Saint Joan* was first produced in London in 1924, so contemporaneously with *Parade's End*. In this play she tears up her recantation in scene 6, on learning she is not to be released from prison, and is swiftly burned.

with dignity at the crucial moment of your life! It was fitting: it
was proper. It justified your former philosophic life. And it was
cunning. Cunning!

For now she said:[32]

"My child! my little child! You have sacrificed all your life to
me and my teaching. How can I ask you now to deprive yourself
of the benefit of them?"

She said:

"I *can't* persuade you to a course that might mean your eternal
unhappiness!" . . . The *can't* was like a flame of agony!

Valentine shivered. That was cruel pressure. Her mother was
no doubt doing her duty; but it was cruel pressure. It was very
cold. November is a cold month. There were footsteps on the
stairs. She shook.

[33]"Oh, he is coming. He is coming!" she cried out. She wanted
to say: "Save me!" She said: "Don't go away! Don't. . . . Don't[34]
go away!" What do men do to you: men you love?[35] Mad men. He
was carrying a sack. The sack was the first she saw as he opened
the door. Pushed it open; it was already half-open. A sack was a
dreadful thing for a mad man to carry. In an empty house. He
dumped the sack down on the hearth stone. He had coal dust on
his right forehead. It was a heavy sack. Bluebeard would have had
in it the corpse of his first wife. Borrow says that the gipsies say:
"Never trust a young man with grey hair!" . . . He had only half-
grey hair and he was only half young. He was panting. He must
be stopped carrying heavy sacks. Panting like a fish. A great,
motionless carp, hung in a tank.

He said:

"I suppose you would want to go out. If you don't we will have
a fire. You can't stop here without a fire."

At the same moment her mother said:

"If that is Christopher I will speak to him."

She said away from the mouthpiece:

"Yes, let's go out. Oh, oh, Oh.[36] Let's go out. . . . Armistice. . . .
My mother wants to speak to you." She felt herself to be suddenly
a little Cockney shop-girl. A midinette* in an imitation Girl
Guide's uniform. "Afride of the gentleman, my dear." Surely one

* A French word for a young Parisian shopgirl, especially one who works in a dress shop.

could protect oneself against a great carp! She could throw him over her shoulder. She had enough Ju Jitsu* for that. Of course a little person trained to Ju Jitsu can't overcome an untrained giant if he expects it. But if he doesn't expect it she can.

His right hand closed over her left wrist. He had swum towards her and had taken the telephone in his left. One of the window panes was so old it was bulging and purplish. There was another. There were several. But the first one was the purplishest. He said: "Christopher Tietjens speaking!" He could not think of anything more recherché to say than that—the great inarticulate fellow![37] His hand was cool on her wrist. She was calm but streaming with bliss. There was no other word for it. As if you had come out of a bath of warm nectar and bliss streamed off you. His touch had calmed her and covered her with bliss.†

He let her wrist go very slowly. To shew that the grasp was meant for a caress! It was their first caress!

Before she had surrendered the telephone she had said to her mother:

"He doesn't know. . . . Oh realise that he doesn't know!"

She went to the other end of the room and stood watching him.

He heard the telephone from its black depths say:

"How are you, my dear boy? My dear, dear boy; you're safe for good." It gave him a disagreeable feeling. This was the mother of the young girl he intended to seduce. He intended to. He said:

"I'm pretty well. Weakish. I've just come out of hospital. Four days ago." He was never going back to that bloody show. He had his application for demobilisation in his pocket. The voice said:

"Valentine thinks you are very ill. Very ill, indeed. She came to you because she thinks that." She hadn't come, then, because. . . . But, of course, she would not have. But she might have wanted them to spend Armistice Day together! She might have! A sense of disappointment went over him. Discouragement. He was very raw. That old devil, Campion! Still, one ought

---

*   Ju Jitsu is a form of martial art. Loosely translated it means 'science of softness' or 'gentle art' and comprises a grappling style.

†   There is a different but equally powerful touch on the wrist in *The Good Soldier*, when, at 'M— [Marburg]', Florence 'laid one finger upon Captain Ashburnham's wrist' (37).

not to be as raw as that.[38] He was saying, deferentially:

"Oh, it was mental rather than physical. Though I had pneumonia all right." He went on saying that General Campion had put him in command over the escorts of German prisoners all through the Lines of several Armies. That really nearly had driven him mad. He couldn't bear being a beastly gaoler.

Still—Still!—he saw those grey spectral shapes that had surrounded and interpenetrated all his later days. The image came over him with the mood of repulsion at odd moments—at the very oddest; without suggestion there floated before his eyes the image, the landscape of greyish forms. In thousands, seated on upturned buckets, with tins of fat from which they ate at their sides on the ground, holding up newspapers that were not really newspapers; on grey days.[39] They were all round him. And he was their gaoler. He said: "A filthy job!"

Mrs. Wannop's voice said:

"Still, it's kept you alive for us!"

He said:

"I sometimes wish it hadn't!" He was astonished that he had said it; he was astonished at the bitterness of his voice. He added: "I don't mean that in cold blood of course," and he was again astonished at the deference in his voice. He was leaning down, positively, as if over a very distinguished, elderly, seated lady. He straightened himself. It struck him as distasteful hypocrisy to bow before an elderly lady when you entertained designs upon her daughter. Her voice said:

"My dear boy . . . my dear, almost son. . . ."

Panic overcame him. There was no mistaking those tones. He looked round at Valentine. She had her hands together as if she were wringing them. She said, exploring his face painfully with her eyes:

"Oh, be kind to her. Be kind to her. . . ."

Then there had been revelation of their . . . you couldn't call it intimacy![40]

He never liked her Girl Guides' uniform. He liked her best in a white sweater and a fawn-coloured short skirt. She had taken off her hat—her cowboyish hat. She had had her hair cut. Her fair hair.

Mrs. Wannop said:

"I've got to think that you have saved us. To-day I have to think that you have saved us.... And of all you have suffered." Her voice was melancholy, slow, and lofty.

Intense, hollow reverberations filled the house. He said: "That's nothing. That's over. You don't have to think of it." The reverberations apparently reached[41] her ear. She said: "I can't hear you. There seems to be thunder." External silence came back. He said: "I was telling[42] you not to think of my sufferings." She said:

"Can't you wait? You and she? Is there *no* ..." The reverberations began again. When he could again hear she was saying:

"Has had to contemplate such contingencies arising for one's child. It is useless to contend with the tendency of one's age. But I had hoped...."

The knocker below gave three isolated raps, but the echoes prolonged them. He said to Valentine:

"That's the knocking of a drunken man. But then half the population might well be drunk. If they knock again, go down and send them away." She said:

"I'll go in any case before they can knock again."

She heard him say as she left the room—she could not help waiting for the end of the sentence: she *must* gather all that she could as to that agonising interview between her mother and her lover. Equally, she must go or she would go mad. It was no good saying that her head was screwed on straight. It wasn't. It was as if it contained two balls of string with two ends. On the one her mother pulled, on the other, he.... She heard him say:

"I don't know. One has desperate need. Of talk. I have not really spoken to a soul for two years!" Oh, blessed, adorable man! She heard him going on, getting into a stride of talk:

"It's that that's desperate. I'll tell you. I'll give you an instance. I was carrying a boy. Under rifle-fire. His eye got knocked out. If I had left him where he was his eye would not have been knocked out. I thought at the time that he might have been drowned, but I ascertained[43] afterwards that the water never rose high enough. So I am responsible for the loss of his eye. It's a sort of monomania. You see, I am talking of it now. It recurs. Continuously. And to have to bear it in complete solitude . . . "

She was not frightened going now down the great stairs. They whispered, but she was like a calm Fatima. *He* was Sister Anne, and a brother, too. The enemy was fear. She must not fear. He rescued her from fear. It is to a woman that you must come for refuge from regrets about a boy's eyes.

Her physical interior turned within her. He had been under fire! He might never have been there, a grey badger, a tender, tender grey badger leaning down and holding a telephone. Explaining things with tender care. It was lovely how he spoke to her mother; it was lovely that they were all three together. But her mother would keep them apart. She was taking the only way to keep them apart if she was talking to him as she had talked to her.

There was no knowing. She had heard him say:

He was pretty well. . . . "Thank God!" . . . Weakish. . . . "Ah, give *me* the chance to cherish him!" . . . He had just come out of hospital. Four days ago. He had had pneumonia all right, but it had been mental rather than physical. . . .

Ah, the dreadful thing about the whole war was that it had been—the suffering had been—mental rather than physical. And they had not thought of it. . . . He had been under fire. She had pictured him always as being in a Base, thinking. If he had been killed it would not have been so dreadful for him. But now he had come back with his obsessions and mental troubles. . . . And he needed his woman. And her mother was forcing him to abstain from his woman! That was what was terrible. He had suffered mental torture and now his pity was being worked on to make him abstain from the woman that could atone.

Hitherto, she had thought of the War[44] as physical suffering only: Now she saw it only as mental torture. Immense miles and miles of anguish in darkened minds. That remained. Men might stand up on hills, but the mental torture could not be expelled.

She ran suddenly down the steps that remained to her and was fumbling at the bolts of the front door. She was not skilful at that: she was thinking about the conversation that dreadfully she felt to be continuing. She must stop the knocking. The knocker had stayed for just long enough for the abstention of an impatient man knocking on a great door. Her mother was too cunning for them. With the cunning that makes the mother wild-duck tumble apparently broken-winged just under your feet to decoy you away from her little things. STORGE, Gilbert White calls it! For, of course, she could never have his lips upon hers when she thought of that crafty, beloved, grey Eminence sitting at home and shuddering.... But she *would!*

She found the gadget that opened the door—the third she had tried amongst incomprehensible, painted century-old fixings. The door came open exactly upon a frustrated sound. A man was being propelled towards her by the knocker to which he held.... She had saved *his* thoughts. Without the interruption of the knocker he might be able to see that mother's device was just cunning. They were cunning, the great Victorians.... Oh, poor mother!

A horrible man in uniform looked at her hatefully, with piercing, hollow, black eyes in a fallen away face. He said:

"I must see that fellow[45] Tietjens; you're not Tietjens!" As if she were defrauding him. "It's urgent," he said. "About a sonnet. I was dismissed the Army yesterday. *His* doing. And Campion's. His wife's lover!"

She said fiercely:

"He's engaged. You can't see him. If you want to see him you must wait!" She felt horror that Tietjens should ever have had to do with such a brute beast. He was unshaven; black. And filled with hatred. He raised his voice to say:

"I'm McKechnie.[46] Captain McKechnie of the Ninth. Vice-Chancellor's Latin Prizeman! One of the Old Pals!" He added: "Tietjens forced himself in on the Old Pals!"

She felt the contempt of the scholar's daughter for the Prizeman; she felt that Apollo with Admetus* was as nothing for sheer disgust compared with Tietjens buried in a band of such beings.

She said:

"It is not necessary to shout. You can come in and wait."

At all costs Tietjens must finish his conversation with her mother undisturbed. She led this fellow round the corner of the

* Also a reference to the *Alcestis*: Apollo the god and Admetus, a (compromised) mortal, both feature here.

hall. A sort of wireless emanation seemed to connect her with the upper conversation. She was aware of it going on, through the wall above, diagonally; then through the ceiling in perpendicular waves. It seemed to work inside her head, her end of it, like waves, churning her mind.

She opened the shutters of the empty room round the corner, on the right. She did not wish to be alone in the dark with this hating man. She did not dare to go up and warn Tietjens. At all costs he must not be disturbed. It was not fair to call what her mother was doing, cunning. It was instinct, set in her breast by the Almighty, as the saying is. . . . * Still, it was early Victorian instinct! Tremendously cunning in itself.

The hateful man was grumbling:

"He's been sold up, I see. That's what comes of selling your wife to Generals. To get promotion. They're a cunning lot. But he overreached himself. Campion went back on him. But Campion, too,[47] overreached *himself*. . . . "

She was looking out of the window, across the green square.[48] Light was an agreeable thing. You could breathe more deeply when it was light. . . . Early Victorian instinct! . . . The Mid-Victorians[49] had had to loosen the bonds. Her mother, to be in the van† of Mid-Victorian[50] thought, had had to allow virtue to "irregular unions". As long as they were high-minded. But the high-minded do not consummate irregular unions.[51] So all her books had showed you high-minded creatures contracting irregular unions of the mind or of sympathy; but never carrying them to the necessary conclusion. They would have been ethically at liberty to but they didn't. They ran with the ethical hare, but hunted with the ecclesiastical hounds. . . . Still, of course, she could not go back on her premises just because it was her own daughter!

She said:

"I beg your pardon!" to that fellow. He had been saying:

---

* A reference back to the sergeant's talk of 'hinstinck'. And, behind this, possibly a reference to the location of the pearl in the fourteenth-century poem of the same name (edited by Gollancz during the First World War for its 'consolatory' nature): 'Lo, even inmyddes my brest hit stode. / My Lorde the Lombe, that schede hys blode, / He pyght hit there in token of pes' (ll. 740-42) (*Pearl, Cleanness, Patience, Sir Gawain and the Green Knight* [London: Everyman, 1988], 30).

† Or 'vanguard'.

"They're too damn cunning. They overreach themselves!" Her mind spun. She did not know what he had been talking about. Her mind retained his words, but she did not understand what they meant. She had been sunk in the contemplation of Early Victorian Thought. She remembered the long—call it "liaison"—of Edith Ethel Duchemin and little Vincent Macmaster. Edith Ethel, swathed in opaque crêpe, creeping widow-like along the very palings she could see across the square, to her high-minded adulteries, amidst the whispered applause of Mid-Victorian England. So circumspect and right!... She had her thoughts to keep, all right.* Well under control!... Well, she had been patient.

The man said agonisedly:

"My filthy, bloody, swinish uncle, Vincent Macmaster. *Sir* Vincent Macmaster! And this fellow Tietjens. All in a league against me.... Campion too.... But he overreached himself.... A man got into Tietjens' wife's[52] bedroom. At the Base. And Campion sent him to the front. To get him killed. Her other lover, you see?"

She listened. She listened with all her attention straining. She wanted to be able to ... She did not know what she wanted to be able to do! The man said:

"Major-General[53] Lord Edward Campion, V.C., K.C.M.G., tantivy tum tum, etcetera. Too cunning. Too b—y cunning by half. Sent Tietjens to the front too to get him killed. Me too. We all three went up to Division in a boxcar—Tietjens, his wife's lover, and me. Tietjens confessed that bleedin' swab. Like a beastly monk. Told him that when you die—*in articulo mortis*,† but you won't understand what that means!—your faculties are so numbed that you feel neither pain nor fear. He said that death was no more than an anaesthetic. And that trembling, whining pup drank it in.... I can see them now. In a box-car. In a cutting."

She said:

"You've had shell-shock? You've got shell-shock now!"

He said, like a badger snapping:

---

* A reference to a poem by Alice Meynell (1847–1922), 'The Shepherdess'; cf. *Some Do Not ...* I.i.

† A Latin phrase meaning at the point, or moment, of death.

"I haven't. I've got a bad wife. Like Tietjens.[54] At least she isn't a bad wife. She's a woman with appetites. She satisfies her appetites. That's why they're hoofing me out of the Army. But at least, I don't sell her to Generals. To Major-General Lord Edward Campion, V.C., K.C.M.G., etc. I got divorce leave and didn't divorce her. Then I got second divorce leave. And didn't divorce her. It's against my principles. She lives with a British Museum Palaeontologist and he'd lose his job. I owe that fellow Tietjens a hundred and seventy quid. Over my second divorce leave. I can't pay him. I didn't divorce, but I've spent the money. Going about with my wife and her friend. On principle!"

He spoke so inexhaustibly and fast, and his topics changed so quickly that she could do no more than let the words go into her ears. She listened to the words and stored them up. One main line of topic held her; otherwise she could not think. She only let her eyes run over the friezes of the opposite houses. She gathered that Tietjens had been unjustly dismissed by Campion, whilst saving two lives under fire. McKechnie grudgingly admitted heroism to Tietjens in order to blacken the General. The General wanted Sylvia Tietjens. So as to get her he had sent Tietjens into the hottest part of the line. But Tietjens had refused to get killed. He had a charmed life. That was Provvy spiting the General.[55] All the same, Providence could not like Tietjens, a cully* who comforted his wife's lover. A dirty thing to do. When Tietjens would not be killed the General came down into the Line and *strafed* him to Hell. Didn't she, Valentine, understand why? He wanted Tietjens cashiered so that he, Campion, might be less disgustingly disgraced for taking up with the wife. But he had overreached himself. You can't be cashiered for not being on the spot to lick a General's boots when you are saving life under rifle-fire. So the General had to withdraw his words and find Tietjens a dirty scavenger's job. Made a bleedin' gaoler of him!

She was standing in the doorway so that this fellow should not run upstairs to where the conversation was going on. The windows consoled her. She only gathered that Tietjens had had

---

* A fop, fool or dupe to women. The Routledge *Dictionary of Historical Slang* (2000) provides as an example of usage a quotation from the comedy that made William Congreve famous, *The Old Bachelor* (1693): 'Man was by nature woman's cully made'. Cf. *No More Parades* I.i.

great mental trouble. He must have. She knew nothing of either
Sylvia Tietjens or the General except for their beautiful looks.
But Tietjens must have had great mental trouble. Dreadful!
  It was hateful. How could she stand it! But she must, to keep
this fellow from Tietjens, who was talking to her mother.
  And ... if his wife was a bad wife, didn't it ...
  The windows were consoling. A little dark boy of an officer
passed the railings of the house, looking up at the windows.
  McKechnie had talked himself hoarse. He was coughing. He
began to complain that his uncle, Sir Vincent Macmaster, had
refused him an introduction to the Foreign Office. He had made
a scene at the Macmasters' already that morning. Lady
Macmaster—a haggard wanton, if there ever was one—had
refused him access to his uncle, who was suffering from nervous
collapse. He said suddenly:
  "Now about this sonnet: I'm at least going to show this
fellow...." Two more officers, one short, the other tall, passed
the window. They were laughing and calling out. " ... that I'm
a better Latinist than he...."
  She sprang into the hall. Thunder again had come from the
door.
  In the light outside a little officer with his half profile towards
her seemed to be listening. Beside him was a thin lady, very tall.
At the bottom of the steps were the two laughing officers. The
boy, his eye turned towards her, with a shrinking timidity you
would have said, exclaimed in a soft voice:
  "We've come for Major Tietjens.... This is Nancy. Of
Bailleul, you know!" He had turned his face still more towards
the lady. She was unreasonably thin and tall, the face of her skin
drawn. She was much the older. Much. And hostile. She must
have put on a good deal of colour. Purplish. Dressed in black. She
ducked a little.
  Valentine said:
  "I'm afraid.... He's engaged...."
  The boy said:
  "Oh, but he'll see us. This is Nancy, you know!"
  One of the officers said:
  "We said we'd look old Tietjens up...." He had only one arm.
She was losing her head. The boy had a blue band round his hat.

She said:

"But he's dreadfully urgently engaged. . . ."

The boy turned his face full on her with a gesture of entreaty. "Oh, but . . ." he said. She nearly fell, stepping back. His eye-socket contained nothing; a disorderly reddish scar. It made him appear to be peering blindly; the absence of the one eye blotted out the existence of the other. He said in Oriental pleading tones:

"The Major saved my life; I must see him!" The sleeveless officer called out:

"We said we'd look old Tietjens up. . . . IT's armi . . . hick. . . . At Rouen in the pub. . . ." The boy continued:

"I'm Aranjuez, you know! Aranjuez. . . ." They had only been married last week. He was going to the Indian Army to-morrow. They *must* spend Armistice Day with the Major. Nothing would be anything without the Major. They had a table at the Holborn.*

The third officer: he was a very dark, silky-voiced, young Major, crept slowly up the steps, leaning on a stick, his dark eyes on her face.

"It *is* an engagement, you know!" he said. He had a voice like silk and bold eyes. "We really did make an engagement to come to Tietjens's house to-day . . . whenever it happened . . .[56] a lot of us. In Rouen. Those who were in Number Two."

Aranjuez said:

"The C.O.'s to be there. He's dying, you know. And it would be nothing without the Major. . . ."

She turned her back on him. She was crying because of the pleading tones of his voice and his small hands. Tietjens was coming down the stairs, mooning slowly.

---

* A large restaurant on the corner of Holborn and Kingsway, central London.

CHAPTER II[1]

STANDING at the telephone Tietjens had recognised at once that this was a mother, pleading with infinite statesmanship for her daughter. There was no doubt about that. How could he continue to ... to entertain designs on the daughter of this voice? ... But he *did*. He couldn't. He did. He *couldn't*. He did.... You may expel Nature by pleading ... *tamen usque recur....*[*] She must recline in his arms before midnight. Having cut her hair had made her face look longer. Infinitely attracting. Less downright: with a refinement. Melancholy! Longing! One must comfort.

There was nothing to answer to the mother on sentimental lines. He wanted Valentine Wannop enough to take her away. That was the overwhelming answer to Mrs. Wannop's sophistications of the advanced writer of a past generation. It answered her then; still more it answered her now, to-day, when a man could stand up. Still, he could not overwhelm an elderly, distinguished and inaccurate lady! It is not done.

He took refuge in the recital of facts. Mrs. Wannop, weakening her ground, asked:

"*Isn't* there any legal way out? Miss Wanostrocht tells me your wife ... "

Tiejtens answered:

"I can't divorce my wife. She's the mother of my child. I can't live with her, but I can't divorce her."

Mrs. Wannop took it lying down again, resuming her proper line. She said that he knew the circumstances and that if his conscience ... And so on and so on. She believed, however, in arranging things quietly if it could be done. He was looking down mechanically, listening. He read that our client Mrs. Tietjens of Groby-in-Cleveland requests us to inform you that after the late

---

* Ford's use of suspension dots here truncates the quotation from Horace's *Epistles* (Book 1, no. 10, l. 24): 'Naturam expelles furca, tamen usque recurret' ('You may drive out nature with a pitchfork, yet she'll be constantly running back'). A famous line, it makes it into Hansard on 15 March 1870, for example, when quoted in a debate later adjourned (perhaps because it ran out of time).

occurrences at a Base Camp in France she thinks it useless that you and she should contemplate a common life for the future. . . . He had contemplated that set of facts enough already. Campion during his leave had taken up his quarters at Groby. He did not suppose that Sylvia had become his mistress. It was improbable in the extreme. Unthinkable![2] He had gone to Groby with Tietjens' sanction in order to sound his prospects as candidate for the Division. That is to say that, ten months ago, Tietjens had told the General that he might make Groby his headquarters as it had been for years. But, in that communication trench he had not told Tietjens that he had been at Groby. He had said "London". Specifically.

That *might* be an adulterer's guilty conscience but it was[3] more likely that he did not want Tietjens to know that he had been under Sylvia's influence. He had gone for Tietjens bald-headed, beyond all reason for a Commander-in-Chief speaking to a Battalion Commander.[4] Of course he might have the wind up at being in the trenches and being kept waiting so near the area of a real *strafe* as he might well have taken that artillery lark to be. He might have let fly just to relieve his nerves. But it was more likely that Sylvia had bewildered his old brains into thinking that he, Tietjens, was such a villain that he ought not to be allowed to defile the face of the earth. Still less a trench under General Campion's control.

Campion had afterwards taken back his words very handsomely—with a sort of distant and lofty deprecation. He had even said that Tietjens had deserved a decoration, but that there were only a certain number of decorations now to be given and that he imagined that Tietjens would prefer it to be given to a man[5] to whom it would be of more advantage. And he did not like to recommend for decoration an officer so closely connected with himself. He said this before members of his staff . . . Levin and some others. And he went on, rather pompously, that he was going to employ Tietjens on a very responsible and delicate duty. He had been asked by H.M. Government to put the charge over all enemy prisoners between Army H.Q. and the sea in charge of an officer of an exceptionally trustworthy nature, of high social position and weight. In view of the enemy's complaints to the Hague of ill-treatment of prisoners.

So Tietjens had lost all chance of distinction, command pay, cheerfulness, or even equanimity. And all tangible proof that he had saved life under fire—if the clumsy mud-bath of his incompetence could be called saving life under fire. He could go on being discredited by Sylvia till kingdom come, with nothing to shew on the other side but the uncreditable fact that he had been a gaoler. Clever old General! Admirable old godfather-in-law!

Tietjens astonished himself by saying to himself that if he had had any proof that Campion had committed adultery with Sylvia he would kill him! Call him out and kill him. . . . [6] That of course was absurd. You do not kill a General Officer commanding in chief an Army. And a good General too. His reorganisation of that Army had been everything that was ship-shape and soldierly; his handling it in the subsequent fighting had been impeccably admirable. It was in fact the apotheosis of the Regular Soldier. That alone was a benefit to have conferred on the country. He had also contributed by his political action to forcing the single command on the Government. When he had gone to Groby he had let it be quite widely known that he was prepared to fight that Division of Cleveland on the political issue of single command or no single command—and to fight it in his absence in France. Sylvia no doubt would have run the campaign for him!

Well, that, and the arrival of the American troops in large quantities, had no doubt forced the hand of Downing Street. There could no longer have been any question of evacuating the Western Front. Those swine in their corridors were scotched. Campion was a good man. He was good—impeccable!—in his profession; he had deserved well of his country. Yet, if Tietjens had had proof that he had committed adultery with his, Tietjens', wife he would call him out. Quite properly. In the eighteenth century traditions for soldiers. The old fellow could not refuse. He was of eighteenth century tradition too.[7]

Mrs. Wannop was informing him that she had had the news of Valentine's having gone to him from a Miss Wanostrocht. She had, she said, at first agreed that it was proper that Valentine should look after him if he were mad and destitute. But this Miss Wanostrocht had gone on to say that she had heard from Lady Macmaster that Tietjens and her daughter had had a liaison lasting for years.

And ... Mrs. Wannop's voice hesitated ... Valentine seemed to have announced to Miss Wanostrocht that she intended to live with Tietjens. "Maritally", Miss Wanostrocht had expressed it. It was the last word alone of Mrs. Wannop's talk that came home to him. People would talk. About him. It was his fate. And hers. Their identities interested Mrs. Wannop, as novelist. Novelists live on gossip.* But it was all one to him.

The word "Maritally!" burst out of the telephone like a blue light! That girl with the refined face, the hair cut longish, but revealing its thinner refinement.... That girl longed for him as he for her! The longing had refined her face. He must comfort....

He was aware that for a long time, from below his feet a voice had been murmuring on and on. Always one voice. Who could Valentine find to talk or to listen to for so long? Old Macmaster was almost the only name that came to his mind. Macmaster would not harm her. He felt her being united to his by a current.[8] He had always felt that her being was united to his by a current. This then was the day!

The war had made a man of him! It had coarsened him and hardened him. There was no other way to look at it. It had made him reach a point at which he would no longer stand unbearable things. At any rate from his equals! He counted Campion as his equal; few other people, of course. And what he wanted he was prepared to take....[9] What he had been before, God alone knew. A Younger Son? A Perpetual Second-in-Command? Who knew? But to-day the world changed. Feudalism was finished; its last vestiges were gone. It held no place for him. He was going—he was damn well going!—to make a place in it for....[10] A man could now stand up on a hill, so he and she could surely get into some hole together!†

He said:

"Oh, I'm not destitute, but I was penniless this morning. So I ran out and sold a cabinet to Sir John Robertson.‡ The old fellow

---

* Cf. *English Novel* 10–11 for a discussion of the social importance of gossip – and other reasons for Ford's attention to it.

† See discussion in the Introduction, but also *No More Parades* II.ii when Mark writes to Christopher, 'I dare say these hell-cats have so mauled you that you are glad to be able to get away into any hole.' Significantly, he continues, '[b]ut don't let yourself die in your hole'.

‡ Cf. *Last Post*, in which this particular plot thickens.

had offered me a hundred and forty pounds for it before the war.
He would only pay forty to-day—because of the immorality of my
character." Sylvia had completely got hold of the old collector.
He went on: "The Armistice came too suddenly. I was determined to spend it with Valentine. I expected a cheque
to-morrow. For some books I've sold. And Sir John was going
down to the country. I had got into an old suit of *mufti* and I
hadn't a civilian hat." Reverberations came from the front door.
He said earnestly:

"Mrs. Wannop.... If Valentine and I can, we will.... But to-
day's to-day!... If we can't we can find a hole to get into.... I've
heard of an antiquity shop near Bath. No special regularity of life
is demanded of old furniture dealers. We should be quite happy!
I have also been recommended to apply for a vice-consulate. In
Toulon, I believe. I'm quite capable of taking a practical hold of
life!"

The Department of Statistics would transfer him. All the
Government Departments, staffed of course by non-combatants,
were aching to transfer those who had served to any other old
Department.

A great many voices came from below stairs. He could not
leave Valentine to battle with a great number of voices. He said:

"I've got to go!" Mrs. Wannop's voice answered:

"Yes, do. I'm very tired."[11]

He came mooning slowly down the stairs. He smiled. He
exclaimed:

"Come up, you fellows. There's some Hooch for you!" He had
a royal aspect. An all-powerfulness. They pushed past her and
then past him on the stairs. They all ran up the stairs, even the
man with the stick. The armless man shook hands with his left
hand as he ran. They exclaimed enthusiasms.... On all celebrations it is proper for His Majesty's officers to exclaim and to run
upstairs when whiskey is mentioned. How much the more so to-
day!

They were alone now in the hall, he on a level with her. He
looked into her eyes. He smiled. He had never smiled at her
before. They had always been such serious people. He said:

"We shall have to celebrate! But I'm not mad. I'm not destitute!"[12] He had run out to get money to celebrate with her. He had meant to go and fetch her. To celebrate that day together.

She wanted to say: "I am falling at your feet. My arms are embracing your knees!"

Actually she said:

"I suppose it is proper to celebrate together to-day!"

Her mother had made their union. For they looked at each other for a long time. What had happened to their eyes? It was as if they had been bathed in soothing fluid: they could look the one at the other. It was no longer the one looking and the other averting the eyes, in alternation. Her mother had spoken between them. They might never have spoken of themselves.[13] In one heart-beat a-piece whilst she had been speaking they had been made certain that their union had already lasted many years. . . . It was warm; their hearts beat quietly. They had already lived side by side for many years.* They were quiet in a cavern. The Pompeian red bowed over them; the stairways whispered up and up. They would be alone together now. For ever!

She knew that he desired to say[14] "I hold you in my arms. My lips are on your forehead. Your breasts are being hurt by my chest!"

He said:

"Who have you got in the dining-room? It used to be the dining-room!"

Dreadful fear went through her. She said:

"A man called McKechnie.[15] Don't go in!"

He went towards danger, mooning along. She would have caught at his sleeve, but Caesar's wife must be as brave as Caesar.† Nevertheless she slipped in first. She had slipped past him before at a hanging-stile. A Kentish kissing-gate. She said:

"Captain Tietjens is here!" She did not know whether he was a Captain or a Major. Some called him one, some another.

McKechnie looked merely grumbling: not homicidal. He grumbled:

---

* Cf. the opening of *Some Do Not . . .* and the poem quoted (as by Rossetti) by Macmaster.

† In Shakespeare's *Julius Caesar* Calpurnia tries to prevent Caesar from going to the Senate on the morning of his death because of her dreams. She almost succeeds, but he finally rebukes her: 'How foolish do your fears seem now, Calpurnia!' after the conspirator Decius Brutus offers him another interpretation of her dreams (II.ii.105).

"Look here, my bloody swine of an uncle, your pal, has had me dismissed from the army!"

Tietjens said:

"Chuck it. You know you've been demobilised to go to Asia Minor for the Government. Come and celebrate." McKechnie had a dirty envelope. Tietjens said: "Oh, yes. The sonnet. You can translate it under Valentine's inspection. She's the best Latinist in England!" He said: "Captain McKechnie: Miss Wannop!"

McKechnie took her hand:

"It isn't fair if you're[16] such a damn good Latinist as that . . ." he grumbled.

"You'll have to have a shave before you come out with us!" Tietjens said.

They three went up the stairs together, but they two were alone. They were going on their honeymoon journey. . . . The bride's going away! . . . She ought not to think such things. It was perhaps blasphemy. You go away in a neatly shining coupé with cockaded footmen!

He had re-arranged the room. He had positively re-arranged the room. He had removed the toilet-furnishings in green canvas: the camp bed—three officers on it—was against the wall.[17] That was his thoughtfulness. He did not want these people to have it suggested that she slept with him there. . . . Why not? Aranjuez and the hostile thin lady sat on green canvas pillows on the dais. Bottles leaned against each other on the green canvas table. They all held glasses. There were in all five of H.M. Officers. Where had they come from? There were also three mahogany chairs with green rep, sprung seats. Fat seats. Glasses were on the mantelshelf. The thin[18] hostile lady held a glass of dark red in an unaccustomed manner.

They all stood up and shouted:

"McKechnie! Good old McKechnie!" "Hurray McKechnie!" "McKechnie!" opening their mouths to the full extent and shouting with all their lungs. You could see that!

A swift pang of jealousy went through her.

McKechnie turned his face away. He said:

"The Pals! The old pals!" He had tears in his eyes.

A shouting officer sprang from the camp bed—her nuptial couch! Did she *like* to see three officers bouncing about on her nuptial couch. What an Alcestis! She sipped sweet port! It had been put into her hand by the soft, dark, armless major! The shouting officer slapped Tietjens violently on the back. The officer shouted:[19]

"I've picked up a skirt.... A proper little bit of fluff, sir!"

Her jealousy was assuaged. Her lids felt cold. They had been wet for an instant or so: the moisture had cooled! It's salt of course!... She belonged to this unit! She was attached to him ... for rations and discipline. So she was attached to it. Oh, happy day! Happy, happy day!... There was a song with words like that.* She had never expected to see it. She had never expected....

Little Aranjuez came up to her. His eyes were soft, like a deer's, his voice and hands caressing.... No, he had only one eye! Oh, dreadful! He said:

"You are the Major's dear friend.... He made a sonnet in two and a half minutes!" He meant to say that Tietjens had saved his life.

She said:

"Isn't he wonderful!" Why?

He said:

"He can do anything! Anything!... He ought to have been...."

A gentlemanly officer with an eyeglass wandered in.... Of course they had left the front door open. He said with an exquisite's voice:

"Hullo, Major! Hullo Monty!... Hullo, the Pals!" and strolled to the mantelpiece to take a glass. They all yelled "Hullo, Duckfoot.... Hullo Brassface!" He took his glass delicately and said: "Here's to hoping!... The mess!"

Aranjuez said:

"Our only V.C...." Swift jealousy went through her.

Aranjuez said:

"*I* say ... that *he*...."[20] Good Boy! Dear Boy! Dear little brother!... Where was her own brother? Perhaps they were not

---

* In the negro spiritual, the 'happy day' is the one when 'Jesus washed all our sins away'.

going to be on terms any more![21] All around them the world was roaring. They were doing their best to make a little roaring unit there: the tide creeping into silent places! The thin woman in black on the dais was looking at them. She drew her skirts together. Aranjuez had his little hands up as if he were going to lay them pleadingly on her breast. Why pleadingly?... Begging her to forget his hideous eye-socket. He said: "Wasn't it splendid ... wasn't it ripping of Nancy to marry me like this?... We shall all be such friends."

The thin woman caught her eye. She seemed more than ever to draw her skirts away though she never moved.... That was because she, Valentine was Tietjens' mistress.... There's a picture in the National Gallery called *Titian's Mistress*....* She passed perhaps with them all for having.... The woman smiled at her: a painfully forced smile. For Armistice.... She, Valentine, was outside the pale.† Except for holidays and days of National rejoicing....

She felt ... nakedish, at her left side. Sure enough Tietjens was gone. He had taken McKechnie to shave. The man with the eyeglass looked critically round the shouting room. He fixed her and bore towards her. He stood over, his legs wide apart. He said: "Hullo! Who'd have thought of seeing *you* here? Met you at the Prinseps'.[22]‡ Friend of friend Hun's, aren't you?"

He said:

---

* A nice pun on the similar names, but there is no painting with this title in the National Gallery Collection. There is, however, one called *An Unknown Lady called 'Titian's Mistress'* at Apsley House, London. It dates from 1550 [?] and is probably by a follower of Titian. Apsley House was the London residence of the Duke of Wellington and his descendants, and there was limited access to its art works (which may also have been loaned temporarily to the National Gallery). The work was given to Wellington by the Spanish royal family in 1813 after the Battle of Vitoria, so was in his collection by Ford's time.

† The English Pale was the name given in the fourteenth century to that part of Ireland where English rule was effective. The word 'pale' is taken from the Latin meaning a stake, hence a fence, a territory with defined limits. Its meaning has been argued to extend logically (though some linguists disagree about this) to include the 'bounds of civilization' or of 'civilized behaviour'.

‡ See newsletter no. 13 of the Ford Madox Ford Society (2007, accessible at www.open.ac.uk/Arts/fordmadoxford-society) on a possible source for the name Prinsep. Bill Greenwell writes that James Frederick Macleod Prinsep (1861–95) is likely to have informed Edward Ashburnham's character in *The Good Soldier*, but notes also that James Hunter (father to James Frederick) had a cousin, the Pre-Raphaelite circle painter Valentine Cameron Prinsep (1838–1904), who was a member of the Hogarth club, founded by Ford Madox Brown in 1858.

"Hullo, Aranjuez! Better?"

It was like a whale speaking to a shrimp: but still more like an uncle speaking to a favourite nephew! Aranjuez blushed with sheer pleasure. He faded away as if in awe before tremendous eminences. For him she too was an eminence. His life-hero's . . . woman! The V.C. was in the mood to argue about politics. He always was. She had met him twice during evenings at friends' called Prinsep. She had not known him because of his eyeglasses: he must have put that up along with his ribbon. It took your breath away: like a drop of blood illuminated by a light that never was.

He said:

"They say you're receiving for Tietjens! Who'd have thought it? you a pro-German and he such a sound Tory.²³ Squire of Groby and all, eh what?"

He said:

"Know Groby?" He squinted through his glasses round the room. "Looks like a mess this . . . Only needs the *Vie Parisienne* and the *Pink Un*. . . .* Suppose he has moved his stuff to Groby. He'll be going to live at Groby, now. The war's over!"

He said:

"But you and old Tory Tietjens in the same room . . . By Jove the war's over. . . . The lion lying down with the lamb's nothing. . . ."† He exclaimed "Oh damn! Oh, damn, damn, damn. . . . I say . . . I didn't mean it. . . . Don't cry. My dear little girl. My dear Miss Wannop. One of the best I always thought you. You don't suppose. . . ."

---

* La Vie Parisienne was one of the more well-known of Parisian magazines. Originally intended as a guide to social and artistic life in the capital, it soon evolved into a mildly risqué publication. The magazine was banned in some neighbouring countries, and General Pershing was said to have warned American servicemen against purchasing it. The *Sporting Times* or 'Pink 'Un' was known less for its sporting news than for its anecdotes and gossip (it was a very different class of sporting publication from the *Field*, referred to in *The Good Soldier*, 14). In Conan Doyle's Sherlock Holmes story 'The Blue Carbuncle' (first published in *Strand* magazine in January 1892), Holmes notes 'when you see a man with whiskers of that cut and the "Pink 'un" protruding out of his pocket, you can always draw him by a bet' (*The Complete Sherlock Holmes* [Harmondsworth: Penguin, 1981], 253). The publication also features in *No More Parades* I.ii.

† Isaiah 12:6: 'The wolf also shall dwell with the lamb, and the leopard shall lie down with the kid; and the calf and the young lion and the fatling together; and a little child shall lead them.' The misquoted version given by Tietjens is very much part of common parlance.

She said:

"I'm crying because of Groby....[24] It's a day to cry on anyhow.... You're quite a good sort, really!"

He said:

"Thank you! Thank you! Drink some more port! He's a good fat old beggar, old Tietjens. A good officer!" He added: "Drink a *lot* more port!"

He had been the most asinine, creaking, "what about your king and country," shocked, outraged and speechless creature of all the many who for years had objected to her objecting to men being unable to stand up.... Now he was a rather kind brother!

They were all yelling.

"Good old Tietjens! Good old Fat Man! Pre-war Hooch! He'd be the one to get it." No one like Fat Man Tietjens! He lounged at the door; easy; benevolent. In uniform now. That was better. An officer, yelling like an enraged Redskin dealt him an immense blow behind the shoulder blades. He staggered, smiling into the centre of the room. An officer gently pushed her into the centre of the room. She was against him. Khaki encircled them. They began to yell and to prance, joining hands. Others waved the bottles and smashed underfoot the glasses. Gipsies break glasses at their weddings. The bed was against the wall. She did not like the bed to be against the wall. It had been brushed by....

They were going round them: yelling in unison:

"Over here! Pom Pom Over here! Pom Pom!

That's the word, that's the word; Over here...."

At least they weren't[25] over there! They were prancing. The whole world round them was yelling and prancing round. They were the centre of unending roaring circles. The man with the eyeglass had stuck a half-crown in his other eye. He was well-meaning. A brother. She had a brother with the V.C. All in the family.

Tietjens was stretching out his two hands from the waist. It was incomprehensible. His right hand was behind her back, his left in her right hand. She was frightened. She was amazed. Did you ever![26] He was swaying slowly. The elephant! They were dancing! Aranjuez was hanging on to the tall woman like a kid on a telegraph pole. The officer who had said he had picked up a

little bit of fluff.... [27] well, he had! He had run out and fetched
it.[28] It wore white cotton gloves and a flowered hat. It said: "Ow!
Now!" ... There was a fellow with a most beautiful voice. He led:
better than a gramophone. Better....
    Les petites marionettes, font! font! font.... *
On an elephant. A dear, meal-sack elephant. She was setting
out on....

TOULON, 9ᵗʰ January, 1926
PARIS, 21ˢᵗ July   "

---

* From a traditional comptine, or children's song: 'Ainsi font, font, font / Les petites
    marionettes / Ainsi font, font, font / Trois petits tours / Et puis s'en vont / elles revien-
    dront / Les petites marionettes / Elles reviendront / Quand les autres partiront.' Cf. *A
    Mirror to France* (London: Duckworth, 1926), 249, and also Conrad's epigraph to *A
    Set of Six* (1908). 'Marionettes' (puppets) feature in *Provence* (231), and in *A Call*'s
    'Epistolary Epilogue', in which Ford imagines himself, the 'poor Impressionist',
    packing his marionettes into their case after the telling of his tale (163). This is very
    like his reference in *English Novel* to Thackeray, who 'must needs write his epilogue
    as to the showman rolling up his marionettes in green baize and the rest of it' (7); cf.
    March 587, and the novelist's related appearance in *Last Post* I.i. The last page of *No
    More Parades* makes reference to the 'pierrots of a child's Christmas nightmare'.

TEXTUAL NOTES

Conventions used in the Textual Notes

The textual endnotes use the following abbreviations and symbols:

UK First United Kingdom edition of *A Man Could Stand Up –* (London: Duckworth, 1926)
TS Typescript of *A Man Could Stand Up –*
US First American edition of *A Man Could Stand Up –* (New York: Albert & Charles Boni, 1926)
Ed Editor
< > Deleted passages
[ ] Conjectural reading (or editorial comment that a passage is illegible)
↑ ↓ Passage inserted above a line; often to replace a deleted passage
↓ ↑ Passage inserted below a line; often to replace a deleted passage

Most of the textual notes compare a passage from UK with the corresponding passage from TS, or with TS and, where appropriate, other witnesses. In these notes the abbreviation for the witness is given in bold typeface. Where witnesses agree, their abbreviations are listed, separated by commas. Semi-colons are used to separate the different quotations. The first quotation is always from UK; it is followed by the corresponding segment(s) from the typescript and/or other witness(es). With segments longer than a single word in UK, the first and last words are identical in all versions, to enable ready comparison. In the (imagined) example:

> **UK, TS** a tobacco shop; **US** a sweet shop

the UK text prints 'a tobacco shop', following the typescript; but US prints 'a sweet shop'.

Deletions in the typescript are quoted within angled brackets; insertions are recorded between vertical arrows, beginning with an up-arrow if the word is inserted from above the line, or with a down-arrow if inserted from below. Thus:

> **UK** had taken a cab from; **TS** had <marched> ↑taken a cab↓ from

indicates that where UK prints 'had taken a cab from', in the corresponding passage in the typescript, the word 'marched' has been deleted, and the phrase 'taken a cab' inscribed above. In this instance, US will have followed UK.

The abbreviation **Ed** is only used where the editor adopts a reading different from all the witnesses. This is mainly used for grammatical corrections.

The abbreviation **AR** stands for 'Autograph Revision', indicating a hand-written revision to a typescript.

Discursive notes (which don't compare versions) are differentiated by not using bold face for the witness abbreviations.

The symbol ¶ is used to indicate a paragraph break in a variant quoted in the textual endnotes. For verse quoted in the footnotes, a line break is indicated by '/'.

Textual Note for Title

1   **UK, US** A MAN COULD STAND UP – ¶ A NOVEL; **TS**, A MAN COULD STAND UP........ <A NOVEL> **AR**

Textual Notes for Dedicatory Letter

1   **UK** GERALD DUCKWORTH; **TS, US** GERALD DUCKWORTH ESQ.
2   **UK** the heavy strain; **TS** the great strain
3   **UK, TS** great—in mortal—danger; **US** great—in moral—danger

Textual Notes for I.i

4   **UK** *PART I* ¶ CHAPTER I; **TS** PART THE FIRST ¶ Chapter I; **US** A MAN COULD STAND UP— ¶ CHAPTER I
5   **UK, TS** asphalte; **US** asphalt
  The *OED* lists the less common '-e' form of 'asphalt' – also the French spelling, which may have influenced Ford.
6   **UK** " .... that; **TS** "..... that; **US** "... that
7   **UK** to her that; **TS** to <Valentine> ↑her↓ that **AR**
8   **UK** world needed; **TS** world <probably> needed **AR**
9   **UK, TS** She; **US** *She*
10 **UK** with joy! ¶ She; **TS** with <hysterical> joy! ¶ She **AR**
11 **UK, US** it's; **TS** it<'>s **AR**
12 **UK, TS** girl's voices; **US** girls' voices
13 **UK, TS** factory-hooters' ululations, amongst; **US** factory-hooter's ulula-tions, amongst
14 **UK** to.... . Then: Miss; **TS** to. ¶ ...... Then: Miss; **US** to.... Then: Miss
  It is possible the extra dot crept into UK due to the confusion about para-graphs in TS. US adopted in this case.
15 **UK** ago ... Before; **TS** ago .... Before; **US** ago.... Before
16 **UK** sirens, whichever; **TS** syrens, whichever
  'Syren' is given in the *OED* as a variant form of 'siren', but indicates that English spelling has been assimilated to the form given in UK. Milton, for example, uses the 'i' spelling. 'Sirens' is spelt with a 'y' throughout the chapter in TS.

17 **UK** Blastus. She; **TS** Blastus <and supplied the word 'Ought'>. She **AR**

18 **UK** for the superannuated; **TS** for <a> ↑the↓ superannuated **AR**

19 **UK** school had had before; **TS** school <must have>↑had↓ had **AR**

20 **UK** herself the venerable; **TS** herself <a> ↑the↓ venerable **AR**

21 **UK** almshouse, probably. Placed; **TS** almshouse, <no doubt> ↑probably↓. Placed **AR**
'No doubt' appears in the following line of text, so there would have been repetition if it had not been deleted here.

22 **UK** a situation; a; **TS** a 'situation'; a

23 **UK, TS** be no omen; **US** be an omen

24 **UK** before.... before; **TS** before..... before; **US** before .... before
US adopted in this use of ellipsis, as it may well be an indication of extended hesitation, while not punctuating a complete sentence, which is the implication of UK.

25 **UK** nonconformist chapel, High, bare walls; **TS** nonconformist chapel. High, bare walls; **US** nonconformist chapel, high, bare walls
The US editor has evidently chosen a solution to the error here that differs from the one available in TS. TS version given here.

26 **UK** show; **TS** shew

27 **UK** shew; **TS** show

28 **UK, TS** the popularly festival; **Ed** the popular festival
The last two letters of the word 'popularly' have a ring around them in TS, probably indicating (as happens elsewhere in TS) an error to be corrected. This correction has not been made in UK, or US.

29 **UK** martyrdoms, her impressive taste in furniture, her large rooms and; **TS** martyrdoms ↑her impressive taste in furniture, her large rooms↓ and

30 **UK** All Critic's wives; **TS, US** All Critics' wives

31 **UK** Savage Lander, a; **TS, US** Savage Landor, a
TS is not completely clear in this case, and it's easy to see it being misread as UK was being prepared.

32 **UK** And she was being disrespectful; **TS** And ↑she was being↓ disrespectful **AR**

33 **UK, TS** sense on the; **US** sense in the

34 **UK, TS, US** Mistress's conference; **Ed** Mistresses' conference

35 **UK, TS, US** Mistress's conference; **Ed** Mistresses' conference

36 **UK** really frightening them was; **TS** really ↑frightening them↓ was **AR**

37 **UK** keep them—the; **TS** keep Them - the

38 **UK, TS, US** Mistress's conference. So; **Ed** Mistresses' conference. So

39 **UK** the—eh—noises; **TS** the ↑- eh -↓ noises

40 **UK** suppose they will; **TS** suppose They will

41 **UK, US** Edith Ethel's story, had; **TS** Edith Ethel's had
There is no indication of the missing word in TS, and it hasn't made it into the Duckworth proofs either.

42 **UK** of the adenoidy, noncomformistish; **TS** of that adenoidy, nonconformistish

43 **Ford** uses three short dashes in TS that stand in for the missing letters that are repeated in the proofs and then in UK and US. See the Introduction to this volume for discussion of Ford's textual treatment of swearing.

44 **UK** his enterprise. She; **TS** his Enterprise. She

45 **UK** telephone had been saying to her inattention, rather crawlingly, after; **TS** telephone, rather crawlingly had been saying to her inattention, after

Textual Notes for I.ii

1 **UK** CHAPTER II; **TS** II
2 There is no line-break in US.
3 **UK** reappearance of a man she hoped she had put out of her mind. A man who had "insulted" her. In one way or the other he had insulted her! ¶ But; **TS** reappearance <referred to> ↑of a man she hoped she had put out of her mind. A man who had "insulted" her. In one way or the other he had insulted her!↓ ¶ But **AR**
4 **UK** Vallambrosa; **TS** Vallombrosa
5 **UK** she has been; **TS** she had been
   Correction made in line with TS because of surrounding sentence structure.
6 **UK** Acts. Nevertheless, she had been thinking of the man who had once insulted her as the Bear, whom she would have to fight again! But; **TS** Acts. ↑Nevertheless she had been thinking of the man who had once insulted her as the Bear, whom she would have to fight again!↓ But **AR**
7 **UK** forgotten. Years ago, Edith Ethel, out of a clear sky, had accused her of having had a child by that man. But she hardly thought of him as a man. She thought of him as a ponderous; **TS** forgotten. ↑Years ago↓ Edith Ethel, out of a clear sky, had accused her of having had a child by that ↑man. But she hardly thought of him as a↓ ponderous **AR**
8 **UK** or, Hell! oh, Hell!; **TS** oh Hell, oh Hell!; **US** or Hell!, oh, Hell!
9 At this point on the leaf the text ceases, though it is only half full. It is the first insert in the text, added as a result of revision. The next leaf of TS originally began mid-sentence, with the words 'she had been talking'. See note below. I.i concludes with these same words.
10 **UK** Valentine had realised that she; **TS** ↑Valentine had realised that↓ she **AR**
   These words were added to the top of the leaf, as a result of the revision noted above.
11 **UK** that Edith; **TS** that <all the while> Edith **AR**
12 **TS** the wall by the mere sound of the offer.... What was the offer? ¶ "I thought that you might, if I were the means of bringing **AR**
   These words are added to the bottom of the TS leaf.
13 **UK** that man, that grey; **TS** that ↑man, that↓ grey **AR**
14 **UK** penetrating nauseously to; **TS** penetrating ↑nauseously↓ to **AR**
15 **UK** pitiful, For; **TS, US** pitiful. For
16 **UK** reclaimed.... ¶ Now, in the empty rooms at Lincoln's Inn—for that was probably what it came to!—that man was; **TS** reclaimed.... ¶ <She could not think of what was> ↑Now,↓ in the empty rooms at Lincoln's Inn – for that was probably what it came to! – <as a human male. It> ↑that man↓ was **AR**
17 **TS** Calling to *her*! **AR**
18 **UK** that did not exist in a girl's head without someone to put it there, but; **TS** that <had to be put into a girl's head.> ↑did not exist in a girl's head without someone to put it there,↓ but **AR**
19 **UK** as affected by; **TS** as <worn> ↑affected↓ by **AR**
20 **UK** into that man's intolerable; **TS** into <the Problem of> ↑that man's↓ intolerable **AR**
21 **UK** alone with you.... ¶ Her; **TS** alone ↑with you....↓ ¶ Her **AR**

22 **UK** grey, grizzly; **TS** grey grizzly
   Correction made in line with **TS** as it supports better the sense of 'grizzly'
   being used as a noun.
23 **UK, TS, US** twenty minutes; **Ed** twenty minutes'
24 **UK** maroons. The impoverished War Heroes would; **TS** maroons. <They>
   ↑The impoverished War Heroes↓ would **AR**
25 **UK** the man's Society; **TS** the ↑man's↓ Society **AR**
26 **UK** Godfather. The man's rather; but; **TS** Godfather. <One of theirs> ↑The
   man's rather↓; but **AR**
27 **UK** these; **TS** those
   The grammatical weight is with 'those' as Valentine is remembering an
   earlier military dress code.
28 **UK** times! ¶ That had been in 1912; **TS** times! ¶ ↑That had been in↓ 1912
   AR
29 **UK** although Mr. So and So was; **TS** although <the lacuna> ↑Mr So + So↓
   was **AR**
30 **UK** of acquaintance with; **TS** of <intimacy> ↑acquaintance↓ with **AR**
31 **UK, TS, US** lama; **Ed** llama
32 **UK** to be said to have; **TS** to ↑be said to↓ have **AR**
33 **UK** When, during the late Hostilities, he; **TS** When, ↑during the late
   Hostilities,↓ he **AR**
34 **UK** her again to; **TS** her ↑again↓ to **AR**
35 **UK** loony: John Peel with his coat so grey, the; **TS** loony: ↑John Peel with
   his coat [so grey],↓ the **AR**
   The last two words of Ford's insertion, made at the top of the TS leaf, are
   nearly illegible.
36 **UK** to ring me up. He; **TS** to ↑ring me up↓. He **AR**

Textual Notes for I.iii

1 **UK** CHAPTER III; **TS** III
2 No line-break at this point in US.
3 **UK** woman's colleges; **TS** women's colleges
4 **UK** Wanostrocht, said, "how; **TS, US** Wanostrocht said, "how
5 **UK** father ... And; **TS, US** father.... And
6 **UK** you; **TS** *you*
7 **UK** He; **TS** *He*
8 **UK** existed between her and him might; **TS** existed ↑between her and him↓
   might **AR**
9 **UK** Girls. She had no doubt been described as having had a baby. A; **TS**
   Girls. ↑She had no doubt been described as having. had a baby!↓ A **AR**
10 **UK** incidentally in; **TS** incidentally <as the last thought she had had> in
   AR
11 **UK** people.... the; **TS** people.... The; **US** people ... the
   UK's standardisation of ellipses is somewhat questionable here, as elsewhere
   in I.iii.
12 **UK** brilliant Victorians; **TS** Brilliant Victorians
13 UK, TS and US all carry this less common, and more antiquated, form of the
   parenthetical phrase, 'by the by'.

14 **UK** friend.... perhaps; **TS** friend..... perhaps; **US** friend ... perhaps
15 **UK** irritating.... and; **TS** irritating... and; **US** irritating ... and infectious
16 **UK** Institutions ... Military Sanatoria.... for; **TS** Institutions.... Military
Sanatoria... for; **US** Institutions ... Military Sanatoria ... for
Ford himself indicates a difference in the length of hesitation in these two
cases in TS, although that decision is reversed in UK.
17 **UK** war; **TS** War
18 **UK** one... Because it's because of the War ..." **TS** one...... Because it's
because of the war......" **US** one.... Because it's because of the War...."
Extra dot given to first ellipsis above in the text, in line with US, as this looks
to be a mistake in UK – because of the lack of a space before the first dot if
an incomplete sentence was being signified.
19 **UK** ".... behaved very badly indeed."; **TS** "...... appears to have behaved
very badly indeed."
In the Duckworth proof of *A Man Could Stand Up* –, the text corroborates
that in TS.
20 **UK** containing," that; **TS, US** continuing, "that
21 **UK** you seem to; **TS** you appear to
22 **UK** Tietjens. I would have. I would at any time. I have always thought of
her as beautiful and kind. But I heard you say the words: '*has been behaving
very badly*,' and I thought you meant that Captain Tietjens had. I denied it.
If you meant that his wife had, I deny it, too. She's; **TS** Tietjens. <If anyone
attacked her I should certainly defend her.> ↓I would have. I would at any
time. She appeared to me to be beautiful and kind. But I heard you say the
words: *has been behaving very badly* and I thought you meant that Captain Tietjens had. I denied it. If you meant that his wife had, I deny it too.↑ She's **AR**
This whole section in TS is handwritten, at the bottom of the page, to
replace the deleted sentence. TS is replicated in the Duckworth proofs. Note
also that Valentine gets it wrong in the published text – Miss Wanostrocht
said (though is interrupted) 'behaved very badly indeed'. See note 19 above.
23 **UK** offspring ... That's; **TS** offspring... That's; **US** offspring.... That's
24 **UK** that ... And; **TS** that.... And; **US** that.... And
25 **UK** But my father couldn't; **TS** But <he> ↑my father↓ couldn't **AR**
26 **UK** should lead a; **TS** should <have led> ↑lead↓ a **AR**
27 **UK** We...." she began again: "We; **TS** We.... She began again: "We; **US**
We...." she began: "We
28 **UK** stripling that her father had been.... They; **TS** stripling ↑that her father
had been↓.... They **AR**

Textual Notes for II.i

1 **UK** *PART II* ¶ CHAPTER I; **TS** PART II ¶ Chapter I; **US** PART II
CHAPTER IV
There is a page-break in US between the PART II and CHAPTER IV.
2 **UK** MONTHS and months before Christopher; **TS** ↑Months and months
before↓ Christopher
3 **UK** was in; **TS** was <precisely> in **AR**
4 **UK** rooster; it gleamed, with five; **TS** rooster; <five-lobed:> it gleamed, with
<those> five **AR**

5 UK, TS just filtering; US just flickering
6 UK there than in the surrounding desolation because; TS there ↑than in the surrounding desolation↓ because
7 UK of just-illuminated rift; TS of ↑just-↓illuminated rift
8 Though it seems likely that Ford meant 'motif' here, rather than 'motive', TS confirms the word as UK prints it.
9 UK No doubt half-past eight; TS No doubt about half-past eight
    TS version imported here due to its clearer distinction from its partner ('or at half-past eight to the stroke').
10 UK, TS shew; US show
11 UK methodical, That; TS methodical, <those fellows.> That; US methodical. That AR
    The sentence alteration possibly led to the end punctuation confusion in this case.
12 TS has a full stop here. There is no full stop at this point in UK, though there is a space on the line for one. There is neither a full stop nor a space in US.
13 In general, TS does not include an apostrophe in place of dropped letters in dialect speech. This is an exception, as in TS there is an apostrophe at the start of the word. Apostrophes are in the Duckworth proof, as well as in UK and US.
14 UK would'n, be; TS wouldn be; US would'n be
15 UK The Acting Sergeant-Major said; TS The Acting <Quarter Master> ↑Sergeant Major↓ said AR
16 UK The Sergeant said; TS The <Quarter> ↑Sergeant↓ said AR
17 UK that Tietjens had; TS that <he> ↑Tietjens↓ had AR
18 UK to bayonet attachment. Tietjens; TS to <barrel> ↑bayonet-attachment↓ . Tietjens AR
19 UK did'n'; TS did'n
20 In TS Ford has not placed speech marks around this paragraph, or the preceding one. They are in the Duckworth proof but have been dropped again from UK. US includes them. I have dropped them here, following TS and UK, because it's not direct speech that is being signified – as shown in the reference to the lance-corporal in the third person. This rationalisation is complicated slightly, but not impossibly, by the information in the next note. See note 10 in the next chapter and the discussion in the Introduction to this volume.
21 UK "Yes sargint, no sargint!"; TS Yes sargint, no sargint!
    TS has no speech marks around what is clearly speech.
22 UK The doctor said; TS <He> ↑The doctor↓ said AR
23 UK, TS nights; US night
24 UK faces; Why? TS faces. Why? US faces; why?
25 UK inwards. Like the; TS inwards, <too,> like the AR
    The Duckworth proofs give the text produced in UK.
26 UK colour they were. Chucked; TS colour ↑they were↓. Chucked AR
27 UK be a hundred and eleven; TS be ↑a hundred and↓ eleven AR
28 Speech marks are added to this phrase AR in TS. See notes 19, 20 in this chapter.
29 UK drooping like the dishevelled veils of murdered bodies. They; TS drooping like the dishevelled veils of murdered brides. They; US dropping like the dishevelled veils of murdered bodies. They

30 **UK** of corpses of vast dimensions; in; **TS** of <unthinkable> ↑corpses of vast dimensions;↓ in
The deletion to TS is AR in this case, while the addition is typed.

31 **UK** the askew, blind-looking eyeholes; **TS** the ↑askew, blind-looking↓ eyeholes

32 **UK** din so; **TS** din <that was> so **AR**

33 **UK** dark tumult, in; **TS** dark <row>, ↑tumult↓ in **AR**

34 **UK** fellows were reliefs. They shot past you clumsily in a darkness spangled with shafts of light coming from God knows where and appeared going forward, whilst you at least had the satisfaction that, by order, you were going back. In; **TS** fellows ↑were reliefs.– ↓ <who> ↑They↓ shot past you clumsily in a darkness spangled with shafts of light coming from God knows where and <who> appeared, going forward, whilst you at least had the satisfaction that, by order, you were going back. In **AR**
TS, then, originally had one long sentence here. The commas were added as part of the revision.

35 **UK** of ... Damn; **TS** of.... Damn; **US** of... Damn

36 In **UK, TS** and **US**, McKechnie is rendered Mckechnie. This issue recurs in subsequent chapters. See the beginning of *No More Parades*, where the character is introduced, for further details as to Ford's use of this name. In general, it causes fewer textual problems in the earlier novel.

37 **UK** longer. The ghostly Huns would have been in the trenches. But; **TS** longer. ↑The ghostly Huns would have been in the trenches.↓ But

38 **UK** subalterns before getting killed. Still, that; **TS** subalterns<?> ↑before getting killed.↓ Still, that

39 **UK** never that day get; **TS** never ↑that day↓ get

40 **UK** not traditionally supposed; **TS** not ↑traditionally↓ supposed

41 **UK** were built of; **TS** were↑built↓ of **AR**

42 This sentence added AR to TS on the line.

43 **UK, TS** was it n smashed. Hin; **US** was it not smashed. Hin
The 1948 Penguin edition, for example, reproduces UK (without apostrophes here, note), but the 1982 Penguin reproduces the US version – and evident difficulty with dialect. See also notes 13 and 19 in this chapter.

44 **UK, TS** beind; **US** behind

45 **UK** the 'Uns' beck; **TS** the Uns'<gas> beck; **Ed** the 'Uns beck
This grammatical confusion may have arisen because the original TS version necessitated a possessive apostrophe after 'Huns'. However, 'gas' was deleted in Ford's hand, and this apostrophe should have gone with it.

46 **UK** it! ¶ The; **TS** it. <Well then......> ¶ The **AR**

47 **UK** The Sergeant said that 'e wished 'e could *feel* the Germans 'ad ruined theirselves: they seemed to be drivin' us into the Channel." Tietjens **TS** The Sergeant said that 'e wished 'e could ↑feel↓ the Germans 'ad ruined theirselves: they seemed to be drivin' us into the Channel. Tietjens; **US** The Sergeant said that "'e wished 'e could *feel* the Germans 'ad ruined theirselves: they seemed to be drivin' us into the Channel." Tietjens
The UK and US editors try in slightly different ways to sort out the curious fact that dialect is reproduced in free indirect style here. (See also note 20, and the two notes below, in this chapter.) The Duckworth proofs carry the same version that US then adopts. TS is reproduced in the text as it has neither set, which of course is grammatically correct. See the Introduction

to this volume for further discussion.

48 There is some inconsistency here in the published versions – in relation to the previous note – as neither UK nor US reproduces any speech marks in this paragraph. The TS, however, is consistent, and has none.

49 UK, US pleasure. "Hit was", he said, "good to 'ave prise from Regular officers." Tietjens TS pleasure. Hit was, he said, good to 'ave prise from Regular officers. Tietjens
  TS version given in text as the form of the text (in any version) doesn't indicate speech – a new line would have been begun. See also the two notes above.

50 UK for at least that TS for ↑at least↓ that AR

51 UK Derby men. Small; TS Derby-men. Small; US Derby Men. Small

52 UK Well, he was that, officially! TS Well, he was that[.] [O]fficially!
  This sentence was added as an AR to TS. Though the TS is unclear, it looks more as if Ford, in fact, has two sentences here.

53 UK the pit-face, hundreds; TS the ↑pit-↓ face, hundreds AR

54 UK disagreeable feelings, thinking; TS disagreeable <sensations>, ↑feelings↓ thinking AR
  See line above in text for probable cause of revision: repetition.

55 The word is not signalled for italicisation (underlined) in TS.

56 UK heavenly powers in decency suspended their activities at such moments. But; TS heavenly powers in decency suspended their activities; in decency, at such moments. But

57 UK lightning. They didn't! A; TS lightning. ↑They didn't!↓ A

58 UK showed to Tietjens, just; TS shewed <him>, ↑to Tietjens↓ just AR

59 UK there ... He; TS there.... He; US there.... He

60 UK subaltern stated that; TS subaltern <suggested the fact> ↑stated↓ that AR

61 UK By signs and removing; TS By ↑signs and↓ removing AR

62 UK the tin hat that covered the face; TS the ↑tin hat that covered the↓ face AR

63 UK instruments. The performers threw; TS instruments. <They> ↑The performers↓ threw

64 UK, TS triger; US trigger

65 UK uber; TS ueber; US uber

66 UK bearers for the corpse. And; TS bearers with a stretcher, positively. And

67 UK Half-a-dozen Germans had; TS Half-a-dozen <of them> ↑Germans↓ had AR

68 No line-break in US here.

69 UK a ghostly visit; TS a ↑ghostly↓ visit AR

70 UK, TS, US O9 Evans; Ed O9 Morgan
  At the beginning of No More Parades, O Nine Morgan, a runner, is killed. Tietjens, then his captain, has just refused his request for leave, made because his wife is having an affair with Red Evans Williams. In this retelling of the story, Ford seems to have confused the two characters' names.

71 UK, TS, US O9 Evans'; Ed O9 Morgan's

72 UK, US unpleasant... Like; TS unpleasant... Like; Ed unpleasant ... Like
  UK emended here as though sentence being signified is an incomplete one. In UK there is a space after the final dot, indicating either that an extra dot was intended, or, more likely (due to the general witness agreement in

numbers of dots), that the dots should have been shifted one space to the right.

73 Both UK and US add this final sentence to the paragraph ("A dream!"). It is absent from TS, and also from the Duckworth proofs, so it was a reasonably late addition, made possibly for reasons of clarity.

74 **UK** Not really as bad as the falling dream: but quite as awakening. . . . ; **TS** Not really as bad as falling: but quite as awakening.
The TS version of this sentence – without specific mention of a dream – is linked of course to the content of note 73 above. An editorial decision must have been taken that the issue of the dream needed to be made explicit.

75 **UK** darkness. Down below, the; **TS** darkness. ↑Down below,↓ [t]he **AR**

76 **UK** perhaps the Country might; **TS** perhaps <they> ↑the Country↓ might **AR**

Textual Notes for II.ii

1 **UK** CHAPTER II; **TS** PART II ¶ Chapter Two; **US** CHAPTER V

2 In many cases of military terminology throughout this chapter, as in 'Sergeant' here, Ford does not use capitals in TS.

3 **UK** efficient working beneath the; **TS** efficient ↑working beneath↓ the **AR**

4 Throughout this chapter, in UK, TS and US, McKechnie is rendered Mckechnie. References have been corrected in all cases.

5 There are no dialect apostrophes in UK and US (or in TS) here and they are absent from later sections of the chapter too: compare frequency instead in the last chapter.

6 **UK, US** Tietjen's; **TS** Tietjens'

7 **UK, US** Tietjen's; **TS** Tietjens'

8 **UK** scarcely refer to Sylvia; **TS** scarcely <be> ↑refer to↓ Sylvia **AR**

9 **UK** to-day? Or; **TS** today? Or; **US** to-day, Or

10 **UK** and US both place speech marks around this whole paragraph, which is inaccurate in so far as the second sentence is not direct speech. TS has the version that is reproduced in the text.

11 **UK** so, without bombs, they; **TS** so ↑without bombs,↓ they **AR**

12 **UK** do! Take orders! It; **TS** do? Take orders? It

13 **UK** C. and D. Companies; **TS** C & D companies

14 From 'Perowne was known to have been his wife's lover [...]' to the end of the paragraph ('up together.') is an autograph addition to the l/h margin of the TS leaf. This is a case in which Ford decides to develop the back story, unpacking the 'triangle' of Perowne, Tietjens and McKechnie, and spelling out Sylvia's adulterous relationship with Perowne.

15 **UK** was not going; **TS** was <never> ↑not↓ going **AR**

16 **UK** Tommies, blond; **TS** Tommies. Blond

17 **UK** to allow Tietjens to persuade; **TS** to ↑allow Tietjens to↓ persuade

18 **UK** He had enough intellectual authority [...] he had used.
In TS this section is an autograph addition to the l/h margin.

19 **UK** the image of; **TS** the <thought> ↑image↓ of **AR**

20 **UK** his Acting Commanding; **TS** his ↑Acting↓ Commanding **AR**

21 **UK** of muddy odd-come; **TS** of ↑muddy↓ odd-come

22 **UK** were men of; **TS** were ↑men↓ of **AR**

23 **UK** 'As; **TS** Has
24 **UK** best!" He was anxious to wipe out the remembrance of the last spoken word. "Give; **TS** best!" <He had heard complimentary references to Tietjens that Tietjens had missed> ↑He was anxious to wipe out the remembrance of the last spoken word↓ "Give **AR**
25 **UK** McKechnie, with; **TS** Mckechnie, <whispering and> with
If left, this would have been a repetition in the sentence.
26 **UK** who had wanted; **TS** who ↑had↓ wanted
27 **UK** McKechnie's present relatively; **TS** Mckechnie's ↑present↓ relatively
28 **UK** fear; **TS** Fear
29 **UK** your; **TS** you
Error (repeated in US) likely to have been made because of subsequent 'four' in text.
30 **UK** b—rs!"; **US** z—rs!"
There are no further examples of this particular formation in US 'bleeping'. The assumption is therefore made that this was a compositor's error in the US edition.
31 **UK** a; **TS** the
TS variant imported in this case as it makes better sense in relation to the next line of text.
32 **UK** the Colonel memsahib's; **TS** the ↑Colonel↓ memsahib's **AR**
33 **UK, US** Corporal's and Sergeant's; **TS** Corporal's and Sergeants'; **Ed** Corporals' and Sergeants'
34 **UK** least to have; **TS** least ↑to↓ have

Textual Notes for II.iii

1 **UK** CHAPTER III; **TS** PART II ¶ Chapter Three; **US** CHAPTER VI
2 **UK** and upset compensations; **TS** and ↑upset↓ compensations **AR**
3 **UK** certain customs of; **TS** certain <survivals> ↑customs↓ of **AR**
4 In many cases of military terminology in this chapter, as in 'Colonel' here, Ford does not capitalise in TS. See previous chapter note also. This applies to subsequent chapters in the volume.
5 **UK** manifested—though always with a sort of Field-Officer's monumental courtesy—towards; **TS** manifested – <at times openly> ↑though always with a sort of Field-Officer's monumental courtesy↓ – towards
6 **UK** that his mind; **TS** that <the man's> ↑his↓ mind **AR**
7 **UK** It; **TS** <And> I **AR**
Revision made on top of existing (lower-case) typed letter in TS.
8 **UK** ought to—and; **TS** ought ↑to↓ – and
9 Though this is technically a mis-spelling, the *OED* includes examples of it in the definitions of the adverb it offers; one is in an article by William James (1907).
10 **UK** you. It may; **TS** you. <and> ↑It↓ may **AR**
11 **UK** had been able to line his; **TS** had ↑been able to↓ line <d> his **AR**
12 This last sentence is an autograph addition on the TS line.
13 **UK, TS, US** remarkable; **Ed** remarkably
14 **UK** still less? No one; **TS** still less ↑?↓ – <n>No one **AR**
15 **UK** some personal stubbornness; **TS** some ↑personal↓ stubbornness **AR**

16 **UK** with such great; **TS** with ↑such↓ great
17 **UK, TS** moral; **US** morale
18 **UK** The easterly winds were needed for the use of the gas without which, in the idea of the German leaders, [**Ed** it] was impossible to attack; **TS** The easterly winds needed for the use of the gas without which the enemy troops could not be induced to attack; **US** The easterly winds were needed for the use of the gas without which, in the idea of the German leaders, it was impossible to attack

This is an interesting case. The Duckworth proofs preserve the TS reading, and so the alteration was made at a late stage, perhaps due to last-minute anxiety about the worrisome inference that could be made about insubordinate, potentially mutinous troops. Note the grammatical error in UK, perhaps a sign of the lateness of the decision; the missing 'it' is instated by US.

19 **UK** position, nevertheless, had; **TS** position <in short> ↑nevertheless↓ had **AR**
20 **UK** breeze, Tietjens; **TS** breeze Tietjens; **US** breeze. Tietjens
21 The last three sentences of the paragraph are an autograph addition to the bottom of the TS leaf.
22 **UK** senior non-commissioned officers; **TS** senior ↑non-commissioned↓ officers **AR**
23 **UK** For; **TS** <And> F **AR**

Revision made on top of existing typed letter. TS originally had no new paragraph here. Ford writes 'n.p.' in the margin, places a square bracket before 'For' and capitalises its initial letter.

24 **UK** *moral*; **TS** morale; **US** *morale*
25 **UK** bucked up; **TS** backed up

The Duckworth proofs give the TS variant, so this is a late editorial decision. Confusion possibly due to the repetition of the vowels in 'patched' and 'drugged'.

26 Throughout this chapter, in UK, TS and US, McKechnie is rendered Mckechnie. References have been corrected throughout. See also relevant note in last chapter.

27 **UK** realise; **TS** realize
28 **UK** squit; **TS** squi<r>t
29 **UK** Derry; **TS, US** Terry

In II.ii the Medical Officer is referred to as Terence. The correct abbreviation is in place here in the TS, and in the Duckworth proofs, but the mistake is carried into UK.

30 **UK** pooping off; **TS** popping off; **US** poping off

Two pages later in TS (see note 39) Ford corrects 'pop off' to 'poop off' AR. See *No More Parades* II.ii for similar editorial difficulties with this word.

31 **UK** up. . . . It was rising on Bemerton! Or; **TS** up where. . . . <Sinking> ↑It was rising↓ on Bemerton! Or **AR**

The Duckworth proofs retain the TS 'where' but it has gone from UK.

32 **UK** no shells falling in that; **TS** no shells in that

The Duckworth proofs retain the TS version.

33 **UK, US** neighbourhood; **TS** neighbo↑u↓rhood **AR**

The AR in this note corrects US spelling to UK, suggesting that if Ford was dictating at this point, as is likely (see the Note on the Text and also see other mis-spellings of words Ford knew well in this chapter), he was also dictating to someone who was American.

34 **UK** Albert-Bécourt-Bécordel; **TS** Albert-<Bicairt> ↑Bécourt↓-Becordel **AR**

35 **UK** realised; **TS** realized

36 **UK** more when all; **TS** more <than> ↑when↓ all **AR**

37 **UK** and Mametz Wood; **TS** and <Manitz> ↑Mametz↓ Wood **AR**

38 **UK** all, as like as not! No; **TS** all, <very likely> ↑as like as not↓ ! No **AR**
Note what would have been repetition in the subsequent sentence.

39 **UK** men poop off; **TS** men <pop> ↑poop↓ off **AR**

40 **UK** artillery *can* do; **TS** artillery <u>can</u> do; **US** artillery can *do*

41 **UK** and Bécourt-Bécordel; **TS** and <Bicairt> ↑Bécourt↓-Bécordel **AR**

42 **UK** dirty-nosed pantomime-supers came; **TS** dirty-nosed <ragtime heroes> ↑pantomime-supers↓ came **AR**

43 **UK, US** came; **TS** come
The mistake is in place in the Duckworth proofs.

44 **UK** of ghosts! **TS** of ghosts really!
The Duckworth proofs retain the TS variant. The deletion is made in UK probably due to what would have been a repetition from the previous line.

45 In TS Ford leaves a space on the line, as though he had to go away and check the word before adding it in later, which he does AR. Or, as suggested in the Note on the Text, this could have been down to a typist who did not understand this word.

46 **UK** signalling officer! And; **TS** signalling <affair> ↑officer↓! And **AR**

47 **UK** What a; **TS** <But> W **AR**
Revision made on top of existing typed lower-case letter.

48 **UK** Parsonage that mattered! What; **TS** Parsonage ↑that mattered↓! What **AR**

49 **UK** they'd had it! He; **TS** they'd <got> ↑had↓ it! He **AR**

50 **UK** O Nine Griffiths; **TS** O'- ; **US** Oh Nine Griffiths
In TS Ford leaves a space on the line after the typed hyphen, as though he meant to come back to complete it once checking the character's number. He didn't. The version in UK is different here from the earlier (and later) 'O9'.

51 **UK, TS, US** O9 Evans; **Ed** O9 Morgan
See the relevant note in II.i 70 on the possible reasons for confusion over these names.

52 At this point in TS a space – enough for a word – is left on the line. A line has been drawn from the space to the l/h margin as though extra text is to be added. This is not visible. No extra text made it into UK, or US, but there is a slight space left on the relevant line in the Duckworth proofs. See the Note on the Text for more relevant detail and discussion – concerning possible dictation, for example. This applies to subsequent notes about spaces left on lines also.

53 At this point in TS a space has been left on the line, into which 'chits' has been added AR.

54 At this point in TS a space has been left on the line, into which 'Conticuere' has been added AR. None of this Latin is underlined, Ford's usual practice to indicate text for italicisation.

55 **UK** surprised; **TS** surprized

Textual Notes for II.iv

1 **UK** CHAPTER IV; **TS** PART II ¶ Chapter Four; **US** CHAPTER VII
2 **UK** Corporal, with; **TS** Corporal with
    TS variant makes better grammatical sense.
3 **UK** continually rubbed his ankles with his shoe when he talked earnestly;
    TS continually kicked his ankles with his heels when he talked earnestly;
    US continually moved his ankles with his soles when he talked earnestly
    It looks as though copy-editors didn't know what to do with this phrase, espe-
    cially the American one – this version is nonsense. TS is preserved in the
    Duckworth proofs. The matter recurs in II.v and there the references are all
    to 'rubbing'.
4 As in previous chapters, McKechnie has appeared as Mckechnie throughout
    UK, TS and US. Decision made to correct in line with previous notes.
5 In TS this word is spelt 'intellectuality' but has a circle around it – the symbol
    often used to denote a necessary correction.
6 **UK** been so kept; **TS** been ↑so↓ kept
7 **UK** minds of affording; **TS** minds by affording
    TS variant makes better grammatical sense.
8 **UK** P. R. I. funds, whilst; **TS** P. R. I. <and> funds whilst **AR**
    'Funds' is added on the end of the TS line.
9 **UK** backgammon; **TS** backgann↑mm↓on **AR**
10 **UK** The Horse Guards was; **TS** Whitehall was; **US** The House Guards was
    The Duckworth proofs concur with TS. This correction was, therefore, a late
    one, when 'Whitehall' and 'the Horse Guards' in this paragraph were
    reversed. In the second case a stray 'the' remains (see note 11 below).
11 **UK** But the Whitehall was; **TS** But the Horse Guards were; **US** But White-
    hall was
    See note above.
12 **UK** Lance-Corporal Duckett; **TS** L. /Cpl Duckett **AR**
    After the initial 'L.' a space has been left on the line, into which the abbre-
    viation for 'Corporal' has been inserted.
13 **UK** the zero of; **TS** the zero of **AR**
    In TS a space has been left on the line, into which 'zero' has been inserted.
14 **UK** of bowls—in fact; **TS** of <books> ↑bowls↓ — ↑in↓ fact **AR**
15 **UK** papers to Duckett. ¶ "Give; **TS** papers <of> ↑to↓ Duckett. ¶ "Give **AR**
16 **UK** Mckechnie amiably to; **TS** Mckechnie ↑amiably↓ to; **Ed** McKechnie
    amiably to
17 **UK, TS, US** affair; **Ed** affairs
18 **UK** were not only endorsed; **TS** were now endorsed
19 **UK** a lonely affair; **TS** a <lucky> ↑lonely↓ affair **AR**
20 **UK** Aranjuex; **TS** Aranjuez
21 **UK** an Oporto Protestant; **TS** an Oporto Protestant **AR**
    In TS a space has been left on the line, into which 'Oporto' has been inserted
    AR. See the Note on the Text for discussion of the possibility of Ford
    dictating portions of these chapters. This applies to subsequent similar notes
    in this chapter.
22 **UK, US** O-Eleven Griffith; **TS** O-Eleven Griffiths; **Ed** O-Nine Griffiths
    This character was introduced at the beginning of II.ii (as O9 Griffiths). I
    have corrected the number, but preserved the current form it takes.

23 **UK, US** against.... say; **TS** against..... say

24 It's 333 on 71, 328 on 98 and 343 men on 151 (UK). Even including the 16 Worcesters it's not absolutely clear how these figures add up – possibly due to losses running throughout Part II. 328 plus the 16 new men is 344, which is what Tietjens says he has until he realises O Nine Morgan has gone – so 343 should be correct. But the earlier 333 sounds anomalous; perhaps Ford did not check the figure from earlier in TS.

25 **UK** of oddity to; **TS** of oddity to **AR**
In TS a space has been left on the line, into which 'oddity' has been inserted.

26 **UK** of drying out; **TS** of <carrying> ↑drying↓ out **AR**

27 **UK** hold an establishment; **TS** hold <our> ↑an↓ establishment **AR**

28 **UK** couldn't! **TS** couldn't!
In TS underlining indicates words for italicisation.

29 **UK** a time writing; **TS** a <tune> ↑time↓ writing **AR**

30 **UK, US** of Tietjens' watch; **TS** of Tietjen's watch
The Duckworth proofs have the corrected version too.

31 **UK** It's presumably coming; **TS** It's <positively> ↑presumably↓ coming

32 **UK, US** Tietjen's mouth; **TS** Tietjens' mouth
On this occasion (see note 30) the mistake is preserved in the proofs too, as well as in US.

33 **UK** wind! ¶ They; **TS, US** wind!" ¶ They
The error is already in the proofs, but it is corrected in US.

34 **UK** to face the gas-screens. It's; **TS** to <carry> ↑face↓ the gas ↑-screens↓ . It's **AR**

35 **UK** *moral*; **TS** moral; **US** *morale*

36 **UK** Noircourt; **TS** Noir<caut> ↑court↓ **AR**

37 **UK** tantalising. But; **TS** tantalizing. But

38 **UK** the Trasna Valley trenches; **TS** the Trasna Valley trenches **AR**
In TS a space has been left on the line, into which 'Trasna' has been inserted.

39 **UK** the Mametz Wood affair; **TS** the Mametz Wood affair **AR**
In TS a space has been left on the line, into which 'Mametz' has been inserted.

40 **UK, US** shut his men; **TS** shut the men
The proofs follow TS. US has the same text as UK here.

41 **UK** the off-chance, might give the Enemy a scunner at; **TS** the off chance might give the <fellows> ↑Enemy↓ a scunner at **AR**
In TS a space has been left on the line, into which 'a scunner' has been inserted.

42 **UK** these owlish fellows; **TS** these owlish fellows **AR**
In TS a space has been left on the line, into which 'owlish' has been inserted.

43 **UK** with rage.... So; **TS** with terror.... So
The TS version (preserved in Duckworth proofs) seems still to best express the likely reaction of the Germans in the face of potential Japanese troops; the UK version (also in US) best expresses the likely reaction if they thought they were being made fun of.

44 **UK** thoughts; **TS, US** thought
The Duckworth proofs preserve the TS version in this case.

45 **UK** realised; **TS** realized

46 **UK** Clean, blond, small: with the ordinary face; **TS** Clean, blond, small: with the ordinary face

In TS there is a space left on the line after 'small' and before ':'. A line is drawn to the margin and the words '? word here' added AR. No word is added here, though, and the proofs have none either.

47 **UK** some old thorn trees; **TS** some old thorn trees **AR**
In TS a space has been left on the line, into which 'old thorn' has been added.

48 **UK** the mining Germans; **TS** the mining Germans **AR**
In TS a space has been left on the line, into which 'mining' has been added.

49 **UK** Now it came only; **TS** <Then> ↑Now it came↓ only

50 **UK** accidental, so it; **TS** accidental, <as> ↑so↓ it **AR**

51 **UK** and square on her feet. As; **TS** and square on her feet. As **AR**
In TS a space has been left on the line, into which 'square on her feet' has been added.

52 **UK** Ethel!" when Edith Ethel Duchemin; **TS** Ethel!" ↑when Edith Ethel↓ Duchemin **AR**

53 **UK** slowly expand like; **TS** slowly expand like **AR**
In TS a space has been left on the line, into which 'expand' has been added.

54 There is no new paragraph at this point in US.

55 **UK** twenty-four-hour day; **TS** twenty-four ↑hour↓ day **AR**

56 **UK** if this were; **TS** if there were

57 **UK** coal would fly; **TS** coal <wait to> ↑would↓ fly

58 **UK** from Bn. H. Q. way, shepherding; **TS** from <Bon H. Z.> ↑Bn. H. Q↓ way shepherding; **US** from Bn.H.2 way **AR**
The AR was initially misread as 'H.2.' which is how it appears in the Duckworth proofs and US.

59 **UK** compulsorily; **TS** compuls<ive>↑ori↓ ly **AR**

Textual Notes for II.v

1 **UK** CHAPTER V; **TS** PART II ¶ CHAPTER FIVE; **US** CHAPTER VIII
2 **UK, US** from Whitehall that; **TS** from the Home Guards that
3 **UK** a Company at; **TS** a company at
As has been the case in previous chapters, Ford tends not to capitalise ranks, and other army nomenclature, in TS (with some occasional exceptions, such as 'Colonel' at the beginning of this chapter, for example).
4 **UK** now, sir?" It; **TS** now, sir? It
5 **UK** great *strafe* that; **TS** great strafe that
In TS 'strafe' is not underlined (and therefore not indicated for italicisation) throughout this chapter.
6 **UK** from Whitehall. He; **TS** from the Horse Guards. He
7 **UK** paper over; **TS** paper from the Horse Guards over; **US** paper from Whitehall over
UK omits mention of the paper's origins in this case. The US editor makes a different decision, perhaps deciding that UK needed clarification. The Duckworth proofs retain the TS version.
8 **UK** unsurprised; **TS** unsurprised
9 **UK** not have. It; **TS** not ↑have↓ . It **AR**
10 **UK** Mckechnie's; **Ed** McKechnie's
With one exception, noted later, Mckechnie is spelt with a lower-case 'k' throughout this chapter in TS. In line with previous notes on this issue, it

has been corrected to McKechnie.

11 In this instance all textual witnesses, including the Duckworth proofs, agree.

12 **UK** realised; **TS** realized

13 **UK** door at; **TS** door-way, at

14 **UK, US** He added! "You; **TS** He added: "You
Correction made in line with TS.

15 **UK** had solicitors' letters; **TS** had solicitors' letters **AR**
In TS a space is left on the line, into which 'solicitors" has been added.

16 In TS 'Glam' has been typed, with a space left on the line, into which 'organs'
has been added **AR**. There is no apostrophe here, but UK added one, as did
US. The correction has been made to this text.

This, and subsequent notes in the chapter, suggest that there may well
still have been a typist taking Ford's dictation at this point in the text. Particular cases include mis-spellings of words with which Ford would have been
familiar (as in the note immediately following this one) and those instances
where, in line with recent chapters, spaces have been left in TS for words to
be inserted later. See the Note on the Text for more discussion.

17 **UK** Messines village; **TS** M<us> ↑ess↓ ines village **AR**

18 **UK** With Major Tietjens'; **TS** With <Captain> ↑Major↓ Tietjens' **AR**

19 **UK** of women or; **TS** of <prostitutes> ↑women↓ or **AR**

20 In TS after 'unclean' and before 'scoundrel' a long gap is left on the line, as
though to be filled with another adjective, perhaps two, later. But the gap
remains.

21 **UK** shoulders indeed collapsed; **TS** shoulders ↑indeed↓ collapsed

22 **UK** a cheque on; **TS** a <check> ↑cheque↓ on **AR**

23 **UK, TS, US** By jove: if; **Ed** By Jove: if

24 In II.iii the name of the Medical Officer, Terence, was abbreviated to 'Derry'
in UK, and to 'Terry' in TS and US. In this case, and in the two subsequent
cases in the next few lines, it has been abbreviated to 'Derry' in UK, TS and
US. The decision is taken to emend UK in line with the previous decision,
the authority for which was taken from TS and US.

25 The final exclamation mark is not included in TS.

26 **UK** might seem to; **TS** might <run> ↑seem↓ to **AR**

27 **UK** Campion was taking over; **TS** Campion <had taken> ↑was taking↓ over

28 **UK** our men stayed under; **TS** our ↑<no?>↓ men stay↑ed↓ <only> under
In TS only the 'no?' has been added in type; the second amendment, to the
verb, is an AR. That first insertion is possibly a sign of mis-hearing by a typist
taking Ford's dictation, who was not sure whether 'no' or 'our' had been said
and then signalled that fact. This is supported by the fact that 'no?' is then
deleted AR, probably by Ford.

29 **UK** self-defence; **TS** self-defense

30 **UK** less heavy masses; **TS** less heavy masses **AR**
In TS a space has been left on the line, into which 'heavy' has been added.

31 **UK** their beastly bullet-distributing; **TS** their <hastily built> ↑beastly bullet-
↓ distributing **AR**

32 **UK** shining, silvery things; **TS** shining, <still> ↑silvery↓ things **AR**

33 **UK** in these beastly; **TS** in the<ir> ↑se↓ beastly

34 **UK** various minds spread; **TS** various <armies> ↑minds↓ spread **AR**

35 **UK** men armed with; **TS** men <around> ↑armed↓ with **AR**

36 **UK** on our side; **TS** on <one> ↑our↓ side **AR**

37 At this point on the leaf in TS the text ceases, and the remaining two thirds of it is left blank. The text recommences with 'would strain themselves' on the following leaf. It is a later insertion, indicating revision at this point in the text. See the Note on the Text (this is also the point at which there is a significant shift in Ford's numbering of TS).

38 **UK** two months' later; **TS** two month's later; **Ed** two months later

39 **UK** Mckechnie; **TS** McKechnie
This is the instance in which this name is correct in the TS (see note 10). It is part of a section of the typescript that, according to a change in one of the systems of numbering the leaves, may well predate others in the drafting process (see the Note on the Text). There is also no evidence for some time of a possible typist at work, although the typewriter problems detailed at the end of II.vi may be relevant here.

40 **UK** the Intelligence officer; **TS** the <signalling> ↑Intelligence↓ officer **AR**

41 **UK** The last sentence of this paragraph is added AR on the TS line.

42 **UK** had been sheer; **TS** had ?been (Printer) sheer **AR**
In TS the word 'had' is the last on a page, while the next begins with 'sheer'. A note has been added either to, or by, the Printer, to make sure that the necessary addition is made.

43 **UK** The two previous sentences ('They had no food […] dumps') are an AR to TS. A pencil line is drawn from after 'order.' into the l/h margin, in which the extra text is written.

44 **UK** front and that threw a self-burying shell containing an incredible quantity of H.E., the; **TS** front ↓and that threw a self-burying shell containing an incredible quantity of H.E.↑ the **AR**

45 **UK** the German soldiers, circulars; **TS** the <troops> ↑German soldiers↓ , circulars **AR**

46 **UK** interest—mostly statistics of influenza cases. But; **TS** interest ↑- mostly statistics of influenza cases↓ . But **AR**

47 **UK** N.C.O's; **TS** N.C.O.s
Correction made in line with TS.

48 **UK** poor General Puffles' unpopularity; **TS** poor ↑General↓<Ri>↑Pu↓ffles' unpopularity **AR**
This TS leaf is a late insert. It contains only nine lines of text, from the AR 'General' detailed above, to 'didn't appear to be coming'.

49 **UK** force. He might then be a hero! … But; **TS** force. Still hero! … But

50 **UK** into immediate danger; **TS** into immense danger

51 **UK** plans. That would inconvenience them. It; **TS** plans. ↑That would inconvenience them.↓ It **AR**

52 **UK** marl; **TS** marle
See also note 57.

53 **UK** in the training camps at; **TS** in <schools> ↑the training camps↓ at

54 **UK** up. It was fairly thorough but it's all; **TS** up. <That's> ↑It was fairly thorough but it's↓ all

55 **UK** sand-hills, say—and; **TS** sand-hills ↑, say,↓ - and **AR**

56 **UK** lance-corporals, section leaders and oldest privates of platoons. And; **TS** lance-corporals, <and section commanders> ↑section leaders and oldest privates of platoons↓ . And

57 **UK** marle; **TS** marle; **US** marl
In TS there is a ring round the word; in previous examples this has been an

indication that a correction is necessary. The UK printer/editor seems not to have picked this up, however.

58 **UK** Army Commanders; **TS, US** Army Commander's
59 **UK** back if the; **TS** back ↑if↓ the

Textual Notes for II.vi

1 **UK** CHAPTER VI; **TS** PART TWO ¶ CHAPTER SIX; **US** CHAPTER IX
2 **UK** he had suddenly; **TS** he ↑had↓ suddenly
3 **UK** suddenly remembered that; **TS** suddenly <reflected> ↑remembered↓ that **AR**
4 **UK** machine guns, or; **TS** machine guns, <their positions> or
5 **UK** eaten practically nothing since; **TS** eaten nothing since
   The Duckworth proofs print the same version as TS in this case.
6 **UK** Commander; **TS** commander
   As in many instances throughout the volume, TS employs lower-case initials for military terms that are routinely made upper case in the proofs, and then in UK too.
7 **UK** be choosers! The; **TS** be choosers [!] The; **US** be choosers. The
   TS is difficult to read here, and in general throughout this chapter exclamation marks are indistinct.
8 **UK** why not leave them to their monastic engrossedness? ¶ Even; **TS** Why not <let> ↑leave↓ them <alone in> ↑to↓ their monastic engrossedness? ¶ Even **AR**
9 **UK** the German men; **TS** the ↑German↓ men **AR**
10 **UK** flail. Another; **TS** flail. <In circulars.> Another **AR**
11 **UK, TS** trenches! ¶ They; **US** trenches. ¶ They
   See note 7 above, and 16 below.
12 **UK** the drawing-room. You; **TS** the drawing ↑room↓. You **AR**
13 **UK** decimating them. ¶ Anyhow; **TS** decimating them-prostrating them. ¶ Anyhow
   In TS the first six letters of 'prostrating' are underlined, indicating they are to be italicised. The Duckworth proof both prints these extra words (unlike UK), and italicises the letters, though in this case it's the first seven of the word.
14 **UK** to redd up; **TS** to reed [?] up
   TS is unclear, though it looks as though the letter that was originally a 'd' has been typed over several times with an 'e' to create 'reed' instead of 'redd'. The proofs print 'reed', but UK has the change.
15 **UK** can't otherwise talk. You; **TS** can't ↑otherwise↓ talk. You **AR**
16 **UK** not.... He; **TS** not! ... He
17 **UK** was perfectly; **TS** was <, now,> perfectly **AR**
18 **UK** who had once made; **TS** who ↑had once↓ made **AR**
19 **UK** postcard! For two years! A sort of Hamlet all right! Or a swine! ¶ Well; **TS** postcard! ↑For two years!↓ A sort of Hamlet all right! Or a swine! ¶ Well **AR**
   The last sentence is also an AR, on the line.
20 **UK** say: "This is to tell you that I propose to live with you as soon as this

show is over. You will be prepared immediately on cessation of active hostilities to put yourself at my disposal; Please. Signed, "Xtopher Tietjens, Acting O. C. 9ᵗʰ Glams." A; **TS** say: This is to tell you that I propose to live with you as soon as this show is over. <Please therefore> ↑You will↓ be prepared immediately on cessation of active hostilities to put yourself at my disposal; <we will inhabit a hut because I shall be penniless.> Please. Signed Xtopher Tietjens Acting O./C 9ᵗʰ Glams." A;

Two corrections have been made to the punctuation in the UK passage as it appears in the text. The first, the full stop after 'disposal', was necessitated because the original semi-colon from TS was reproduced, even though text had been edited out, as can be seen above. The second correction involved the removal of the inverted commas in front of 'Xtopher'.

21 **UK**, **TS** was commanding; **US** was a commanding

22 **UK** a Pro-German. She; **TS** a pro-German. She

23 **UK** purposeless. Well there; **TS** purposeless- <and> ↑Well,↓ there

24 **UK** marle; **TS** marle; **US** marl
See both notes on this in the previous chapter. In one instance there, UK corrects TS to 'marl'; in another, though the word is circled in TS, a signal that correction is needed, UK also has 'marle'.

25 **UK** myriad—two myriad— corks at; **TS** myriad <-two-corks-> ↑-two myriad-corks↓ at

26 **UK** "hinstinck"; **TS** hinstinck

27 **UK** swell too! ¶ He; **TS** swell too! <The swine!> ¶ He **AR**

28 See II.iv, note 3 for examples of editors' difficulty with this phrase.

29 **UK** right hand a; **TS** right a
A word is clearly missing from TS, which is underlined at this point, with a question mark in the margin. The Duckworth proofs include 'hand'.

30 **UK** War.... If; **TS** war.... If
In each instance in this paragraph, and just after the next main one (beginning 'Certainly, I shall…') too, 'war' has a lower-case initial letter in TS.

31 **UK** then exploded; **TS** then <presumably> exploded
See use of deleted word earlier in the same sentence.

32 **UK** Gibb's trench; **TS** Gibbs's trench; **US** Gibbs' trench

33 **UK** from Brother Mark; **TS** from brother Mark
In each use of 'Brother Mark' in this paragraph, there is the same difference between UK (and US) and TS.

34 **UK** provided them with; **TS** provided ↑them↓ with

35 **UK** devil's pockets; **TS** devils' pockets

36 **UK** their dung-and-seed-money on; **TS** their dung and seed money on; **US** their dung "and seed" money on

37 **UK** of their money; **TS** of ↑their↓ money

38 **UK** their communion was; **TS** their <love> ↑communion↓ was

39 **UK** Tietjens shouted. He; **TS** Tietjens <said> shouted. He

40 **UK** end of mud; **TS** end mud
The proofs have the correction.

41 At this point in TS the text on this leaf ceases. A hand-drawn line extends down the rest of the page (nearly half) to indicate that no text is missing. It recommences on the subsequent leaf with 'Cockshott and the Corporal…'

42 At this point in TS, problems seem to develop with the typewriter or concentration of the typist (see notes 44 and 45 here also). From the end of this

sentence, instead of a full stop, '%' appears as end punctuation in many cases, until nearly the end of the chapter – possibly the full stop key had ceased to work.

43 **UK** enormous It; **TS** enormous. It
The proofs do have this punctuation, following TS.

44 In this instance of inverted commas, and the one in the line above, a '2' appears on the TS instead of ". The 'shift' key, too, may have been faulty therefore.

45 **UK** or fun! Hatred; **TS** or fun? Hatred
It is clear from TS – due to the problems being experienced at the time with exclamation marks on the typewriter – that a question mark is intended at this point. It's an exclamation mark by proof stage, however.

46 In this paragraph, and for the next three pages of TS, instead of exclamation marks there are '½'s instead, corrected by hand. All of these technical difficulties could equally well be explained by someone working with an unfamiliar machine, however. It has been some time since the signs of potential dictation have been visible; perhaps if it's not simply Ford's machine proving faulty a new typist has taken over briefly here.

47 **UK** "Do you know how to apply artificial respiration." ¶ "To the drowned?" ¶ Cockshott said: ¶ "I; **TS** "Do you know how to apply artificial respiration? To the drowned?" ¶ Cockshott said: ¶ "I
US and the proofs confirm TS in its presentation of this dialogue. UK does not make sense as it suggests Cockshott replies twice.

48 **UK** E aint rubbin' 'is ankles; **TS** E ain't rubbin is ankles; **US** 'E ain't rubbin' is ankles
The Duckworth proofs represent this cockney dialogue differently again. Though the version is close to UK, there is no apostrophe in place of the 'h' of 'his'. In a related point, in UK on the next page (p. 180 here) a paragraph begins "'E wasn't on'y twenty-two" and in this case the missing initial letter is signified by an apostrophe.

49 **UK** Company Cmander is; **TS, US** Company C'mander is

50 **UK** men but only an officer. As; **TS** men. As
The additional phrase is not in the proofs either, so was added, probably for reasons of clarity, at a later stage.

51 **UK** certain greater responsibility, they; **TS** certain ↑greater↓ responsibility, they

52 **UK** a small tin-hat; **TS** a <slight> ↑small↓ tin-hat

53 **UK** Tietjens could hear his heart beat, little dry scraping sounds out of his lungs. The; **TS** Tietjens could hear his heart little dry scraping sounds from his lungs. The; **US** Tietjens could hear his heart beat out of little dry scraping sounds from his lungs. The
The Duckworth proofs provide a transitional stage in the change from TS to UK, in the addition of a comma after 'heart' ('Tietjens could hear his heart, little dry scraping sounds from his lungs'). In TS 'heart' is the last word on a page, so at first it seemed likely that the word 'beat' may have been added, by Ford perhaps, somewhere on the page but no longer visible; the proof variant suggests otherwise, and that this sentence or section of text was more likely edited and added to in stages – differently in the case of US. See also the Note on the Text for discussion as to the role textual history may have played here (this is the case of the three typed '182's).

54 **UK** go mad. We; **TS** go <u>mad</u>. We
   The underlining indicates 'mad' was to be italicised, as it is in the proofs, but
   not finally in UK.
55 **UK** took over. Notting; **TS** took after. Notting
   In TS 'after' is encircled (a common way of indicating a mistake) and there
   is a pencil note in the adjacent margin: '? over (Printer.)'

Textual Notes for III.i

1 **UK** PART III ¶ CHAPTER I; **TS** A Man Could Stand UP ¶ Part III ¶
   Chapter One; **US** PART III [page break] CHAPTER X
   In TS the title is an AR at the top of the page, above an intriguing deleted
   detail: 'Of ¶ HOPE AND GLORY'. See also relevant footnote at the end of
   II.vi.
2 **UK** and silver-grey and rigid; **TS** and ↑silver-grey and↓ rigid
3 **UK** to-day; **TS** today
4 **UK** empty room; in; **TS** empty <house> room; in
5 **UK** this madman. It; **TS**, **US** this mad man. It
6 **UK** eighteenth century. ¶ She; **TS** eighteenth century! ¶ She
7 **UK** the shadows; she; **TS** the <hall> ↑shadows↓; she
8 **UK** was Armistice Day. She; **TS** was armistice day. She
   In general, as in previous chapters, TS tends to capitalise words much less
   than UK. This relates primarily to military terms (e.g. 'major') but is the case
   here too.
9 **UK** her night; too. . . . Armistice; **TS** her night too. . . . . . Armistice; **US** her
   night, too. . . . Armistice
10 **UK** empty room. He; **TS** empty room! He
11 **UK** he hadn't Always; **TS**, **US** he hadn't. Always
12 **UK** light from between; **TS** light ↑from↓ between
13 At this point the TS leaf (typed no. 187; handwritten 214) comes to an end.
   At the top of the next leaf, the text runs on as in UK ('others too. Normally
   her mother was irritated…'), but at the same time, between the UK lines,
   are three interspersed lines of reverse type. In the top left corner of the leaf
   there is also a reverse typed no. 193. The reversed text reads as follows: 'when
   occasion served Mrs Tietjens would remove the furniture wh[ich] was all hers
   from No 64 Great Square. ¶ She had removed the furniture! She <u>had</u>
   removed the furnit[ure] […].' The reversed text then ceases. Words run off
   the l/h edge of the leaf, as indicated above, and some further text may be
   missing from those lines. This is not the text that is found at the top of the
   leaf with typed no. 193, although it would conceivably follow on from the
   bottom of that found on 192 ('For surely the rest of the letter must say that
   Mrs Tietjens had removed the furniture. And […]'). This section of the text
   has undergone fairly significant revision. The leaf following that with the
   reversed type is a late insert, as is the next but one. Perhaps, in the confusion that resulted, Ford began to type on a leaf he intended to keep, stopped
   and then restarted on a new '193' (the one we still have), changing his mind
   at the same time as to the direction the text would take. There is no mention
   of 'Great Square' anywhere else.
14 **UK** the War. A; **TS** the war. A

15 **UK** was. He would; **TS** was. <u>He</u> would
   'He' is italicised in the Duckworth proofs.
16 **UK, US** capable... *You*; **TS** capable.... *You*; **Ed** capable.... *You*
   UK emended in line with TS in this case, as the typescript has the same
   number of dots here as after 'not' in the next line.
17 **UK** like an ill-arranged; **TS** like ↑an↓ ill-arranged
18 **UK** dozen typed pages; they; **TS** dozen <letters>; ↑typed pages↓ they
19 This sentence is not underlined in TS, and is not italicised in the proofs.
20 **UK** house-fronts; **TS** housefronts
21 **UK, US** being.... ruined; **TS** being..... ruined
22 **UK** him. I; **TS** him. <I don't even know whether he wants me.> I **AR**
23 **UK** sane. He; **TS** sane. <I came here as a nurse.> He **AR**
24 **UK** out?" She pondered for a long time. "I; **TS** out? <I will never abandon
   you. I will always back you>." ↑She pondered for a long time↓ "I **AR**
25 **UK** good." A rustling sound. "But; **TS** good." ↑A rustling sound.↓ "But **AR**
26 **UK** down, unthinkingly ... as one does when; **TS** down, ↑unthinkingly....
   as one does↓ when
27 **UK** came, turned; **TS** came, <measured, and> turned **AR**
28 **UK** I can't. I; **TS** I <cannot order you to come back>.↑can't↓ I **AR**
29 **UK** cannot order; **TS** cannot <come back> order **AR**
30 **UK** That was reasonable: she wrote books like that; **TS** She wrote books like
   that: it was reasonable.
   The Duckworth proofs carry the same version as TS, so the decision to switch
   these clauses was a later one.
31 **UK** in conscience go; **TS** in ↑conscience↓ go **AR**
   The added word is the very last one on the TS leaf. There is a further erased
   addition which is illegible.
32 **UK** For now she said; **TS** For she said now
33 The TS leaf has five lines of text that have been deleted AR at this point in
   the text. They are the first five lines on the leaf, and form an earlier version
   of the section just above in UK that begins "'My child! my little child!" [...]
   shook.' The deleted passage reads "'↑My child, my↓ little child. You have
   sacrificed your whole life to me. Do you suppose that I am unaware of that?
   And could I then persuade you to a course that may mean your eternal
   unhappiness?" ¶ Valentine was shivering. It was very cold. November is a
   cold month. There were footsteps on the stairs. She shook.' The first three
   words are an AR.
     It is very likely that the previous TS leaf (which contains the version of
   this passage that appears in UK) is an insert, as it is short, with blank lines
   – enough for 5–6 lines of text – at the bottom. There has been a process that
   led to Ford rewriting this section of text, then, and shortening it too, adding
   in a new leaf carrying the changes.
34 **UK** Don't go; **TS** <u>Don't</u> go
   The underlining indicates italics, but none appear in the proofs.
35 **UK** love? Mad; **TS** love. Mad
36 **UK** oh, oh, Oh. Let's; **TS** Oh, oh. Oh. Let's
37 **UK** that—the great inarticulate fellow! His; **TS** that. ↑- the great inarticulate fellow!↓ His **AR**
38 **UK, TS, US** be as raw of that. He; **Ed** be as raw as that. He
39 **UK** days. They were all round him. And; **TS** days. ↑They were all round

him.↓ And **AR**
40 **UK** her...." ¶ Then there had been revelation of their ... you couldn't call it intimacy! ¶ He; **TS** her...." ¶ ↑Then there had been revelation of their ... you couldn't call it intimacy!↓ ¶ He **AR**
The AR is made between the existing lines of text in this case.
41 **UK** Reverberations apparently reached her; **TS** reverberations <seemed to> ↑apparently↓ reached her **AR**
In TS the necessary 'ed' addition to 'reach' is made on the line.
42 **UK** was telling you; **TS** was begging you
43 **UK** I ascertained afterwards; **TS** I <discovered> ascertained afterwards
44 **UK** War; **TS** war
45 **UK** see that fellow Tietjens; you're; **TS** see ↑that fellow↓ Tietjens; you're
46 McKechnie appears as Mckechnie at this point in TS. The decision has been made, in line with earlier comment (see, for example, II.ii), to correct.
47 **UK** Campion, too, overreached; **TS** Campion ↑too↓ overreached **AR**
48 **UK** green square. Light; **TS** green Square. Light
In the first line of the chapter, UK also capitalises here, but a different decision has been made in this instance.
49 **UK** The Mid-Victorians had; **TS** The <early> ↑Mid↓ Victorians had **AR**
50 **UK** of Mid-Victorian thought; **TS** of <early> ↑Mid↓ Victorian thought **AR**
51 **UK** high-minded. But the high-minded do not consummate irregular unions. So; **TS** high-minded. ↑But the High-minded to not consummate irregular unions.↓ So
52 **UK** Tietjen's wife's; **TS, US** Tietjens' wife's
53 **UK** Major-General Lord; **TS** Major ↑General↓ Lord
54 **UK** Like Tietjens. At; **TS** like Tietjens's. At
55 **UK** General. All the same, Providence; **TS** General. ↑All the same↓ Providence **AR**
56 **UK** engagement to come to Tietjen's house to-day ... whenever it happened ... a lot; **TS** an engagement ... a lot
The additions are not in the proofs either. UK is reproduced here of course, but grammatical correction has been made to 'Tietjen's'. US has 'Tietjens" here.

Textual Notes for III.ii

1 **UK** CHAPTER II; **TS** PART THREE ¶ Chapter Two; **US** CHAPTER XI
2 **UK** extreme. Unthinkable! He; **TS** extreme. ↑Unthinkable!↓ He **AR**
3 **UK** was more; **TS** was <very unlikely. It was> more **AR**
4 As noted in previous chapters, Ford often does not capitalise military terms in TS. The same is true throughout this final chapter. In this sentence, for example, he doesn't capitalise Commander-in-Chief or Battalion Commander.
5 **UK** to a man to; **TS** to ↑a↓ men to **AR**
In TS, 'men' is altered AR to 'man' by writing over the relevant letter.
6 **UK** would kill him! Call him out and kill him.... That; **TS** would <have> kill<ed> him! ↑Call him out and kill him↓ ..... That **AR**
7 **UK** would call him out. Quite properly. In the eighteenth century traditions for soldiers. The old fellow could not refuse. He was of eighteenth century

tradition too. ¶ Mrs. Wannop; **TS** would <have killed him!> ↑call him out.↓ Quite properly. In the eighteenth century tradition for soldiers. <He would not have wanted to, but he would have!> ↑The old fellow could not refuse.↓ ¶ Mrs Wannop; **US** would call him out. Quite properly. In the eighteenth century traditions for soldiers. The old fellow could not refuse. He was of eighteenth century traditions too. ¶ Mrs. Wannop **AR**
As can be seen from this note, the final sentence of the paragraph is not in TS. There is a cross on the line, which may be some editorial sign for a later insertion to be made. There is only a very slight variation in US: the word 'tradition' in this final sentence is again pluralised, matching that in the previous sentence-but-one.

8   Although both UK and US have 'his' instead of him, TS has a circle around 'his', perhaps querying a later change.

9   In TS the previous four sentences are added AR in l/h margin.

10 **UK** for.... A; **TS** for <him. And for her.> A **AR**

11 **UK** In Toulon, I believe. I'm quite capable of taking a practical hold of life!" ¶ The Department of Statistics would transfer him. All the Government Departments, staffed of course by non-combatants, were aching to transfer those who had served to any other old Department. ¶ A great many voices came from below stairs. He could not leave Valentine to battle with a great number of voices. He said: ¶ "I've got to go!" Mrs. Wannop's voice answered: ¶ "Yes, do. I'm very tired."; **TS** In Toulon, I believe↑d↓. The Department of Statistics would transfer <me> ↑him↓... I'm quite capable of taking a prac-tical hold of life!" ¶ ↑All the government departments, staffed of course by non combatants, were aching to transfer those who had served to any other old department. He finished:↓ A great many voices came from below stairs. He could not leave Valentine to battle with a great number of voices. He said: ¶ "I've got to go!" Mrs. Wannop's voice answered: ¶ "Yes. I'm very tired."; **US** In Toulon, I believe. I'm quite capable of taking a practical hold on life!" ¶ All the Government Departments, staffed of course by non-combatants, were aching to transfer those who had served to any other old Department. The Department of Statistics would transfer him.... ¶ A great many voices came from below stairs. He could not leave Valentine to battle with a great number of voices. He said: ¶ "I've got to go!" Mrs. Wannop's voice answered: ¶ "Yes; do. I'm very tired." **AR**
In the proofs the past tense 'believed' is preserved; the AR 'him' is carried forward, and the section beginning 'All the Government Departments, staffed [...] old Department' features too. All of this (AR) section was trans-ferred from the l/h margin of TS. The last two words – 'He finished' – didn't make it from TS and proof into UK or US. Both UK and US alter the posi-tion of the sentence 'The Department of Statistics would transfer him.' Its position in TS (which is preserved in the proofs) is confusing as it does not match the first-person, direct speech of the previous sentence. But these witnesses move it to different locations: UK to the beginning of the subse-quent paragraph, while US chooses the end (with added suspension dots).

12 **UK** mad. I'm not destitute!" He had; **TS** mad. And I'm not destitute!" <She gathered that> he had

13 **UK** spoken of themselves. In; **TS** spoken. In; **US** spoken of themselves! In

14 At this point in TS there is a page-break, even though only half of the leaf is complete. The following leaf begins with text crossed out that, in an edited

version, formed an earlier part of this chapter ('hair had given refinement to her face. They were both changed. He desired to say:') The text then continues, as is shown in UK, with "I hold you in my arms. [...]".

15 **UK, TS, US** Mckechnie; **Ed** McKechnie
   As in previous chapters, this spelling is corrected throughout.

16 **UK** "It isn't fair if you're such; **TS** "If your such; **US** "It isn't fair. If you're such

17 At this point in TS an insert arrow leads in pencil to the l/h margin, in which this section, comprising the next three sentences in all – 'That was [...] Why not?' – is visible AR.

18 **UK** The thin! hostile; **TS** The thin!, hostile; **US** The thin, hostile
   The US editor decided to remove this stray exclamation mark, and, in general, the copy-editing and proofreading is sharper in US. It was still in the proofs (though the comma also in TS has been deleted there).

19 **UK** back. The officer shouted: ¶ "I've; **TS** back. <He> ↑The officer↓ shouted: ¶ "I've **AR**

20 **UK** "*I* say ... that *he*...." Good; **TS** I say.... We all say that he ......" Good
   The underlining indicates words to be italicised.

21 **UK** Perhaps they were not going to be on terms any more! All; **TS** Perhaps they were not on terms! All

22 **UK, TS, US** Prinsep's; **Ed** Prinseps'

23 **UK** it? you a pro-German and he such a sound Tory. Squire; **TS** it? Such a sound Tory. Squire; **US** it? You're a pro-German—he's such a sound Tory. Squire
   The proofs carry the same version as TS.

24 **UK** of Groby.... It's; **TS** of Groby really.... It's

25 **UK** least they weren't over; **TS** least <it wasn't> ↑they weren't↓ over **AR**

26 **UK** ever! He; **TS** ever!!!! He
   Extravagant punctuation has not always received comment (especially in the case of numbers of suspension dots, as explained in the Introduction), but as the novel is building towards its climax here, Ford's use of four excla-mation marks seemed worthy of mention.

27 **UK, US** fluff.... well; **TS** fluff[;;; .] well

28 **UK** had! He had run out and fetched it. It; **TS** had! It
   The sentence is missing from the proofs too.

SELECT BIBLIOGRAPHY

Works by Ford (whether as 'Hueffer' or 'Ford')

Ancient Lights and Certain New Reflections: Being the Memories of a Young Man (London: Chapman and Hall, 1911); published as *Memories and Impressions* (New York: Harper, 1911)

Between St. Dennis and St. George (London: Hodder and Stoughton, 1915)

A Call (1910) (Manchester: Carcanet, 1984)

The Cinque Ports (Edinburgh and London: William Blackwood and Sons, 1900)

The Correspondence of Ford Madox Ford and Stella Bowen, ed. Sondra Stang and Karen Cochran (Bloomington and Indianapolis: Indiana University Press, 1994)

Critical Essays, ed. Max Saunders and Richard Stang (Manchester: Carcanet Press, 2002)

England and the English, ed. Sara Haslam (Manchester: Carcanet, 2003) (collecting Ford's trilogy on Englishness with *The Heart of the Country* and *The Spirit of the People*)

The English Novel from the Earliest Days to the Death of Joseph Conrad (London: Constable, 1930)

The Fifth Queen (London: Alston Rivers, 1906)

The Fifth Queen Crowned (Eveleigh Nash, 1908)

The Ford Madox Ford Reader, with Foreword by Graham Greene; ed. Sondra J. Stang (Manchester: Carcanet, 1986)

The Good Soldier, ed. Martin Stannard (Norton Critical Edition; New York and London: W. W. Norton & Company, 1995)

The Heart of the Country (London: Alston Rivers, 1906)

'A House (Modern Morality Play)', *The Chapbook*, 21, March 1921 (London: The Poetry Bookshop, 1921)

It Was the Nightingale (1933) (New York: The Ecco Press, 1984)

Joseph Conrad: A Personal Remembrance (1924) (New York: The Ecco Press, 1989)

Last Post (London: Duckworth, 1928) – the fourth and final novel of

Parade's End
Letters of Ford Madox Ford, ed. Richard M. Ludwig (Princeton, NJ:
    Princeton University Press, 1965)
A Man Could Stand Up – (London: Duckworth, 1926) – the third novel
    of Parade's End
The March of Literature (London: Allen and Unwin, 1939)
The Marsden Case (London: Duckworth, 1923)
Mightier Than the Sword (London: Allen and Unwin, 1938)
A Mirror to France (London: Duckworth, 1926)
Mister Bosphorus and the Muses or a Short History of Poetry in Britain.
    Variety Entertainment in Four Acts. . . with Harlequinade, Transfor-
    mation Scene, Cinematograph Effects, and Many Other Novelties, as
    well as Old and Tried Favourites, illustrated by Paul Nash (London:
    Duckworth, 1923)
New York Essays (New York: William Edwin Rudge, 1927)
No More Parades (London: Duckworth, 1925) – the second novel of
    Parade's End
No Enemy (1929), ed. Paul Skinner (Manchester: Carcanet, 2002)
On Heaven and Poems Written on Active Service, The Bodley Head
    (London: John Lane, 1918)
The Panel: A Sheer Comedy (London: Constable, 1912)
Portraits from Life (Boston and New York: Houghton Mifflin Company,
    1937)
Pound/Ford: the Story of a Literary Friendship: the Correspondence between
    Ezra Pound and Ford Madox Ford and Their Writings About Each Other,
    ed. Brita Lindberg-Seyersted (London: Faber & Faber, 1982)
Privy Seal (London: Alston Rivers, 1907)
Provence: From Minstrels to Machine (1935), ed. John Coyle
    (Manchester: Carcanet, 2009)
Return to Yesterday (1931), ed. Bill Hutchings (Manchester: Carcanet,
    1999)
Selected Poems, ed. Max Saunders (Manchester: Carcanet, 1997)
Some Do Not ... (London: Duckworth, 1924) – the first novel of
    Parade's End
The Spirit of the People (London: Alston Rivers, 1907)
Thus to Revisit (London: Chapman and Hall, 1921)
War Prose, ed. Max Saunders (Manchester: Carcanet, 1999)
When Blood is Their Argument (London: Hodder and Stoughton, 1915)
When the Wicked Man (London: Jonathan Cape, 1932)

Other Works

Angier, Carole, *Jean Rhys: Life and Work* (Boston, Toronto, London: Little, Brown, 1990)

Bowen, Stella, *Drawn from Life* (London: Collins, 1941).

Ferguson, Niall, *The Pity of War* (Harmondsworth: Penguin, 1998)

Harvey, David Dow, *Ford Madox Ford: 1873–1939: A Bibliography of Works and Criticism* (Princeton, NJ: Princeton University Press, 1962)

Nicolson, Juliet, *The Great Silence 1918–1920: Living in the Shadow of the Great War* (London: John Murray, 2009)

Saunders, Max, *Ford Madox Ford: A Dual Life*, 2 vols (Oxford: Oxford University Press, 1996)

Wiesenfarth, Joseph, *Ford Madox Ford and the Regiment of Women: Violet Hunt, Jean Rhys, Stella Bowen, Janice Biala* (Madison, WI: University of Wisconsin Press, 2005)

Further Critical Reading on *Parade's End*

Armstrong, Paul, *The Challenge of Bewilderment: Understanding and Representation in James, Conrad, and Ford* (Ithaca, NY, and London: Cornell University Press, 1987)

Attridge, John, '"I Don't Read Novels ... I Know What's in 'em": Impersonality, Impressionism and Responsibility in *Parade's End*', in *Impersonality and Emotion in Twentieth-Century British Literature*, ed. Christine Reynier and Jean-Michel Ganteau (Montpellier: Université Montpellier III, 2005)

Auden, W. H., 'Il Faut Payer', *Mid-Century*, 22 (Feb. 1961), 3–10

Becquet, Alexandra, 'Modernity, Shock and Cinema: The Visual Aesthetics of Ford Madox Ford's *Parade's End*', in *Ford Madox Ford and Visual Culture*, ed. Laura Colombino, International Ford Madox Ford Studies, 8 (Amsterdam and New York: Rodopi, 2009), 191–204

Bergonzi, Bernard, *Heroes' Twilight: A Study of the Literature of the Great War* (Manchester: Carcanet, 3rd edn, 1996)

Bradbury, Malcolm, 'The Denuded Place: War and Ford in *Parade's End* and *U. S. A.*', in *The First World War in Fiction*, ed. Holger Klein (London and Basingstoke: Macmillan, rev. edn, 1978), 193–209

—'Introduction', *Parade's End* (London: Everyman's Library, 1992)

Brasme, Isabelle, 'Between Impressionism and Modernism: *Some Do Not . . .*, a poetics of the *Entre-deux*', in *Ford Madox Ford: Literary Networks and Cultural Transformations*, ed. Andrzej Gasiorek and

Daniel Moore, International Ford Madox Ford Studies, 7 (Amsterdam and New York: Rodopi, 2008), 189–99

Brown, Dennis, 'Remains of the Day: Tietjens the Englishman', in *Ford Madox Ford's Modernity*, ed. Robert Hampson and Max Saunders, International Ford Madox Ford Studies, 2 (Amsterdam and Atlanta, GA: Rodopi, 2003), 161–74

Brown, Nicholas, *Utopian Generations: The Political Horizon of Twentieth-Century Literature* (Princeton, NJ: Princeton University Press, 2005)

Buitenhuis, Peter, *The Great War of Words: British, American and Canadian Propaganda and Fiction, 1914–1933* (Vancouver: University of British Columbia Press, 1987)

Calderaro, Michela A., *A Silent New World: Ford Madox Ford's Parade's End* (Bologna: Editrice CLUEB [Cooperativa Libraria Universitaria, Editrice Bologna], 1993)

Caserio, Robert L., 'Ford's and Kipling's Modernist Imagination of Public Virtue', in *Ford Madox Ford's Modernity*, ed. Robert Hampson and Max Saunders, International Ford Madox Ford Studies, 2 (Amsterdam and Atlanta, GA: Rodopi, 2003), 175–90

Cassell, Richard A., *Ford Madox Ford: A Study of his Novels* (Baltimore: Johns Hopkins University Press, 1962)

—*Ford Madox Ford: Modern Judgements* (London: Macmillan, 1972)

—*Critical Essays on Ford Madox Ford* (Boston: G. K. Hall, 1987)

Colombino, Laura, *Ford Madox Ford: Vision, Visuality and Writing* (Oxford: Peter Lang, 2008)

Conroy, Mark, 'A Map of Tory Misreading in *Parade's End*', in *Ford Madox Ford and Visual Culture*, ed. Laura Colombino, International Ford Madox Ford Studies, 8 (Amsterdam and New York: Rodopi, 2009), 175–90.

Cook, Cornelia, 'Last Post', *Agenda*, 27:4–28:1, Ford Madox Ford special double issue (winter 1989–spring 1990), 23–30

Davis, Philip, 'The Saving Remnant', in *Ford Madox Ford and Englishness*, ed. Dennis Brown and Jenny Plastow, International Ford Madox Ford Studies, 5 (Amsterdam and New York: Rodopi, 2006), 21–35

Deer, Patrick, *Culture in Camouflage: War, Empire, and Modern British Literature* (Oxford: Oxford University Press, 2009)

DeKoven, Marianne, 'Valentine Wannop and Thematic Structure in Ford Madox Ford's *Parade's End*', *English Literature in Transition (1880–1920)*, 20:2 (1977), 56–68

Erskine-Hill, Howard, 'Ford's Novel Sequence: An Essay in Retrospection', *Agenda*, 27:4–28:1, Ford Madox Ford special double issue (winter 1989–spring 1990), 46–55

Frayn, Andrew, '"This Battle Was not Over": *Parade's End* as a Transitional Text in the Development of "Disenchanted" First World War Literature', in *Ford Madox Ford: Literary Networks and Cultural Transformations*, ed. Andrzej Gasiorek and Daniel Moore, International Ford Madox Ford Studies, 7 (Amsterdam and New York: Rodopi, 2008), 201–16

Gasiorek, Andrzej, 'The Politics of Cultural Nostalgia: History and Tradition in Ford Madox Ford's *Parade's End*', *Literature & History*, 11:2 (third series) (autumn 2002), 52–77

Green, Robert, *Ford Madox Ford: Prose and Politics* (Cambridge: Cambridge University Press, 1981)

Haslam, Sara, *Fragmenting Modernism: Ford Madox Ford, the Novel, and the Great War* (Manchester: Manchester University Press, 2002)

Heldman, J. M., 'The Last Victorian Novel: Technique and Theme in *Parade's End*', *Twentieth Century Literature*, 18 (Oct. 1972), 271–84

Hoffmann, Charles G., *Ford Madox Ford: Updated Edition* (Boston: Twayne Publishers, 1990)

Holton, Robert. *Jarring Witnesses: Modern Fiction and the Representation of History* (Hemel Hempstead: Harvester Wheatsheaf, 1994)

Hynes, Samuel, 'Ford Madox Ford: Three Dedicatory Letters to *Parade's End*, with Commentary and Notes', *Modern Fiction Studies*, 16:4 (1970), 515–28

—*A War Imagined: The First World War and English Culture* (London: The Bodley Head, 1990)

Judd, Alan, *Ford Madox Ford* (London: Collins, 1990)

Kashner, Rita, 'Tietjens' Education: Ford Madox Ford's Tetralogy', *Critical Quarterly*, 8 (1966), 150–63

MacShane, Frank, *The Life and Work of Ford Madox Ford* (New York: Horizon; London: Routledge & Kegan Paul, 1965)

— ed., *Ford Madox Ford: The Critical Heritage* (London: Routledge, 1972)

Meixner, John A., *Ford Madox Ford's Novels: A Critical Study* (Minneapolis: University of Minnesota Press; London: Oxford University Press, 1962)

Mizener, Arthur, *The Saddest Story: A Biography of Ford Madox Ford* (New York: World, 1971; London: The Bodley Head, 1972)

Monta, Anthony P., '*Parade's End* in the Context of National Efficiency', in *History and Representation in Ford Madox Ford's Writings*, ed. Joseph Wiesenfarth, International Ford Madox Ford Studies, 3 (Amsterdam and New York: Rodopi, 2004), 41–51

Moore, Gene, 'The Tory in a Time of Change: Social Aspects of Ford

Madox Ford's *Parade's End*', *Twentieth Century Literature*, 28:1 (spring 1982), 49–68

Moser, Thomas C., *The Life in the Fiction of Ford Madox Ford* (Princeton, NJ: Princeton University Press, 1980)

Munton, Alan, 'The Insane Subject: Ford and Wyndham Lewis in the War and Post-War', in *Ford Madox Ford: Literary Networks and Cultural Transformations*, ed. Andrzej Gasiorek and Daniel Moore, International Ford Madox Ford Studies, 7 (Amsterdam and New York: Rodopi, 2008), 105–30

Parfitt, George, *Fiction of the First World War: A Study* (London: Faber & Faber, 1988)

Radford, Andrew, 'The Gentleman's Estate in Ford's *Parade's End*', *Essays in Criticism* 52:4 (Oct. 2002), 314–32

Saunders, Max, 'Ford and European Modernism: War, Time, and *Parade's End*', in *Ford Madox Ford and 'The Republic of Letters'*, ed. Vita Fortunati and Elena Lamberti (Bologna: Editrice CLUEB [Cooperativa Libraria Universitaria, Editrice Bologna], 2002), 3–21

—'Introduction', Ford Madox Ford, *Parade's End* (Harmondsworth: Penguin, 2002), vii–xvii

Seiden, Melvin, 'Persecution and Paranoia in *Parade's End*', *Criticism*, 8:3 (summer 1966), 246–62

Skinner, Paul, '"Not the Stuff to Fill Graveyards": Joseph Conrad and *Parade's End*', in *Inter-relations: Conrad, James, Ford, and Others*, ed. Keith Carabine and Max Saunders (Lublin: Columbia University Press, 2003), 161–76.

—'The Painful Processes of Reconstruction: History in *No Enemy* and *Last Post*', in *History and Representation in Ford Madox Ford's Writings*, ed. Joseph Wiesenfarth, International Ford Madox Ford Studies, 3 (Amsterdam and New York: Rodopi, 2004), 65–75

Snitow, Ann Barr, *Ford Madox Ford and the Voice of Uncertainty* (Baton Rouge: Louisiana State University Press, 1984)

Sorum, Eve, 'Mourning and Moving On: Life after War in Ford Madox Ford's *The Last Post*', in *Modernism and Mourning*, ed. Patricia Rae (Lewisburg, PA: Bucknell University Press, 2007), 154–67

Stang, Sondra J., *Ford Madox Ford* (New York: Ungar, 1977)

Tate, Trudi, 'Rumour, Propaganda, and *Parade's End*', *Essays in Criticism*, 47:4 (Oct. 1997), 332–53

—*Modernism, History and the First World War* (Manchester: Manchester University Press, 1998)

Trotter David, 'Ford Against Lewis and Joyce', in *Ford Madox Ford: Literary Networks and Cultural Transformations*, ed. Andrzej Gasiorek and Daniel Moore, International Ford Madox Ford Studies, 7

(Amsterdam and New York: Rodopi, 2008), 131–49

Weiss, Timothy, *Fairy Tale and Romance in Works of Ford Madox Ford* (Lanham, MD: University Press of America, 1984)

Wiesenfarth, Joseph, *Gothic Manners and the Classic English Novel* (Madison, WI: University of Wisconsin Press, 1988)

Wiley, Paul L., *Novelist of Three Worlds: Ford Madox Ford* (Syracuse, NY: Syracuse University Press, 1962)

THE FORD MADOX FORD SOCIETY

Ford c. 1915   ©Alfred Cohen, 2000   Registered Charity No. 1084040

This international society was founded in 1997 to promote knowledge of and interest in Ford. Honorary Members include Julian Barnes, A. S. Byatt, Hans-Magnus Enzensberger, Samuel Hynes, Alan Judd, Bill Nighy, Ruth Rendell, Michael Schmidt, John Sutherland, and Gore Vidal. There are currently over one hundred members, from more than ten countries. Besides regular meetings in Britain, we have held conferences in Italy, Germany, the U.S.A, and France. Since 2002 we have published International Ford Madox Ford Studies; a series of substantial annual volumes distributed free to members. *Ford Madox Ford: A Reappraisal* (2002), *Ford Madox Ford's Modernity* (2003), *History and Representation in Ford Madox Ford's Writings* (2004), *Ford Madox Ford and the City* (2005), *Ford Madox Ford and Englishness* (2006), *Ford Madox Ford's Literary Contacts* (2007), *Ford Madox Ford: Literary Networks and Cultural Transformations* (2008), *Ford Madox Ford and Visual Culture* (2009), and *Ford Madox Ford, Modernist Magazines and Editing* (2010) are all still available. Future volumes are planned on Ford and France, on his pre-war work, and on *Parade's End* and the First World War. If you are an admirer, an enthusiast, a reader, a scholar, or a student of anything Fordian, then this Society would welcome your involvement.

The Ford Madox Ford Society normally organises events and publishes Newsletters each year. Future meetings are planned in Glasgow, London, the Netherlands and Germany. The Society also inaugurated a series of Ford Lectures. Speakers have included Alan Judd, Nicholas Delbanco, Zinovy Zinik, A. S. Byatt, Colm Tóibín, and Hermione Lee. To join, please see the website for details; or send your name and address (including an e-mail address if possible), and a cheque made payable to 'The Ford Madox Ford Society', to:

Dr Paul Skinner, 7 Maidstone Street, Victoria Park, Bristol BS3 4SW, UK.
Telephone: 0117 9715008; Fax: 0117 9020294 Email: p.skinner370@btinternet.com

Annual rates: **Sterling:** Individuals: £12 (by standing order; otherwise £15); Concessions £8; **Euros:** €15.00 (by standing order; otherwise €20.00); Concessions €8.50. **US Dollars:** Any category: $25

For further information, either contact Paul Skinner (Treasurer) at the above address, or Sara Haslam (Chair) by e-mail at: s.j.haslam@open.ac.uk
The Society's Website is at: **http://open.ac.uk/Arts/fordmadoxford-society**